George Albert Brown, a graduate of Yale University and Stanford Law, started as a hippie in San Francisco's Haight Ashbury and retired at age 40 after having co-founded a successful international finance company. Following stints thereafter as a humorous author (*The Airline Passenger's Guerrilla Handbook)* and an angel investor in over a score of high-tech university spinouts, he built a catamaran in Chile and for more than a decade, cruised it across the globe with his significant other. Today, as a father of three grown children, a grandfather of four not-yet-grown children, and an involuntary lover of stray cats, he continues his peripatetic lifestyle by other means.

Who Killed Jerusalem? is the book that George, a life-long devotee of William Blake, had always wanted to write.

WHO KILLED JERUSALEM?

A ROLLICKING LITERARY MURDER MYSTERY
BASED ON WILLIAM BLAKE'S CHARACTERS & IDEAS
UPDATED TO 1970s SAN FRANCISCO

GEORGE ALBERT BROWN

Galbraith Literary Publishers Incorporated

This is a work of fiction. Names, characters, places, events, and incidents are the products of the imagination of the author or are used fictitiously and are not construed to be real. Any resemblance to actual persons (living or dead) or actual events, locales, organizations, or persons, living and dead, is purely coincidental.

Published by Galbraith Literary Publishers Incorporated, Sheridan, Wyoming, USA (www.galbraithliterarypublishers.com).

Library of Congress Control Number: 2021946119

Publisher's Cataloging-in-Publication data:

Names: Brown, George Albert, author.

Title: Who Killed Jerusalem? A rollicking murder mystery based on William Blake's characters & ideas, updated to 1970s San Francisco / George Albert Brown.

Description: Sheridan, WY: Galbraith Literary Publishers Incorporated, 2022.

Identifi ers: ISBN: 978-1-7377744-2-6 (hardcover) | 978-1-7377744-1-9 (paperback) | 978-1-7377744-0-2 (epub) | 978-1-7377744-3-3 (audiobook retail) | 978- 1-7377744-4-0 (audiobook library)

Subjects: LCSH San Francisco (Calif.)--History--20th century--Fiction. | Blake, William, 1757-1827--Characters--Fiction. | Mystery fi ction. | Humorous fi ction. | BISAC FICTION / Literary | FICTION / Mystery & Detective / Historical | FICTION / Humorous / General

Classifi cation: LCC PS3602.R69768 W47 2022 | DDC 813.6--dc23

Cover creation by Damonza.com, based in part on William Blake's 1795 painting, *Satan Exulting over Eve,* image courtesy of the Getty's Open Content Program.

To Melinda,

for keeping me safe in dangerous waters.

CONTENTS

Part One | 1

Key Facts To Know Before Reading This Book 3
Epigraph 5
Chapter 1: The Prisoner 7
Chapter 2: How The Chains Were Fitted 13
Chapter 3: The Expert In The Cave 16
Chapter 4: The Dancing Shadows—Section 1 23
Chapter 5: The Dancing Shadows—Section 2 45
Chapter 6: Feeling The Chains 58
Chapter 7: Stress-Raisers In The Metal 71

Part Two | 85

Chapter 8: The Weakest Link 87
Chapter 9: The Chains Slip 103
Chapter 10: The Intimation Of Freedom 120
Chapter 11: The Turn Of The Head 130
Chapter 12: Seeing The Others 142
Chapter 13: Is That A Man Or A Specter? 155
Chapter 14: Rubbing The Eyes In Disbelief 163

Part Three | 183

Chapter 15: Fallen Vs. Unfallen Chains 185
Chapter 16: Hearing The Puppeteer's Voice 199
Chapter 17: The Light Flickering From The Side 212
Chapter 18: The Body Turned Around 219

Chapter 19: The Glare Of The Flames 237

Part Four | 263

Chapter 20: Fire Blindness 265
Chapter 21: The Dancing Shadow Puppets 289
Chapter 22: The Puppeteer 304
Chapter 23: The Origin Of The Shadows 314
Chapter 24: Blinded By The Light Coming From Outside 328
Chapter 25: Fleeing Back Inside 344
Chapter 26: Glimpses Out Of The Mouth 352

Part Five | 371

Chapter 27: The Shadows On The Ground 373
Chapter 28: The Reflections In The Water 387
Chapter 29: Ding An Sich—Ein 397
Chapter 30: Ding An Sich—Zwei 409
Chapter 31: Raising The Eyes To The Heavens 421
Chapter 32: Blinded By The Golden Sun 437

Part Six | 453

Chapter 33: Beyond The Burning Gas Ball 455
Chapter 34: The Faintest Of Moons 461
Chapter 35: The Revolving Planets 476
Chapter 36: Reaching For The Stars 489
Chapter 37: A Galaxy Far, Far Away 499
Chapter 38: The Enormous Black Void 514
Chapter 39: What Didn't Happen 522
Chapter 40: Bottom's Truth 532
Epilogue 553
Acknowledgements 561

PART ONE

KEY FACTS TO KNOW BEFORE READING THIS BOOK

1: William Blake's Nonexistence

In the following story, all the quoted poems, aphorisms, words of wisdom, marked-up drafts, paintings, and drawings (you can look the latter two up on the web if you're interested) that are attributed to Ickey Jerusalem, a fictional 1970s San Francisco artist and poet, as well as almost all the amalgamated names and general traits of his coterie, are derived from the writings of the English artist and poet, William Blake (1757-1827).

I acknowledge Blake now because in this story, there never was an artist and poet named William Blake. Accordingly, you will not have to worry about Ickey Jerusalem eventually confessing to plagarization; there is no way Jerusalem could plagiarize someone who never existed.

2: It is Unnecessary to Know Anything about Blake

While *Who Killed Jerusalem?* is a riff on William Blake's work, it is not necessary to know anything about the real-life Blake or his work to appreciate the story.

Blake's personality and life story bear no relation to the personality and life story of the fictional Ickey Jerusalem, and Blake's work, produced over a fifty-year career, is often inconsistent, not to mention downright baffling. So, if you *do* happen to know something about the subject, you'd probably enjoy this book more if you just ignore all that and go with the flow.

3: 200-Year-Old Spelling, Grammar, and Punctuation

Ickey Jerusalem's works quoted herein are precisely as Blake wrote them. Thus, despite Jerusalem living in 1970s San Francisco, his works have the spelling, grammar, and punctuation existing in late 1700s and early 1800s London. My proofreader has insisted I include this notice so her reputation does not suffer.

4: My Apology for Difficult Names

Let me apologize for the strange and difficult names of some of the characters herein. All I can say in mitigation is that despite Blake's failures in this sphere, he still became one of the greatest poets of the English language.

Enjoy the story!

I give you the end of a golden string,

Only wind it into a ball:

It will lead you in at Heaven's gate,

Built in Jerusalem's wall....

—William Blake, circa 1804

CHAPTER 1

THE PRISONER

Just after midnight on Sunday, October 23rd, 1977, in the first-class section of a droning 747, Ickey Jerusalem, the thirty-three-year-old poet laureate of San Francisco, a man who appeared to have everything—looks, wealth, genius, passion, the love of a beautiful woman—was sitting alone and motionless in a backward-facing toilet cubicle, the door securely locked.

Jerusalem's pants were puddled around his ankles. His wrists were tied behind him. His back was leaning against the front wall. His plum-purple face was frozen in a look of terror. His mouth was soundlessly screeching inside a transparent plastic cleaning bag that shrouded his head.

Ickey Jerusalem was dead.

Jerusalem's eyes, however, seemed still alive. So wide and frenzied, and yet so focused, it was as though they were now seeing what a living person couldn't. Piercing with X-ray vision straight through the veil of the locked toilet door toward the back of the plane, through the upholstered partition at the rear of first class, through the shabby gentility of business class, through a clutch of overused toilets with their tissue-clogged bowls and suspicious wet spots on the floor, through a metallic-neon food galley, and then into the long, sweatily compressed bowels of tourist economy, where, after driving onwards to the very last row, Jerusalem's penetrating vision stopped dead at the hard outer surface of a pair of Coke-bottle spectacles sturdily shielding two closed eyes.

They were the eyes of a man who appeared to have neither looks, nor wealth, nor genius, nor passion, nor the love of any woman, let alone a beautiful one.

Ded Smith opened his eyes and stared through his thick glasses.

When he had booked this red-eye flight from New York to San Francisco, he had assumed there would be plenty of empty seats on which he could stretch out and sleep, once he had completed his necessary tasks. He had not counted on being accompanied by a hundred cowboy-hatted members of the New York State Used Car Dealers Association, who were traveling to a national convention at San Francisco's Cow Palace, nor on finding himself crammed between what had to be the two fattest and drunkest of the lot, monopolizing his armrests with their elbows while shouting locker-room ribaldries to their friends.

Ded had gone through the motions of trying to join in, letting rip at the wrong times with an awkward "Whoopee!" or "Yessiree!" In the end, though, he had reverted to his long-established role of the severely myopic, highly intelligent, forgotten, only child of aged parents—alone in his room, drawing stick figures of the other kids playing far below on the street. He had withdrawn into his airplane seat, overwhelmed with his usual feelings of isolation, loneliness, and suffocating claustrophobia.

Luckily, Ded had been able to escape to do his business. During a severe bout of turbulence, the less sedate of his seatmates—the one blocking him from the aisle—had clambered up onto the back of the temporarily empty seat in front of him, straddled it as though it were a bucking Brahman bull, and begun waving his cowboy hat in the air, yelling, "Yippee-Yi-O!" in a high-pitched Brooklyn accent.

The salesman, his riding skills on par with his yodeling, had soon fallen off. More precisely, he had been bucked off when an accidental flick of his spurless heel on the seat-adjuster lever had combined with a fortuitous, forward-driving air pocket to hurl his 350-pounds yippee-yi-o-ing headfirst into the next row up, where he became the topic of conversation for some time thereafter.

No one had noticed Ded slip into the aisle and head toward the front.

The turbulence had long since ceased. Most of the passengers were asleep. The huge, breathing carcass of the ride'em cowboy had been repatriated to the aisle seat next to Ded, where it was currently slumped, obstructing any escape. Its stupefied head was rotated towards Ded, its gaping, aspirating whirlpool of a mouth threatening to suck him, ear-first, into oblivion.

On Ded's left, in the window seat, sat the other, still conscious salesman, who, having discovered Ded did not own a car, was eagerly peppering him with sales pitches, like a hydra-headed monster looking for an opening.

"I can see," the salesman said, his huge, stubbled jaw jiggling, "that you are a man who appreciates the better things in life."

In his mind, Ded saw his long-dead father, a senior accountant at the Buffalo, New York, water company, working away in his paper-stacked office. "There is no better thing in life," he was telling his son, "than a sense of duty."

Young Ded, awed at being invited into the sanctum where his father spent almost all his waking hours, had written down every word. His father spoke to him so seldomly that when he did, it was an event to be remembered.

Ded's mother was not there that day. But then, Ded already knew what she thought. In her view, the better things were not in this life at all. As a devout Catholic, she spent almost every one of *her* waking hours in the local cathedral, kissing the cold, polished toe of the statue of St. Jude. "The patron saint of lost causes," she often pointed out to young Ded. The saint's name was so close to "Judas" that, according to legend, the only way he could get anyone to pray to him was to specialize in causes no other saint would touch with a barge pole.

Ded couldn't help but take his mother's veneration of this particular saint as reflecting adversely on her only child.

"That's why I know I've got just the car for you," the salesman enthused, his eyes fixed on his prey. "A brand-spanking-*used* Oldsmobile. Your classic cloth-top convertible. Four-on-the-floor. Tuck-and-roll upholstery. Humongous tail fins. Glasspack mufflers. Low-rider lifter shocks. Chrome-reverse wheels. Bright orange, flame detailing. And with only one owner, a little old lady who drove it to and from church on Sunday mornings."

Ded did not respond.

The salesman cleared his throat. "And the price is a steal, all due to a minor accident."

The salesman put his lips to the glass of beer in his right hand, his bloodshot eyes raised in an imitation of trustworthiness, waiting for Ded to take the bait. When Ded didn't, the salesman continued.

"One Sunday morning, on her way to church, the little old lady was rocketing up New York City's East River Drive at ninety miles an hour. Coming upon a Maserati hogging the fast lane, she accelerated to the right. Reaching the top of fourth gear, she attempted a rapid, double-clutch shift into fifth—forgetting the Oldsmobile doesn't have a fifth gear—and accidentally jammed the stick into reverse. The inertia of her still-speeding car tore through the gearbox, causing the frontend of the drive shaft to break loose, drop to the ground, and pole-vault the car into the air, where, despite the little old lady's vigorous application of the brakes, it bounced off the right edge of an overhead sign and pinwheeled into the river."

Ded turned to the salesman.

The salesman, thinking he had hit Ded's hot button at last, shifted into a higher gear with his many-pronged attack. "The little old lady was totaled. But the car was fine. The water was—"

"I don't need a car," Ded cut him off. "Do you know why?"

The salesman's hippo jowls quivered a no.

"Because I don't have a home. It's my job, you see." Ded settled back in his seat. "I'm traveling all the time."

A statement that was true. Having no community of his own, Ded traveled all the time, perpetually dipping into other communities, becoming responsible in each for yet another death before hastily flying away.

In every case, the people he encountered seemed so wrapped up in where they were—their local politics, their social clubs, their sports teams, their schools, their family, their friends, their enemies. Meanwhile, to Ded, always the outsider, none of it meant a thing.

Eight years earlier, around Christmas, just after he'd first started traveling for his current job, Ded was sitting at a stool in a diner in Beulah, North Dakota—population 3000—when a local businessman next to him, full of the holiday spirit, invited him on a four-hour, guided tour of the town. Having nothing better to do, Ded went along.

Certainly, even the most ardent booster of small-town America would have to admit that a four-hour tour of the tiny town of Beulah, North Dakota, was some kind of world record. After all, how much can a sane person say about a motley collection of characterless, low-rise boxes set in a grid against the barren plain, and providing, as its only color, neon signs on fast-food franchises along the highway?

The Beulah businessman, however, thought his hometown the greatest place on earth. At one point, he had gestured proudly over the nine-hole municipal golf course, buried under three feet of ice for as far as the eye could see—which, because of the raging blizzard, was not all that far—and declared, "You know, I couldn't imagine living anywhere else."

Which, to Ded, was the point.

Now, after eight years of business travel, Ded had come to believe that this limited outlook didn't afflict just the people of Beulah, North Dakota, but people everywhere—in whatever city, or state, or country, or, in fact, on the whole goddamn planet.

A limited outlook, I guess, Ded mused, *is what allows them to live their lives unafflicted by claustrophobia.*

In the aisle seat, the comatose salesman made a slight strangling sound in his throat. Ded turned and peered deep into the black void of the man's yawning mouth.

The trained-to-be-persistent salesman by the window, his curiosity getting the better of him, asked, "So, what type of business requires you to travel so much?"

Ded disconnected himself from the void. Before he could stop himself, he answered, "The business of death."

The fleshy face registered a flicker of anxiety. "Death?" He studied Ded's thick glasses and skinny body. "What… what exactly is it that you do?"

Ded, trapped between the whirlpool and the many-headed monster, chose to stare straight ahead towards the front of the plane. *Damn. What should I say now?*

CHAPTER 2

HOW THE CHAINS WERE FITTED

The plane landed without further incident and docked at the gate. The window-seat salesman had just recounted for the newly awakened aisle-seat salesman the job title Ded had volunteered. The aisle-seat salesman was laughing uproariously.

Why couldn't I have kept my big mouth shut? Ded reprimanded himself. He sighed. *At least, I'll be out of here soon.*

There was a crackle on the public address system. "I'm afraid your disembarkation will be held up for a while," the captain announced. "During our descent, we had an incident in the first-class section. We'll have to wait for the police to arrive."

The police? Ded thought. *Am I going to have to run a gauntlet at the front of the plane? Or worse, are they going to search economy class?"*

Ded recalled the stunningly beautiful, strawberry-blond young woman in dark glasses, a paisley silk dress, and a white leather coat he'd glimpsed entering first class at the beginning of the flight. Ded had been presenting his boarding pass to a steward, had looked up, and caught sight of her face. That was all, for maybe half a second, before she disappeared behind the curtain. Against her shades, the woman's pink skin had seemed so soft, so innocent. He could almost feel his fingers stroking her delicate cheek.

He wondered whether she was okay.

Ever since his divorce, he had been so lonely that he'd found himself becoming instantly infatuated with every halfway decent-looking woman who crossed his path. Glancing at the date indicator on his watch, he saw that the midnight that had just passed marked the third anniversary of the final decree.

My ex-wife had the same soft pink skin, he thought. *God, do I miss her.*

Ded had met his wife, Harriet, shortly after graduating from Buffalo State College. His social isolation at college had been a continuation of his experience at school—primary, middle, and high. As a day-student lacking the skills to relate to others, he had confined himself to the classroom and the library. While he made a few acquaintances, he had no friends. Each evening, he would retreat to his room at his parents' house to eat leftovers from the refrigerator, reduce everything he had learned that day to a cryptic logic tree on a piece of paper, and on Friday evenings between 10:45 and 10:50 p.m., engage in a perfunctory, though usually successful, act of self-knowledge, to take care of what Ded called, "the sexual side of my personality."

Harriet had rescued him from all that.

Still, Ded knew it wasn't fair to say his college years without her had been *all* bad.

It was there he had discovered something arguably much more important than human relationships could ever be, something—

His thoughts were interrupted by another crackling sound, followed this time by the captain's announcement that deplaning was about to begin.

The salesmen struggled to their feet. Ded let them out and then returned to his seat as the mob of conventioneers slowly exited. Ded, eager to be rid of his two sniggering companions, was happy to wait until the plane had emptied.

Several minutes later, Ded retrieved his case from under the seat, his garment bag and coat from the overhead rack, and trudged up the long, empty aisle. At the front, on the other side of the perpendicular exit corridor, a policeman guarded the entrance to first class, arms folded across his chest.

Ded knew he shouldn't show any interest, but he couldn't help himself.

He glanced past the cop into the cabin in the hope the beautiful young woman was still there. He couldn't see anybody. He did, however, hear a couple of muffled masculine voices. Slowing his exit, he kept both ears pointed to first class, hoping to make out what the voices were saying. Soon, his head was facing almost completely backwards, like an owl.

Ded suddenly felt strong hands gripping his shoulders from the front.

"You're under arrest, Smith!"

Ded spun his head around to come face to face with a burly, disheveled man standing in the jetway.

"At last," the man gloated, loudly chewing his gum, "I've got the infamous Dr. Deadly."

CHAPTER 3

THE EXPERT IN THE CAVE

"*Inspector* O'Nadir," the puffy gum-chewer said, letting go of Ded.

"*Inspector*?" Ded stammered. "Good God. Don't tell me you've been promoted?"

"Yep," the inspector beamed. "The Knife case. That's what did it." The inspector put his hand on Ded's shoulder. "I owe you for letting me take the credit."

"It was nothing. Evidence in court always looks better when it comes from the police. Anyway, I got what I wanted. The Olympian Life Insurance Company no longer had to pay out under the policy."

O'Nadir smiled politely at Ded's professional modesty. "Sorry for rattling you with the phony arrest. I just couldn't resist."

Yes, Ded was a life insurance claims adjuster. To most people, including those sniggering fat salesmen, the job title conjured up the mental image of some middle-level bureaucrat sitting at his desk before an overflowing inbox, matching the items in his checklist against those in the doctor's death certificate. Yet Ded was about as far from that kind of life insurance claims adjuster as one could get. In the first place, he was never at a desk. More importantly, though, was that no checklist could ever hope to resolve the cases he was brought in to adjust. They were the tough ones, where the facts were so unclear that they required a detailed, on-scene investigation from someone with exceptional deductive skills.

The Knife case, which he had investigated the last time he had been in San Francisco, four years earlier, was a prime example. It began with the coroner concluding, "All I can say is that the expression on the dead man's face leads me to believe that when he sat down, he was not aware of the butcher's knife wedged in the center of his chair, sharp end up. His expression, although not fitting neatly into any category I could think of, was perhaps, on the whole, closer to one of astonishment."

Following the local Olympian Life representative's memo to the home office, in which the representative had been forced to admit that after spending quite some time locked in a room with a butcher's knife and a chair, he still hadn't been able to figure it out, the company, at last, sent for Ded.

Examining the body, Ded noticed right away the tattoo on the right bicep: a large anus being stabbed by a dagger and the word "MOM" on a semi-circular banner across the top.

Ded laid out for O'Nadir side-by-side photos of the central tattoo and the unlucky orifice, showing an almost perfect match, apart from an enormous gash.

"Damn," the inspector said. "So, it's not a tattoo of a black-and-blue sunflower?"

After that, some quick interviews by Ded of various barflies in a nearby saloon revealed that the night before the incident, the drunken insured had made repeated death threats to "his asshole"—evidence even the coroner had to admit clinched the case.

Although Ded's skills far exceeded those of your average insurance claims adjuster, he had no delusions of grandeur. Just the opposite. As he saw it, no one with an outsider's view like his could have any delusions whatsoever. Far from thinking he was anything more than he was, Ded knew he was something much, much less.

⁂

"So, what brings you back to this neck of the woods, Dr. Deadly?"

"I'm waiting for the six-thirty connecting flight to Tokyo this morning."

O'Nadir showed his watch face to Ded. It said 3:01 a.m. "Great. You've got time. I'm here to investigate the death of some guy on your flight. How'd you like to join me?"

"Why not?" Ded answered, while thinking, *So, that's what happened in first class. Doesn't sound like it was the young woman, thank heavens.*

Ded stood aside as O'Nadir entered the plane. Although a loner, Ded had a soft spot for old acquaintances. He often daydreamed that when he was elderly, decrepit, and ready to die, he would meet for a few minutes all the people he had ever met. He had nothing in particular to say to them, but he somehow believed the mere existence of such a meeting would tie up the loose ends of the rather bald and unconvincing narrative that was his life.

Of all his old acquaintances, San Francisco Police Inspector O'Nadir was Ded's favorite. O'Nadir had a special quality that made him endearing: he was one of the few who actually liked Ded. Why was never clear. True, O'Nadir was grateful that Ded had let him take the credit for a bit of detective work, but the inspector had liked him even before that. With his down-to-earth, almost subterranean manner, O'Nadir was immune to Ded's detached objectivity, logical thinking, and other such social inadequacies. To him, Ded was simply one hell of a good investigator.

O'Nadir flashed his credentials to the cop and led Ded into the first-class cabin, which had the standard 747 design. A row of two seats ran along each wall, coming together at the front. A triangular-shaped table with fruit and newspapers on it sat in the middle. On Ded's immediate right was a blank partition; in front of that, a galley; and in front of that, a spiral staircase leading to the upper deck, where Ded knew there were more seats, a toilet, and the door to the flight deck.

Ded trailed the inspector as he circled around the front to the right-side aisle, where the row of paired seats continued back along the wall to a closet compartment. Opposite the aisle from the closet, behind the central galley, was a small corridor leading inward across the plane. At the far end of that corridor was the blank partition Ded had seen when entering. On the forward, galley side of the corridor were a couple of toilet compartments.

Two men were in the corridor. One was an airport security officer who was standing with his back to the aisle. The other was a brown-suited man on his knees, bent so deep into the far toilet cubicle that only his trouser cuffs and shoes were in view.

"Hey," O'Nadir hollered, "is this the line for blowjobs?"

The security officer turned around sharply, a look of confused non-recognition on his face. The man in the brown suit leaned back on his haunches and grinned at O'Nadir. "I didn't know you were into necrophilia, Inspector."

"Shit, I've been married for twenty years to a Catholic convent-school graduate. What more proof do you need?"

The brown-suited man held forensic tweezers. He looked up at the security officer. "Officer Jarvis, may I introduce Inspector O'Nadir. One of the city's finest."

The security officer extended his hand.

O'Nadir gave Officer Jarvis's hand a perfunctory pump and cocked the back of his head at Ded. "This is Ded Smith, a trained investigator."

"The kneeler with the tweezers," O'Nadir said out of the side of his mouth to Ded, "is Ben, my best forensic guy."

Ben waved in acknowledgment.

"You okay inside of a plane, Ben?" O'Nadir asked.

"As long as it's not up in the air."

"Ben's just like me," O'Nadir said in another aside to Ded. "Terrified of flying. So, neither of us have ever taken a flight."

O'Nadir leaned forward. "All right, Mr. Best Forensic Guy, what've we got here?"

"He's pretty much as we found him. Seems he had a plastic bag over his head. It was removed before we got here and placed in the next-door toilet for safekeeping."

Ben and Jarvis stepped aside to give O'Nadir and Ded a view into the cubicle.

The victim was sitting on the toilet, hands behind his back, pants around his ankles. His face was streaked purple and pink, and contorted with fear.

O'Nadir, blanching, turned to Ben. "You *sure* you didn't give this guy a blowjob?"

Ben pretended to chuckle.

Ded didn't crack a smile. "He have a name?"

Ben supplied it. "Ickey Jerusalem."

"No shit." O'Nadir whistled. "Didn't recognize him with all the facial contortions." The inspector rotated his head to give Ded the lowdown. "He's San Francisco's poet laureate. Fucking rich, supposedly. I saw him in person, several years ago. Once, at the Condor strip joint, playing his favorite game with Carol Doda, the city's first topless dancer. She would put a breast under each arm. He'd place his nose in between them, cry, 'Arms up!' and then luxuriate in the resultant blubbering against his cheeks. Another time, I had to arrest him for disturbing the peace outside Finocchios, the transvestite show on Broadway. He was drunk on the sidewalk, loudly announcing to a small crowd his guesses concerning the sexual predilections of the middle-aged Iowans stepping out of the tour bus."

O'Nadir, mimicking Jerusalem, took on the bellowing demeanor of a head butler announcing guests at a party. *"Mr... Jethro... Spotsbottom, Jacob's sheep... bondage and discipline. Mr... Homer... Butterball, Guernsey cows... missionary position only."*

O'Nadir clucked his tongue. "Look at him now."

Bucking up, Ded stepped past the inspector into the cubicle to peer behind Jerusalem's back. "Wrists tied with two shoelaces twisted together, a slip loop on each end."

He knelt, avoiding eye contact with Jerusalem's private parts sprawling from between his naked white thighs onto the hard-plastic surface of the toilet-seat lid. Ded examined the running shoes on the dead poet's feet. "Laces missing."

Ded swapped places with O'Nadir so he could see for himself. "What do you think, Ben?"

"Looks like suicide to me. Made the loops himself, placed the plastic bag over his head, put a wrist in each loop, and then pulled the loops tight. Neat. Clean. And deadly."

Ded eyed Jerusalem's staring, fear-deformed face. The poet's suicide—*if* it was suicide—had been anything but peaceful. Whatever Jerusalem had intended when he had begun, in the end, he had died horribly and unwillingly, desperately trying to gasp in the life-giving air a mere micro-millimeter beyond the plastic bag.

Ded suffered a brief burst of claustrophobia.

"The door was apparently locked from the inside when he was found," Ben said, to bolster his suicide hypothesis. "There isn't any latch on the outside. And see the farewell message on the mirror?"

Starting in the lower left corner of the mirror above the basin, written in soap, were two four-inch-high block letters: B I. The vertical line and bottom horizontal line of the "B" were aligned with the respective edges of the mirror.

"Anybody else in first class with him at the time?" Ded asked.

It took Security Officer Jarvis a few seconds to realize he was being addressed. "Six others. I've got them back in the main terminal. I didn't want to let them go until the inspector had a chance to interview them. They're being fingerprinted right now."

O'Nadir let out a sigh. "Let's get it over with. Since it's clearly suicide, not much to investigate."

"I'm not so sure," Ded said, about to point out some discrepancies in the evidence.

"In that case, Deadly," O'Nadir called, already halfway down the aisle, "why don't you come along and check 'em out? Your sharp investigator's eye might see things I can't."

ஃ

Ded got into the back seat of the electric cart with his bags, while Security Officer Jarvis got into the driver's seat with Inspector O'Nadir next to him. The cart then beeped its way to the main terminal through the empty concourse.

"Who were the six passengers?" Ded asked the security officer.

With one hand on the wheel, Officer Jarvis pulled a folded piece of paper out of his breast pocket, and after eying O'Nadir for approval, gave it to Ded.

The claims adjuster unfolded the paper. He skimmed the list of names. "Robert N. William. Adam Ghostflea. Beulah Vala. Tharmas Luvah. Bacon Urizen. Dr. Bromion Ulro. Hmmm, Robert N. William sounds okay, but are these other names for real?"

"They're the ones they gave me."

"Sounds like some kind of joke," Ded said as he studied the list more closely. "Hey, O'Nadir, you mind if I copy these names down?"

"Knock yourself out," O'Nadir called back, as Ded pulled a small, loose-leaf notepad from his inside suit jacket pocket.

Notations by each name were apparently written by Officer Jarvis. All six were Bay Area residents. Two appeared to have no connection with Jerusalem: Robert N. William, the flight purser, and Dr. Bromion Ulro, a physician. The remaining four were Adam Ghostflea, Jerusalem's chauffeur; Tharmas Luvah, his business manager; Bacon Urizen, his lawyer; and Beulah Vala, his personal assistant.

Recognizing the latter as the only obvious female name on the list, Ded felt a slight anticipation quickening inside. *Beulah? Is the name a coincidence?*

From the glimpse he'd caught of her face, he wouldn't have thought she was from North Dakota.

CHAPTER 4

THE DANCING SHADOWS—SECTION 1

The interrogation room, lit by overhead neon lights, had an institutional table in the middle. O'Nadir sat at the table in front of a tape recorder, facing the door, next to which was a hat stand with the inspector's coat. On the other side of the table was a folding metal chair where the interviewee would sit. In the wall on the policeman's left was a large two-way mirror.

Ded, sitting in a darkened observation chamber behind the mirror, his bags and overcoat next to him, watched through the slight haze of the glass as O'Nadir tested the tape recorder, leaned back, and rested the outside of his right ankle on his left knee. The hidden sound system filled Ded's space with the noise of the inspector's cracking gum.

Here I am, Ded yawned wryly, *back in the Cave, once again.*

❧

Ded saw himself sitting virtually alone in the gloom of the red-eye flight from Miami to L.A., three years before, the night his divorce became final.

A week after Harriet filed for divorce, he had signed the house over to her and arranged to receive his assignments in the field. At that point, he'd already been traveling on his job for several years. From then on, without anyone or anything left to anchor him down, he'd become completely rootless.

On the outside, Ded had acted as if his wife's rejection meant nothing to him, but on the inside, it had evoked an emotional response so powerful it made all other emotions he had ever experienced during his life seem but anemic parodies of the real thing. The pain was unbearable, as though a huge claw had ripped out his internal organs and left him bleeding and empty, floating alone, backwards through space.

He had hoped, too optimistically, that the agonizing pain would soon be dampened by his increasingly frenetic travel. Instead, it had become more acute, growing in intensity, until the last night of the six-month waiting period, when Ded sat on the near-empty red-eye flight from Miami to L.A., he'd begun—for the very first time—to wonder whether perhaps suicide was the only logical solution.

The drinks service, the meal service, the movie, and the post-movie trip to the toilets had all come and gone. Ded adjusted his thick glasses and stared at his watch. In a few minutes, it would be midnight. His marriage would be over. He rotated his wristwatch until the face was out of sight, then leaned against the pressure of his seatbelt to examine the contents of the seatback pocket, looking for something—anything—to keep his mind off the gnawing hollowness inside him.

Grabbing the first thing that caught his eye, he pulled out the airline's fold-over of safety instructions. With great concentration, he scrutinized the two-dimensional passengers passing wordlessly through the stations of the crash, sliding out of the plane, leaving behind an empty, dying hulk, devoid of—

Pitching the fold-over away and returning to the contents of the pocket, Ded retrieved an unused air-sickness bag stamped with the airline's motto.

With forced concentration, he recited the words out loud.

"Flying through the air with the greatest of ease."

In the context of airsickness, it was not all that reassuring a motto.

The graphic images conjured up in Ded's mind made him feel emptier than ever.

After dropping the bag on the floor, he reached deeper into the seatback pocket. There was something crumpled up, way at the bottom. He lifted it out and smoothed it flat onto his tray.

It was a pair of soiled pages torn from a comic book. On the top left of the first page was a header: "Universal Comics, History of Philosophy, Part 1." Below that, in the center, was the title: "Chapter 1: Plato's Cave."

Ded had heard of Plato, but he had never gotten around to studying his works—or those of any other philosophers, for that matter. If he'd known the ancient Greek philosophers had written comic books, he might have taken a greater interest.

All Philosophy 101 students (of which Ded was never one) know Plato's parable about prisoners chained from birth in a cave, facing the back wall, onto which are cast by a flickering fire behind, the shadows of moving stick puppets. The prisoners, unable to see anything but the shadows, believe them to be the only reality. The parable has the well-known plot in which a prisoner breaks loose and sees, step by step, each time rubbing his eyes in initial confusion, what he has never seen before—the other prisoners, the puppets, the dazzling fire, the bright mouth of the cave, and then outside, the ground, the stars, the planets, the moon, and eventually, the blinding sun. After having learned the truth, the lone prisoner returns to the cave to tell the others that everything they thought was reality was but a mere shadow.

In the comic-book version, however, the chained and blinkered prisoners were anthropomorphic cartoon animals. The main character, like Bottom the weaver in *A Midsummer Night's Dream*, had a man's body and a donkey's head, the latter all rolling eyes and lolling tongue.

The other characters, although dressing and behaving like humans, were physically wholly animal: a black goat with a goatee; a voluptuous pink cow with movie-star dark glasses; a pale fat pig with a top hat and tails; a vain python twined around a staff; a neatly clipped poodle with a trimmed mustache; and a carapace-backed, musclebound insect standing on his hind legs with a too-small head sporting bulging-out, crossed eyes and a skinny sucking tongue between tiny fangs at either end of his mouth.

The dialogue in the voice balloons was peppered with Bottom's "hee-haws" and "guh-yucks," as well as other comic touches that Plato patently lacked the creativity to imagine. Such as in one of the later pages, when Bottom returned, hee-hawing, to the darkened cave to give the prisoners the word, and due to his eyes not yet having adjusted from the brightness of the sun, failed to notice a low stone platform around the fire. 'Yikes!" he yelled as he banged his big cartoon toe on the corner. Instantly gathering his injured digit up into both hands instead of first paying attention to stopping completely his forward momentum, he slowly rotated counterclockwise an involuntary 180 degrees on his barely balancing other leg, fell backwards over the platform, landed bottom-first on the fire with a pathetic "Oh, no," and immediately thereafter, while letting out an echoing "WHAA-HOO-HOo-Hoo-hoo," and using nothing more than his arms, legs, donkey's head, and flaming rear end, created what the prisoners agreed to be an award-winning wall shadow.

After which, for some reason, no one took him seriously—other than to exchange a few thoughtful murmurings about the necessity of killing this deranged fruitcake before he hurt someone.

The remainder of the comic-book parable was missing. But Ded didn't need more pages to know what had happened. Moments before his divorce became final, the perpetually traveling claims adjuster intuitively understood that Bottom, having seen the light, had only one choice: to turn away from the prisoners and head out of the cave and into the glorious sunlight, guh-yucking as he went, never to return.

Ded laid the comic-book pages onto his lap and gazed out over the near-empty cabin of the 747.

"Two-and-a-half millennia ago, the ancient Greeks had already come to the same conclusion as I did," he marveled out loud, his painful emptiness having briefly faded in the brilliant light of Plato's parable. "The only way to see what is really going on is to widen your perspective until you are outside the cave."

He put the fingertips of his right hand to his heart. *I am Bottom,* he thought, without irony. *Unlike the bulk of mankind, enamored of the shadows on the wall, unable to imagine themselves in a position other than that which they are in, I've been able to so widen my perspective that I can look up and see—*

Ded turned to the airplane window. Putting his face near the glass to block out the reflection in the low-lit cabin, he peered into the night sky, past the remaining thin atmosphere, past the planets, past the stars, into the enormous black vacuum in which the earth, the sun, and all the other meandering accidental specks of matter seemed lost—doomed to spread out forever into an energyless nothingness. Or was it, instead, to contract into a geometric point? Ded could never remember. Either way, the vastness of it all made human concerns seem so small, so transitory, so meaningless.

Ded's excruciating emptiness returned.

For some time, he sat forlorn in the plane, gazing into the enormous black vacuum, searching for something, anything. *Why did Bottom's widened perspective lead to a guh-yucking happiness*, he wondered, *while mine leads only to emptiness and despair?*

Then, in a flash, he understood.

Of course!

He sat up straight and smacked his thigh with his hand. *That's where Bottom went wrong!*

❧

Blinding light poured through the opening side door to the interview observation chamber. Ded sat up straight in the chair and squinted, wresting himself out of the dreamy realm of remembering and into the present, where a poet was dead and an interrogation was about to begin.

"I've been thinking," O'Nadir said as he entered. "You're the better investigator. Unlike me, being unconvinced it's really suicide, maybe you should conduct the interviews. I don't want you saying I didn't give you a fair chance."

"Is that allowed?"

"I don't see why not. This is merely a preliminary interview of potential witnesses, and I'll be by your side to step in with the necessary Miranda warnings, should anyone promote themselves to suspect."

Not having slept during the red-eye, Ded was exceptionally tired. On the other hand, the opportunity to demonstrate the holes in O'Nadir's thinking was not one he could pass up. He followed the inspector into the interview room, pulled up a spare chair, and sat down next to the now cross-legged O'Nadir.

❧

The door to the brightly lit interview room opened. A small man with short hair, a pinched face, a pencil mustache, and an excessively neat uniform entered.

"Robert N. William?" Ded inquired as he motioned to the chair on the opposite side of the table. "The flight purser?"

The man nodded, primly lowered himself into the seat, crossed one knee over the other, grasped the top knee with his interlaced fingers, and sized up his two interviewers with an air of speculation.

O'Nadir did not respond. Ded knew that while growing up, O'Nadir had naturally absorbed the Catholic Church's then view that homosexuals were an abomination to God, and that this view occasionally surfaced in small ways in the inspector's behavior, such as his having just unconsciously put his feet flat on the floor. However, Ded also knew that as a policeman, O'Nadir believed gays were fully entitled to their lifestyle, and he always made a point of treating them as politely as he would treat anybody else. "I'm not prejudiced against homosexuals at all," O'Nadir had told Ded during the Knife investigation. "I mean, with some of them, you can't even tell, can you? The only ones that get my goat are those who talk to straight people like me in way that suggests, as far as they're concerned, it's us, and not them, who are the freaks of nature."

To Inspector O'Nadir, it looked like the purser was one of those.

Ded himself had no problems with any kind of homosexual, nor with homosexuality itself. As he saw it, once you looked at things on the purely physical level, there was very little to distinguish gay sex from straight. "It's all the same in the dark," he often summed it up—usually to some hapless male passenger sitting next to him on a night flight. In truth, Ded had no direct experience on which to base this assertion.

Ded cleared his throat. "Thank you for coming, Mr. William. My name is Ded Smith, and I am assisting Inspector O'Nadir."

The purser bobbed his head to Ded and then, more slowly and intently, with a great air of superiority, at the inspector.

"Maybe we can start with you telling us what the 'N' in your name stands for?"

"Nebuchadnezzar." The purser's ostentatiously camp manner confirmed his pride in the eminence of his middle name.

"Right," the claims adjuster said, adding "Nebuchadnezzar" between "Robert" and "William" in the list of weird names. "You were in charge of first class?"

"I was, I'm sorry to say."

"Were there any other flight attendants working with you, Mr. William?" Ded asked.

A martyred veneer came over the purser's face. "Two stewardesses on the roster didn't show up. Since there were only six first-class passengers, the company said I ought to be able to handle them on my own. They suggested I borrow a flight attendant from economy if I got in trouble. But that wouldn't have been fair." His voice registered a genuine concern. "Economy was packed to the armpits with drunken cowboys."

The purser leaned forward confidentially and lowered his voice. "Once, when I looked in, one of them had actually mounted a seatback like a bull!"

Ded had been sitting right next to that particular salesman, so he knew what was being described. But he could see O'Nadir blinking at the interviewee, manifestly unsure whether the phrase "like a bull" was meant to modify the noun "seatback" or the verb "mounted."

Not wanting to enlighten O'Nadir as to the proper grammatical interpretation, Ded simply allowed himself an ambiguous, sympathetic scowl before proceeding. "You saw Ickey Jerusalem during the flight?"

The purser drew his right shoulder forward under his chin. "What kind of service do you think I give in first class?"

Ded did not answer this rhetorical question.

"Obviously, I saw him," Robert N. William said. "How could I miss him? The tall, perfectly proportioned body. The handsome, somewhat snooty face. A dead ringer for my twin brother."

Ded reviewed the purser's slight physique and pinched face. "Your *twin* brother?"

"Fraternal," the purser clarified. He raised his hands, palms-forward, fingers-spread, thumbs at his temples, and tilted his head, an ironical, clown-like smile on his face. "The greatest high school quarterback Chautauqua, Kansas, had ever seen."

Ded, not sure what to make of the purser's peculiar performance, listened for a moment to O'Nadir placidly chewing his gum. "Did Jerusalem seem depressed to you?"

Robert N. William pursed his lips, trying to recollect. "No, not really. Remote, maybe, as though off in another world. He spent a lot of time scribbling in his spiral notebook. Now and then, he talked quietly to his seatmate."

"Seatmate?"

"Miss Vala. Very young. Beautiful. Strawberry-blond hair. Rosy skin. Dark glasses."

Ded found his interest suddenly rising.

"Dark glasses on a night flight?" O'Nadir cut in. His manner indicated he found the young woman's behavior pretentious.

"She was blind," the purser explained in a tone one might use when talking to an idiot.

"Right," O'Nadir acknowledged, struggling to maintain his Joe Friday exterior. Then, blustering, "How did you know?"

The purser reflected. "Well, as she boarded, Mr. Jerusalem led her by the arm. She was facing steadily ahead, as though trying to see with her ears, and was reaching out with her free hand. When he let go of her to give me their coats to hang in their closet, she took a step and fell over the center fruit table. That type of thing."

"Thank you," the inspector stated in a small, highly controlled voice, before making a careful, if superfluous, entry in his notebook. "Fell… over… the… center… fruit… table."

Blind. Ded savored the concept. Somehow, the revelation of this vulnerability served only to increase the woman's perfection in his mind. Making her more approachable, less likely to judge, more in need of protection.

Ded looked once more at his list of first-class passengers. "Beulah Vala, Ickey Jerusalem's personal assistant." He looked at the purser. "How did you know her name was Miss Vala?"

"We're always given a plan of the first-class seating assignments, so we can address each passenger by name and also be aware of any special needs."

"Do you still have your copy?"

The purser nodded and handed Ded a folded sheet from his inside jacket pocket. "You'll notice there's no indication Miss Vala was visually impaired. She must not have mentioned it in her booking."

The plan showed Ickey Jerusalem and Beulah Vala in the seats on the right side of the cabin, just in front of the coat closet and across the aisle from the corridor with the two toilets. Dr. Bromion Ulro was at the front of the right side of the cabin. The other passengers sat in the middle of the left side. The galley in the center would have blocked their view of Jerusalem's seat.

"Did you see Jerusalem go to the toilet?"

"No." The purser smirked. "He closed the door on me. Some hang-up he had about privacy, I guess." He turned to O'Nadir. "Something, Inspector, you have certainly encountered while trying to boost your arrest tally by busting cruisers at the public toilets under the Marina Green grandstand."

O'Nadir traced his thumb down the length of a thin scar on the left side of his forehead and cheek, a badge of honor he had received at the hands of a cornered pedophile. Ded knew his fellow interviewer did not agree with wasting police resources on the activities of consenting adults. But the inspector was clearly beginning to tire of the purser's relentlessly superior airs. Despite O'Nadir's self-proclaimed lack of prejudice, Ded imagined the man's thoughts at the moment were less forgiving. Some obscure concatenation of associations beginning, perhaps, with seldom used appellations such as "sodomite" and "Hostess Twinkie," before degenerating into dark ruminations on the Decline of Western Civilization.

Ded rephrased his question. "Did you see Jerusalem leave his seat at any time?"

"No," the purser answered, this time without the smirk. He seemed to realize that even though he was no longer, thank heavens, living in Chautauqua, Kansas, it was still a good idea to keep on the right side of the cops.

"Would any business class passengers behind have seen Jerusalem leave his seat?"

The purser shook his head. "Screened off by a curtain."

Ded recalled seeing the curtain from the other side when, freed by the yippee-yi-o-ing salesman's headfirst dive into the next row up, he had avoided the long line at economy's rear toilets by heading up the aisle to sneak into the restroom at the back of business class.

"Did you see anybody other than Beulah Vala near Jerusalem?" Ded asked. "On their way to the toilet, perhaps?"

"Given that it was a night flight, most people slept. And I used the toilets upstairs, where there were no passengers. Not the ones opposite where Mr. Jerusalem was sitting." The purser nibbled his lower lip. "But now that I think about it, I do remember seeing one passenger heading back into that area. Mr. Urizen."

Although the purser's pronounciation of the name was the same Ded had used when he read out loud the first-class passenger list Officer Jarvis gave him, this time the claims adjuster could hear that the name sounded a lot like "your reason."

Ded slid the list of passengers closer. "Bacon Urizen?" The notation by the name indicated he was Jerusalem's lawyer.

"Yes, that's it," Robert N. William confirmed. "Older man. Bald. Heavy. Weary. Distinguished-looking."

"Distinguished-looking?"

"He wore a monocle."

"A monocle," Inspector O'Nadir interrupted, writing with great deliberation in his notebook. As an Irish-American born and raised in San Francisco's Mission District, O'Nadir obviously ranked monocles—and those who wore them—right up there with Robert Nebuchadnezzar William on the Decline-of-Western-Civilization index.

"When was the last time you saw Jerusalem alive?" Ded asked the purser.

Robert N. William melodramatically racked his memory before answering. "A little before midnight. He asked if I could give him a bottle of wine to keep at his seat, so he wouldn't have to keep hassling me for a drink. I gave him a bottle of Pinot Noir."

"And after that?"

"I, uh, went back to a rear seat on the left side of first class for a rest."

From the seating plan, Ded could see the purser would have been sitting just on the other side of the thin partition at the end of the toilet corridor.

"Did you hear any unusual noises coming from behind the partition across the aisle?"

The purser took a split second to reply. "No, no, I didn't. But then, the plane was going through an extended patch of turbulence. It could have drowned out any noises Mr. Jerusalem might have made."

Ded leaned back, stretching his arms in the air. The jet lag was getting to him.

"When did you first notice Jerusalem was missing?"

"I checked all the first-class passengers when the turbulence ended. Miss Vala was in her reclined seat, curled up under her coat, asleep, but Mr. Jerusalem was nowhere to be seen."

"Did she know where he'd gone?"

"No, not exactly. When I woke her to bring her seat back up for landing, she felt his empty seat but didn't seem all that concerned. She said that Mr. Jerusalem had difficulty sleeping on planes, and often, to relieve his boredom, would go for walks down one aisle, all the way to the end, and then up the other. She figured he might've met somebody he knew in economy and stayed to talk. I wasn't too concerned. I mean, he obviously hadn't left the plane. I was going to take a look in the corridor toilets, but before I could, Mr. Urizen started banging on his call button, so I had to attend to him."

"When was Jerusalem found?"

"Shortly thereafter, after another passenger, Mr. Tharmas Luvah, overheard me telling Mr. Urizen that Mr. Jerusalem was missing and got into quite a lather about it. 'You better find him,' he kept telling me, implying that it was me who was responsible."

The purser assumed the mien of the genuinely offended.

"As the two followed me on my search, I noticed the locked lavatory door, forced it open, and there was Mr. Jerusalem, sitting on the toilet seat with a cleaning bag over his head, staring at us with that terrorized expression, his open mouth pressed against the plastic. Dead."

The purser closed his eyes with a shiver. He put his right palm to his chest, sighed, and then, having regained his composure, opened his eyes. "I remember turning to Mr. Luvah, who was standing in the corridor behind me. 'Goodness,' I said, 'I hope you don't think this is any fault of *mine*.'"

"Did you touch anything in the cubicle?"

"No. I ushered Mr. Luvah back into the aisle, told Mr. Urizen—who had the necessary bulk—to block the entrance to the corridor, and then shot off to get one of the first-class passengers, Dr. Ulro, to examine Mr. Jerusalem. After that, I told the captain, so he could alert the police in San Francisco to meet the plane."

"And then?"

"I went up into the upstairs toilet and had a good cry."

Ded contemplated the vision of the haughty Robert N. William weeping in the upstairs toilet.

"I've been under a lot of personal stress recently," the purser explained, "having just broken up with my partner. Finding Mr. Jerusalem in the toilet cubicle was the last straw."

The inspector stopped masticating. With a snort, he put his hand on Ded's arm. "Thank you," he said to the purser, courteously but nonetheless evincing zero interest in the man's personal problems. "I think that'll be all, for now."

Ded, although he had a couple more questions he wanted to ask, went along.

Robert N. William gathered up his hands, stood, gave a patronizing smile, turned, and minced out of the room.

"We'll contact you if we need you for anything more," Ded called after him.

"Let me know ahead of time if he's coming into the station," O'Nadir said to Ded under his breath. "I'll make sure to call in sick."

ఌ

Ded's tired eyes were fixed on the door that had just closed behind the purser. Was Miss Vala next?

In answer, the door snapped opened, revealing a tall, strikingly good-looking blond.

It was not, however, Miss Vala—this tall, strikingly good-looking blond being a man.

He was in his mid-thirties. He wore a powder blue tracksuit, clay-colored running shoes, and a casual, Marin County look. The well-groomed hair. The perfect teeth. The tanned skin. The flat stomach. The air of condescending friendliness so characteristic of the nation's richest and hippest county, lying immediately north of San Francisco, across the Golden Gate Bridge. There was also a doctor's antiseptic smell about him.

"Dr. Bromion Ulro?" Ded said.

The man stood motionless for a moment in the doorway, the air of condescending friendliness frozen about him. Then, his blue eyes, under the control of some lagging internal rheostat, brightened. "Yes, that's right," he replied in a rapid-fire, shockingly high-pitched, California-Central-Valley voice.

Ded gave a start. The last time he had heard a similar voice was when his high school science teacher had demonstrated the effects of inhaling helium. He swept his open palm at the chair. "Have a seat."

With movements more wooden than Ded expected, Dr. Ulro stepped into the room, sat down, clasped his very large hands together at his belly button, and in a simulation of masculine *savoir faire*, leaned back, raising his left ankle up onto his right knee.

Ded noticed the heel of the doctor's left running shoe was unworn.

O'Nadir, seemingly relieved he had a male interviewee who crossed his legs in accordance with the Laws of Nature, paid no notice to Dr. Ulro's stilted mannerisms.

After the introductions, Ded began. "You're a medical doctor?"

The doctor's bright eyes remained immobile as he considered what mask to wear. "Yes," he answered in his ultra-falsetto, his choice being a look of humility. "A plastic surgeon."

Ded noticed there was something peculiar about the doctor's faultless hairline. He squinted through his thick glasses, soon confirming what he had suspected. The well-groomed hair was a toupée.

"In fact," Dr. Ulro continued, enhancing his air of humility with a submissive smile unusual for a surgeon, much less for one who spoke like a machine-gunning, Okie-accented Tweetie Pie, "that's why I was in New York. I attended a plastic surgeons' convention."

The doctor broadened his smile and Ded saw his line of upper teeth, without warning, drop away from his upper gum and onto his lower lip. The doctor snapped his mouth shut. When he opened it again to resume his previous expression, his smile was back in place. His perfect teeth were false.

O'Nadir, running his eye over the purser's seating plan, missed this little dental display.

Ded took his cue from the inspector. "Where were you sitting on the plane?"

"At the front row, on the right."

"You're aware Ickey Jerusalem, one of your fellow passengers, died in the lavatory tonight?"

The smile-enhanced humility held for a few seconds before Ulro replaced it with a façade of seriousness. "Yes."

Ded was scrutinizing the skin on the doctor's neck, right behind the jaw. He could see some unevenly colored crease marks. The doctor's tan appeared to be from a bottle.

Ded looked to his right as O'Nadir pulled a stick of shockingly pink gum out of his pocket, and then, looking down, went through the procedure of exchanging the now tasteless wad in his mouth for the fresh piece in its wrapper. The doctor, thinking himself momentarily freed from the interrogators' attention, unclasped his hands, reached under his tracksuit top, and hoisted something underneath.

Ded, turning back more quickly than expected, caught a glimpse of the bottom of a ribbed abdominal girdle. Even the flat stomach was phony.

"During the flight, Doctor, did you see or hear anything that might have had something to do with the deceased's death? Peculiar movements? Noises?"

Dr. Ulro, whose hands had now returned to their motionless clasped position and whose face had adopted an impassive mask, considered the question, before at last replying in a few Uzi-like bursts of E above high C. "I'm afraid I was not in a position to see or hear anything. My schedule called for me to sleep the entire flight. I got up once, to go to the bathroom upstairs, but I didn't see or hear anything unusual."

Ded surveyed Dr. Ulro's unblemished face, hunting for evidence of anything else the doctor might have had done to make his appearance conform to the Marin County image. A nose job? A chin tuck? A lip thinning? A facelift? A skull-swap with a life-sized Ken doll?

"So, you didn't see the deceased at all, Dr. Ulro?"

This time, the doctor's pause before responding was so long that Ded was beginning to suspect he might not answer at all. "Only right before landing, after they found him. The purser woke me, saying he needed a doctor, and took me to the cubicle."

"What did you see when you got there?"

"One of the other passengers, a Mr. Urizen, was in the corridor, holding a clear plastic cleaning bag he said he had just removed from Ickey Jerusalem's head."

"And did you examine the deceased?"

"I felt his carotid artery. That's all." Dr. Ulro answered without emotion. "There was no pulse. His skin was cold. His eyes were frozen open. I could see it wasn't worth me going any further."

"Did you notice anything unusual about the body?"

"No." A long delay. "Other than maybe the look on the face."

"What was unusual about that?"

"It looked as though—" The doctor closed his eyes, searching for, or perhaps trying to suppress, the right simile.

"As though what?" Ded prodded him.

The doctor, his face still impassive, opened his eyes, and let his hopped-up oral interface reply. "As though, at the moment of his death, he had come face to face with Satan Incarnate."

Ded lifted an eyebrow. The description, though apt, was peculiar coming from the lips of a man so intent on conforming to the Marin County image. Religion in Marin County, it was well known, consisted mainly of harmless faiths such as transcendental meditation, Zen Buddhism, Tantric yoga, and the occasional charismatic acceptance of the love of Jesus Christ. Such an unrelentingly puritanical, party pooper as Satan Incarnate just didn't have what it took to be accepted as a valid religious concept.

Even more peculiar to Ded, though, was the look in the doctor's eyes as he uttered the words. Behind all the control, there had been, Ded was sure, a slight flicker of emotion; a certain hardness. A nastiness, even.

Regrettably, O'Nadir, who was untutored in Marin County religions, and had broken eye contact a moment too soon, noticed none of this. Thinking he had everything he needed, he terminated the interview long before Ded would have liked.

This was getting irritating. If O'Nadir wasn't going to let him pursue the case, what was the point of the inspector's having asked Ded to be involved in the interview?

❧

As the door closed after the doctor, O'Nadir swiveled to Ded. "Only four more to go and we're out of here."

Yes, Ded thought as he yawned, *and one of those four will definitely be her*.

He only hoped he could stay awake.

The interview room door opened slightly. There was a sigh. The door opened farther. There was another sigh. Then a pause. A deep breath. A surge of effort. And the door swung all the way open to reveal a huge, bald-headed, fat man gasping for breath and looking every bit as exhausted as Ded felt.

"Take a seat, Mr. Urizen," Ded directed without even glancing at the list of names. The man was wearing a monocle.

"You expect me to sit in that little thing?" Bacon Urizen replied in a voice suitable for Gregorian chants.

Ded indicated he did.

Taking a deep breath, Urizen lumbered into the room. He was in his late sixties, and had a deathly pale, almost albino complexion. His clothes, though nicely cut, were rumpled and sweat-stained. He collapsed onto the straining metal chair and sat there, panting but imperious. His head was enormous. And his body, too. Visible through his open suit jacket, the white silk shroud of his shirt clung to the contours of his flab.

"Do you really think it is right," Urizen complained in *basso profundo*, "keeping me down at baggage claim for over an hour at this time of night, and then making me walk up that broken escalator to get here? Aren't you aware who I am? Of my physical condition? In all my years of airplane travel, I don't think I've ever been treated so shabbily."

"I apologize," Ded offered. "I'm sure if Inspector O'Nadir had known of your physical condition, he would have arranged for a wheelchair."

O'Nadir nodded, although from his manner it was clear he was finding it hard to feel sorry for anyone wearing a monocle.

Urizen scoffed and looked toward the mirror.

His gesture was intended to indicate offense, but it went on too long, as though he had become distracted by the aging physical wreck he saw in the glass. From his quizzical, sorrowful expression, he appeared to be mourning the loss of the young, strong, sinewy body, and dashing good looks he must have had in his twenties. How in God's name had he come to this?

The lawyer returned his gaze to Ded, who immediately had the unsettling sensation that his remaining energy was draining out of his sleepless, jetlagged body and into the lawyer's sorrowful, questioning Cyclopsian eyepiece.

"I've only got a few questions," Ded said, struggling to shake off his sudden lassitude. "The faster we get through them, the sooner you can go."

Urizen studied Ded a few moments more before he relented, his imperiousness regained. "Well?"

"You were Ickey Jerusalem's lawyer?"

"Don't you mean 'are'?" Urizen replied huffily. "Or don't you think my representing his estate and trust, now that he is dead, is the same as representing *him*?"

For Urizen's benefit, Ded, fighting to maintain his flagging attention, made a production of writing the proper tense of the verb "to be" on a piece of paper. Then, singularly worn out by the effort, he glanced at the purser's seating plan. "Mr. Urizen, you sat in the middle on the left side of the plane, in the aisle seat next to Tharmas Luvah, Jerusalem's business manager, just behind Adam Ghostflea, his chauffeur. Is that right?"

"Yes? So?" The trust-and-estates lawyer moved his gaze from Ded and peered disdainfully through his monocle at the inspector—or more accurately, at the inspector's mouth, now re-engaged in an all-too-public mastication of its wad of shockingly pink gum.

Ded put a little mark on the plan by Urizen's name. "Did you see Jerusalem at all during the flight?"

"Given that I used the toilet at the end of the corridor next to his seat several times, to avoid climbing the spiral staircase, I would have had to be blind not to see him, wouldn't I?"

"Did he talk to you?"

Urizen hauled himself up higher. "Would you say asking to borrow my pen qualifies as talking?"

Ded suggested agreement by making a superfluous note.

"And," Urizen continued, "what would you say failing to return my pen qualifies as? Given that it was an expensive, silver ballpoint with my initials on it? A special gift from my predecessor as head of the firm?"

"Unavoidable in the circumstances," Ded answered flatly. He transcribed the description of the pen. "Did Jerusalem say anything when he asked to borrow it?"

Urizen removed his eyepiece and examined its patina of fingerprints in the light. "Do you expect me to reveal client confidences, Mr. Smith?"

"I just want to know if Jerusalem gave any sign that he might be planning to commit suicide. That's all."

The lawyer rubbed his monocle clean with a fold of his silk shirt and gave an indifferent shrug before reinserting it.

Plowing on through his fatigue, Ded asked his next question. "When the purser left you to guard the corridor, you took the bag off Jerusalem's head?"

"It was the least I could do, wouldn't you think, given the bag was mine?"

"Yours?"

Urizen monocled Ded and then O'Nadir. "Are you two students of deductive reasoning?"

"Yes," Ded said, while O'Nadir stopped chewing his gum. Although not sure whether his reasoning was deductive or inductive, the inspector blinked at Urizen as though he engaged in that class of reasoning all the time.

Urizen blinked back. "In that case, what would you conclude from the following facts? I have my mud-splashed overcoat cleaned in the New York hotel. Not needing to wear it in the limo to the airport, I bring it onto the plane still on the hanger with the plastic bag over it, and give it to the purser, who hangs it in the closet behind Mr. Jerusalem and Miss Vala. And after we land, when the purser brings my overcoat back to me, the cleaning bag is missing."

Ded absorbed this information, waves of tiredness sweeping through his body. "You're saying Jerusalem could have noticed your overcoat being hung in the closet, removed the cleaning bag some time later, and taken it into the toilet cubicle to commit suicide?"

"Is Yahweh the God of the Jews?"

Ded set his pen down and tilted back in his chair, steepling his fingers. "Could you tell me the reason for your trip to New York?"

"Don't you read the newspapers, Mr. Smith?"

"Enlighten me."

"So, you weren't aware that Hayley House had decided to publish a complete anthology of Mr. Jerusalem's poems? That the publication marked his transition from a minor Bay Area celebrity with a few slender, locally published collections, to a poet of national stature with epic poems expressing his new metaphysics? That, to celebrate this milestone, Hayley House was holding a week-long series of news conferences, book signings, cocktail parties, and other major publicity events in New York? And that Mr. Jerusalem and all of us flew out last Sunday to participate?"

"Sounds to me like Jerusalem should have been happy."

"'Should' and 'was' are two entirely different concepts, don't you agree?"

"So, you're saying he was *sad* about becoming a nationally recognized poet?"

"Sad? Happy? Rather one-dimensional emotions to expect from San Francisco's poet laureate, don't you think?"

Ded gazed for a moment at the dancing reflections of the overhead neon lights on the wheezing lawyer's glistening bald head. Urizen's tendency to turn every answer into a question was becoming frustrating. "Let me put it another way. If Jerusalem *did* commit suicide, would you be surprised?"

"I can't say I would have expected it, but surprised?" Urizen put his hand on his head, blocking the shimmering lights. "Would you believe me if I tell you that after having been Mr. Jerusalem's attorney for over a decade, nothing he did could ever surprise me?"

Ded reflected on what Inspector O'Nadir had said about his own past encounters with Ickey Jerusalem at the Condor strip joint and outside Finocchio's. There was, without a doubt, strong evidence Ickey Jerusalem's mind did not function in the normal way.

"Thank you, Mr. Urizen." Once more, O'Nadir ended the interview long before Ded was ready. "That's all for now."

Urizen gave O'Nadir a disdainful look that said, "*So,* that's *what you kept me in baggage claim over an hour for?*" He then staggered to his feet.

O'Nadir moved to the door and opened it. "Sorry again about the broken escalator," he said as Urizen hobbled through. "Please ask Security Officer Jarvis for the easiest way to get back to baggage claim. There must be a service elevator nearby that can take you."

The inspector closed the door on Urizen's backward-glancing frown. Turning to Ded, he said, "Three more and we can get out of here."

Ded was exhausted. The lack of sleep, the jet lag, Urizen's energy-draining monocle, and the effort of trying to extract information from an interviewee answering only with questions had done him in. He was also irked at being unable to complete the interviews to his satisfaction because Inspector O'Nadir, convinced it was all a suicide, kept cutting things short before Ded could get to the meaty stuff.

This, after all, is not my case, Ded thought. *It's the inspector's. I should butt out.*

"You know," Ded said to O'Nadir. "I think I've become too tired to go on. That last interview really took it out of me. I'm going to retreat to the observation chamber and become a spectator."

"You sure? I thought you were doing a great job."

"Yeah, well, you know, you can fool some of the people some of the time."

CHAPTER 5

THE DANCING SHADOWS—SECTION 2

During the several minutes' wait for the next interviewee, Ded sat in the darkened observation chamber. His tired, wandering mind transported him back three years to the Miami-to-L.A. red-eye, upon which he had discovered Bottom's error, and discovered why, in Plato's Cave, the protagonist's broadened perspective had led to a guh-yucking happiness, while Ded's had led only to emptiness and despair.

In Socrates's time, Ded mulled as he sat in the plane, *everyone believed that the stars, the planets, the moon, and the sun were different-sized, flat, shiny disks sliding around on the inside surface of a rotating, cozy sphere with the earth at its center. With such a mental boundary, Bottom's eye was naturally drawn to the brightest and warmest light in the sky, the sun, thinking it the ultimate reality.*

Ded peered through the airplane window into the night. *This was Bottom's error.*

Instead, if Bottom the weaver, had known modern astronomy, he would have seen past the sun and other shiny disks on the imaginary sphere, far, far beyond, to the real *ultimate reality, the chaotic, infinite space in which our tiny ball of dirt is floating, and he would have understood from this infinitely widened perspective, that everything, absolutely everything, is ultimately meaningless.*

One would have expected this realization on the Miami-to-L.A. red-eye to have not done anything to lessen Ded's pain, yet, peculiarly, that's what it began to do. Feeling he was on a roll, Ded excitedly pursued his argument further, tapping out the impeccable reasoning on his thigh.

When someone is upset, their acquaintances say, "Hey, get some perspective." What they mean is, "Step back, get above it, and widen your field of view. Distance yourself from the problem, so you can see it doesn't matter all that much." Therefore, if my perspective has now widened to such an extent that I can see nothing at all really matters, then how can I be upset by my divorce? Who cares about an infinitesimal, female life form stuck on a dust speck? What impact on the universe is there of the breaking of a single pair bonding in Buffalo, New York? How important to infinite space and time is a county clerk's ledger entry recording a change of legal status?

As he continued in this nothing-really-matters vein, Ded sensed, powered by a desperate hope and not a little self-delusion, yes… yes… yes… he could sense it… he could sense his terrible pain osmosing through the outer surface of his inner emptiness, dissipating faster and faster into the meaninglessness of the enormous black vacuum of space… until… yes… except for some sporadic traces… miraculously, the pain was gone.

Ded folded the pages of the Plato parable and put them into his suit jacket. *Never again,* he vowed, *will I lose my infinite perspective. From now on, I will live resolutely on the outside. Not just of the Cave, but of myself.*

A vow, which—given that with the pain gone his insides were

now even emptier than they had been before—was not as imprudent as it sounded.

For the next several weeks after Ded's divorce became final, he tried to inform various airplane seatmates about how he had seen the light—or in his case, the darkness—and how everything they thought important was but a shadow. But since their heads were still chained facing the wall, Ded was forced to convey the meaningless of the enormous black vacuum by casting finger shadows on the seatback, with the result he succeeded in eliciting at most a blank stare, a nervous laugh, or, as happened once, a detailed exposition of the intricacies of major league batting averages.

A month-and-a-half later, he made one last attempt. Deplaning from a puddle-jumper in Macon, Georgia, having endured two women seated behind him gossiping the whole flight about what "he said" when "she said" that "they said," he followed the still-at-it women into baggage claim and cornered them at the carousel.

"Excuse me," Ded said, "but aren't you aware that the earth, the sun, and all the other meandering accidental specks of matter in the universe are lost in an enormous black vacuum, doomed to spread out forever into an energyless nothingness or to contract into a geometric point?"

The women gave him cow-like stares. "No," the more talkative of the two admitted. "But then, we've been out of town the last few days."

Ded gave up ever trying to convert others to his widened perspective. But he didn't give up his vision of the ultimate reality, which not even Plato's Bottom had been able to see. In the three years between the revelatory Miami-to-L.A. red-eye flight when his divorce had become final and the New-York-to-San-Francisco red-eye flight he shared with Ickey Jerusalem, Ded built the Cave's abstract, objective logic into a sophisticated Grand Unifying Theory that armored both his outside and his inside surfaces, thereby managing, just barely—on a conscious level, at least—to keep his despair at bay.

Needless to say, at the unconscious level, where Ded was unable to fool himself with logic, he was still as lonely, bitter, and despondent as he'd been before.

❧

Ded watched the door to the interview room crack open. A few seconds later, there appeared a diminutive head with a wide, nervous grin from which slithered a wormlike tongue. The head peered straight at Ded through two gigantic, bulging-out, crossed eyes. It was the comic book insect from the Cave! With the same cartoonist's black outlines of the body and its features. The pixelated, pastel in-fillings. Now, all puffed up with a lightweight, third dimension.

Or so it appeared to Ded. Although he did not know it, his desire to stay awake to see Miss Beulah Vala had not been strong enough to offset his tiredness or his sudden indifference to the investigation due to O'Nadir continually cutting him off. Ded had fallen into an eye-open dream in which, as he would realize later when he read the transcripts, he was hearing and understanding every word spoken, but at the same time beholding each of the remaining interviewees not as themselves but as characters from the Cave. Aurally, he was absorbing all the objective facts, while visually, he was absorbing a subjective message that, had he been more aware, he would have realized was of greater significance to the case than those facts could ever be.

Even stranger, now freed of the obligation or even desire to ask penetrating questions, Ded found himself passively going with the flow. So much so that in his dream, he had become "Inspector Ded," a doppelgänger of Inspector O'Nadir, asking the police inspector's questions and thinking his thoughts.

❧

The imagined Inspector Ded, having seen Urizen out of the interview room, plopped back into his seat just as his next interviewee arrived. He looked at his list of names. "Adam Ghostflea? Jerusalem's chauffeur?"

The insect's smile turned worried, tightening sufficiently to reveal a pair of small fangs hanging over his lower lip.

Inspector Ded pointed to the chair. "Please, sit down."

Bowing repeatedly, the bug bobbed awkwardly on its hind legs, revealing a carapace-backed, muscle-bound body much too large for its head. Eyes down, it positioned itself in the seat to look as small as possible, its multiple handlike forelegs gripping and re-gripping each other on its lap.

During the interrogation, Inspector Ded did not need to take notes. To each question, the bug's response was the same—to dip its head lower, waggle its thin tongue, and mumble in a guttural voice, "I didn't notice."

By the end of the interview, Adam Ghostflea's head had burrowed beneath the folds of his armored chest and could be seen no more.

Inspector Ded gave up. "Thank you, Mr. Ghostflea. You may go."

The insect popped its head from its chest, stood unsteadily, each eye still looking at the other, and bowing again and again, backed away in the general direction of the door.

Sadly, it was not in the precise direction of the door, as was soon attested to by the newly supine orientation of the hat stand bearing Inspector Ded's coat.

The interviewee righted the stand, replaced the coat, scurried toward Inspector Ded, mumbled its embarrassed apologies, and then again backed away, bowing over and over, this time scoring a direct hit on the doorknob with its pestilent rear end.

"Hey!" Inspector Ded growled. "That's enough."

The insect, still bowing and apologizing profusely, reached back with one of its many forearms, pulled open the door and shuffled out, backwards.

"Christ," Inspector Ded muttered, wondering how he could avoid touching the doorknob when he left the interview room.

❧

Almost immediately, there was a knock.

Ded felt a touch of excitement well up inside him. This had to be her!

"Come in."

The door opened, revealing the small, wiry, black goat from the Cave, standing on its hind legs while delicately pinching the doorknob through a handkerchief held between his front cloven hooves.

That insect who was just here, Ded thought, *must have quite a reputation.*

The goat stepped inside and let the door close. Ded studied him, noticing two important differences from the comic-book goat. One was its expression, which now, instead of showing enjoyment of the shadows on the wall, was morose. The other was the erect member, which Ded didn't remember from the parable, now being conspicuously presented. *A good two feet long,* Ded figured.

"Have a seat," Inspector Ded said, unfazed by the goat's bargepole swaying stiffly in the air.

The goat put his handkerchief away and sat down. He hurriedly surveyed the room before coming to rest on his reflection in the mirror. Appraising his appearance, he patted his black curly hair with his hoof and then stroked his chin whiskers. Although his face was forlorn, his dark eyes seemed interested only in the reflection.

Inspector Ded coughed to get the goat's attention. "You are Tharmas Luvah, Jerusalem's business manager?"

The goat cocked his head, avoiding the swaying obstruction rising from his lap. "Yeah, that's me." The goat's voice had a nasal, slightly foreign character.

"I hope you don't mind me asking," Inspector Ded said, "but I couldn't help noticing a slight accent. Where are you from?"

"Here. I grew up in San Francisco. But my parents were Maronite Christians from Lebanon."

Inspector Ded nodded indifferently, before reviewing the seating plan. "During the flight, you sat in the inside seat next to Bacon Urizen, on the left side of the cabin and behind Adam Ghostflea, Jerusalem's chauffeur?"

"That's right. Ghostflea was just in front of us, knocked out with some sleeping pills I gave him." The goat stopped. "No. Wait." Trying to remember, he looked up and stuck out his exceptionally large, forceful tongue, much larger and longer than that of the insect. He absentmindedly flicked the head of his erection. "No, I got it wrong. The sleeping pills was on the flight out to New York. But then, thinking about it, he coulda been sleeping on the flight back to San Francisco, too."

The goat looked apologetic. "It's tough to tell with that guy."

Ded commenced with his questions.

The goat had not talked to Jerusalem during the flight, had used only the upstairs toilet, and had seen nobody near Jerusalem, not even Beulah Vala.

"She musta been there," the goat explained, "but I couldn't see nothing from where I was sitting. Before I sat down, I did see her when her and Ickey came on board. I remember kissing her hand."

The goat's eyes softened. "Such a small hand, yuh know. Like a child's." His attention seemed to drift inward. "Delicate, pink, innocent." He inhaled through his goat's nose. "Smelling like roses."

Ded gave out a long, pleasurable sigh, his mind wandering through the luscious description.

"Goddamn!" The goat's face fell. "I knew Ickey was gonna do something like this."

Inspector Ded's ears perked up. "You thought Jerusalem might commit suicide?"

"In New York, he was acting so peculiar."

"In what way?"

The goat opened his mouth to answer and then hesitated. "I dunno," he mumbled. "Peculiar. Like he was just going through the motions. Hiding some sorta big plan up his sleeve unrelated to his poetry. Yuh know what I mean?"

Inspector Ded dipped his head to one side, trying to make contact with the goat's downcast eyes behind his moving member. "What made you—"

"I just knew, that's all," the goat bristled. "I'd been his business manager since his career began. I knew him like I know myself."

The possibilities of a goat with an erection of such proportions knowing Jerusalem like he knew himself was something Ded would have pursued. But reduced by his dream to a mere mimic of Inspector O'Nadir, Inspector Ded only looked at his watch.

He thanked the goat for his help and released him.

The goat got up, headed to the door, started to reach for the knob, and then, catching himself, stopped, and took out his handkerchief. With a show of abhorrence, he deftly pinched the knob around to the right with both hooves, pulled the door open, and hurried out before it could swing closed onto his member.

⁂

Ded, sitting in the darkened viewing chamber, dwelling on the goat's luscious description of Beulah Vala's delicate hand, lay his head down and closed his eyes. An extraordinary sensation of peace swept over his body, lifting him up off his chair and into the air. Languidly, he drifted out the back wall and into a mellow, moonlit garden.

Somewhere in the clear night sky above, he thought he could hear a woman's soothing voice whispering a single word, over and over again. He strained to make it out.

The word was "mercy."

⁂

Security Officer Jarvis stuck his head through the interview room door. "Miss Beulah Vala," he announced with an odd grin. He withdrew his head. Then, pushing the door open with his back, a white leather coat draped over his forearm, he escorted the blind personal assistant into the room.

Ded, floating through the garden of his dream, searching for the source of the soothing female whisper, raised his eyes to the moon and shot back into the body of Inspector Ded on the chair in the interview room, the moon following just as quickly, metamorphosing into the stunningly beautiful female face of the entering personal assistant. Very young-looking. With pale, soft, pink features. Radiating with a lunar glow of unformed wonder, hope, faith, and due to her dark glasses, a touch of mystery.

Inspector Ded sprang to his feet. "Uh, come in, come in."

Bedazzled, Ded felt himself being drawn forward by a physical attraction stronger than any attraction he had ever felt before. Certainly, much stronger than any attraction he had ever felt for a cow.

For that's what he beheld. A petite, pink cow standing on her hind legs.

It was the cow from the Cave, but changed beyond belief. In the Cave, she had been a mere faded, two-dimensional image, evoking no emotion at all. Here, though, she had become wonderfully alive, devastatingly lovely, and powerfully magnetic.

Ded's eyes traced down the line of her delicate neck, down her smooth, furry shoulders, past her beseeching front legs, and then onwards, farther down, past her sensuous four-part stomach, to her—

Holy Cow! Ded thought as he beheld her udder.

It was immense. Plump. Milk-filled. Comforting. Sticking straight out, teats and all, like a gigantic, over-inflated rubber glove. Pulling Ded in with an irresistible, hypnotic power. Enclosing him within its warm, pulsating, spongy flesh.

A previously unknown contentedness welled up inside him.

Officer Jarvis guided the cow into the chair, grinned at Inspector Ded, and left, taking her leather coat with him.

Inspector Ded remained standing, his eyes glued to the stupendous udder.

The cow in the dark glasses sat demurely in her chair, hind legs crossed at the knee, her dainty front hooves resting on her exploding mammary gland.

Coming sufficiently to his senses, Inspector Ded sat. He cleared his throat. "I apologize, Miss Vala, for putting you through this so soon after the shock of Ickey Jerusalem's death." His voice exuded an almost leering sympathy. "But we need to establish what happened tonight, while it is still fresh in everyone's mind."

"Please, Inspector," the cow insisted in the brave, innocent voice of a high school beauty queen whose team had just lost the championships. "Don't apologize. I'm happy to tell you everything I know."

Inspector Ded adopted Officer Jarvis's grin—the grin of a man who had come to the realization that since his voluptuous interviewee was blind, he could look at her udder to his heart's content.

"During the flight, Miss Vala, you sat next to Ickey Jerusalem?"

"Yes," she exhaled wistfully.

The resulting undulating udder movement caught Inspector Ded's attention, causing him for an instant to forget his next question. "And did you leave Jerusalem's side at all?"

"Only when I went to the bathroom."

Inspector Ded raised his eyebrows. "You went to the bathroom by yourself?"

The cow looked puzzled. "Don't you?"

"Uh, yes," Inspector Ded stammered. "What I meant was, being blind, wouldn't you need some help finding your way around?"

The cow smiled, presenting a line of perfect, ruminant molars. "The toilet was right across the aisle. It's not all that difficult to feel for an empty cubicle, squeeze inside, find the seat, and latch the door." She hesitated. "Although, I have to admit that sometimes, getting out of such cubicles is another matter. Especially with those accordion doors. Once, as a kid, I was stuck inside for half an hour, until a stewardess heard me banging and got me out."

The cow became pensive as though remembering what had taken place years before.

Inspector Ded, his critical faculties submerged in glowing infatuation, became similarly pensive—although, in his case, it was because his eyes, having slipped after his last question, were riveted once again on the soft, pink, palpitating flesh of the cow's milk bag.

With some effort, Inspector Ded unbolted his eyes from the object of his pensiveness and welded them onto his interviewee's dark glasses. "How many times did you go to the bathroom during the flight?"

The cow put her delicate right hoof on her cheek to help her recollect. "Twice. Once after the drinks service. And once right before I fell asleep, about four hours into the flight."

"When you fell asleep, was Jerusalem still sitting next to you?"

"Yes."

"And you didn't hear him get up after that and go to the toilet?"

"No. I'm a very deep sleeper." Her statement was made with such naïveté, such purity, Inspector Ded was certain she had to be telling the truth. He caught his eyes drifting again and dragged them back to the sweet bovine face. "What was Jerusalem doing during the flight?"

"Writing."

"How did you know he was writing?"

"By the sound of his pen on the paper," she answered languorously. "And his breathing when he was straining to come up with the right word. And the feel of his elbow as it brushed my arm whenever he reached the end of a line."

The waves of the cow's voice washed over Ded's body, lowering him back onto the freshly plowed garden earth.

"Did he say what he was writing?"

The cow stroked her longish right ear with the tips of her right hoof. "No. But they must have been poems. Couplets or epigrams, at first. I could tell by the way he quickly tore out the pages and put them in his pocket, to be transcribed later. After that, he was working on something longer. He must not have completed it because he never tore it out."

Inspector Ded made a note to check the contents of the poet's pockets.

"Did Jerusalem say anything unusual to you during the flight?"

"Only once, just as I was falling off to sleep. He put his hand on my arm. 'Beulah,' he said, 'I'm ready. Ready, at last, to unite with the highest level of God's consciousness.'"

Inspector Ded scrunched up his face. "What did he mean by that?"

"I assume," the cow said, her opaque shades aimed disconcertingly at the inspector's forehead, "he was at last on the verge of uniting his subjective self with God's infinite and eternal creativity."

"Right," Inspector Ded drawled, drawing his chin into a skeptical pose. "Did Jerusalem say he was planning to do this in the toilet?"

"No." The cow shifted, setting off another tiny wave of liquid motion.

Transfixed, Inspector Ded waited until the motion stopped. "When Jerusalem said he was going to… what were his words?"

"Unite with the highest level of God's consciousness," the cow repeated serenely.

As Inspector Ded wrote the phrase, he asked, "Did you take that to mean he was intending to commit suicide?"

"No. Just the opposite." Her youthful voice was earnest, almost excited. "I took it to mean he was on the verge of achieving eternal life."

Inspector Ded raised his eyes to the ceiling, dropped his tongue out of his open mouth, and rotated the tip of his index finger around his ear in an expression of his view of the organizing principle of Jerusalem's brain, and the cow's as well.

Inspector Ded considered his sightless interviewee and then, unable to resist, asked, "So, let me get this straight. You think in ending up dead on the toilet, Ickey Jerusalem somehow achieved eternal life?"

The cow smiled as though in complete denial about what had occurred on the plane. "To you, he's dead. To me, he lives on in the eternal and infinite creativity of the highest level of God's mind."

"Right," Inspector Ded deadpanned. "I'll make sure the coroner notes it. 'Although appears dead, in fact lives on in the eternal and infinite creativity of the highest level of God's consciousness.'"

Inspector Ded now had no doubts. This metaphysical crap was the clincher. The deceased had killed himself not in a fit of depression, but in a daft attempt to achieve some poetic state of nirvana, some highfalutin version of *Arms Up!* with Carol Doda.

Inspector Ded thanked the cow for her "enlightening" statement. Then, with much laying on of hands, helped her out the door, going so far as to personally guide her delicate hoof to the insect-blessed doorknob so she could pull it open herself.

Part way through the door, she turned back to the inspector. "Don't feel bad about having ogled my udders. It didn't bother me. After all, it's not your fault that God, the Creator, in his imaginative wisdom, has instilled such a desire in men."

When Inspector O'Nadir entered the darkened room behind the two-way mirror, Ded Smith, now free of the Inspector-Ded strait-jacket, was fast asleep under his overcoat, an intense, dreamy smile spread across his lips, murmuring, "Yes, unite with the highest level of God's consciousness."

Inspector O'Nadir had invited Ded along for a second opinion on whether Jerusalem could have been murdered. But given that Miss Vala's evidence of a suicidal disposition in the poet seemed conclusive, the toilet door had been locked from the inside, Ded's questions hadn't uncovered any evidence of murder during his interviews of the first three from first class, *and* it looked like he'd been asleep during the last three interviews, the inspector saw no reason to wake Ded now.

Instead, he told Officer Jarvis to rouse the life insurance investigator at five a.m. for his flight to Tokyo and went home to his wife to catch a few hours of shut-eye.

As a result, it would take some time before O'Nadir would learn from Ded what he had missed.

And an even longer time for Ded to at last realize how Ickey Jerusalem had fallen victim to Bottom's error.

CHAPTER 6

FEELING THE CHAINS

Around six in the morning, Ded Smith boarded his scheduled flight to Tokyo. His peculiar infatuation with a cow the night before didn't bother him at all, nor did his unusual doppelgänger tour inside the mind of Inspector O'Nadir. He had managed to rationalize them both away almost immediately after Security Officer Jarvis shook him awake in the viewing chamber.

Sicilian Illusions of the severest kind, Ded had categorized them, *unquestionably due to a highly suggestive state induced by falling asleep in the Cave.*

The concept of the Sicilian Illusion had come from something Ded had encountered at Buffalo State College. Something that had rescued him from his inability to form normal human relationships there. Something that, for the first time, had provided him with an authorized framework from which to understand the world. Something that went by the name "sociology."

While most of Ded's fellow students saw a major in sociology as a way to get through college without having to work, Ded saw it as a revelation; a complete and prefabricated world view that suited him perfectly. He worshipped sociology's detached objectivity, its reduction of humanity to desiccated graphs, pie-charts, and scatter-point diagrams on sheets of paper (the discipline's glorified extension of the stick figures Ded had sketched as a boy), and most of all, sociology's apparent ability, through those abstractions, to understand the behavior of a community from the outside much better than its members understood it from the inside.

Ded's favorite professor (who also wore a monocle, by the way) had done a study of a small Sicilian village with a strong prohibition against women engaging in premarital sex. Having examined different cultures from all over the world, seeing where the prohibition against premarital sex existed and where it did not, the professor believed the prohibition arose to prevent premature childbearing in cultures in which effective birth control was not available and/or children were not raised communally.

The Sicilians, unaware of how their culture compared with others, had a somewhat different view.

If a Sicilian father stumbled upon his daughter engaging in premarital sex, the study showed he was unlikely to lean over and say, "I'm sorry to trouble you, my dear, but don't you realize you're living in a culture in which children are not raised communally?" Instead, in 97.8% of the cases reviewed, the actual words of the Sicilian fathers were "Mamma mia!" This was invariably followed (in Italian) by "You've been ruined!" Punctuated almost immediately thereafter by the father pulling out his shotgun and sending the damaged goods back to their maker. (The body of the daughter's piteous lover, minus a few of its severed vandal's tools, would follow sometime later.)

Interviews showed the reason for the Sicilian father's fatal reaction was his unquestioning perception that the mere penetration of his daughter's vagina by an unauthorized penis would make her not just a social outcast, but irrevocably, physically unclean—and once she had become irrevocably, physically unclean, she was better off dead.

This "Sicilian Illusion"—the perception by the father of something that wasn't there—had soon become Ded's term of choice for any emotion-laden perception by someone locked up inside an experience, unable to see the truth a dispassionate observer standing outside the experience could see. Such as the perception of a person in love that his lover was ideal—which Ded could see was nothing more than hormonally induced pair bonding. Or the perception that one's ethnic group was superior—which Ded could see was a mere community cohesion mechanism. Or that the fashionable was beautiful—which Ded could see was mere peer-group conformity. Or that the expensive luxury item was exquisite—which Ded could see was mere status seeking. Or, it eventually seemed, the perception of anything by anyone other than Ded.

After the subsequent development of his Grand Unifying Theory, Ded understood that Sicilian Illusions were just the flip side of what had happened to him on the Miami-to-L.A. red-eye. If widening his perspective to the infinite made everything lose meaning, and thereby wiped out his emotional engagement, then logically, the only way to obtain meaning and emotional engagement was to put blinders on. The more you narrowed your field of view and focused on what was in front of you, while ignoring what those outside could see was really going on, the more meaning and emotional engagement you had. To state it succinctly, meaningfulness and emotional engagement were simply Sicilian Illusions created by a limited perspective.

For the next few days, Ded had no time to think about anything other than his Tokyo investigation. The chairman of one of the major Japanese trading groups died after being mysteriously crushed to death underneath a mass of kids at Tokyo Disneyland. Since the kids had dispersed before they could be identified and questioned, the Japanese detectives were stumped as to motive. Ded, however, able to see things from the outside, promptly deduced and—with the help of a second autopsy and some demanded medical records—soon proved that the chairman suffered from an especially active, limb-waving, full-body-bucking form of grand mal epilepsy, a condition that not only had not been disclosed on his application for insurance, but also naturally had caused the less empathetic kids at the theme park to mistake him for a free ride. Olympian Life was let off the hook once again.

On the final morning, as Ded was in his room writing up his fax report, he got a call from his bureaucrat boss at the home office. "Ded, we've got a claim with respect to a twenty-million-dollar insurance policy on a likely suicide in San Francisco. Our local adjuster was following up with the police, and they mentioned that someone from the company, namely you, already knew about the case, and in fact, had sat in on the initial interviews."

"Yeah. The death occurred on my flight, and the detective on duty was a friend of mine. So, during the layover, I helped him out."

"Well, given your connections, I'd like you to go back to San Francisco and make sure no facts supporting a verdict of suicide are overlooked by the local police. As you know, if it's suicide, the company doesn't have to pay."

Ded bridled. "Rest assured, I will use all my efforts to reconstruct what happened."

Ded was no one's hired gun. He knew that once he started entering into investigations with preconceptions, he would lose the dispassionate objectivity which allowed him to be so good at his job. He would find out the truth, no matter what the consequences.

Plus, he had to admit, he was once again eager for the chance to show his pal, Inspector O'Nadir, how it was done. As a life insurance claims adjuster, he could now conduct his investigation on his own terms, without being cut off by the inspector whenever the inquiry was getting to the juicy stuff.

"Who's the beneficiary?" Ded asked.

There was a ruffling of papers at the other end of the phone. "Miss Beulah Vala, the insured's personal assistant."

At the mention of the lady's name, his bovine infatuation popped out of the Sicilian Illusion category into which Ded had crammed it, and before he could react, inflated his emptiness with incredible pleasure. He instantly reason-wrestled the feeling back into its box, but not before noticing something significant. The face looking up at him as he shut the lid was not that of a cow, but of a woman—a beautiful, young, strawberry blond with pink skin and dark glasses.

Ded told his boss to book him in business class back to San Francisco, so he could sleep the whole flight. It was important to be fresh for what was to come.

Finishing his report, Ded added his signature and then wrote out the date: October 28th, 1977.

Touching the pen's clicker to the end of his tongue, Ded looked up, mulling over the date. He had a feeling the 28th of October held personal importance. But how? Searching his memory, he came across the image of his mother, hobbling up the steps of the massive stone cathedral in which she prayed each day.

St. Jude, Ded realized. On the Catholic calendar, the 28th of October was the day of St. Jude.

Not one to seek meaning in mere coincidences, Ded unceremoniously ushered the saint out of his mind and set about preparing for his trip back to San Francisco.

Hopefully, by the time he got there, the home office would have gotten the contact details of the interviewees from Inspector O'Nadir and set up the necessary appointments.

Ded squinted out the window of his return flight from Tokyo at the bright, late-October sun. Having crossed the International Date Line, Ded was arriving the same day in San-Francisco time that he had left in Japan time, making the trip just one long St. Jude's Day. He lowered his eyes to the brilliant white fog shrouding the Bay Area below, looking for all the world like white North Dakota ice. Ded shivered as claustrophobia engulfed him again. Although the feeling had existed in one form or another since he developed his Grand Unifying Theory, during the last several months, it had become increasingly intense.

In the distance, beyond some scattered business-district high-rises, were two red towers sticking up through the earthbound clouds.

The Golden Gate, Ded thought, recalling his investigation in the holy city of Jerusalem a few months before. That city also had a "Golden Gate." In the old city wall. A now-bricked-up portal leading to Gethsemane, the garden where, according to the New Testament, Christians first knelt when they prayed. The garden where Jesus was betrayed.

Did Jesus feel the claustrophobia, too, Ded mused, *and thus, decide death was the only way out?*

The plane dropped into the fog.

Or was it Judas Iscariot?

❧

The San Francisco Hall of Justice squatted over an entire city block on the southern edge of downtown. Backed up against an elevated freeway, the dreary seven-story building separated itself from the surrounding wooden cafes, vacant lots, and bail bondsmen storefronts with a moat of one-way multi-lane streets. Clad in thin slabs of imitation granite, the structure was devoid of all decoration, except at its entrance, where massive concrete steps marched up between two septic-tank-sized urns holding symmetrical hemlock spruces to a set of three-story-high Cecil B. DeMille doors. The building gave the overall impression that the architects, intending to create one of the grandest edifices in the city, had run out of money after completing the entrance.

In front of the Hall of Justice, Ded got out of his airport cab with his bags. Before going in, he glanced up through the fog at the barred windows on the top floor, lit up by the late afternoon sun. He had always thought it ironic that the prisoners in the Hall of Justice had a much better view than the cops.

Ded entered the building, took the elevator to the basement, and walked down a long corridor to a door at the end. At eye level was a hand-printed, cardboard sign: "Inspector O'Nadir, Special Homicide Division."

Ded went in. The room was small, dingy, and windowless. A single, flickering fluorescent light hung from the ceiling pipes. A disheveled, gum-chewing O'Nadir sat facing the left wall, bent over a pile of files on a dilapidated pedestal desk, oblivious (as usual) to the lack of status of his surroundings.

Ded set his carry-on bags on the floor and moved into the inspector's field of view.

"Dr. Deadly!" O'Nadir exclaimed, his tone a combination of genuine affection and appreciation for an excuse for a temporary respite from his paperwork. "Your boss told me you'd be returning to Baghdad-by-the-Bay. A twenty-million-dollar insurance policy on Ickey Jerusalem's life, huh?"

"Yes, taken out on Monday, October 10th, just under two weeks before he died."

"No shit. Who's the beneficiary?"

"Beulah Vala." Ded spoke her name without betraying a hint of emotion.

"Ah, yes, the lovely *personal* assistant." O'Nadir drew out the word "personal" as lewdly as a happily married man with three grown daughters was allowed to do.

Ded feigned indifference. "You have some evidence on how 'personal' an assistant Miss Vala was?"

"Yeah," O'Nadir grinned. "Her tits."

Ded gave O'Nadir an obligatory smile, while wondering whether O'Nadir would apply the same logic to his well-endowed youngest daughter, who was intent on becoming a nun. "My home office has arranged for me to meet Miss Vala tomorrow."

"You're a *lucky* man," O'Nadir said, lecherously cracking his gum.

Ded kept the obligatory smile a few moments longer before letting it fade, trying to achieve just the right balance necessary to indicate that Miss Vala may or may not have had tits, but that he had more important things on which to focus his attention.

"What did the autopsy show?" Ded inquired.

"Death by suffocation."

"Any bruises on the body?"

"Went over it with a fine-tooth comb. No bruises anywhere, except for some minor ones on the underside of his toes and the balls of his feet. Fits with forensics's confirmation the scuff marks we found on the lower part of the door came from Jerusalem's shoes, probably while kicking during his death throes."

Ded adjusted his thick glasses. "The autopsy show any drugs?"

"No, just a lot of wine. But not enough for him to pass out."

"Any fingerprints on the door handle?"

"The purser's on the outside, probably made when he forced the door open. There is no handle on the inside, just a small button on the latch slide. Too small to take identifiable prints from."

"What about fingerprints in the cubicle, ignoring for the moment the plastic bag, which was removed before Ben got there?"

"Jerusalem's prints are on the front top and bottom edge of the toilet seat cover. The only other identifiable ones in the cubicle belong to Bacon Urizen, the lawyer, and they're everywhere—on the seat, the wall, the door, the sink, the mirror."

"None from Miss Vala?"

"Not in the crime scene, only in the lavatory closest to the aisle. Which fits what we were told by Urizen and—while you were sleeping during the interview—Beulah Vala." He paused. "The problem is the other set in Jerusalem's cubicle."

"There's another set of prints?"

"Yeah. Glove prints. Suede."

Ded pushed his thick glasses up with the knuckle of his writing hand. "What was someone doing in Jerusalem's lavatory wearing suede gloves?"

"Lifting the toilet seat, I'd say. There's a thumbprint on top of the seat cover on the left and another on the right side, and corresponding finger grip marks on the underside of the seat edges." O'Nadir cracked his gum. "So, have you seen anybody recently using suede gloves in a toilet?"

"No, but I'll keep my eyes open next time I go."

"Good idea. You'll find you pee on your feet a lot less that way."

After a perfunctory show of appreciation for O'Nadir's guy-humor, Ded pulled his loose-leaf notepad out of his inside jacket pocket and recorded the information he had just received.

"Oh," O'Nadir remembered, "and we found prints from two fingers and the thumb of Jerusalem's right hand on a bar of soap lying in the basin. Judging from its flattened corner, Jerusalem used it to write the farewell message near the lower left edge of the mirror."

"BI?"

"That's right." O'Nadir wrinkled his forehead. "You'd think a poet would be able to spell."

Ded nibbled the head of his pen. "Unless the poet in question happened to be in the middle of uniting his subjective self with God's infinite and eternal creativity."

"Yeh, right," O'Nadir chuckled. "Talk about shooting your spelling completely to hell."

Ded gave O'Nadir the requisite return chuckle and briskly moved on. "What about the plastic bag?"

"Someone tore off the tag. Just the staple was left. Forensics found fibers from Bacon Urizen's overcoat on the inside of the bag, confirming it must have been his. Surprisingly, there were no fibers of any kind on the outside. Nor any other foreign substances either outside or inside. Only lots of oily fingerprints. Jerusalem's left handprint on the shoulder of the sealed end, likely made when he removed the bag from the hanger and carried it into the cubicle. And his left and right handprints together near the center of the bag's opening end, with thumbs inside and fingers outside, consistent with him pulling the bag over his head with both hands. In addition, Bacon Urizen's prints were all over the bag, and there was a set of the purser's at the sealed end, close to the hole for the hanger hook. There were also two sets of unidentified prints. One, from suede gloves, all over the bag, and the other, from a pair of extra-large hands, at the extreme edges of the bottom opening, this time with fingers inside and thumbs outside."

Ded mulled the results over. "Urizen's prints make sense, given his overcoat fibers being on the inside of the bag. But the purser's prints? Didn't he say in your airport interview he hadn't touched anything in the cubicle? And didn't Urizen say that after removing the bag from the cubicle, he'd put it on the seat in the other toilet, making sure nobody touched it?"

"I guess so."

"As for the glove prints, are they identical to those you found on the toilet seat?"

"Matching glove prints is an experimental technique beyond the department's expertise. So, we've been using a criminology academic at UC Berkeley. He says the two sets of gloves prints are not inconsistent. But since the toilet seat ones were badly smeared, he can't say for sure."

"As for the unidentified large handprints," Ded moved on, "I recall that Dr. Ulro had large hands. Did you check the prints against his?"

"Unfortunately, we failed to get fingerprints from Dr. Ulro. Officer Jarvis was keeping everyone in separate places, and the fingerprinting guy overlooked the back room, where the doctor was. I've meant to do something about it, but since the doctor appears to have no connection with Jerusalem, I haven't pushed it. No problem, though. Since he's a doctor, his prints should be on file with the California Medical Board. It's too late now. Those Sacramento government workers always quit early on Fridays. But on Monday morning, I'll ask them to fax us a copy."

Ded stroked his chin. "The unidentified prints could have come from the packers at the dry cleaners."

"Great minds think alike. I asked the New York hotel that Jerusalem's group stayed in to give us the contact details of their dry cleaners early this week. The hotel just got back to us. Angel Cleaners. I'll ring them tomorrow morning and let you know what they say."

"Good. Nothing else unusual about the bag?"

"Only that from its creases, it appears to have been folded up at one time into a small square."

Ded asked about Ickey Jerusalem's personal effects. O'Nadir went through the list. Other than the clothes he had been wearing at his death, there were his black leather jacket the purser had hung in the closet, a spiral notebook found on his seat, and miscellaneous items from his trouser pockets. O'Nadir removed a manila folder from his desk drawer and poured out the contents for Ded to examine: a spiral notebook with about half its pages missing; a key ring; a wallet containing the usual licenses, credit cards, and cash; and four crumpled notebook pages torn from the wire spiral.

Ded picked up one of the loose pages. In the flickering light, he read its single, hand-printed line:

The tygers of wrath are wiser than the horses of instruction.

He lifted his eyes and gestured to O'Nadir with the piece of paper. "One thing's for certain. Jerusalem could never have gotten a job as a sign writer at the zoo."

Ded studied the line again. Maybe the "BI" message on the mirror had indeed been a misspelling. "Can I borrow these?"

Inspector O'Nadir puffed up his cheeks and then let the air out through his protruding lips. "Against procedure. But then, I don't see how anybody'll care much. Forensics has finished with them. I've got photocopies. You can take the spiral notebook as well, if you want." He opened his desk drawer. "And this transcript of the interviews I conducted at the airport."

Ded put the four torn-out pages under the front cover of Jerusalem's notebook and picked up the transcript. "Oh, last week when we looked into Jerusalem's toilet cubicle together, it was for only a few seconds. Since it wasn't my case, I didn't pay all that much attention. But there was one thing I noticed that didn't make sense."

O'Nadir perked up.

"If Ickey Jerusalem went into that airplane toilet intending to suffocate himself with the plastic bag," Ded said, "why did he take his pants down?"

The inspector's face showed this question had not occurred to him. However, not wanting to look like he had missed something important, he immediately came up with a theory. "People hung on a gallows sometimes drop a load in their pants as they die. Maybe Jerusalem wanted to make sure if the same thing happened to him, it would go into the toilet."

"If that were the case," Ded said, "it wouldn't have been very effective."

"Why not?"

"Jerusalem was sitting on the lid."

O'Nadir scrunched up his face. "Okay. How about this? He started off sitting with the lid up, and then, in his death agonies, he stood, the lid fell closed, and he sat back down."

"Clearly," Ded said, "you're not a devotee of Ockham's Razor."

"Who? What?"

"A 14th-century theologian-monk, William of Ockham, who, according to a Franciscan friar sitting next to me once on a flight, preached that the simplest explanation should always be preferred to the more complex ones."

O'Nadir crossed his arms. "Ded, I don't understand why you're so interested in seat lids, monk razors, and that sort of stuff here. You still worried Jerusalem didn't kill himself? I mean, no matter what evidence you find, the only way you'll prove it was murder and not suicide is to find a murderer who can get out of a locked airline toilet without unlocking the door."

"Put that way," Ded agreed, "I'd say it was a tall order."

"So?" The inspector waited for the explanation.

"All the murderer would've had to do is lock the door from the outside after leaving Jerusalem's body inside."

"How could anyone do that? There's no latch on the outside of the toilet cubicle."

"It could be locked the same way the purser must have unlocked door when he was looking for Jerusalem. You and Ben, having never flown, wouldn't know, but any experienced traveler could tell you. The bolt on the inside door latch is fixed to a small, plastic sign visible on the outside. When the bolt slides over to lock, the sign slides from 'VACANT' to 'OCCUPIED.' In the middle of the sign is a tiny, vertical slot. By sticking a pointed object in that slot, anyone outside can slide the sign in order to unlock or lock the door."

"Shit. So, we *could* have a murder case on our hands."

"Unless, of course," Ded said, enjoying his little moment of triumph, "it's a suicide after all."

CHAPTER 7

STRESS-RAISERS IN THE METAL

Due to a discount arrangement negotiated by his employer, Ded was required to stay only at Holiday Inns. In San Francisco, where there were three, he chose the one variously advertised as "the Financial District Holiday Inn" or "the Chinatown Holiday Inn," depending on which potential clientele the hotel was trying to mislead at the time.[1] The place had everything one might expect of a large San Francisco hotel—from a red-uniformed, Chinese doorman out front looking for tips from passersby to a chirpy reception staff ruled by room-info cards slotted into a pre-computer "rack board" on the wall.

Ded skirted the doorman and went to check in. As he waited at reception for the counter clerk to obtain the necessary instructions from the rack board, he looked around the lobby. Near the elevators, there was a black cat. In a window opposite that was a witch holding a broom. Behind reception, a tall, white skeleton hung by a wire from the top of its head.

---

1 The hotel later became a Hilton.

Ded looked at the date display on his watch. *Monday will be Halloween.*

He returned his gaze to the skeleton, focusing on the dull, vacuous eyes of the desiccated skull.

Yes, Ded thought, *my boss is not going to be happy I put doubts in O'Nadir's mind.*

A dancing light caught the side of Ded's right eye. He turned. On the far end of the reception counter was a huge jack-o'-lantern, its idiotic peepers and square-toothed grin glowing from the candle flame inside its hollowed pumpkin interior.

The best way to determine whether or not a suicide had occurred, Ded was aware, was to get inside the victim's mind. In Ickey Jerusalem's case, however, that was going to be a problem. From prior experience, Ded knew that the mind he had the greatest difficulty getting inside of was the mind of a poet.

Once, back in Buffalo State College, in freshman English, Ded had written a poem—an exceptionally moving piece (for him) about finding his pet goldfish floating belly-up in its bowl. Ded had felt he possessed a real gift for poetry. In fact, he could have written more, had he been given the right encouragement. However, after reading his goldfish poem out loud to his college class, he had concluded that, not being totally selfless, he had no interest in continuing to put himself out for the bawdy and unappreciative.

Since then, Ded had generally avoided poetry. He had read a short poem he'd liked in an in-flight magazine, but it had rhymed. And Ded knew from a budding-poet acquaintance of his at Buffalo State College that real poetry—at least, of the modern sort—was never supposed to rhyme.

Ded considered the inability of modern poets to conform to the requirements of rhyme (not to mention meter, punctuation or—now, it appeared, with Ickey Jerusalem—spelling) to be the natural result of a lack of mental discipline that infected all poets, whether modern or not.

A mind able to scramble memories and recombine them in novel ways, Ded theorized, *is necessarily a mind so undisciplined and confused as to be unable to express the result clearly and explicitly so it can be understood.*

What vexed him most about poets was not just their inability to express themselves clearly and explicitly, but also the exaggerated importance with which they invested their output. To Ded, poetry was nothing more than a little verbal decoration, occasionally pleasing to the ear or the intellect, but having no other significance.

To the few poets he had encountered, though, poetry was evidently much more.

When Ded had been in San Francisco on the Knife case, he had overheard some poet talking to his fellow poets in a local eatery.

"Poetry," the man had pontificated, "proves the inadequacy of abstract and rational ideas, like those you see in philosophy and science; ideas which present only a sterile unity, a mere juxtaposition of bare abstractions, with no creative imagination in the experience. That's because poetry is a communication from the whole mind addressed to the whole body—creating images of the permanent, living reality beyond time and space, reachable only through the imagination."

Ded had been surprised the man's companions didn't laugh him out of the diner. Certainly, as clearly intelligent people, they must have considered these pronouncements as ridiculous as he did. But they just sat there, nodding vigorously, as though agreeing with every word.

While Ded did not think it unusual a group might be so wrapped up in their own little community that they would fall prey to Sicilian Illusions, he did think it unusual when those very same people seemed to be conceptual, lateral-thinking, social outsiders who freely associated outside the box, pulling in analogies and images from every imaginable position in which they were not, in order to describe that which they were in.

Unlike the Sicilians, Ded thought now, as he waited at the Holiday Inn's reception, *poets seem to be consciously setting out to create the illusions with which they are then fooled.*

The face of the jack-o'-lantern at the far end of the counter appeared to transform itself into the face of Beulah Vala, enveloping Ded for a microsecond in the total experience of her being.

He immediately broke eye contact with the pumpkin.

What I have to figure out is how poets can use their broad perspective to create pleasing shadows on the wall, while simultaneously narrowing that perspective so they will believe the shadows are real.

The candle flame in the jack-o'-lantern flared, sputtered, and went out. Two wisps of smoke slithered out of the pumpkin's darkened eyes and rose to the ceiling.

"Your key, sir," the counter clerk chirped, in obedience to the marching orders from the rack board. "And here's a fax, and a message left for you earlier."

Ded looked first at the fax, which came from his home office. It was a list of the phone numbers for those in first class. Notations were made by a couple of the names with an appointment time and place.

He then unfolded the message and deciphered its childish scrawl: "I know who did it. Will contact you later. In the meantime, take care. A friend."

Ded raised his face to the clerk. "Did you see who dropped this message off?"

The clerk shook his head. "I was consulting a file in the office about an hour ago, and when I returned, I found it on the counter with your name written on it."

Ded didn't know what to make of it. How did the message writer know he would be at the Holiday Inn?

Wearily, he slipped the fax and the message into his loose-leaf notepad, turned for the elevators, and headed up to his room.

Ded stepped to the window. His room was above the fog. The sun had set. Four short blocks straight ahead rose the Bank of America tower,[2]

---

2 In 1998 Bank of America merged with NationsBank and moved its headquarters to Bank of America Corporate Center in Charlotte, North Carolina. In 2005 a new owner changed the name of the San Francisco building to 555 California Street.

the tallest building floorwise in San Francisco[3], a hulk of darkness broken by scattered lit windows. His appointment tomorrow evening would take place there, in the top floor office of Jerusalem's overweight, monocled lawyer, Bacon Urizen.

A few years ago, Ded had seen a movie in which a psychopath on top of the Bank of America tower had used a high-powered rifle to shoot a woman swimming in the pool on the roof of this Holiday Inn. *Somebody could be on top of the tower right now, focusing their telescopic sight on me.*

Ded started to close the curtain against the intrusion, but then stopped, deciding that despite the movie, it was absurd to think anyone four blocks away would have any interest looking into his window, never mind shooting at someone inside. Besides, having come from O'Nadir's claustrophobic basement office, he felt a need to leave his vistas as open as possible.

Before removing his suit, Ded went to the desk against the wall and emptied from his pockets his pen, his loose-leaf notepad, the transcript, and Jerusalem's spiral notebook with the four crumpled pages sticking out. He pulled the loose pages free, noting that the top one contained the obscure "tygers of wrath" line he had read in O'Nadir's office. Wondering whether the other pages might have clearer clues as to what had been going on in Jerusalem's mind just before he'd died, Ded spread them out on the desk. He picked one up at random and read out loud what was written, syllable by syllable:

> The Bat that flits at close of Eve
> Has left the Brain that wont Believe.

Ded lowered his hand. It wasn't any clearer than the "tygers of wrath," but at least there were no misspellings, and astoundingly, it rhymed.

---

3 Technically, the TransAmerica Pyramid is taller. However, the Pyramid has a 212-foot, uninhabited spire and thus only 48 inhabited floors—fewer than the 52 for the Bank of America. In 2018 both were dwarfed by the Salesforce Tower.

He dropped the page onto the desk and held the next one up to the fading light.

> Attempting to be more than Man
> We become less

Ded pondered this statement for some time. Perhaps Jerusalem wasn't a poet after all, but a riddle writer for the Egyptian Sphinx.

Giving up on poetry for the moment, Ded pulled out the fax from his home office, located Robert N. William's telephone number on the list, and rang it.

"Yes?" a voice answered tentatively.

"Mr. William?"

It was, so Ded introduced himself as the person who had interviewed him at the airport, and asked the purser two follow-up questions.

"No," the purser answered with an offended lilt, "none of the downstairs toilets were out of order during the flight. And as for storing stuff in them during takeoff, we don't do that sort of thing in first class, although it occasionally happens in economy."

The answers were what Ded had expected. He thanked the purser for his assistance and was about to hang up, when the purser stopped him.

"Wait. Since you called…"

"Yes?"

"This morning, I realized I saw something interesting on the flight that I neglected to tell you about during our airport interview."

"Which was?"

"Well, the coat I hung in the closet—"

A buzzer sounding in the background on the purser's end cut him off.

"Oh, that's a friend at the front door downstairs. He's taking me out on the town. Could you ring me tomorrow? Say, early afternoon? What I have to say is for your ears only."

Intrigued, Ded agreed, and hung up. *What can there be about Urizen's coat that we don't already know?*

Then, realizing he was hungry, he picked up the phone again and ordered his favorite Chinese dishes from the room service menu. In lieu of a knife and fork, he requested chopsticks.

While he waited for the food, he rummaged absentmindedly through the crumpled, free notebook pages lying on the desk. There was one he had not read. The daylight almost gone, he removed his thick glasses and held the paper up close to his eyes.

> I found them blind I taught them how to see
> And now they know neither themselves nor me

Ded set the page back onto the desk. The couplet had brought to his mind the image of his ex-wife, Harriet, as she had been, way back before he had mistakenly taught her to see with a widened perspective.

❧

Harriet had been his first sexual encounter with someone other than himself.

Although he eventually grew to love her, it was not love at first sight. A young secretary trainee with pointed glasses and a frumpy dress sense, her stated goal was to save herself for marriage. Her method for accomplishing this was as simple as it was effective: the moment any man showed the slightest interest in her, she would, without so much as a by-your-leave, provide him with immediate, preemptive, manual relief.

While her directness initially gave her a certain popularity as far as Ded was concerned, his enthusiasm was soon tempered by the severe lack of coordination in her elbows, tending, as it did, to produce a stroke both irregular in tempo and volatile in amplitude. So volatile, in fact, that on their first date, Ded felt lucky to have escaped with his manhood still attached.

As he summed it up when he bid her good night, "On the whole, next time, I think I'd prefer to do it myself."

Sadly, Ded was so inexperienced with women he had no idea how to end the relationship. He politely continued to go out with her for three more harrowing weeks, until, stretched almost to the breaking point, he concluded that the only chance he had of keeping himself together, literally, was to marry the woman and hope she would let go.

Sure enough, as soon as the knot was tied, she released her grip and offered to Ded what she had been saving for so many years: a certain natural orifice, which, though no more coordinated than her elbows, was significantly less life threatening—in reality, if not in appearance.

"Christ Almighty," was all Ded could say at the moment his virgin eyes beheld a woman's private part. "Am I really expected to entrust my one and only to *that*?"

❧

After eating his room-service dinner while watching the totally uninteresting, local news, Ded viewed an hour-long documentary on the sex life of the Australian sand flea solely for the occasional glimpses of the blond female presenter's long, tan, bare legs bracketed by her walking boots at the bottom and her rolled-up outback shorts at the top. When the program ended, Ded took off his clothes, turned the lights out, and got into the queen-sized bed, his ex-wife returning to his mind.

Despite his initial trepidation upon seeing his wife's private part, he'd soon gotten to like it. In the course of time, the attraction he felt for Harriet went beyond mere physical, sexual gratification. He began to feel a protective tenderness towards her, augmented by an extraordinary mooniness when she was around. On a rational basis, he knew it was just another Sicilian Illusion. But he couldn't help himself. He was falling in love.

Sometimes, at night, he now reminisced dreamily, *we'd lie in bed, cuddling each other. Gently. Innocently. Our arms and legs entangled. Talking softly about life. Then our lips would meet and we'd—*

"Fuck each other's brains out," a deep, masculine voice intruded.

It came from the next room through the communicating door. A woman giggled.

Ded cocked his ear and heard a second, higher-voiced man who could have been a hillbilly. "Lips, titties, pussy, and ass," the man was chanting. "Lips, titties, pussy, and ass."

From the content of their dialog, Ded decided the two men were not talking to him.

The woman giggled again.

"Do to me what you're doing to them," Ded heard a third man beg in a Norwegian accent.

"I can't reach," the woman replied indistinctly, as though she were talking through a mouthful of pork sausages.

Ded got out of bed. It had always been his policy as an investigator never to listen at keyholes. People were entitled to their privacy. The current situation, however, piqued his intellectual curiosity.

What kind of board game are they playing? Ded asked himself, knowing full well whatever game they were playing was highly unlikely to be confined to the surface of a board.

He pressed his ear to the door. He could hear heavy breathing.

"Come on, girlie," the hillbilly demanded. "We paid for it."

"All right," the woman muttered with an air of resignation. "Pass the can of lard, will you?"

"Wait a minute," the Norwegian whined. "What about the broccoli?"

"Only if you use a rubber," the woman declared firmly. "It's a bitch to clean up otherwise."

Ded pushed back from the door—not because what he had heard had disgusted him, but because a certain part of his anatomy was becoming too tumescent for him to stand close. He reached down and lifted it up so it no longer pointed out perpendicular from his naked body. His hand tarried. *Hmmmmm.* He considered his options.

He looked back at the window. Except for the faint, urban

light-pollution's faux twilight coming up through the fog, the room was dark. Nobody could see him.

He stood there, his hand still.

After a moment's reflection, he shook his head, and released his grip. He just had too much self-respect to masturbate over a piece of broccoli.

One, after all, had to draw the line somewhere.

"Holy Jesus," Ded heard the man with the deep voice moan. More bizarre noises now began coming from the room beyond. Ded could not imagine what was going on. It sounded like a gang of armadillos having sex with a platypus in a vat of rice pudding.

The disparate noises were gathering into a slow crescendo.

"Great hairy Ned on the mountaintop!" the hillbilly screamed.

The armadillos were getting carried away, banging against the telephone, the furniture, the walls, the ceiling—groaning, gasping, and shrieking.

"Get in there, you little green bugger!" the Norwegian cursed.

Ded assumed the man was addressing a piece of broccoli, although it was possible he could have had some kind of severe birth defect he normally would have been hesitant to display in public. Then again, in light of the other noises Ded was hearing and his limited knowledge of the pigmentation of uncommon species, it was conceivable the little green bugger was an armadillo.

Whatever it was, the Norwegian's exclamation seemed to spark off a concupiscent cacophony of screeching, squealing, braying, bleating, and from one poor person, mooing like a cow, the likes of which Ded had never heard before, eventually reaching its peak in a single, long, hoarse, community "Wha-hooooo!!!"

That was followed by absolute silence.

Three separate male bodies slumped to the floor with a sigh, after which there was another, even longer silence.

"Christ," the woman griped, "this hammock's a mess."

Ded heard the sounds of her struggling to her feet followed by the rustle of clothing, the zip of a zipper, and the click of a purse. The door to the hallway opened and closed.

"Not bad for a dwarf, huh?" the hillbilly wheezed.

His curiosity overcoming his sense of propriety, Ded rushed to his door and cracked it enough to see. The hallway light outside his door was lit, but beyond the orgy room, the lights were out. Standing at the cusp between light and dark, primping the flaming-red hair piled high on her head, was not a dwarf, but an exceedingly short, roly-poly woman, wearing lots of eye makeup, a glittering spaghetti-strap blouse, a super-tight miniskirt, and high-heeled mules. A plague of orange freckles covered her from head to toe. She was bedecked in imitation gold, precious stones, and pearls set in a myriad of anklets, rings, bracelets, armbands, necklaces, earrings, barrettes, and an elaborately sequined headband etched with some mysterious script like ancient Babylonian. In the middle of the headband was a golden sunburst brooch framing what looked like a stubby, striated, dull-gray metal phallus.

The woman, noticing Ded spying from his door, flashed her dark eyes at him in a way that was both suggestive and explicit. Smiling seductively, she strode up, and before he could stop her, pushed his door wide-open, driving him back into a room now indirectly lit by the hallway lights, exposing his still somewhat erect member to her necessarily (given her height) level gaze.

Greedily, she licked her lips. Then, as her mouth began impersonating the hungry orifice of an orange-spotted fish, she advanced on his member. A tantalizing one inch before her target, she stopped and angled her head so her line of sight went straight up the front of Ded's naked body to meet his eyes. Maintaining her gaze, she brought her cupped right hand up to the side of her mouth.

"Beware of the doctor," she whispered. "He—"

In the adjoining room, the three men began talking as they dressed. The woman inhaled sharply through her nose, returned to the door, peeked around the jamb to see if the coast was clear, looked back at

Ded with an expression of utter fear, and then scurried off down the corridor.

Ded slammed his door before he could be seen by anyone who might be in the hall.

Jesus Christ, Ded thought, breathing heavily and listening for footsteps. *Who in the hell was that woman? Was she the person who left the message for me downstairs?*

He sniffed. In the woman's wake was a faint cleaning-liquid odor he'd smelled before, but he couldn't identify where.

And who was the doctor she warned me about? Dr. Bromion Ulro? The Marin County plastic surgeon? The one who said the dead Ickey Jerusalem looked like he had come face to face with Satan Incarnate?

There had been no suggestion during the interview that the doctor had any connection to the poet, other than checking for signs of life after Jerusalem was discovered.

The claims adjuster made a mental note to find out more about Dr. Ulro.

He stopped still, staring at the doorknob. Someone was trying it. The rattling became more insistent until there was a hard thump, as though that someone had banged a shoulder against the door in frustration. Everything went silent.

"Hello?" Ded asked hesitantly.

There was no answer.

Ded crept up, set the bolt lock, and fastened the chain. Then he slid the desk chair over to the door. Discovering that the back of the chair was too low to jam under the doorknob, he balanced his small suitcase on the top of the seatback. If someone tried to enter, the suitcase would fall, making a loud noise.

He stood there for a while, facing his jerry-rigged alarm.

Oh, well.

After all that had just happened, he was going to need some help falling asleep.

Ded got the hotel services folder from the desk and checked the schedule card for the in-room, set-time, pay-per-movie channels.

Ded knew the hotel didn't charge for a movie until a customer watched it for more than five minutes. Therefore, observing his usual routine, rather than accessing the targeted movie when it began, he instead watched seven and half minutes of an *I Love Lucy* rerun on regular TV, giving the porn stars sufficient time to get past the bad acting and into the good action. Then, positioning himself, a hand towel, and everything else just right, he set his watch timer for four minutes and fifty-five seconds and pushed the movie button on the remote control.

Before his watch beeped, Ded, upholding an unbroken tradition of punctuality, had climaxed and turned off the set.

It wasn't great, he knew, but it was better than nothing, and unlike most sex, it didn't cost a thing.

PART TWO

CHAPTER 8

THE WEAKEST LINK

The Holiday Inn lobby sat at the top of a ten-foot-high flight of broad concrete steps, facing Kearney Street, a major one-way thoroughfare coming from the left of the hotel. The hotel was set back between two small side streets, Merchant and Washington. Along the front of the steps was a driveway into which cars entered from Merchant. After around thirty yards, the driveway curved to the left, exiting back onto Kearney.

The next morning, Saturday, Ded got up early to read through the airport interview transcripts over a meager continental breakfast. By nine, he was dressed in his suit, waiting below the steps near the Merchant Street side for the car Beulah Vala had arranged to pick him up and drive him over to meet her in Marin County. Ded had put out of his mind his infatuation with the glimpse of Miss Vala he'd caught when entering the plane and his having been swept away by her manifestation as a cow during her interview. This upcoming meeting was a crucial first step in the investigation. On the one hand, being so close to Jerusalem and his metaphysics, she would likely know better than anyone what was going through the poet's mind. On the other hand, if Jerusalem had, in fact, been murdered, Beulah would be a top suspect—having both motive ($20 million from the insurance policy) and opportunity (sitting next to Jerusalem on the red-eye flight, hidden from the view of the other passengers).

A roaring sound caused Ded to turn to the left just in time to see a huge, black, beat-up old hearse, its chassis jacked up high above its wheels, speeding up the middle of Kearney Street. Abruptly, it swerved right across traffic and into Merchant Street, tires screeching, and then left into the hotel's driveway. Burning lots of rubber, it sped straight at Ded.

As the hearse jumped the curb in front of him, Ded fell back onto the concrete steps, feeling the passing vehicle's wheels touching but not running over his toes.

The hearse, having missed its prey, lurched up the short driveway. Exiting onto Kearney Street, it executed a sharp left turn and headed the wrong way up Kearney, weaving amongst the blaring horns and squealing wheels of oncoming cars. It then cut left onto Merchant Street, turned left again into the hotel's driveway and aimed once more at Ded, who began scrambling backwards on his bottom up the steps. The jacked-up hearse, in pursuit, clumped up the steps on a higher and higher diagonal until, just as it approached Ded, its engine began lugging with the strain. The slowing vehicle, unable to maintain its upward climb, turned, brushing by Ded's outstretched palms, and headed back down the steps and rightwards onto the driveway, where it passed exceptionally close to the red-uniformed, Chinese doorman holding his hand out for a tip. Ten yards up the driveway later, it at last slid to a halt. The hearse's driver, an ungainly, muscular man with a small head, leapt out of the vehicle and began running in Ded's direction.

Ded turned to sprint up the stairs, before noticing the driver come to an abrupt stop in front of the red-coated doorman. The doorman was no longer extending his palm for a tip. Instead, he was hopping around, holding one foot in both hands and yelling what Ded took to be powerful Chinese expletives.

Before Ded's amazed eyes, the driver began assailing the doorman with a rapid and explosive street-fighting attack.

"Huh! Huh! Huh!" The driver's hands, elbows, knees, and feet flew in rapid succession at the cringing, still-hopping doorman.

The doorman, somewhat disadvantaged in this martial engagement by having to pogo around on one leg while holding his foot in both hands, would for sure have been a goner had any of the blows connected. But they didn't. Not a single one.

All at once, the hearse operator, satisfied he had made his point, stopped, and awkwardly put his knuckles on his hips. The doorman, his hands now over his eyes rather than his foot, continued hopping for a while before noticing the attack had ceased. He lowered his sore foot to the ground and limped to within inches of his assailant. The two men stood, face to face, both glowering in a menacing manner, until ultimately the doorman blinked, spit out a word which sounded like the Chinese for "shithead," wheeled about, and hobbled up the hotel's entryway steps.

Removing his glowering eyes from the retreating doorman, the driver caught sight of Ded high up on the steps to the right. The man's ugly face split into a broad smile. Muttering repeatedly in a guttural voice a generally unacceptable four-letter Anglo-Saxon word implying sexual congress, he lurched resolutely toward the doomed claims adjuster.

Ded nervously returned the man's smile and checked his avenues of escape.

Reaching Ded near the top of the steps, the driver's gloved hands shot up into the air. Ded instinctively ducked, covering his head with his arms.

When blows failed to land, Ded peeked up from under the crook of his elbow and realized that the man's arm motion, as well as his continuing repetition of the four-letter word, was not a prelude to attack but rather a clumsy gesture of apology for an egregious *faux pas.* Attempting to run Ded over with the hearse, perhaps? Or failing to run him over? Ded couldn't tell.

Ded quickly examined the disconcerting, muscle-bound man before him. His head was too small for his body. His skin was a ruddy red, with the broken texture of a dried-out lakebed. His hair, even though he appeared to be only in his twenties, was thinning, scraggly, and swept back, as were his ears, like Mercury's head-wings. His large nose was a mere continuation of his sloping-back forehead. His mouth was wide and thin, with gold-capped eye-teeth protruding at each side, and peeking from between his lips, a thin, hungry tongue. His burning eyes were gigantic, bulging out, and crossed.

Ded finally twigged. *The cartoon insect at the interview! This guy must be Adam Ghostflea, Ickey Jerusalem's chauffeur!*

"Excuse me," Ded said, speaking as slowly and distinctly as he could, assuming that anyone so grotesque had to be obtuse as well. "Have you come to take me, Ded Smith, to meet Miss Beulah Vala?"

Ghostflea ceased swearing and studied Ded's moving lips as though something were wrong with them. "Uh, yes," the chauffeur croaked when Ded had at last finished his question. "At the funeral for Mr. Jerusalem."

Ded raised an eyebrow. Miss Vala had not said anything about him attending Ickey Jerusalem's funeral, and certainly not in the hearse with the body. Keeping a wary eye on Adam Ghostflea, Ded walked down the steps and over to the hearse sitting high above its wheels. There was no coffin in the back.

"Where's Jerusalem, then?"

Ghostflea gave Ded an odd look. "He's dead."

"I mean, where's the body?"

The chauffeur made a series of spastic gestures which Ded took to mean either "cremated" or, just possibly, "blown to smithereens by an atomic bomb."

"Then why the hearse?" Ded asked.

"The hearse is Mr. Jerusalem's limousine."

Ded peered through the window at the back seat. The inside had been outfitted with all the modern comforts of home: leather seats, plush carpeting, a wall telephone, a TV, and two paneled cabinets marked "Refrigerator" and "Bar."

Ghostflea opened up the back hatch to the storage space behind the leather seats and looked at the ground. "Where's your luggage, Mr. Smith?"

"Luggage?"

"Lug - gage," the chauffeur repeated, mouthing the word so as to be understood by even the most mentally challenged.

"In my hotel room," Ded replied dubiously.

"I'll get the bellboy to bring it down."

"I don't think that will be necessary," Ded stopped him. "I've got everything I need with me."

Ghostflea shrugged, closed the back hatch, and opened the door to the back seat for Ded to climb in.

"It's no skin off my nose," the chauffeur growled as Ded passed into the car, "if tonight you're going to have to sleep in the nude."

❧

Ded sat in the back of the raised-up, tanklike hearse as it headed for Marin County.

In truth, based on Adam Ghostflea's manifested sense of direction, "headed for" should not be taken literally. The chauffeur's route seemed to require an extraordinary number of right-, left-, and U-turns, designed, as far as Ded could make out, to take in every congested alleyway, double-parked shopping street, and grid-locked intersection in San Francisco. By happy chance, the chauffeur could not make up his mind which side of the road he was supposed to drive on, or the hearse would not have made any progress at all.

Speculating that if he distracted Ghostflea from looking at the road, his driving might improve, Ded leaned forward and slid aside the glass partition behind the driver's petite head.

"Could you tell me, please, Mr. Ghostflea," Ded asked, using a tone not unlike the tone one would use to address an unexploded bomb, "whether—"

"I'm not *Mr.* Ghostflea," the chauffeur interrupted gruffly. "Ghostflea is the name my parents gave me."

"Didn't your parents have a family name?"

"They gave it up so the government couldn't trace them."

"Why would—"

"They were afraid of the UN black helicopters. My parents were survivalists. We lived in a compound in the mountains on the Oregon-California border."

"What about your last name when you went to school?"

"I was homeschooled."

"I assume your homeschooling also covered hand-to-hand combat."

"Yes. And lots about guns and knives, too."

Ded decided it was best to go onto another subject. "Then how did you get the name Adam?"

"Mr. Jerusalem. When he first met me, six years ago, at the Condor off Broadway. I was the bouncer."

"A bouncer?

"Yes. I got the job because of my muscles, martial arts training, and according to the manager, scary face."

Ded studiously avoided any comment on the chauffeur's face. "A bouncer is an occupation that seems completely at odds with the meek persona you presented to Inspector O'Nadir at your airport interview last week."

"I clam up whenever I meet cops. Been that way since I was twelve, when my parents died in a shootout with the ATF."

"Goodness, that's terrible. What happened to you after that?"

"After the ATF found me hiding in the basement, I was sent to live with my grandparents on a farm in Mendocino County."

"Were your grandparents survivalists, too?"

"No, unlike Mother and Father, who never talked about God, my grandparents were devout Christians."

"Did you become devout, too?"

"I have no interest in anything I can't see in the flesh with my own eyes. I'd felt the same way about the UN black helicopters. As soon as I turned eighteen, I left the farm for San Francisco."

"So, why did Ickey Jerusalem call you Adam?"

"He said I reminded him of the first man created by God. 'Made of red clay.' That's what Mr. Jerusalem said 'Adam' means."

Ded cocked his head. "Did Jerusalem say why you reminded him of Adam?"

"'Most men have feet of clay,' he told me. 'But you, Adam, have clay all the way up through your head.'"

Ghostflea's mirror-framed, cracked-mud face looked proudly at Ded.

Ded wanted in the worst way to ask the chauffeur how closely related his parents were but decided against it. He peeked out the front window at the twenty or thirty screaming pedestrians running down the sidewalk ahead of the hearse.

"Mr. Jerusalem said on the seventh day after creation, when God fell asleep, God's consciousness shrunk from the whole universe into Adam's mind."

"No kidding?" Ded said with some irony. "I must have been home ill the day they talked about that in Sunday school."

Ghostflea seemed disappointed. "I was hoping you had. Nobody else, not even my grandparents, ever told me about God falling asleep. But, true or not, Mr. Jerusalem saying I'd ended up with God's brain inside my skull was kind of nice, don't you think?"

"Without a doubt," Ded said.

The chauffeur stared briefly into space. "Anyway, only Mr. Jerusalem and Miss Vala have ever called me Adam. Like everybody else, you can just call me Ghostflea."

As he pondered what Jerusalem could have meant by this preposterous story, Ded's eyes drifted left from the back of the chauffeur's head to the dashboard on the passenger's side.

That's odd, he thought.

"Ghostflea, why does this hearse have the steering wheel on the right?"

The chauffeur glanced back, seemingly surprised his passenger did not know. "To steer the car."

"No, I mean why is it on the right?"

"Right?"

"Look at that car over there," Ded instructed, pointing at a Plymouth which had just jammed on its brakes at the sight of the hearse barreling toward it the wrong way up a one-way street. "Do you see anything different about that car's steering wheel?"

Ghostflea looked at the Plymouth. "Yes. The top part of the steering wheel is in the driver's mouth."

Giving up on the comparisons, Ded decided a more concrete approach was required. "Where did Jerusalem get this hearse?"

"England, when he was a student at Oxford."

"Oxford?" Despite himself, Ded was impressed. "Were you with him then?"

"No. During my years as a bouncer, I'd gotten to know Mr. Jerusalem when he came into the club. Then, three-and-a-half years ago, he approached me. Said he'd decided to move from San Francisco to the Oakland hills, and so would be taking his hearse out of storage. He asked me to be his bodyguard, keeping people away, and also to be his chauffeur. I leapt at the job. I was tired of people making fun of me. Calling me a flea head. Or worse. Mr. Jerusalem gave me a book on how to drive. He let me live in a cabin behind his house. And six months later, Miss Vala joined him there, so I got to drive her around as well."

Ded saw Ghostflea's dreamy expression reflected in the rearview mirror. "So, since you took the job, you must have gotten to know Jerusalem well."

"Yes." Ghostflea's bulging eyes indicated his association with Jerusalem was a source of great pride.

"Other than calling you the shrunken consciousness of God, did he talk to you much at the house or when you were chauffeuring him around?"

"Yes."

"What about?"

"My driving."

"Anything else?"

"No."

"What did he say about your driving?"

"He liked it," Ghostflea beamed.

"He liked it," Ded said, careful to hide his incredulity. "Did he say what he liked about it?"

"He said it had 'the virtue of not being mediocre.'" As Ghostflea parroted Jerusalem's words, his pleased, crossed eyes glowed in the mirror.

"When did Jerusalem say that to you?"

Ghostflea thought back. "Three days before our flight to New York."

"That would be Thursday, October 13th," Ded said, calculating from Urizen's interview statement that they had flown to New York on the Sunday a week before the return flight on which Jerusalem died.

"If you say so," Ghostflea said. "I remember it as the day I took Mr. Jerusalem for his appointment with Dr. Ulro."

"Dr. Bromion Ulro? The plastic surgeon who was on the plane?"

"Yes."

Ded scooted to the edge of his seat. "How long had Dr. Ulro been Mr. Jerusalem's doctor?"

"The whole time I've been Mr. Jerusalem's chauffeur. I think before that, too. But Dr. Ulro was not Mr. Jerusalem's doctor after the appointment."

"Why not?"

"They had a big fight. Dr. Ulro told Mr. Jerusalem if he wanted to live, he should never see Dr. Ulro again."

Ded arched his eyebrows, hearing again the red-headed sex guppy's whispered warning the night before. "What was the argument about?"

"I don't know. I was in the waiting room. I heard Mr. Jerusalem shout something about the doctor having the eye of a vegetable. Or maybe it was a tongue. I don't remember. And fruit. He said the doctor was the fruit of the Tree of Mystery. Whatever. The doctor did not agree with Mr. Jerusalem. He yelled something back about killing all the fruitcakes."

"Killing all the fruitcakes?"

Ghostflea gesticulated with his left hand that he had no idea what the doctor had meant, causing his right hand, gripping the wheel, to veer the hearse toward the sidewalk. "It was not a normal conversation." Returning his left hand to the wheel, he overcorrected in the opposite direction. "At least, that's what the patient next to me in the waiting room said when he left early."

"What about the vegetable and fruit stuff? Do you know what Jerusalem meant?"

"No. But then, I seldom knew what Mr. Jerusalem meant when he said things. He was a poet, you know."

Ded knew only too well. The deceased being a poet was definitely going to present a real obstacle to any kind of rational or logical solution to the case. "Did Jerusalem say anything to you after you left the doctor's office?"

"No, he just laughed to himself and muttered, 'Bullshit. Bullshit. Bullshit.'"

"Did he normally laugh that way after meetings?"

"No. Never. Sometimes, just the opposite. He'd look sad. Like after his visit to Mr. Urizen's office the Monday before his Thursday appointment with the doctor."

That'll be Monday, October 10th, Ded thought. *The same day the policy on his life was purchased with Beulah as the beneficiary.*

"Coming back from Mr. Urizen's office," Ghostflea said, "Mr. Jerusalem sat for a while in the back, peering down sadly at his lap, saying nothing. Then, he slid open the glass and asked me to give him one of the books on the front seat."

"What was in the book?"

"All of Mr. Jerusalem's poems," the chauffeur answered. "And a small piece of raw broccoli."

"Broccoli?"

"It stuck out of the book. Marking a page. It had been there for many days. Since right after Mr. Jerusalem received the book from his publisher in the mail. When he was reading it at the kitchen table, I'd pulled a head of broccoli from the shopping bag there and a small piece had fallen off. He picked it up as a bookmark."

"What did Jerusalem do after you gave him the book from the front seat?"

"Opened it at the broccoli and read a poem out loud." The throaty Ghostflea spoke as though the reading had been for his benefit.

"What was the poem about?"

"I don't know. Night. Day. God. Human. Something."

"And what did Jerusalem do then?"

"Nothing. Just stared at the book all the while I was driving him home. When I stopped in the driveway, he sucked in air very loud, opened his eyes wide, took the piece of broccoli from the book, and ran into his house. Since he'd forgotten the other book on the front seat, I left that one in his study, although he wasn't there at the time."

"What was that book?"

"I don't know. It was black, extra-wide, about two inches thick, with no title on the cover." Ghostflea paused. "The next morning, Mr. Jerusalem came to my cabin and took my shoes."

"Took your shoes?"

"In the afternoon, he gave them back," Ghostflea said right away, as though exculpating his employer from any taint of theft.

Ded, deciding he had little more than an ice cube's chance in hell of the chauffeur enlightening him further about Ickey Jerusalem's state of mind, dropped the subject. "Ghostflea, were you aware that Dr. Ulro was going to be on the flight?"

"No. He must have come onto the plane at the very last. Only when he'd stored his parka and case above his head did I smell him and see the side of his head."

Ded remembered the doctor's antiseptic odor at the airport interview.

"He was taking a little black medical bag down from his case," Ghostflea added.

The hearse stopped at a light. It was green. The chauffeur looked both ways several times until the light turned yellow, and then stepped on the gas.

Ded asked Ghostflea a few more questions about the flight but didn't get much. The trip to New York had been his first on an airplane. On the flight back, apart from the two times he used the upstairs bathroom following the lead of Jerusalem's business manager, Tharmas Luvah (Ghostflea was not even aware there *were* downstairs toilets), he seemed to have spent the whole time in his seat, unable to see anyone behind him, or even the doctor in front, once Dr. Ulro sat down. Since it was a red-eye flight, Ghostflea mostly, quite sensibly, slept.

Ded started to slide the partition closed in order to spend the rest of the drive contemplating the new information gleaned from the chauffeur. As he did, he noticed the wood trim around the partition seemed newer than the leather padding beneath it. Then, he changed his mind. *No reason to close it,* he thought. *I'm not going to be talking to myself. And it'll make it easier to communicate with Ghostflea if I need to.*

Ded sat back, steadying himself with his palms on either side of his seat. Feeling something grainy, he lifted his palms back up, looked at them, and then looked at the seat. There were sprinklings of what looked like cookie crumbs everywhere. He hadn't noticed them before.

Brushing his hands clean, he took out his loose-leaf notepad and scrabbled in his suit jacket for his pen to make some notes about his conversation with Ghostflea.

Damn, he realized after a moment's search, *I've left my pen back in my hotel room.*

As Ded returned his loose-leaf notepad into the inside pocket of his jacket, the back of his fingers brushed against something hard. It was Ickey Jerusalem's spiral notebook. Ded had brought it with him from the hotel.

Ded fingered the cover in his pocket. He had not yet read the poem Beulah Vala said Jerusalem was working on before he died.

He pulled the poet's notebook out. *What'll it be this time? Another misspelled epigram? Another rhyming* non sequitur? *Or if I'm really lucky, something longer, say step-by-step instructions on how to achieve eternal life by uniting with the highest level of God's consciousness?*

Ded opened the notebook's cover, noticing on its underside, written upside down, "150010/31GHUA843." Ded couldn't say for sure but it had the appearance of an offshore bank account number.

He riffled through the pages that remained, a small number, due to Jerusalem's apparent practice of tearing out completed poems to be transcribed. All the pages were blank, except the first. Ded inhaled and charily read what was written:

The Sick Rose
O Rose thou art sick.
The invisible worm,
That flies in the night
In the howling storm:
Has found out thy bed
Of crimson joy:
And ~~her~~his dark secret love
Does thy life destroy.

Ded exhaled, gazing at the ceiling of the hearse. *Wrathful tygers, instructive horses, unbelieving bats, and now, invisible, flying worms.*

He shook his head. The overall meaning of the poem was no more intelligible to Ded than the four epigrams he had read earlier. And yet, he had a nagging feeling there was something more there, some kind of story.

Scanning the poem again, his eyes came to rest on the third line. That flies in the night. *Is that the red-eye flight?*

In the howling storm. *The turbulence that night?*

Does thy life destroy. *Destroys Jerusalem's life? On the plane? In the storm? If so, then the sick rose must be Ickey Jerusalem.*

Ded scratched his scalp. *But if Jerusalem is the sick rose, who is the invisible worm? The word "her" has been crossed out and replaced with "his." If the worm is a person, how could Jerusalem have not known its sex? Maybe it wasn't a person at all, but the plane? Or something more abstract. A problem? Something gnawing at him like a worm? A dark secret love? On his crimson bed of joy? Driving him to suicide?*

Ded frowned at the poem a while longer before giving up in exasperation.

If only poets could learn to be clearer and more explicit about what they mean.

ഴ

The hearse, now moving parallel to the Bay, was passing a block-long playground on the left. Ded looked up through the open space at the jumble of houses on Pacific Heights. In San Francisco, almost everyone seemed to live on a hill with a view.

How different from Buffalo, Ded mused, *where almost everyone seems to live in a basement apartment.*

San Franciscans had the much wider perspective. Which was the reason, doubtlessly, they also had a much greater suicide rate.

But then, he had to agree, *it is hard to kill yourself by jumping out of the window of a basement apartment.*

Ded recalled he had lived with Harriet in such a basement apartment in Buffalo when they were first married.

ഴ

Marriage had brought about a change in Ded's life that went beyond his new feelings for his wife. Overnight, he went from veritable hermithood to becoming enmeshed in Harriet's extensive social life. Intimate dinner parties. Church bazaars. Massive, in-law get-togethers. Thursday evenings at the Multi-Ethnic Folk Dancing Club.

So, this is what life is all about, Ded marveled to himself one Thursday evening as, in response to the Balkan step caller, he set off hopping yet one more time in a one-legged *do-si-do* around Harriet, trying as best he could to look like a Bulgarian.

Despite the long periods of solitary recuperation Ded needed after such events, he was amazed how much he enjoyed them. It was the sense of, if not belonging, then at least *appearing* to belong.

When, by their third anniversary, having moved out of the basement apartment into a house, his wife suggested that the next step was to fill it with children, Ded not only agreed but found the idea positively attractive.

If life had continued in this manner, Ded would, no doubt, ultimately have been able to pass for a normal person. But before Harriet could start on her string of pregnancies, his metamorphosis occurred.

∞

Ded looked up. The hearse was approaching the Golden Gate Bridge.

Some years earlier, to cut down on staff and speed up traffic, the bridge had provided that drivers going north into Marin County paid no toll, while those going south into San Francisco paid double. North-going cars did not have to stop, but they had to slow down to negotiate the narrow lanes between the old, now-empty tollbooths.

As Ghostflea approached the toll plaza at a speed varying erratically between 45 and 75 miles per hour, weaving the hearse from side to side, trying to get a bead on the gap between the empty booths, Ded's attention shifted from his life in Buffalo to certain Biblical odds involving a camel and the eye of a needle.

From Ded's vantage point, there were three possible outcomes: the hearse would take out the left booth, the hearse would take out the right booth, or, considering the significant probability the hearse would enter the gap sideways, it would take out both booths at once.

Just before Ghostflea got to the gap, he slammed on his brakes. The fishtailing hearse miraculously skidded to a stop between the two abandoned booths. The chauffeur slid over to the English passenger side, rolled down his window, and due to the height of the jacked-up hearse, handed a dollar bill horizontally to the nonexistent toll-taker.

Curiously, none of the speeding cars following behind hit the hearse. When Ded screwed up enough courage to look back, he could see most, if not all, had managed instead to hit each other.

Tiring of holding his dollar out of the window, Ghostflea brought his arm back in, slid back over to the driver's side, put the car in gear, and tore off at a great speed, cursing to himself about how, whenever he crossed the bridge in this direction, those goddamn toll-takers weren't at their posts.

Apparently, Ickey Jerusalem had never set him straight.

CHAPTER 9

THE CHAINS SLIP

Mount Tamalpais, a 2604-foot peak still largely in an undeveloped, natural state, lay in Marin County, on the northern end of the Golden Gate Bridge. A slender road wound up the mountain, offering spectacular drop-away views of the Pacific Coast. It was not a road one would want to take at an excessive speed.

Twenty-nine minutes after clearing the bridge toll booths, near the top of Mount Tamalpais, Adam Ghostflea parked the hearse on the hill side of the road among a long line of perpendicularly parked cars. He got out and opened Ded's door.

The insurance investigator removed his hands from his eyes.

Normally, Ded was not one to see things in religious terms. However, to the extent there had ever been any doubt, he had to say that Ghostflea's reckless hurtling up the narrow, winding road that clung to the side of the mountain had conclusively proved God did not exist. Or if He did exist, He certainly wasn't deserving of worship. Creating such an incompetent and—Ded read the chauffeur's disturbing face more closely—*angry* driver is not something your everyday Almighty should be going around bragging about.

Ded staggered out of the hearse, forgetting to account for the jacked-up vehicle's excessive distance from the ground.

A moment later, picking himself up from where he'd fallen, he had another, more disturbing thought. *Did Beulah Vala send this nightmare on wheels to dispose of me in an unfortunate "accident" in order to stop my investigation?*

Taking a steadying breath, Ded checked his surroundings. Parked adjacent was a pristine, VW hippie bus covered with brightly colored flowers, stars, sunbursts, and paisley patterns that reached up over the side windows. Laid onto that background on the side facing Ded was a dramatic picture showing a kneeling, young woman face-on. She was clothed in a flowing dress, her golden hair flying against a stormy sky, her large angel wings behind. A huge, orangey-red, bat-winged man hovered horizontally above her, looking down into her upturned gaze. The top of his goat-horned head pointed towards Ded, his muscular arms stretched out sideways from his organically armored shoulders, his equally muscular legs spread out behind. In line with his enlarged backbone, his long, serpentine tail coiled into the background. A title ran along the bottom: *The Great Red Dragon and the Woman Clothed with the Sun*.

"Whose VW bus is this?" Ded asked.

"It belongs to Tharmas Luvah, Mr. Jerusalem's business manager."

"And the painting?"

"Mr. Jerusalem did it."

Ded pointed at the VW's driver's door, which hung ajar.

Ghostflea nodded. "Mr. Luvah never locks his bus."

Curious, Ded walked around to the back of Tharmas Luvah's vehicle. There, against a fiery background, Ickey Jerusalem had painted a naked, androgynous contortionist with his or her sinewy legs in full stretch, as though running from right to left, flames licking at the character's crotch, while simultaneously the upper body and head, arms spread wide, palms down, were turned away towards the inferno.

The title along the bottom read: *Furious Desires*.

Below the picture was a vanity California license plate: LUV TREE.

Ded continued around to the far side of the van.

Under the painting on that side was the title: *Satan Exulting over Eve*. Against a background of hellish flames, a young woman, perhaps the same "Woman Clothed," was lying supine on the ground, right side to the viewer, completely naked. Her right hand capped a golden apple on the ground, undoubtedly the fruit of the tree of the knowledge of good and evil, and her head was cast backward, as though she was zonked, her blank, Little-Orphan-Annie eyes staring blindly offstage to the left. A large serpent was coiled loosely around her body, from her feet to her private parts, where it disappeared behind the hidden left side of her body to reappear beyond her hair spread-out on the ground and then curve back and over her face to rest its sizable head on her breasts, its cartoonishly arched eye evidencing self-satisfaction as it looked offstage to the right. Floating prone a couple of feet above the supine Eve, was the serpent's controller, Satan, not as the over-muscled "Great Red Dragon" but as a naked, attractive man in his prime, ordinary in all ways apart from his human-sized, bat-like wings. His tousle-haired head and physically toned upper body were turned towards a spot just to the picture-viewer's right. His arms were spread wide in a formal manner, his right forearm fastened to the underside of a shield behind, his left hand holding a near-horizontal spear pointed towards his floating feet. His full face had large eyebrows and broadly positioned eyes framing a classically Greek nose, while below, his fleshy lips and curved chin were no wider that his nostrils. Despite the painting's title, Satan's expression was one not of exultation but of a wan, apathetic weariness, as though he had just completed yet another boring task on his list.

"The newest painting," Ghostflea said. "Mr. Jerusalem finished it at the end of May this year."

Ded carried on to the front of the vehicle, wondering what the image there would be. Perhaps the so-far unseen face of the red dragon? Or, more logically, the frontal view of the contortionist in the *Furious Desires* picture at the rear? Or Satan's now pointing forward spear and shield. Any of them would make a kind of ship's figurehead leading the bus's charge.

The figurehead, though, was entirely different. In a small, square frame, Ded found a black and white etching of a swaddled baby caterpillar with a human face lying on its back on a leaf sprouting from a branch. Overarching it, another leaf from the same branch hung with a larger, prone adult caterpillar looking over the edge at the baby. At the bottom of this picture was the title: *What Is Man?* Below that was a plaque that said:

The Sun's Light when he unfolds it
Depends on the Organ that beholds it

Ded massaged the back of his neck with his palm, trying to digest the four pictures he'd seen. *Ickey Jerusalem's paintings are as obscure as his poetry.*

It could all take an eternity to decipher.

Adam Ghostflea motioned clumsily at a broad pathway heading up through a gently sloping grove of evergreen trees. Against his better judgment, Ded followed the stumbling, brawny chauffeur up the hill. For the first time, he noticed how Ghostflea's exaggerated backbone crept up his massive, bull-like neck beneath the stringy hair hanging from the back of his little head, and he realized that the chauffeur's muscular body, absent the horns, wings, and tail, was almost identical to that of the dragon-man painted on the VW bus.

After about two hundred yards, they reached the crest. Ded froze at the view before him. It was—there was only one word for it—Olympian. Cut into the hill below was a huge, stone amphitheater. Here and there, patches of grass grew from cracks in the seats. Lizards darted in the sunlight. At the bottom of the amphitheater, on an expanse of flat, hardened dirt, was a raised, wooden stage with tall trees behind. On the stage, 25 to 30 people faced upstage like a chorus in a Greek tragedy. Beyond the amphitheater, fifteen miles or more down the mountain, past the nearest finger of the blue Bay, was the city of San Francisco, a hazy pile of white blocks shimmering in the sun. In the far distance on the other side of the eastern expanse of the Bay, beyond Berkeley and Oakland, Ded could see the pointed peak of Mount Diablo, the Mountain of the Devil, a natural landmark so prominent navigators and surveyors used it to plot their position.

Suitably awed, Ded started down the amphitheater steps toward the gathering, causing San Francisco, the Bay, Berkeley, Oakland, and even Mount Diablo to drop behind the trees.

On stage, someone standing on a small platform was addressing the gathered crowd. When Ded reached the ground just in front, all he could see, floating above the assembly, was a woman's face, young-looking, with baby-pink skin, wreathed in long, fine, strawberry-blond hair. The face radiated with a lunar glow of unformed wonder, hope, faith—and due to the dark glasses, a touch of mystery.

Ded's heart sprung to his throat. *Beulah Vala!*

He stopped and swallowed. Determined not to succumb to another embarrassing Sicilian Illusion, as had happened with the cow, he forced his mind outside of the temporary community in which he had become immersed. This allowed him the objective detachment necessary for looking back at himself and at what he was experiencing. Then, monitoring his every move, he climbed onto the stage, raising his perspective relative to the blocking crowd and thereby bringing the rest of Miss Vala into view. First, the line of her delicate neck. Second, her smooth, naked shoulders. Then, gaping from the plunging décolletage of her filmy peasant blouse, her breasts.

"My God!" Ded murmured.

From her childlike face, Ded would have expected her breasts to be the modest, nubile, champagne-glass features of ballerinas and wood sprites. But, no. They were immense. Plump. Comforting. Like the milk-filled bosoms of an enormous earth mother. Projecting out in a soft, jiggling cantilever without any independent structural support.

As in the cow's-udder dream he'd had during Inspector Ded's airport interview, Ded imagined himself being pulled in by the udder's irresistible, hypnotic power, until he was completely enclosed within its warm, pulsating, spongy flesh, totally contented.

Ded jerked his mind out of his daydream and pushed to the front of the congregation, only to find his eyes now drifting down, past the delicate outline of Miss Vala's nipples, over the rest of her more-out-of-its-clothes-than-in body. Small, electric shocks of libido pulsed through him with each new, anatomical feast. Below her billowing, cut-off blouse, her waist—so naked, tight, pivoting—spoke to unbelievable varieties of motion. Her hips—firm, curving, sensuous, and rocking ever so slightly in a low-slung, brown suede micro-skirt. Her incredibly long legs—thin, tapered, barefoot, touching at the ankles, yet still showing light between the upper thighs, advertising a space longing to be filled.

In a desperate bid to regain perspective, Ded drew back his focus to take in Miss Vala as a whole. But now, her effect was even more powerful, as the hyper-sexiness of each part of her anatomy became, in the context of her angelic face, almost demure. Hesitant, even, betraying a slight lack of confidence, which, like the small, fading bruises Ded noticed on the tops of her knees, gave her an irresistible air of vulnerability and innocence.

Ded sighed, sinking into the amorphous pleasure of the Beulah Vala experience, before once again frog-marching himself back.

Get a grip, he lectured himself. *Your reaction is no different than a rooster sexually aroused when presented with a huge tail feather and a ping-pong-ball hen's head suspended from a string. It's absurd. More than that, it's meaningless; a mere evolutionarily created, chemically driven, patterned response triggered by perceiving an arbitrary combination of a few objectified physical characteristics—youth, clear skin, large breasts, full hair, symmetrical features, a certain curve from the hip to the waist—that studies have shown correlate strongly with health and fertility.*

Sternly, he eyed Miss Vala's objectified physical characteristics once again. *Beneath that arbitrary combination, Miss Vala is a woman, like any other—nothing more, nothing less.*

A statement, despite its iron logic, he couldn't help suspecting was not entirely true.

⁂

Beulah had been speaking. She paused and shifted toward Ded.

Before he could stop himself, Ded gave her a smile.

She offered no response.

Ded noticed a harnessed seeing-eye dog at her feet, and remembered Beulah Vala was blind.

Beulah surveyed the group through her unseeing, dark glasses while holding her level right hand at her midriff. "Since Ickey is no longer in the mid-level of God's consciousness in which most of us live, where we appear separate from the physical world around us—" She spoke in the slow, chirpy, singsong voice an ex-cheerleader would use to instruct a kindergarten class, emphasizing the last few words of each phrase, and then pausing to let it sink in. "It might seem easiest to seek him in the lowest level of God's consciousness—" She lowered her right hand, palm down, to thigh level. "In which our minds are cut off from everything else, reflecting only on our own abstractions." A mock scowl formed on her forehead. "But to do so would be a mistake. All that we would find there would be the pale shadow of Ickey's reality. Vague remembrances. Dry generalizations."

Kind of technical for a funeral oration, Ded critiqued, trying to maintain his emotional distance from Jerusalem's personal assistant.

"If we want to discover Ickey's reality," she continued blithely, "we must look in the highest level of God's consciousness—in which the distinction between us and the physical world has been obliterated by divine creativity. Only there will we find the eternal body of Ickey Jerusalem."

She raised her angelic face to the heavens, and then, after a pause, dropped it, gesturing with her small, open hands to something next to her platform.

His line of sight blocked by the crowd, Ded, with Ghostflea trailing, hurried around to the right to get a better view.

Lying on the wooden platform before Beulah was a six-foot, cookie-flat, gingerbread man with dot eyes, hyphen brows, a Mr. Happy smile, an icing bow tie, and crucifix-wide, welcoming arms.

Ded raised his right eyebrow. *THIS is the eternal body of Ickey Jerusalem?*

His new vantage point also allowed him to see a balding, thirtyish man struggling to restrain an old woman, his back to the eternal gingerbread. The woman, sobbing uncontrollably, stretched her gnarled and bony arms out at the cookie. "He was such a good boy," she blubbered. "Such a good boy."

Without losing his grip on the woman, the balding man looked over his shoulder at the spread-eagled biscuit. "A little peculiar, though, Grandma, you gotta admit."

"Who are they?" Ded asked Ghostflea.

"The old lady is Mr. Jerusalem's grandmother. Her name's Enion. The man is Mr. Jerusalem's brother, Theo. He takes care of her."

Beulah pointed a mildly condemnatory finger at the cookie. "This is the memory of Ickey. Generalized. Abstract. One-dimensional. Deflecting us from seeking his eternal body in the highest level of God's consciousness."

Ded raised his eyebrow again. *So, this is* not *the eternal body of Ickey Jerusalem?* Due to Beulah's breezy voice and pubescent face being so out of kilter with the ponderous content of her lecture, he was having trouble keeping track of the proper location of the deceased.

Beulah directed her face vaguely to her left. "Tharmas?"

A nasal voice answered, "Yeah?"

A Middle-Eastern-looking man toward the back of the crowd raised his gloved hand. He had curly black hair, dark eyes, and a hawk-like nose. He was wearing an orangey-red, short-sleeved shirt in the same shade as that of the goat-horned, winged bodybuilder in the VW bus paintings.

Next to him, standing about waist-high and therefore partly obscured by others, Ded saw a woman whose head was piled high with flaming-red hair. *The pint-sized prostitute from last night! What's she doing here? And why's she with Tharmas Luvah, Jerusalem's business manager? Was he the one who sent her to give me the whispered message implicating the doctor?*

Ded's office had tried to set up a meeting with Luvah, but he hadn't responded.

Before I leave this funeral, Ded vowed, *I've got to confront Luvah and the redhead for some answers.*

Beulah, with the giant, humanoid cookie lying at her feet, zeroed her ears in on Tharmas's voice. "Could you please bring out the paper plates?"

"No," Grandma Enion bawled, "I won't let you!" She broke past Theo and threw herself, wailing, onto the gingerbread man's chest.

It was a pitiful scene, rendered even more so by the old woman landing with such force that she broke off the gingerbread man's head. The grainy, brown face, now rotated a few degrees to the left, grinned inanely, as if to say, "That's the way the cookie crumbles."

Following several minutes of unseemly commotion, Theo and the others were at last able, with the help of Beulah's seeing-eye dog, to wrest the gingerbread man's head from Grandma Enion's grip.

With great reverence, the head was placed back where it belonged.

Not your typical funeral, Ded observed, finding it easier and easier to keep his emotional distance.

"I know it's hard to do," an empathetic Beulah counseled the sniveling Grandma Enion, "but if we are to discover the true reality of Ickey, we must let go of his memory."

Beulah took a large, serrated knife from a railing behind her, felt her way down from the raised platform onto the stage, got onto her hands and knees (affording Ded a heart-stopping view of her breasts), and began cutting the re-capitated cookie—grin, dogtooth marks, and all—into three-inch squares that were passed on the paper plates to the assembled mourners.

~

Ded got an eye. Even in its most generalized, abstract, and one-dimensional form, an eye was not the easiest thing to eat—although, based on the loud and excessive protestations from Grandma Enion when offered the cookie's icing bow tie by Ickey's brother, Theo, not the most difficult.

"She doesn't seem to be taking this at all in the right spirit," Ded remarked to the man sitting to his left on the edge of the stage.

The man was in his mid-sixties, of a stocky build, with muscular arms reminiscent of a village blacksmith. His callused hands indicated a life of physical labor. On his wrist, he wore a large, elaborate watch.

"She hasn't been right in the head since her husband left," the man said in an Oklahoma accent, pensively nibbling at the one-dimensional memory of Ickey Jerusalem's big toe.

"When was that?"

"A long time ago," the man replied, as though barely able to recall how long ago it actually was. "Back when she was young and pretty. He was a sailor. Highly emotional, disorganized, out of control. Went off on a voyage in the Pacific one autumn and never returned."

Ded gave a desultory poke at his gingerbread eye. There was something unsettling about the way the damn thing stared up at him. "She took it bad, huh?"

"At first she just sat there, weaving on her loom, moaning his name, 'Tharmas, Tharmas, Tharmas—"

Ded looked up. "But that's the name of Ickey's business manager."

"Nickname," the man corrected him. "That Tharmas's real name is Thomas. Thomas Luvah." His eyes hardened. "Though the name 'Satan Incarnate' is more accurate, if you ask me."

Ded wasn't sure what to make of that. He looked uneasily at his plate and covered the staring eye with his left hand. He then scoured the crowd for Tharmas. Although he caught a glance of the prostitute's flaming-red hair, the business manager was nowhere to be seen.

Sitting on the ground in front of the stage, Grandma Enion let out a plaintive moan.

The man peered down at her with a sad face. "She's lost her faith in the Holy Spirit."

Ded surmised this was bad news.

The man sighed. "Now, at the least little thing, she'll break down."

Ded clucked his tongue.

The man turned. He searched Ded's face.

What? Ded worried to himself. *Wasn't clucking my tongue the right response?*

Ded tried hard to look concerned about the Holy Spirit.

It wasn't easy.

The man indicated the gray-haired woman sitting primly beside him, a paper plate on her lap. She was thin, immaculately groomed, her face showing the wrinkled residual of what in earlier days must have been heavenly looks. Her manner was aloof, almost queen-like. She was eating the remains of the gingerbread man's groin.

"My wife, Enith," the man announced with an air of resignation.

The woman acknowledged Ded with a regal dip of her head, tiny crotch crumbs falling from her lower lip.

The man reached out to shake Ded's hand. "My name is Los."

"As in the opposite of profit?" Ded joked, for that was the way the man had pronounced his name.

"The opposite of *prophet*?" Los gave Ded a look of incomprehension. "No, as in Los Jerusalem. Enith and I are Ickey's parents."

Ded instantly withdrew his smile. "Oh, I'm so sorry about your son."

It seemed the right thing to say in the circumstances.

Los suppressed a sob.

Queen-like Enith stared right through Ded's head. "My son was destined to be a great man, you know," she incanted in an Oklahoma accent identical to Los's. "A hero. A messiah. It was written in the stars." She drew her hands apart to demonstrate the awesomeness of space and then looked up through them. "Up there."

"You bet." Ded wasn't about to disagree with a mother who was eating her son's private parts.

Los dabbed his eyes with his fingers. "I don't know about the stars, but we certainly thought we could make something out of him, some kind of lasting contribution to mankind." He looked at his watch. "It was just a matter of time, you know."

"Yes, siree," Ded agreed. "Just a matter of time."

At a loss for further *bon mots*, Ded palmed the gingerbread eye, brought it cake-side up to his mouth, and had a nibble.

"Mmm, not bad," he concluded.

After this brief nod to propriety, he pinched the cookie with his fingers, lifted it up in the air, eye-side still facing away, and brought it to his mouth, intending to gobble it down before the damn thing could flip over and start blinking at him.

Just as the cookie reached his lips, it exploded and was gone. Simultaneously, he heard in his stage-side ear a thud in the wooden floor, and in his amphitheater-seats-side ear, the slight echo of what sounded like a distant, muffled cap gun with an automatic reloading mechanism.

He looked back up to the crest of the hill where he had entered with Ghostflea and saw someone disappearing down the other side, elbows out, as though holding something in both hands. The person's head was covered by a blue knit cap.

Christ, he thought, *was that guy shooting at me?*

Or was it merely a weak cookie?

He scanned the stage floor, sure he would see a burn-ringed hole in the wood. Yes, there it was, not six feet away.

Los, who had not seen the cookie explode but must have heard the cap gun and thud, was looking around with an uncertain expression. His wife was gnawing regally on the last of her gingerbread son.

Ded glanced up to the currently empty ridge.

If it had been a shooter, it looked like he would not risk taking a second shot now the target was aware.

While keeping an occasional eye on the crest of the mountain to make sure the blue-knit-hat guy had not returned, Ded forced his agitated mind back to his investigation, forming the precise words to say next to Los.

"This isn't the proper time or the place, Mr. Jerusalem, but I'm a claims adjuster for an insurance company that issued a policy on your son's life. Do you think I could see you briefly later this week to ask you about him?"

"Go ahead and ask me now. Better than my sitting here, brooding."

"Thanks. That's very kind. I'll make it quick. Do you have any idea why your son might have wanted to kill himself?"

Los tightened his mouth, tears in his eyes, and shook his head. "He had everything going for him. Looks, brains, education. He even went to study in England. At Oxford. And then, of course, my Uncle Urthon set up the trust for him."

"Uncle Urthon?"

Urthon, Enion, Theo, Los, Enith, Ded thought. *Is there some kind of family in-joke I'm missing here?*

Los gave the uncle's full name. "Urthon Spectre."

Ded knew that name. The policy on Ickey Jerusalem's life naming Beulah Vala as beneficiary had been taken out by the Urthon Spectre Trust. At the time, Ded had assumed the name had been made up.

"Last I heard," Los added, shaking his head at the tragedy of it all, "the trust had over a hundred million dollars in it."

Ded whistled at the figure. "What happens under the trust now that Ickey has died?"

"Assuming Ickey hasn't modified the trust, the default beneficiary is my next living son." Los dipped his head in the direction of the bald-headed Theo, Ickey's brother, crouching in front of his grandmother.

"Come on, Grandma," the new potential suspect urged, "a little bow tie isn't going to kill you."

Ded watched this touching scene for a minute before turning back to Los. "Did Theo know he was the default beneficiary?"

"All my children knew. Any one of them, if they'd ended up being the oldest of Ickey's survivors, could have been the default beneficiary."

"And how many children do you have?" Ded asked, looking to expand his list of potential suspects.

"Twelve," Los answered, parental pride shining through his tear-filled eyes.

Los's wife, Enith, still regally silent in her grief, gave Ded a pained look.

Ded replied with a gesture of sympathy.

"All of them boys, thank the Lord," Los said. "After Ickey there was Orc. Died sophomore year of high school. Then there was Theo." Los watched as Theo, making aircraft engine noises, flew the icing bow tie like a toy plane in an ever-tightening spiral aimed at the wide open hangar of Grandma Enion's mouth.

"Such a nice young man," Los declared as Grandma Enion peered up at Theo, her hangar still wide open, the rapidly dissolving bow tie hanging precariously on her lower lip. "'Do unto others as you would wish them to do unto you.' That's Theo's motto. He works for the Social Services Department. Says if he ends up the beneficiary of the trust, he's going to give it all to charity."

Ded studied Theo, trying to tell from his demeanor whether he could have been capable of murder.

"And then there's Ozo," Los said, continuing to count off his sons. "He's over there. Soth, there. Tamon. Rint. Palam…"

Ickey? Orc? Theo? Ozo? Soth? Tamon? Rint? Palam? Ded recited Los's expanding list of offspring. This was beyond a family in-joke. Child abuse was more like it.

Ded waited for the poet's father to finish his list before following a hunch. "Where are you from, Los?"

"The Central Valley. A small town called Eden."

Right, Ded thought. *That explains the names.*

The Central Valley of California was a huge former desert. Through the miracles of irrigation and human cultivation, it now produced two-thirds of America's nuts, fruits, and vegetables. Its inhabitants were mostly immigrants from Oklahoma, North Dakota, and other such garden spots, and reflected altogether the products of their new land.

"Did Ickey grow up in Eden?" Ded asked.

"Yes." Los sighed once again. "He should never have left."

"Why's that?"

Los contemplated his rough palms, avoiding an answer. "If only he'd stayed, he'd never have fallen—"

A clanging came from behind them.

Los and Ded got on their feet to see.

Ded saw Beulah Vala standing at the rear of the platform, leaning back against the railing, holding before her an upturned garbage can lid piled high with gingerbread crumbs. She was banging on the lid edge with the back of the serrated knife.

Everyone fell silent.

"The last of Ickey's memory," Beulah declared light-heartedly in her primary school teacher voice. She lifted the lid over her head like a sacrificial offering, turned about, and with a tremendous effort, flung it between the tall trees backing the stage, down the steep slope behind. "For the worms," she exulted, "the final guests at natural man's last supper."

The group listened as the tin lid bounced and clattered down the rock-strewn mountain on its way to oblivion.

Beulah cast her unseeing face toward the sun, following its heat. "And now," she continued, as if the appallingly tasteless display just completed was not enough, "to help us find Ickey's eternal body in the highest level—"

What now? Ded speculated, looking up into the sky. A *giant balloon filled with the dead poet's farts?*

One could say that, at this point, Ded's ability to keep himself on the outside of the Beulah Vala experience had become fairly secure.

Beulah opened her hands, dropped her head, and gestured once more to her feet. "—I give you… the Word."

Before her, on the platform, as though hurriedly left behind by a departing divinity, was a pile of leather-bound books. Beulah motioned the group forward. "For each of you, in a single volume, in chronological order, the complete collection of Ickey's poems, published just before he died."

She picked up a book and pressed it between her diminutive palms. "Only in this book will you discover the eternal body of Ickey. The eternal body of humanity. Of the imagination. Of God Himself."

Ded joined the throng to grab a copy. He got one and turned it over in his hand. "Must be one hell of a book," he muttered, forgetting what acute hearing sightless people can have.

From behind her dark shades, Beulah turned a blind eye to Ded, first in the literal sense, and then in the figurative. Her face lit up with reverence. "In the book is a poem which Ickey wrote about a famous portrait painter."

She wet her rose-petal lips and recited from memory with the same optimism and emphasis had the poem been *Little Bo Peep*:

When Sir Joshua Reynolds died
All Nature was degraded;
The King dropped a tear into the Queen's ear;
And all his Pictures Faded.

Beulah clasped the book to her breast. "Now, Ickey, as well, has died. If we aren't careful, all nature, the world he illuminated with his vision, will become degraded. Even worse, his poems, faded."

She opened the book and turned it out for her audience to see the page. "You must read his words, not with your eyes, but with your imagination," she said, speaking in a tone which, although inspirational, was oddly reminiscent of a child addressing a recuperating houseplant. "Seeing as Ickey saw, into the luxuriant and colorful world hidden beneath the faded surface the mediocre call reality."

She closed the book and brought it back to her bosom. "If you can do that, then Ickey Jerusalem, I assure you, will not have lived in vain."

CHAPTER 10

THE INTIMATION OF FREEDOM

The gathering was breaking up. Ded was sitting on the edge of the stage once more, watching the departing guests, while coming to the realization that at some point, while his head had been turned, Ickey Jerusalem's business manager, Tharmas Luvah, and his red-headed sidekick had vanished.

Adam Ghostflea sat down beside Ded, looking adoringly ahead. On the ground before the stage, about ten feet away, where the amphitheater steps began their upward sweep, a tag-end of the funeral attendees passed by Beulah Vala, giving their condolences, a task made difficult by the fact that her seeing-eye dog, which she held by a harness in her left hand, kept lunging at them, trying to bite them.

The dog caught hold of the trouser leg of a pale, bald-headed, fat man wearing a monocle. Bacon Urizen, Jerusalem's lawyer—Ded recognized him immediately. Urizen attempted to maintain an air of imperious indifference toward the animal while simultaneously hopping away on his free leg.

Ded nudged Ghostflea with his elbow and pointed with his chin.

"The dog bites everybody who gets close to Miss Vala," the chauffeur said in his rasping tone. "But Miss Vala doesn't see. Not because she's blind in her eyes. Her other senses more than make up for that. She's always very aware of what is happening around her. When it comes to the dog, though, Miss Vala has an unexplained blind spot. She likes him so much, no one dares say anything."

Unable to keep his balance, Urizen collapsed ignominiously to the ground, from where, after a struggle, he succeeded in extricating himself from the dog's clutches. Exhausted, he located his monocle, which had popped out during the fall, reinserted it, got to his feet, and with as much dignity as he could muster—inasmuch as he had had to leave his trousers behind—bid Beulah farewell.

"I look forward to seeing you on Monday morning," she said amiably, her dark glasses aimed in Urizen's general direction.

"And I, you," Urizen replied, his deep voice betraying an excusable lack of sincerity.

The lawyer rotated his immense bulk around. On cue, a mountain of a man with a haunted face lumbered up from behind the stage, where he had apparently been hiding, turned, and squatted. Urizen put his arms around the man's neck and fell onto the offered broad back. The giant reached behind him, gathered up Urizen's bare, fat legs, and struggled to his feet.

"Who's he?" Ded asked Ghostflea as they watched the giant piggyback the lawyer up the amphitheater steps.

"One of Jerusalem's relatives, Cousin Ijim. Owns Ferrous Peak above Eden."

"Strong," Ded commented.

"Strong," Ghostflea agreed.

Ded watched Ijim carry his burden all the way to the crest of the amphitheater. He wanted to gauge whether, at that distance, Ijim matched in size the suspected gunman glimpsed there earlier.

It was difficult to say.

ɷ

Beulah stood contented and alone, listening to the retreating footsteps of Cousin Ijim and the few remaining guests who had wisely decided to give their condolences later by mail. Beulah's dog lay at her feet, blissfully chewing the zipper on Bacon Urizen's trousers.

Ded touched his fly as he debated whether it was all that important to interview Ickey Jerusalem's personal assistant at this time. *Perhaps I'll slip away now and—*

Beulah addressed the air in Ded's vicinity. "Adam?"

"Yes, Miss Vala," God's shrunken consciousness answered before Ded could shut him up. Ghostflea's face was evidencing great pleasure at having been addressed by Beulah.

"Did you pick up the insurance man who wanted to see me?"

"Yes, Miss Vala. He's here. I'll bring him to you now."

Ded assessed the situation. If he wheeled around and ran, the dog would catch him before he reached the top of the amphitheater. He could try to back casually away, but that would likely agitate Ghostflea, who already had hold of Ded's arm, which, in turn, would cause Beulah to become confused—which, in turn, would cause the dog to decide to take matters into his own jaws.

No. Ded's only course of action was to avoid exciting the beast and go along with whatever the woman wanted.

"Miss Vala," Ded called out warily, as Ghostflea ushered him forward to greet her.

"Beulah, please," she demurred, extending her hand in a manner as open and friendly as the neckline of her peasant blouse.

The claims adjuster gulped at the view, stretching his arm to shake her fingertips with his own. "Ded Smith."

The dog raised his head from Urizen's zipper and growled, causing Ded to whip his hand back.

Beulah reached down to pat the evil canine head with the fingers

Ded had just shaken. "Poor Scofield. I think something's wrong with his tummy."

Ded anxiously chimed in with several effusive expressions of sympathy for the dog's tummy, although, frankly, given the cur's diet, Ded found it hard to be all that supportive.

Tummy, hell, Ded silently sniped. *It's his hemorrhoids I'm looking forward to seeing.*

Beulah turned her attention from the dog. "Dead? Like a doornail? That's really an unusual name."

"No. Not D-e-a-d. Just D-e-d. It's short for Dedalus. My parents took it from Greek mythology." Secretly, Ded had always felt the etymology of his name gave him a certain class.

"Dedalus? Dedalus?" Beulah mulled over the name, having apparently not heard it before. "So, you must be from the Central Valley, too?"

"Uh, no," Ded stammered. "Buffalo, New York."

"Oh," Beulah remarked, as though Ded had at that moment taken off his hat to reveal his head ended at his eyebrows.

Ded changed the subject. "That was an original funeral, Miss Va—I mean, Beulah."

Beulah bowed her head humbly, her long, reddish-blond hair touching her waist. "I was only following Ickey's instructions."

"That part with the gingerbread man," Ded continued, "where we all symbolically ate Jerusalem's body—"

"Symbolically?" Beulah interjected, arching an eyebrow over her dark glasses.

"Er, you know, it was like holy communion." Ded spelled it out. "Take and eat this in remembrance of—" Ded stopped at his sudden uneasy suspicion. "It wasn't symbolic?"

Beulah smiled sweetly. "Ickey taught us that the thing itself is always more powerfully poetic than its symbol." She moved her hand as though stirring a bowl. "We mixed his ashes into the gingerbread."

"Yes," Ded agreed, as calmly as he could, "that *is* more powerfully poetic."

In his mind, however, Ded was not quite so calm, picturing himself hauled up before the Olympian Life Insurance Company disciplinary committee for having violated the company rule against a claims adjuster eating the insured. "Honestly, I didn't know," he imagined his defense. "That damned woman said it was just his memory we were eating. She swore the poet was still alive and kicking in the highest level of God's consciousness. Even so, I had only a small nibble of his right eyeball."

All at once, Ded had a horrible thought. *Christ, don't tell me cannibalism is a strict liability offense—like bigamy, where you're convicted even if you had no reason to suspect that your Las Vegas divorce was not valid, or like statutory rape, that the young woman was underage. So, my being unaware the cookie contained human remains just isn't going to cut it in court as a valid defense.*

Ded seized control of his otherwise soon-to-be hyperventilating brain and forcibly returned his attention to the poet's personal assistant, his gaze drifting down Beulah's body.

Scofield looked up from his trouser meal and eyed Ded's fly with disquieting interest. Ded swiftly refocused his attention on Beulah's face. "From our interview at the airport a couple of weeks ago plus your funeral oration today, Beulah, it appears that when Jerusalem was on the plane, he felt he was on the verge of uniting with something called the highest level of God's consciousness. I wonder if you could give me some background."

"Ickey's ideas are hard to get at the first sitting," Beulah said, appearing to sense his skepticism. "I know I had a tough time at the start. Plus, frankly, in my experience, when most people hear the word 'metaphysics,' they become immediately bored, switching off their ears before anything is said, no matter how interested they might have been had they taken the effort to listen."

"I'm willing to make the effort," Ded said. He knew that to figure out what Jerusalem had been thinking on the plane, he had to understand the poet's beliefs, no matter how illogical. And although the ideas Beulah had expressed so far had seemed patently illogical, they were illogical in a way he had never encountered before.

❧

Ded Smith, it should be noted, had some very definite views on metaphysics and God.

"Atheistic fundamentalism" was perhaps the most accurate description of his beliefs. Ded felt about the literal facts of the objective world the same as a Christian fundamentalist feels about the literal words of the Bible: the literal says it all, and thus, any attempted non-literal interpretation must be reading into the literal something that is not there.

"Except for a few loonies," Ded would argue to the occasional seatmate unable to escape the claims adjuster's rampant didacticism, "people who believe in God have never seen, heard, tasted, touched, or smelled Him. Their belief arises solely from an extra-textual interpretation of those things they can see, hear, taste, touch or smell: 'Nature is organized, so God must exist.' 'A sunset is beautiful, so God must exist.' 'Sometimes, when I pray for things, I get them, so God must exist.' 'When the preacher lays his hands on my head, I start babbling incoherently, so God must exist.'"

Belief in God, to Ded, was a Sicilian Illusion writ large. As long as the belief was kept at the level of an inchoate feeling, the illusion could be sustained. But once the believer looked at his belief from outside the Cave, trying to justify it with objective, logical thought, its absurdity became obvious. It was as though a tiny fly, perched on the edge of a colossal, slowly turning, industrial cogwheel, set about constructing arguments to prove that the sole purpose of the wheel was to give him a ride. No matter how elaborate and sophisticated the arguments necessary to support this belief became, in the end, they'd always run up against the indifference of the cogwheel, at which point the believer, in order to save himself embarrassment, would have to fall back on mystery.

"Three hundred thousand people are wiped out by an earthquake in China," Ded would often state to illustrate the point. "What do the religious say? 'God works His wonders in mysterious ways.' What do I say? Geologic stresses in the earth's crust built up, the land shook, and a lot of Homo sapiens were crushed in the falling debris. Period. That's it. Where's the mystery?"

If you believe in God, the world is ultimately mysterious. If, instead, you simply accept the objective world as it is, there's no mystery whatsoever.

There also isn't much meaning. But then, Ded didn't see his job as giving the world meaning—only dispelling its mysteries.

Beulah fiddled for a moment with a tiny jack-o'-lantern brooch on her blouse over her heart, its grin disturbingly similar to that on the pumpkin at the Holiday Inn. "To make it easier to keep the interest of the average person, I've tried to figure out a way to explain Ickey's metaphysics using cute cats. But it just can't be done."

"I don't need cute cats," Ded declared. "Cute cats are for wimps."

"Okay, then, here it goes," Beulah began cheerfully. "I'm sure you, like most thinking people, have at one time or another wondered whether everything you experience as separate from your mind, including your own body, in fact, exists *only* in your mind, a mere figment of your imagination."

"I have. And I decided there was no way logically to disprove it—although I don't actually believe it's all in my mind."

"Okay, now, gross that up and imagine that everything everywhere exists only in the mind of God, the creator, as a figment of *His* imagination."

"Sure," Ded said. "Piece of cake."

"If everything exists only in the mind of God, then everything God imagines, by definition, exists."

"The tautology is clear," Ded agreed.

"Since God's creative imagination is omnipotent," Beulah continued, "if He imagines, say, a white rose, He takes in at once everything possible to see in the rose—the soft petals, the purity of the Virgin Mary, the paleness of death, the pollination by bees, the medieval War of the Roses, aphid infestations, etcetera—producing for Him an infinitely total experience of the rose's reality, the greatest reality possible."

"So, let me guess," a confident Ded said, "what you are describing here, where God sits around imagining the totality of everything about everything, is what you call the highest level of God's consciousness?"

"You're right. It *is.* But unfortunately, God sat around at that level imagining things only before the Fall."

"The Fall?"

"Before the creation of humanity and the physical world."

Beulah reached her hands out and moved them sinuously, as though modeling a female sculpture in the air. "After a few eons of randomly imagining everything about everything, God, in an act of play, turned instead to focus on creating a complete physical world in His mind, using in its construction only those elements which could be perceived by the five senses—touch, taste, sight, sound, and smell."

Ded was silent. From his point of view, Beulah's invisible, female sculpture outlined precisely its curvaceous creator behind it.

Beulah struck an admiring posture in the general direction of her imaginary creation. "God found the physical world unbelievably beautiful."

"Unbelievably beautiful," Ded sighed, drinking in Beulah's concrete reality—the absurdly lovely face, the ingénue voice, the soft, soft skin, with its rosy, rosy perfume, and like as not, sweet, sweet taste.

"So absorbed did He become in its beauty," she continued, "He forgot it was a mere part of His mind and fell into a deep, deep sleep."

"Deep, deep sleep." Ded's eyelids were becoming heavy.

Beulah took a step forward until her face was as close to Ded as her breasts would allow. "Shrinking His consciousness."

Ded's heavy-lidded field of view contracted down to focus intently on the dainty way Beulah's full, yielding lips moved as she spoke.

"Until the consciousness of God contracted into what became the human mind, inculcated first into the physical body of the newly created Adam, then passed on to Eve when she was molded from his rib, and thereafter, to all their progeny. Although everything was still a figment of God's omnipotent imagination, God's shrunken consciousness, the human mind, could see only the small part perceivable through the five senses. The sleeping God was reduced to peering out from a myriad of subjective human selves at what looked like separate physical objects, believing those objects to be all there was to reality."

"All there was to reality," Ded murmured.

"This is the mid-level of God's consciousness, where most of humanity passes their existence, unable to see past the physical world to the total true reality of God's infinite and eternal imagination, and thus, are condemned to live their lives as nothing more than a shallow parody of that reality."

Beulah's mouth came to a stop.

For a brief eternity, Ded stared at her stopped mouth before jerking his eyes wide, conscious that Beulah was waiting for him to comment on Jerusalem's ideas.

Urgently, he racked his brain for the right word. *Drivel? Claptrap? Twaddle? Blather? Gibberish?* There were so many to choose from.

"Very interesting," he managed at last, which in its own way was true. Never had Ded heard a religious interpretation so extra-textual as to have no connection at all to the objective facts it was interpreting. Still, he had to admit, Miss Vala had a much more intriguing mind than her youthfully innocent voice and teenybopper dress sense would have led one to believe. And despite her weird ideas, when she expressed them, he felt something elegant. Emotionally attractive. Comforting. Desirable, even.

Ded considered asking Beulah to outline the lowest level of God's consciousness, but he needed time to absorb the parable of the sleeping God. Plus, he had more immediate matters he wanted to ask Beulah about.

"If you don't mind, Beulah, I've got a few questions about—" Ded managed to stop himself before saying the word "reality." "Uh, well, you know, about the circumstances of Ickey Jerusalem's death."

Beulah's smile manifested her openness on the subject.

"A little under two weeks before Jerusalem died," Ded began in his most professional manner, "a twenty-million-dollar insurance policy was taken out on his life, for which you were named the beneficiary."

Beulah's raised her guileless eyebrows. "There was? Ickey never told me."

Ded made a quick note to check this assertion that evening when meeting with Bacon Urizen. The lawyer had signed the insurance application for the Urthon Spectre Trust.

"Under Section Eight of the policy, no proceeds are to be paid if the insured's death is due to suicide."

"I see." Beulah's tone evidenced no particular interest in this fact.

Ded stiffened up. "It's my job to confirm Jerusalem killed himself."

"There's doubt?" Beulah asked.

"There's always doubt," Ded stated portentously. "All I want to do is reduce that doubt to a size that can be comfortably ignored."

Beulah pursed her lips as she considered what Ded was saying. "Perhaps we should discuss this on our way to the East Bay."

"The East Bay?"

"That's where Ickey's house is. Where I live. We'll have lunch there. And then, after I've told you everything I know, I'll show you whatever it is you might want to see."

Ded swallowed the remainder of what he was going to say, as assorted interpretations of Beulah's offer ran uncontrollably through his brain.

CHAPTER 11

THE TURN OF THE HEAD

Beulah Vala and Ded sat in the back of the hearse, she on the right, Ded on the left, a large, empty gap between them. Beulah, despite her earlier openness, had covered everything from her neck on down with a soft, earth-colored cloak, and retreated into a quiet, internal space. Ghostflea, cursing like a hoarse sailor, and the seeing-eye dog, Scofield, were in the front of the glass partition. The dog's harness had been tied to the door handle on the left side—the English vehicle's passenger side—so he couldn't interfere with Ghostflea's driving by biting off his small head.

Actually, given the way the hearse was now careering uncontrollably down Mount Tamalpais, Ghostflea losing his head probably wouldn't have made much difference.

As on the trip up, a sense of foreboding bordering on panic flooded through Ded's being. *What am I doing here, stuck inside a hearse with a cross-eyed, foul-mouthed, totally out-to-lunch driver, a rabid carnivore riding shotgun, and sitting next to me, a blind occult enchantress, who, for all I know, is taking me back to her gingerbread house to shove me into her oven as a late-morning snack?*

As Ded closed his eyes to avoid the view out the window, he saw himself being crammed into a coffin-shaped oven by a strawberry-blond witch, and sliding out twenty minutes later as a six-foot long, cookie-flat gingerbread man, shrink-wrapped in the clear plastic remains of the sleeping God's contracted mind, a subjective self cut off from life-giving air, suffocating, suffocating—

Ded opened his eyes and sucked in a lungful of air. *Christ! Perhaps the parable of the sleeping God* does *have a connection to Ickey Jerusalem's death.*

Using all the willpower at his disposal, Ded forced his mind once more outside of his self, distancing his fear, if not his sense of foreboding. He glanced at Beulah. Despite the wild ride, her sublime face seemed so relaxed, so serene, so lacking in anxiety. He knew it wasn't due to her sightlessness. Based on what Ghostflea had said, Beulah was always very aware of what was happening around her. She probably knew at that very moment he was looking at her.

Ded imagined himself as Ickey Jerusalem sitting next to the similarly placid Beulah during the turbulence on the plane. At once, he pictured her springing alive, leaping on top of him, and pulling a plastic cleaning bag over his head.

No, he concluded. Skinny as he was, he'd have no problem fighting her off. After all, on average, men have about twice the upper body strength as women. Plus, the violence of such a struggle would inevitably leave telltale bruises on his arms—which Jerusalem's autopsy did not show—as well as Beulah's fingerprints on the bag—which also weren't there.

Something tapped Ded's left thigh. He looked down. It was his leather-bound anthology of Jerusalem's poetry, which, in response to an extraordinarily sharp swerve by Ghostflea, had fallen open on his lap. Ded adjusted his glasses, and consciously trying to divert his attention from the dangerous driving, skimmed the page on the right. Noticing a poem about eternal and infinite love, Ded slowed his reading speed to take in the words.

> Embraces are Cominglings from the Head even to the Feet;
> And not a pompous High Priest entering by a Secret Place.

Ded scratched behind his ear, then read the lines again, this time out loud. "A pompous High Priest entering by a Secret Place?"

Belatedly realizing what the poem was alluding to, he clapped the book shut and looked embarrassedly over at Beulah. She said nothing. The only reaction Ded could detect was the addition of a slight wistfulness to her serenity.

Scofield interrupted Ded's thoughts with a machine-gunned line of barks at two hikers who, having rapidly leapt up to cling to the rock-face on the inside of the road, stared terror-stricken, at the hearse as it zoomed past at something approaching the speed of sound. The dog, satisfied he had sufficiently warned the hikers about getting unduly close to his mistress, turned and assessed Ded impassively through the glass partition.

Ded pressed against his side of the car before addressing Beulah again. "So, what sort of seeing-eye dog training has Scofield had?"

"I know it's hard to believe, but none. He's entirely self-taught."

Ded gave the dog a forced-friendly smile. The dog's top lip curled upwards to reveal a row of yellowed fangs set in gums the color of bad meat.

"Ickey found him at the pound," Beulah said fondly. "Told me he knew he'd be perfect for my needs."

Ded kept his eyes on the beast. "Where was Scofield during the flight from New York?"

"In the hold. Poor ol' Scolie is not a good flier."

Ded wondered what sins subsumed in the description "not a good flier" had been committed the last time poor ol' Scolie was let into the passenger cabin. "His being in the hold was, I assume, a great relief to Bacon Urizen."

"Why?" Beulah's face indicated she didn't have a clue.

"You know when he was speaking to you at the end of the funeral today?"

"Yes. He has such a pleasantly deep voice."

"You couldn't see, but he wasn't wearing any trousers."

"Really?" Beulah looked genuinely surprised. "I've always thought of him as too conservative for that sort of thing."

Ded glanced at Scofield. In the opposite of the dog's top lip, his bottom lip was now curled *downwards*, exposing a whole new set of fangs.

Ded sensed it wouldn't be in his interest to try to explain why Urizen had been trouserless. Much more profitable would be an end run around attorney-client privilege. "On the flight from New York, when Jerusalem asked Urizen for his pen, what else did the two talk about?"

"Ickey wanted to know if Bacon had made changes to the Urthon Spectre Trust and his will."

"What kind of changes?"

Beulah gave her head a superficial shake. "They didn't say. Whatever they were, Bacon told Ickey he couldn't make the changes until he got back to San Francisco."

Was Jerusalem going to change the beneficiary of the trust, wiping out his brother Theo? Gazing into Beulah's dark glasses, Ded noticed the reflection of his own, thick spectacles. Suddenly, he realized how glad he was she was blind. She had no way of knowing how unappealing he looked—nor, apart from perhaps the occasional compliments of others, how dazzling she was.

"Do you know why Jerusalem was going to a plastic surgeon?"

"Plastic surgeon?" Beulah took a moment to work it out. "Oh, you mean Brom Ulro. He's a plastic surgeon, that's true. But for Ickey, he was acting merely as a primary care physician. Ickey had known him since Eden, before Brom even went to medical school. Ickey wouldn't trust anyone else with his medical matters."

"Three days before the trip to New York, Thursday, October 13th, to be precise, Jerusalem and Ulro had an argument. Do you know anything about it?"

"Only that it occurred. But their relationship had always been prickly. Probably because of Theo."

"Theo? Ickey's brother? What did he have to do with Dr. Ulro?"

Beulah gathered her cloak more closely around her body. "It's a long story."

Ded surveyed the panoramic, drop-away view zigzagging in Beulah's window, his sense of foreboding growing again. "How about giving me the abridged version? I'm not sure we've got time for anything longer."

Beulah then proceeded to tell the story of what had happened in Eden.

ಯ

Roughly a decade and a half earlier, when Ickey Jerusalem was approaching the end of his senior year at Eden High School, his younger brother, Theo, a quiet and timid virgin, gave a lift to a petite teenage girl hitchhiking through the Central Valley on her way to San Francisco's Haight-Ashbury. The girl, Rahab Oothoon, was one of the original flower children, a free spirit, filled with life and impulsive energy, thirsting after new experiences and new pleasures, with absolutely no need to explain or rationalize her actions to anyone.

What she saw in Theo, God only knew.

Nonetheless, one thing led to another in Theo's convertible, and before they had gone more than half a mile, the boy was experiencing his first oral sex.

"I almost ran the car off the road," he later recounted to an Ickey preoccupied with finishing a rhyming couplet on something or another. "Miss Oothoon was straddling my shoulders from the front and I couldn't see a thing."

Rahab reached orgasm shortly after a cop used his siren to pull the convertible over.

"I can't repeat what the policeman said," Theo told his barely listening older brother. "Miss Oothoon's thighs were clamped too tightly over my ears for me to hear anything but a muffle."

Theo, a good Christian boy, was not one to shirk his responsibilities. He realized he'd had carnal knowledge of Rahab Oothoon (although not in the manner he had expected). Accordingly, as soon as he got his mouth sufficiently free to speak, he dutifully proposed marriage.

"Why not?" Rahab immediately replied. She knew when she was on to a good thing.

The next day, the couple were married across the border in Reno, Nevada, at a place that didn't care if they were underage. The day after that, when they returned to settle in Eden, Rahab found herself in immediate conflict with the town's conventional views on married life. A socially backward farming community, Eden was not ready for a newly wedded woman who kept her maiden name, nor for one who publicly espoused the virtues of free love.

Although Ickey hardly blinked an eye about Rahab, Ickey's best friend, Bromion Ulro, was more critical. "The woman's a harlot!" he proclaimed in his rapid, cartoon-canary voice whenever anyone mentioned Rahab's name.

Granted, Bromion Ulro had been a little unstable around that time. His father, the town drunk (he had been psychologically damaged while working in the Office of Strategic Services in World War II), and his mother, the town's designated woman of easy virtue, had died in a car crash earlier that year. They'd been on their way back from a visit to Cousin Ijim's place, up on Ferrous Peak. Cousin Ijim blamed the crash on Satan Incarnate, whom he said had been tormenting him that morning in the outhouse. An impressionable Bromion reacted by becoming a born-again Christian, adopting the name "Nobodaddy," and striding around town, denouncing Satan and his works with the grand gestures of the God of the Old Testament.

A week after Rahab's marriage to Theo, Bromion caught her making what he assumed was a surreptitious call from a sidewalk telephone booth. He spent over an hour standing outside, haranguing her and passersby in the voice of a stentorian chipmunk with quotes from the Bible about extramarital sex.

"A good quarter of which," Rahab recounted to Theo, "were actually in favor of it."

It wasn't until several months into the marriage that Theo finally got around to looking up the definition of "free love" in the family dictionary and discovered, to his astonishment, the exact import of his wife's beliefs.

"So, that's what that guy dressed as a donkey was doing in our bed last night!" he exclaimed.

Rahab tried her best to convince Theo that her belief in free love would not interfere with their relationship. "Don't worry about the donkey, dear. You can still perform oral sex on me any time you want."

Uncertain what to do, Theo turned to Bromion for advice.

"Thou must expel this Jezebel from thy house!" Bromion declared without hesitation in speedy falsetto. "Free love is an abomination unto God's Law. For it is written, a man's wife should lay only with him, and not with another, particularly if the 'another' doth present himself unto the wife clothed as a beast of burden."

Theo suspected Bromion might be overstating his case, but he had neither the courage nor the energy to argue back. At Bromion's urging, Theo left the marital home and went back to his parents.

Soon thereafter, Rahab Oothoon left town.

❧

"So, that's why Jerusalem didn't like Dr. Ulro?" a dubious Ded queried Beulah as she appeared to finish her story. "Ulro convinced Theo he shouldn't share his wife with another?"

Beulah amicably shook her head to indicate there was more.

❧

"Aeiiiiiiiiiiiiiiiiiiiiiiiiiiiiiiiiiiii!"

Startled, Ded looked out of the front windshield as an upside-down bicyclist slid rightwards off the sharply left-turning hearse's hood. The investigator swiveled his eyes back to Beulah, who showed no reaction, apparently experiencing the passing Doppler-shifted frequency of the *Aeiiiiiiiiiiiiiiiiiiiiiiiiiiiiiiiii* as a normal background noise associated with a Ghostflea-chauffeured ride in the hearse.

That's it, Ded made up his mind. *I'm getting the hell out of here.*

But how? As a formal representative of the Olympian Life Insurance Company, he couldn't just blurt out, "Stop the fucking hearse!"

"A few weeks after Rahab Oothoon left town," Beulah continued in a gossipy tone, as Ded struggled to distance himself from his panic once again, "Ickey headed off to Oxford and Brom to UC Berkeley. Four years later, and several months after returning from England, Ickey went to see the then UCSF medical student, Brom, at his rented tract home in San Francisco's Sunset District. When Ickey rang the doorbell, to his astonishment, Rahab opened the door."

Beulah put on a scandalized face. "It turned out not only were she and Brom living together, they had been lovers from almost the day she'd married Theo. The rumor is Brom might even have been the guy in the donkey suit."

Ded furrowed his brow. "What did Jerusalem do?"

Beulah gave a nervous, girlish laugh. "He moved in with them."

"Moved in with them?"

She nodded.

Ded screwed up his lips. "It doesn't sound like Ickey Jerusalem was all that upset with Bromion Ulro for cuckolding his brother."

"Oh, he was. I'm sure. That's why a few years later, when Brom and Rahab finally got married, Ickey refused to go to the wedding."

Ded studied Beulah's blithe, schoolgirl face. He had the feeling she had left something vital out of her story, but was unsure whether he should press her on it at the moment.

"So, what did Jerusalem say when Bromion Ulro showed up on your flight?"

"Nothing at all. I didn't even know Brom was on the plane until I heard him examining Ickey's mortal remains near the end of the flight."

The mention of Ickey's mortal remains reminded Ded of a line of questioning he wanted to pursue. "Beulah, at your interview at the airport, you said Jerusalem indicated on the plane he was ready, at last, to unite with the highest level of God's consciousness. Then, later at the funeral, you said we should look for Jerusalem in that highest level. So, I take it, you think Jerusalem's union was successful?"

Beulah didn't skip a beat. "Of course. Ickey had been repeatedly uniting his mind with the highest level for years."

"He had? How?"

Beulah swiveled her earthen-cloaked body around to face Ded. "You remember I said that everything that exists is in the mind of God, a being of infinite and eternal imagination?"

"Yes, I remember," Ded replied, adding to himself, *Although, I can't say I put much credence in it at the time.*

"And that this God, after creating the physical world, fell asleep admiring its beauty, and his consciousness contracted into the human mind? And although the rich imaginings of the fully conscious God's mind continued to exist, His shrunken consciousness, confined to the five senses, could no longer see those imaginings? So, instead, God was reduced to peering out from myriad subjective human selves at what looked like separate physical objects, believing those objects to be all there was to reality?"

"Yep. How could I forget?"

"Well, after God fell asleep, a certain residual creative imagination continued to exist in human minds, but it was much more limited—in part, because humans tend to focus only on what they can perceive with their five senses, and in part, even without that focus, the scope of the human mind is so much narrower than the mind of the omnipotently creative, fully conscious God. Most humans, therefore, use their limited creative imagination primarily to dream up new ways of manipulating the physical world for their benefit. There are, however, some—such as painters, musicians, sculptors, playwrights, and poets—who use their creative imagination to produce works of art that can pierce the façade of the physical objects, capture a glimpse behind, and to the extent of that small glimpse, reunite the sleeping God's shrunken consciousness with the normally hidden highest level of God's consciousness."

Ded felt himself starting to lose the thread. "Could you give me an example?"

At that moment, the hearse turned northwards onto the flatlands, bringing the warmth of the mid-morning sun flooding into Beulah's side of the vehicle. She rotated her head to face the warmth.

"Take the sun," she offered.

"The sun?"

"What do you see when you look at the sun?"

"What it is: an eighty-thousand-mile-diameter burning ball of gas ninety-three million miles away in space."

"Ickey, too, saw that burning ball of gas. But that was just the lowest-common-denominator physical object that all humans can see. Using his God-given creative imagination, Ickey was able to pierce the façade of the physical sun and perceive a much greater reality: an innumerable company of the Heavenly Host crying, 'Holy, Holy, Holy is the Lord God Almighty.'"

Ded reflected on this for a moment. Sensing where the conversation was going, he was overcome with an urge to cut Beulah short. "I don't mean to be critical," he said testily, "but I hardly think someone who looks at a burning ball of gas and sees an innumerable company of the Heavenly Host crying 'Holy, Holy, Holy is the Lord God Almighty' is seeing a greater reality."

Chancing Scofield, he slid closer to Beulah so he could look out of her window at the sun shining in the sky. "The sun is not an innumerable company of anything. It is simply a burning ball of gas. Nothing more, nothing less." He pointed at the burning ball for Beulah's edification. "I mean, ask your own eyes."

When she did not do so, Ded blanched, lowered his finger, and slid back over to his seat. *I don't know what it is in my makeup that leads me to come out with such statements,* he rebuked himself. *It must be genetic.*

There's just no way that telling a blind woman to ask her own eyes could be a learned behavior. Who would ever teach it?

Beulah ignored Ded's intemperate outburst. "Of course, the innumerable company is just one of the near infinite things the fully conscious, infinitely imaginative God can perceive in the sun, but even that one glimpse is still a lot deeper and hence a lot more real than your pedestrian burning ball."

Shamed by his ask-your-own-eyes *faux pas* into accepting, solely for the purposes of the discussion, that the entirety of existence is merely part of God's mind, Ded wrinkled his forehead. "So, all Jerusalem had to do was catch a glimpse of the Heavenly Host in the sun, and bingo, he was united with the highest level of God's consciousness?"

"No," Beulah answered cheerily. "He had to capture that glimpse in a poem. Which, in fact, he did. The first poem of his I ever read, and therefore, a poem I will never forget."

"You mean, all it took was his putting a few descriptive words down on a scrap of paper?" Ded asked, trying very hard to understand.

Beulah shook her head with the patience of a nun helping a four-year-old Ded unable to cut a figure out of poster paper with his tiny blunt scissors. "It wasn't merely a matter of writing down a few descriptive words. It was organizing those words into a perfect unity of meaning and image, of intellect and emotion, of the necessary and the desired, taking everything in all at once on multitudinous, integrated levels, thereby reimagining the fully conscious God's holistic experience of the sun's Heavenly Host as part of His mind, obliterating, to the extent of the innumerable host, the fallen world's fictitious distinction between the self and the physical world."

"Goodness." Ded slapped his cheek lightly. "That's a horse of a different color. How could Jerusalem do anything *but* obliterate the fictitious distinction between the self and the physical world?"

Ded closed his eyes. He found Beulah's mind fascinating; but this stuff, she couldn't seriously believe. *Is this really what Jerusalem thought he was doing while scribbling his poems in the plane?*

"Yes, yes! You've got it," Beulah bubbled. "And since the poet's mind, as everything else, is just part of God's omnipotently imaginative mind, the glimpse afforded by the poem of the sun's innumerable Heavenly Host in the highest level of God's consciousness will now burn as a beacon forever in the shrunken consciousness of the sleeping God."

Ded didn't know what to say.

Taking Ded's silence as confirmation that he now understood, Beulah retreated into the private reverie with which she had begun the journey, leaving Ded, in the silence that followed, to engage in a half-hearted attempt to use this further piece of the puzzle to trace a logical path from the parable of the sleeping God to Ickey Jerusalem's death.

If a poem would do the uniting trick, then why did Jerusalem have to kill himself in the toilet? Or was Jerusalem, in fact, aiming for something more than just uniting with a small part of God's mind? Maybe he was aiming at the whole shebang.

CHAPTER 12

SEEING THE OTHERS

Ded broke his thoughts with a silent *Oh, shit!* Having focused his attention so intently on the relevance of the burning ball of gas to his investigation, Ded had failed to keep his eye on more pressing matters.

Ghostflea, gunning the hearse to eighty miles an hour, was trying to pass a forty-ton truck on a blind corner.

Passing forty-ton trucks on blind corners at eighty miles an hour was probably not unusual for Ghostflea. In this case, however, there were three additional factors giving rise to Ded's concern. First, the forty-ton truck was parked at the pumps of a service station on the right of the highway. Second, the hearse was speeding not on the highway but along the narrow shoulder between the highway and the truck. Third, according to the rightward-pointing sign on the wall twenty feet in front of the truck, the blind corner led around the side of the service station building to a dead end.

As the hearse swerved around the front of the stationary truck and down the far side of the building, hurling Ded into the left car door, the claims adjuster could see through the front window, jutting out from the far end of the building, a fifteen-foot-long, ten-foot-high metal rack filled with new tires. Ghostflea jammed on his brakes, slinging Ded forward. The rear of the turning hearse spun out, whirling the vehicle around 180 degrees before it smashed backwards into the rack, simultaneously heaving Ded into his seatback and driving the rack, several hundred tires and all, back to just outside the service station's public toilets, where the weakened structure, after teetering and tottering for the longest time, collapsed, burying the hearse beneath a mountain of rubber.

While Ded cowered in the darkness, Ghostflea idled his engine, punching out four-letter words, apparently trying to decide which way to go. At last, Ghostflea jammed his foot down on the gas, the engine roared, and a mere sixty seconds later, shortly after the chauffeur realized he was still in neutral and shifted into first, the hearse jerked fitfully out of the pile of tires amidst the sound of grinding gears and a minute's worth of accumulated exhaust fumes, and headed for the front of the station.

&

Meanwhile, standing side by side, the service station attendant and the driver of the forty-ton truck watched as the hearse lurched in their direction on its elevated chassis, assorted tires falling from its roof.

"Funeral drivers nowadays certainly aren't what they used to be," the attendant remarked.

Scofield, still in the front seat and tied to the passenger door, lifted his head from under his front paws, sat up, and after discovering that the mysterious rubber deluge had subsided, demonstrated his courage by barking contemptuously at his reflection in the windshield.

"Well, no wonder!" the truck driver replied to the attendant, not realizing that the passing hearse was a British vehicle. "The damn thing's being driven by a dog!"

&

For the balance of the journey, as the hearse wended its way through the cities of Richmond, Berkeley, and Oakland, and then up into the

Oakland Hills, Scofield treated the vehicle's occupants to an impressive demonstration of perfectly repeated barks—not once varying his pitch, volume, rhythm, or pronunciation, or even, as far as a thoroughly disheveled Ded could detect, taking a breath.

Now and then, when at a stoplight a curious pedestrian would catch Ded's eye, the defeated claims adjuster would acknowledge the inherent question with a mock graciousness and indicate by his facial language that while, yes, the dog was indeed barking, it was important for the beast's personal development he be allowed to express himself whenever and however he saw fit.

At last, the hearse reached the house, with Scofield still going at it. Ded and Beulah waited in the passenger compartment as the powerful Ghostflea hauled the dog out of the vehicle and around the house to the kennel, where, although Ded could still hear him barking, the sound was sufficiently distant and muffled as to no longer have the power to jam human speech.

Ded turned to Beulah, wrapped in her soft, earth-colored cloak and the protective world of her sightlessness. She appeared as accepting and unconcerned about the barking Scofield as she had so far seemed about everything—including, Ded realized, the recent death of Ickey Jerusalem.

There's something not quite right about Beulah, he mused. *Almost spooky.* During Ghostflea's gas-station tour, Ded had been thrown violently around the inside of the hearse. The car phone had even fallen out of its holder. But Beulah hadn't moved at all. As though she had so precisely anticipated each lurch, her relative position to the seat did not change.

Now, Beulah stirred, letting her cloak slip gradually from her shoulders, past her peasant blouse, past her micro-skirt, and all the way down to her dainty feet.

"Let me help you," Ded rasped, rising from his seat and stepping past her to open her door from the inside. As he did so, Beulah rotated in the same direction, accidentally catching his leg between her bare knees. His leg began to shake.

Ded opened the door, hurried out, and turned to help Beulah down. Grasping his hands, she stood up, and without hesitation, stepped blindly into the air, landing with both of her feet between his, her silk-covered nipples gently brushing his shirt.

Beulah raised her unseeing face to Ded's. "I'll have Adam bring your bags."

"My bags?" Ded croaked, realizing, at last, the reason Ghostflea had asked for his luggage that morning. "They're back at the hotel."

"But why?" Beulah's face registered her surprise.

"If you're going to be free in this world, you've got to travel light. The road warrior's motto." That was what Ded *should* have said. It would have shown *panache*, philosophical depth, an openness to new experiences. He realized it moments later, after he had retreated into pomposity. "I think it's best that I keep some distance between me and those I'm investigating."

"Yes, that's best," Beulah said, backing away, a barely detectable disappointment in her voice.

"I'm glad you understand," he said as she turned towards the house.

Ded struck the top of his head silently with his fist. *Idiot!* How could he have so thoughtlessly foreclosed such a wonderful, if highly improbable opportunity?

⁂

If Ded had only had a little wider perspective, he would have realized his mere lack of luggage was no impediment to a woman like Beulah.

⁂

From the outside, Jerusalem's house was an old, squat, weathered-wood affair, its shingled skin punctured at regular intervals by heavy beam ends and pasted over with Arts and Crafts shutters and trellises. Although the house itself had only one story, attached on the right was a square, two-story, shingled tower with a cantilevered roof, resonating with that of the house. On the front of the house was a wide, covered porch, shading two heavy windows that peered out through some poplar trees over the Oakland flatlands below, like the beetle-brow of an elderly madam whom age had given an aura of respectability, crowding out the memory of her former vulgarity.

Ded, with Beulah beside him, stopped at the bottom of the steps, stricken with the same foreboding he had felt when he got into the hearse at the top of Mount Tamalpais—likely the same foreboding Hansel must have felt before entering the gingerbread house. Looking for an excuse to delay entry, Ded asked, "How long have you lived here?"

"Around three years. Shortly after Ickey met me. Six months before that, he'd moved here from North Beach to get away from it all."

"Right." Ded turned and examined a luxuriant leafy creeper covering almost the entire front of the house. "And what's this big plant here?"

Beulah took a moment to calculate what plant he was referring to. "That's Ickey's grapevine."

Ded put the knuckles of his right fist on his hip and shook his head. "I've never seen one so large."

"Despite my advice as a trained landscape gardener, Ickey refused to prune it. He couldn't bear to restrain its life in any way." She reached out to feel a leaf. "As a result, it's never borne fruit."

She sighed and headed onto the porch.

Ded still wasn't ready to pass through the front door. In one last attempt to postpone it, he read the sign on the lintel above the door. "Lambeth?"

Beulah paused, keeping her face forward. "Ickey named the house after a part of London he lived in during his first summer vacation from Oxford. He was a real Anglophile, you know. Used a lot of Anglicisms in his poetry. Place names, vocabulary, even spellings. 'The English Ickey' is what he called his poetic side."

Having imparted this information, Beulah got a key from her purse and blindly pointed it with her right hand in the direction of the lock on the front door.

Ded's chivalry overcoming his unease, he hurried up to her, intending to help her insert the key.

As his foot hit the stoop, Beulah took a step ahead, effortlessly slipped in the key, rotated it, and pushed the door open. After giving Ded a proud smile, she lifted her foot to stride into the foyer.

"Stop!" Ded screamed, grabbing her trailing left arm and yanking her back.

A split second later, a confused Beulah Vala, three feet behind and reoriented ninety degrees sideward, staggered as she tried to catch her balance.

"Stay here," Ded commanded after he had stabilized her. He moved cautiously toward the open door.

Stretched between two screws, one on each doorjamb, slicing through the faded veil the mediocre call reality, was a taut, single strand of gleaming razor wire, just the right height that if Ded had not stopped Beulah's progress, the wire's repeated line of horizontally oriented, tiny, exquisitely sharpened halberd blades would have slashed open her windpipe, and if she had, in shock, instinctively turned to Ded for help, it would have fatally lacerated her carotid artery as well.

Ded recoiled at of the thought of this innocent, beautiful woman with an open gash in her throat, gasping as pulsing blood gushed from the side of her neck.

"What is it?" Beulah asked.

"Someone has stretched razor wire across the doorway, meaning to kill you."

Beulah smiled cheerily. "Oh, I'm sure it's just someone's idea of a practical joke."

Ded was astounded by her nonchalance. "This is no joke."

"Gosh, okay, if you say so. But I don't want to get anybody in trouble with the police."

"Who do you think could have done this?"

"Maybe Tharmas Luvah. He's a great practical joker. He could have taken some razor wire from my garden, where it's coiled to keep the local pets out."

Ded pictured Beulah gardening on her hands and knees in her current outfit. "Do you work in the garden by yourself?"

"Of course. I love plants, and if I do say so myself, I'm very good with them."

"Isn't working in the garden dangerous with coils of razor wire around it?"

"I wear heavy gardening gloves so I can safely feel where to step over."

Adam Ghostflea, having finished putting Scofield in the kennel, now appeared on the steps, goggle-eyeing the wire in amazement.

Ded pivoted to include both people in his audience. "Who was the last person to go through this door?"

"Adam," Beulah answered. "Early this morning, he came into the house from his cabin in the back, received my instructions, and then left through the front door to pick up the gingerbread man from the local pizza parlor. They're the only place with big enough ovens."

Ded recalled the crumbs he had encountered on the back seat of the hearse.

"There was no wire then," the gravelly Ghostflea confirmed.

"What about after you returned with the gingerbread man?"

Beulah answered for the chauffeur. "Adam took the hearse to the rear of the house to pick up the anthologies of Ickey's poetry stacked inside the back door. I met him there with Scofield, and we headed off to the funeral."

So, if that's true, Ded thought, *the wire could have been strung any time after Ghostflea left for the baker's and before Beulah and Ghostflea returned from the funeral. Anyone attending the funeral, including Tharmas Luvah, would've had very little time to set the trap before or after, although Tharmas did appear to have left early. And what about Dr. Ulro? I didn't see him at the funeral at all.*

On the other hand, Ded continued his analysis, *it's possible either Ghostflea or Beulah is lying. Perhaps they're both lying. But the wire doesn't seem to fit the chauffeur's guns, knives, and martial arts* modus operandum, *and if Beulah wanted to top herself, now that her funeral duties were done, there are plenty more certain, less messy ways to do it.*

"Do you have some gloves and tools I can use to remove this wire?" Ded asked.

Beulah turned to Ghostflea. "Could you go to the tool rack on the garden shed wall and bring back my suede gardening gloves and an appropriate screwdriver hanging there?"

Ghostflea wheeled around to go.

"No," Ded said to halt him. "I'll go. Stay here and keep Beulah safe."

He headed around the two-story square tower towards the back yard, passing on the side a large herb, flower, and tree nursery garden surrounded by multiple coils of razor wire. There were so many coils, it was impossible to say whether a yard-long strip had been removed.

At the far end of the garden, in the back yard, was a shed. As he approached it, Ded noticed a low, rectangular-cuboid cage made from a wooden frame with metal screens on the top, bottom, and sides. Inside were perhaps a hundred toads writhing over and under each other.

Jesus, he thought, *maybe the woman* is *a witch.*

At that moment, he heard a deep, vicious snarling. The snarling exploded into a deafening, crazed barking, punctuated by a crashing, rattling noise. On the far corner of the back yard, next to what Ded took to be Ghostflea's cabin, Scofield was charging the chicken wire walls of his kennel, his raging eyes focused on Ded.

Clearly, Ded needed to complete his errand quickly. As he retrieved the gloves and screwdriver, he noticed a set of wire cutters on the tool rack. Ded then returned posthaste to the front steps.

"Beulah," he said, as he set about removing the trap with his bare hands after finding that Beulah's gardening gloves were too small for him, "what are all those toads doing in the cage?"

"Oh, those. Toads keep invading my garden, but I can't bring myself to kill them. So, I put them in the cage and have Adam buy me live crickets from the pet store to feed them."

To Ded, Beulah feeding the toads instead of killing them was in character, but the fact that she fed them live crickets added to his unease, especially because toads were supposed to be good for gardens, devouring the bugs that ate the plants.

৺

Ded laid down the removed wire. Confident Beulah would not be able to see, he slipped the screwdriver into an evidence bag, and then put the bag and her gardening gloves into his lower outside jacket pocket for O'Nadir's fingerprint guys. He had been careful to touch the screwdriver on only a small part of the handle closest to the end so as to preserve any existing prints on the rest of the handle.

"There," Ded proclaimed loudly. "Done."

"Thank you," Beulah said. After tentatively touching both doorjambs, she entered the foyer.

Ded followed, cautiously. The wire had been strung outside the locked door and he could see no sign of forced entry. Nonetheless, he decided to keep his eye out for any other traps that might have been set inside.

"I'm going to slip into something comfortable," Beulah announced. "If you'd like to freshen up, the bathroom is at the back on the right."

"Thank you, I would," Ded responded, his foreboding briefly eclipsed by an excited speculation concerning what form of clothing would be more comfortable than a peasant blouse and a micro-skirt that barely covered a fifth of her body.

৺

Beulah sat in the middle of the couch in the cathedral-ceilinged livingroom while Ded sat opposite her on a straight chair with back slats running all the way to the floor. Both items of furniture were made of heavy wood, exceptionally right-angled, gigantic, and designed, Ded assumed, to make their occupants look small and superfluous.

As promised, Beulah had slipped into something more comfortable: a high-collar, floor-length, natural-linen caftan. Ded, sipping mineral water, stared at her diminutive, rose-colored toenails peering shyly up at him from beneath her hem.

"Do you have a will, Beulah?" Ded asked, wondering who, if she had died from the razor wire, would have inherited her new $20 million estate.

"Yes. Ickey had Bacon Urizen draft me one several years ago after we got together."

"Who's the beneficiary?"

"Ickey was. But now that his physical body is no longer with us, Tharmas Luvah."

"Why Tharmas Luvah?"

"Apart from Ickey, he was at the time the only other person I knew well."

Ded's mind instantly turned from Tharmas Luvah's financial incentive for Beulah's death to the possible implications of the phrase "knew well." Quickly, he forced his mind back to his fact-gathering mission. "Does Tharmas know about your will?"

"I'm sure I told him."

Which means, Ded realized, *if Tharmas also knew about the $20 million insurance policy, he, as well, had an incentive to kill Ickey Jerusalem. The poet's death would trigger the insurance payout to Beulah. And if she died after that, Tharmas would inherit the funds.*

Earlier, on his trek to the toilet, Ded had peeked into the rooms on either side of the hallway and seen in each a curious jumble of furniture, books, and other odds and ends arranged around the walls, leaving the center of each room bare.

"You've laid out the things in your house in an interesting manner, Beulah."

Beulah lifted her chin with a look halfway between hope and defiance. "Yes. I did it yesterday. Moved all of Ickey's things to the edges of each room so I wouldn't trip over them any longer."

"Naturally." Ded took another sip of his mineral water as he repeated her words in his mind. Was she talking about more than the objects on the floor? Perhaps also about the memory of Jerusalem now pushed to the edges of her mind?

"Reminds me of a case I had once involving a child who was blind," Ded said, to continue the conversation. "Whenever his parents wanted to punish him, they rearranged the furniture in the house."

Beulah seemed slightly taken aback.

"Your parents ever do the same?"

"No. But then, I wasn't blind as a child. I lost my sight about three-and-a-half years ago. Six months before I met Ickey."

"Oh, I'm sorry," Ded said, genuinely upset by her revelation. Beulah having lost her sight recently was, for him, much more of a tragedy than never having been able to see at all. "How did it happen?"

"I was working as a landscape gardener in Golden Gate Park, shortly after I'd arrived from Florida. It was spring. Everything was in bloom. I felt as though I was about to be reborn." Beulah's countenance took on a strange, euphoric hue. "At lunchtime, someone I'd met at the dentist's office that morning visited the Park's rose garden. I remember I was admiring the crimson bed of joy spread before me—"

Ded gave a start. *Crimson bed of joy*?

"—when my new friend materialized at my side. He pulled out a sheet of blotter paper as blue as the sky and placed it in my hand. Printed in a calligraphic script across its front was a poem. He told me it was by Ickey Jerusalem, the poet laureate of San Francisco. He instructed me to read the first line. I did. When I'd finished, he took the poem back, tore out the line's last word, 'sun,' and placed it on my tongue. The paper had a slight acid taste. Then, he handed the poem back to me and told me to read the rest.

"With the 'sun' dissolving on my tongue, I read on, delving deeper into the poem. By the time I'd reached the end, all the shapes of the physical world I'd so long taken as permanent had melted away, revealing in their stead the infinite and eternal reality of the poet's vision.

Raising my eyes to the sky, I beheld for the very first time not a burning ball of gas but an innumerable company of the Heavenly Host, crying, 'Holy, Holy, Holy is the Lord God Almighty!'"

Beulah sat, enraptured by her memory.

"I couldn't take my eyes off it," she said softly. "Two hours later, I was blind." She paused, contemplating something behind her dark glasses. "The doctors said it was because the sun had seared my retinas. But *I* knew it was because I'd looked upon the face of God."

Ded stared sorrowfully at Beulah. *If only the piece of paper you'd read had summarized my Grand Unifying Theory,* he wanted to point out, *you would have looked instead into the enormous black void and still have your eyesight today.*

Realizing, however, that this obvious point would serve only to make Beulah feel worse about the loss of her eyesight, he restricted his response to the straightforward follow-up question, "Who was your friend?"

"Tharmas," she admitted.

"Were you angry with him for the loss of your sight?"

"No. How would he know what I'd do?"

"What about the author of the poem?"

Beulah dismissed the suggestion with a friendly, girlish laugh. "Ickey hadn't even met me. When he eventually heard what had happened, he took me in. In the three glorious years since, I've ended up, thanks to him, seeing much more than I ever did when I had sight." Beulah sighed dreamily. "Our relationship was the best thing that ever happened to me, a lonely, unattractive girl from a broken home."

Unattractive? Ded thought. *How can she think that?*

Beulah leaned back on the sofa, her legs parting. "And I'm sure our relationship was good for Ickey, too."

I bet it was, Ded thought, his wistful eyes tracing the front of Beulah's caftan as it cascaded sensuously from her overhanging breasts into the newly opened space between her upper thighs.

"My little place of seed," Beulah breathed. "That's what Ickey called me." She rested her head on the back of the couch. "His little garden. The nourishing earth in which his poetic genius could grow into a unified and coherent form." She capped her left hand with her right and placed it over her womb. "Ever since he'd moved to Lambeth, he'd been suffering from writer's block. That all ended the very first time he found refuge in me. Lying in my post-coital embrace, he worked backwards logically from his blotter-paper poem having united my mind with the sun's Heavenly Host. Gathering together all the disparate images and concepts that had been flooding through his mind since the death of Urthon Spectre had set him free, he soon arrived at the key concept: the universe is the mind of an omnipotently creative God whose consciousness has shrunk into ours. Ickey immediately commenced writing his epic poems to lay it out for all to see."

The detective in Ded interrupted the spell. "Could you tell me, Beulah, how the death of Uncle Urthon Spectre set Jerusalem free?"

"Sure. But we need to start at the beginning."

CHAPTER 13

IS THAT A MAN OR A SPECTER?

Los's uncle, Ickey's great uncle, Urthon Spectre, was a self-made man, although unhappily, as one of the more snobbish who met him noted, undeniably the product of unskilled labor. Despite earning millions from strip-mining coal in Wyoming, Uncle Urthon still saw himself as socially and culturally inadequate. In particular, as he confessed to his nephew, the young, newly married Los, he was terribly embarrassed by his grammar.

"What?" Los looked askance at Uncle Urthon. "I can't believe that." Los put his hand on his uncle's shoulder. "I agree, the woman may have been peculiar, but good God, she's been dead nigh on twenty years."

"Not my *gramma*, you fool," Uncle Urthon swore. "My *grammar*."

Los was suitably contrite. "In that case, Uncle," he said, "I've got just the thing for you." He dug out an old, weathered copy of the *Concise Oxford English Dictionary* he had won as a prize years before in a school spelling bee.

To Los's amazement, Uncle Urthon greedily grabbed the book.

Over the next few months, he memorized it from cover to cover, markedly upgrading his vocabulary, if not his grammar. In gratitude, Uncle Urthon set up the Urthon Spectre Trust with Los as the trustee, and funded it with a sufficient amount of money to pay for Los's future first-born male child to go to Oxford University and earn a degree in English.

"I ain't got no doubt no-how," Uncle Urthon informed Los, "that if your primogeniture matriculates into that there lexicon curriculum, his verbalizing is gonna eventuate much more gooder'n me, on account of when them sesquipedalian pedagogues necessitate him effectuating his memorization, *he's* gonna be perpetrating it on the *Complete* (rather than *Concise*) *Oxford English Dictionary*."

"You couldn't have said it better if you'd tried, Uncle," Los observed.

Los viewed the establishment of the trust as a sign the Holy Spirit had chosen him to raise his yet-to-be-born son to make some great, permanent contribution to mankind. His wife, Enith, however, as suggested by her appearance at the funeral as a remote, enigmatic beauty, wrapped up in the mysteries of astrology, spiritualism, and herself, found it difficult at the time to show interest in anything as mundane as the destiny of her future offspring.

Nonetheless, nine months later, when the pain of giving birth to Ickey became sufficient to disrupt her indifference, Enith was moved to do the about-to-be-born child's astrological chart.

The chart she produced was incredibly complex and varied, a result she attributed to a once-in-a-millennium alignment of the stars.

Los thought it was more likely due to the lack of writing space on the delivery table.

"That, and the way Enith's right hand kept jerking every time she had a contraction," he tut-tutted to Grandma Enion after it was over. "You should've seen how the doctor had to keep stopping to pick Enith's pencils and papers up off the floor."

When one nurse took baby Ickey away for his tests, another nurse wheeled Enith off to the post-natal ward, where, spurred by the results of her astrological charting, she conducted a one-woman séance with the spirit world, at the conclusion of which she opened her eyes and proclaimed to the heavens, "My son, Ickey, is the great Messiah come again!"

The mothers in nearby beds took this news with amazing equanimity, considering.

Enith then lapsed back into indifference. For the next eighteen years, she showed no interest in Ickey—or Los, for that matter, apart from her passive acceptance of his dutiful, highly confidential, once-a-year deposits to fulfill the Biblical injunction to go forth and multiply. So little interest did she show in Los that Ickey grew up under the distinct impression his had been a virgin birth.

❧

During his early years, Ickey, in imitation of his mother, totally ignored his father, his annually increasing number of brothers, and everyone else but her. He idolized his mother. Night after night, he would sit by her chair while she stared out of their picture window, mesmerized by the stars. There, overwhelmed by her indifference and the indifference of the unbounded black vastness of space in which her eyes were lost, young Ickey felt himself contracting, squeezing into a tiny, claustrophobic shell, helpless, alone, his only means of escape being to idolize her more.

As he grew older, Ickey ceased sitting at his mother's knee, but remained a private person, aloof from others, treating even his brothers as mere acquaintances. Whenever he spoke to someone, he gave the impression his mind was not in the conversation—which was true. After each little encounter, he would retreat to his bed upstairs and compose a simple rhyming couplet about the experience.

In the course of time, Ickey slowly began to develop a relationship with Los, partly due to his father being a much better conversationalist than his mother. ("At least you're willing to use words," Ickey once told him admiringly.) For his part, Los encouraged Ickey to make a permanent contribution to mankind. ("Maybe if I do," Ickey agreed, "Mom will pay some attention to me.") But given that his father usually worked at his blacksmith shop from early morning to late at night, the relationship was never close in the traditional sense.

Still, by the time Ickey was a senior in high school, he had internalized Los's values. Everything Ickey did had to be aimed at producing a permanent contribution. Nothing could be enjoyed for itself. And since there was only a limited amount of time in which to produce the contribution, he granted himself no time off for good behavior.

Then, on Ickey's eighteenth birthday, when the Vietnam War was heating up, Enith came down to breakfast, singled out her firstborn from among her twelve sons and husband at the table, and declared, looking straight into Ickey's eyes, "You must enlist in the army, go to Vietnam, return a great war hero, go into politics, get elected President of the United States, unite the nations of the world, become Emperor of the Universe, and then, at last, reveal yourself as the Messiah come again."

Every one of her sons stared as their awe-inspiring mother drew herself up. "My Ouija board has spoken."

Los shook his head. "Well, dear, now we know why you were taking so long in the bathroom this morning."

Ickey sat, open-mouthed. It was the first time in his life his mother had addressed him as other than a member of an audience. His immediate urge was to rush out and enlist, if only to gain her approval. Luckily, Enith, having delivered her bulletin to Ickey, promptly became engrossed in revealing to the family dog that it would marry a tall, dark stranger, and thus failed to press home her advantage. The result was that Los, with some effort, was able to talk Ickey into forgetting about the army, and instead take a student deferment and enroll at Oxford University to study English, as Uncle Urthon wished.

Ickey's years at Oxford were a time of open exploration, free from conflict and parental pressure—a time in which he finally began to enjoy life's pleasures solely for themselves.

Primary among life's pleasures was poetry.

At Eden High School, Ickey's exposure to poetry had been limited to the analysis of rhyme and meter as it appeared in various disconnected excerpts in a beige-covered poetry anthology certified by the local school board as containing no swear words, atheism, or sex. At Oxford, the poetry to which his tutors introduced him was something completely different: an all-encompassing, bubbling cauldron of imaginatively organized words able, it seemed, to reveal a reality one could otherwise not see.

Partly because of his long-time practice of recording his encounters in rhyming couplets, and partly in reaction to his snobbish Oxford classmates ostracizing him as an unsophisticated philistine from the Central Valley of California, Ickey threw himself wholeheartedly into the universe of poetry.

Ickey let his short hair grow long, acquired a sweeping scarf and a tattered, French peasant's broad-brimmed hat, and spent his evenings, locked up in his garret-like room, not only reading poetry, but eventually writing his own. Short, tentative pieces. Pastoral celebrations of wonder, joy, and love.

"Songs of Innocence," as he later called them.

Spring
Little Lamb
Here I am,
Come and lick
My white neck.
Let me pull
Your soft Wool.
Let me kiss
Your soft face.
Merrily Merrily we welcome in the Year.

"Jesus Christ," Uncle Urthon blurted out when he read those lines, transmitted in a letter from Ickey. "Three years of memorizing the dictionary at Oxford and the boy's become a sheep dorker!"

Happily, Uncle Urthon's mind was put to rest when he thereupon suffered a seizure and fell into an apparently irreversible vegetative state.

❧

Upon graduation, Ickey returned to Eden, and at once, his poetic idyll, his subsidy from the Urthon Spectre Trust, his student deferment from the draft, and his freedom from the bonds of duty all ended. Enith again made Delphic suggestions that he go fight in Vietnam. Los again urged him to find some way out of the military and work on his permanent contribution to mankind.

Thrown into internal turmoil by the conflict between what he wanted and what his parents wanted, compounded by a general culture shock over what he now saw as the barren emptiness of the Central Valley, Ickey withdrew into himself. Day after day, he would sit in the corner of his old room at his parents' home, watching his hand age, and carry on conversations with his dead brother, Orc.

Since only Ickey's side of those conversations was audible to third parties, and since Orc appeared to do most of the talking, precisely what they discussed never became clear. "It sure as hell ain't the weather," Los reported to Cousin Ijim. "I can tell you that much. People talking about the weather just don't use words like 'despair,' 'oblivion,' or 'suicide'—unless perhaps they live in North Dakota."

❧

One Sunday, two or three months after Ickey escaped the draft, the conversations ended. The young man emerged from his room and announced to the world that he was moving to San Francisco to become a poet.

Los, who had been relatively sympathetic to Ickey's turmoil, was horrified. "Words written on a piece of paper, by definition, cannot be a permanent contribution to mankind," he pointed out to his son.

Enith agreed. "Everyone knows," she intoned between trances, "the only permanent words are those written with urine in the snow. How does the boy expect to become the new Messiah if he doesn't know that?"

Seeing that Ickey's mind was set, Los acquiesced. Through a contact of Cousin Ijim's, he got Ickey a job at a small engraving business in San Francisco copying letters and figures onto business cards, invitations, and brochures. In addition, Los contacted Bromion Ulro and promised to pay the struggling medical student's rent if he would let Ickey live with him.

Los's motivation was not entirely altruistic. His hope was that through the combination of holding down a "real" job and associating with a thoroughly practical, religious person such as Brom (Los did not know about Brom and Rahab Oothoon), Ickey would, in time, come to his senses, give up poetry, and start pursuing that all-important, permanent contribution to mankind.

It was a shrewd move. As Ickey became increasingly wrapped up in the everyday details of his engraving job and fell under the influence of the philistine Brom, he spent less time writing poems. Inexorably, poetry shifted in the young man's mind from an obsession to a hobby, and finally, to a distant, almost inchoate desire.

Which would have been the end of it, but for one fortuitous event.

About three years after Ickey had moved to San Francisco, the nurses tending to the comatose Uncle Urthon Spectre in his penthouse hospital suite attempted to halt his developing bedsores by replacing his bottom sheet with a lamb's fleece.

The moment Uncle Urthon's head hit the soft, pulled wool, his eyes sprang open. "Sheep dorker!" he cried, waving his atrophied arms and legs in the air, trying to get away from what he imagined to be the woolly pervert behind and underneath him. In the process, he accidentally hit the mode switch on the hospital bed, and instead of Uncle Urthon making good his escape, the bed folded in the middle, swallowing him and the fleece whole.

The desperate nurses stuck their arms down the bed's gullet, fighting to retrieve their hapless patient. After a tense struggle, they were able to grab hold of his bedgown. On the count of three, they all gave a tremendous, simultaneous yank, and the bed burped its life-sized, living catarrh up, out of his nightshirt, and through the open penthouse window.

"S-h-e-e-e-e-e-e-e-p d-o-r-r-r-r-r-r-r-r-r-r-k-e-r-r-r-r-r-r-r-r-r-r-r-r," the naked Uncle Urthon cried in a feeble, drawn-out protest as he traced a perfect parabolic arc, arms and legs failing, through the air, ceasing abruptly when he was converted into an irregular pancake on the plaza fourteen stories below.

At that moment, under the previously undisclosed terms of the now dead Uncle Urthon's will, his entire fortune poured over into the empty Urthon Spectre Trust for the sole benefit of Ickey Jerusalem.

⁂

Freed of the necessity of work, Ickey quit his job. He moved out of Brom and Rahab's house, and intent on becoming a poet, relocated to San Francisco's North Beach, an old Italian neighborhood on Telegraph Hill.

During the 1950s, it had been the birthplace of the Beat Movement. In hangouts like Caffè Trieste, Vesuvio Café, Specs' Bar, and the City Lights Bookstore, writers such as Allen Ginsberg, Jack Kerouac, and Lawrence Ferlinghetti would meet to drink, argue, and proclaim to the world. Some of the old beatniks were still there, now accompanied by younger, *avant-garde* poets who patronized the local joints to recite their own verses while rubbing shoulders with the greats.

That was where Ickey Jerusalem got his start.

CHAPTER 14

RUBBING THE EYES IN DISBELIEF

As Beulah finished her exposition, Ded was thinking back, about North Beach. When he was in San Francisco on the Knife case, he had, on O'Nadir's advice, spent a free evening there, soaking up the ambience in a fruitless attempt to understand what the Beat movement had been all about. At one point, he'd stopped to read a poem by Ferlinghetti taped to the window of the City Lights Bookstore in which the poet, as far as Ded could figure, was strongly advocating the construction of giant pigeon statues for generals to shit on.

Given all the publicity the Beatniks have received, Ded had thought at the time, *I'd have expected the goals of their movement to have been broader.*

Ded realized Beulah was no longer talking. She was facing sightlessly ahead, her countenance lit with a look of adulation. Following her blind gaze, Ded turned to the back wall of the room. Up over a massive stone fireplace hung a large, gold-framed drawing. It showed, in fine lines, a muscular old man in a white beard and not much else, down on one knee on a cloud, his right arm pointed earthward and casting two vectorial beams of light, one from his lone forefinger and one from his other three straightened fingers pressed together.

The drawing style was like those on Tharmas Luvah's VW bus, but with a clearer line and less vibrancy of color.

"Who did the drawing over the mantelpiece?" Ded asked.

"Ickey. It comes from an engraving. He often made engravings for me, because, unlike a drawing, I can feel the image. I liked this one so much, he made a print for himself and enlarged it to fit into the gold frame."

Ded returned his gaze to the picture, noting with his logical mind that it was necessarily the negative of what Beulah would have felt with her fingers. "I take it the naked senior citizen in the white beard is God."

"Yes, but in his fallen form, Urizen."

"Bacon Urizen?"

"Yes. And no. You can see this Urizen looks nothing like Ickey's lawyer. But that doesn't mean he wasn't the inspiration."

"So, what's this Urizen doing?"

"Bifurcating the appearance of reality for man in the fallen world below, at the moment God fell asleep."

BI-furcating. Ded rolled the word around in his mind, recalling the two letters written with soap on the mirror in the plane. "Bifurcating the appearance of reality into what?"

"Subject and object, of course. But also time and space, energy and form, emotion and reason, mind and matter, life and death."

Ded studied the picture in the light of this symbolism, following the two beams up to the hand from which they emanated. "So, in the same way Jerusalem could unite subject and object in a specific situation through a poem, he could unite these other bifurcations as well?"

"You've got it."

"I'm not sure I do. For instance, how could Jerusalem possibly unite life and death? What does that even mean? Use his poems to create the living dead? Some sort of zombies?"

"No, not zombies." Beulah shook her head patiently. "Because you, like most humans trapped in the middle level, accept bifurcations as real, it's difficult for you to conceive how opposites can be united. The best you can do is mix the opposites together, but that produces only a washed-out result halfway in between. Like mixing black and white to produce grey, your mixing of life and death produces zombies, pale shadows of the life and the death from which they were mixed. To understand how opposites are united, you need to focus instead on how it was before the bifurcations were created at the Fall. If everything exists solely as a figment of an omnipotently creative mind of God imagining everything about everything, then not only can He imagine life and death in all their intensity, but those imaginings are just part of an infinite number of other imaginings unified at the highest level in His mind. Life and death themselves have no relevance to the fully awake God's own existence. It's only from the perspective of the shrunken consciousness of the sleeping God, our billions of illusory subjective selves peering out at the equally illusory objective world, that life and death take on their existential character."

As Ded struggled to absorb what was being said, the muscular Ghostflea lurched into the doorway. He stood, listening, his worshipful bug eyes fixed on Beulah. Ded was sure that Beulah's words had some relevance to the poet's own life and death, but he couldn't quite put his finger on it.

Beulah leaned forward, assuming a perkily pedagogical pose. "You're right in one sense, though, Ded. Uniting life and death is not easy. It takes much more than a single poem. It takes a whole lot of poems."

Ghostflea coughed once. "Lunch is served."

Ded helped Beulah to her feet. "I'm glad that during our ride here earlier you started with something easy like uniting subject and object," he said.

Had we started with uniting life and death, he thought, *my brain would have given up and gone home for good.*

As things were, he could already feel his brain beginning to make disturbing lurches toward the open window.

Following Beulah and Ghostflea out of the room, Ded looked above the fireplace one more time at the drawing of the fallen God bifurcating the appearance of reality. Between the base knuckles of God's first and second fingers, where the common source of the two beams of light would have been, there was a fly. It was moving. Fidgeting about. Randomly. Aimlessly.

Much too close to the surface for it to see it was crawling on the hand of God.

Ded's feeling of foreboding returned.

ꕥ

Ded, Beulah, and Ghostflea were having lunch on the covered porch, where Ghostflea had set out on a circular, glass table luncheon meats, several salads, French bread, ice-cold apple juice, and various accompaniments.

Ded looked through the poplar trees at the silver haze covering the flatlands of Oakland below. Above, the sky was clear.

Beulah lifted her pink face to the heavens and located the October sun from the warmth of its rays. "The sun has passed its midday peak," she intoned reverently, "and begun its long afternoon fall into the sea."

"Let's hope the Heavenly Host brought water wings," Ded quipped, raising his lens-covered eyes to the shining orb.

Beulah turned with great patience to Ded, her preschool student who, once again, had gotten it wrong. "The Heavenly Host can't fall into the sea. Their sun, the unfallen sun, is forever in the sky. It's only the burning ball of gas, the fallen sun, which, locked in a never-ending cycle of death and rebirth, each evening falls into the sea, and then, on the following dawn, emerges reborn on the opposite horizon to move across the sky once again."

Ded picked up his fork. "I don't know if you've read the newspapers recently, but the weight of current scientific opinion is that the burning ball of gas does not fall into the sea at the end of each day. Nor does it pop up on the other side the following dawn. Rather, because of our limited perspective, the rotation of the earth on its axis makes the stationary sun look like it's—" Ded broke off his ironic synopsis of Astronomy 101. Beulah had taken a piece of French bread and begun meditatively chewing it into nothingness. From her features, he could see she was preparing to launch into yet another round of cheery pontification on the sun, something he was beginning to find both endearing and irritating in roughly equal measure. He changed the subject.

Or was it the object? Ded was losing track.

"Since you met Jerusalem only after you lost your sight, I assume you never saw what he looked like." Ded put a forkful of potato salad into his mouth, hoping that Jerusalem's features would be at least one area where he did not need to worry about Beulah drawing invidious comparisons.

"I never saw him," she agreed, reflectively stroking her long, strawberry-blond hair. "But I did something much better. I felt him."

Ded mashed the salad between his molars. "How did he feel?"

"Beautiful, "Beulah glowed. "I held in my hands his hefty head, bulging with genius. Wavy hair cascading between my fingers. Prominent eyebrows above wide-set eyes, their long eyelashes caressing the tips of my thumbs. A straight nose rubbing along my cheek. Full lips of a small mouth devouring mine. A diminutive, stubbled chin brushing my neck. Broad, masculine shoulders projecting winglike over me. Powerful arms embracing my torso. A sinewy chest pressing down upon my breasts. A long, supple spine I could trace with my heels down the deep valley between the muscles of his back. Tight straining buttocks, alive with sweat."

"I see," Ded said, once he had been able to swallow his mouthful of potato salad. He took a sip of ice-cold apple juice, concentrating on the feeling as it slid over his tongue, down his esophagus, and into his stomach.

Based on Jerusalem's broad, masculine shoulders, powerful arms, and sinewy chest, Ded thought, *it's even less likely Beulah could have overpowered him.*

"Did you love Jerusalem?"

"I loved his poetry," Beulah said quietly.

"Did Jerusalem love you?"

Beulah chose her words carefully. "To Ickey, love—the union of a specific subject, the lover, with the reality behind a specific object, the beloved—was the lowest form of the creative imagination, a form which almost anyone could experience, at least temporarily. Consequently, as you might imagine, Ickey preferred to focus his talent on the form of the creative imagination he saw as the highest."

"Which was?"

Beulah put on a brave smile. "His poetry."

Staring at Beulah in a way he could never have done had she had sight, Ded saw a certain melancholy in her face and heard it in her words. With a surge of sympathy, he began, almost involuntarily, to open his eyes wide, trying, although he knew it was silly, to unite the reality behind her illusory separateness with his mind.

"Excuse me," Ghostflea said, leaning his disturbing, cracked-red countenance into Ded's field of vision. "Can you pass the pickles, please?"

After lunch, while Ghostflea went to the garage to perform his regular post-drive bodywork on the hearse, Beulah helped Ded look through Ickey Jerusalem's things. They began with the jumbled piles along the wall of the first room.

"It's all organized," Beulah assured Ded, "but by touch rather than eye. Instead of placing things the same size or shape together, as a sighted person probably would, I've separated them into different piles loosely arranged by subject."

The pile at their feet contained a book, a record, a cassette tape, and half-empty wine bottle mingling with a few eccentric items such as a megaphone with "Eden High School" on the side, a box of string labeled "Too Short to Save," and a three-foot, wooden, Indonesian statuette of a laughing god with an eighteen-inch phallus.

Exactly what the god found so funny, Ded did not know.

Ded turned the statue over. A combination bill of sale and certificate of authenticity from the gift shop in the de Young Asian Art Museum was stuck to the base. The bill of sale was dated Sunday, April 10th, 1977. Easter Day.

As a test of Beulah's prowess, Ded rummaged through another pile, pulled out an ornate frame containing a large photograph, and handed it to her. "What's this?"

She felt its contours. "A picture of me."

Ded took it back. It was, indeed, a picture of her. Smiling sweetly at the camera, with her dark glasses on, Beulah was reclining on her side, her perfect body completely nude. Ded drew in his breath as his eyes followed the graceful curves defining her physical form. Never had he seen such gentle, trusting, natural charm pictured in a woman, least of all in one who held a howling, naked, fat lady scissor-locked in her legs.

Ded was unable to suppress his astonishment. "What were you doing when this photograph was taken?"

"Wrestling."

Ded studied the picture again. The fat woman was losing and did not appear all that happy about it.

Blushing with embarrassment, Beulah provided some background. "After I lost my sight, I had to give up my job in Golden Gate Park. So, during the months before I met Ickey, I worked as a naked lady wrestler at a Broadway nightclub."

Ded strained to fit this bit of biographical data with his existing image of an angelic, childlike Beulah. *Being blind,* he rationalized, *I guess she couldn't be that choosy about the jobs she took.*

"My more acute sense of hearing and touch helped me a lot," Beulah said modestly. "Often, I could tell where my opponents were going to move before they did."

Hmm, Ded thought. *Maybe she* could *have overcome Jerusalem, under the right circumstances.*

Ded put the picture back onto the pile face down, picked up a mounted set of underdeveloped cow horns, and read the name engraved on the mounting board's brass plaque. "Who was Klopstock?"

"That was Ickey's nickname at Oxford. I think it was meant to suggest a country hick. Someone hung the horns on his door a month after he arrived."

Ded returned the cow horns to the pile. He hadn't told Beulah he was looking at them. She must have known just from the name, Klopstock.

He reached into the heap and pulled out a dirty white captain's hat with a smudged black bill.

"To wear when he went out on his sailboat," Beulah said. She could have told what it was only by its rustle as it was withdrawn from the pile. "He'd go every Friday afternoon," Beulah explained. "Alone, on the Bay. To think."

Ded studied the crumbling golden wings tacked on the front of the hat and then traded it for a framed clipping from the *San Francisco Chronicle.* It was part of a column by Herb Caen, the local gossip columnist and humorist so well known (he had invented the term "Beatnik") that even Ded had heard of him. The date was a few months after the Knife case. Ded read out loud a paragraph circled in pen:

> ...Welcome to San Francisco! Local fixture, poet Ickey Jerusalem, was arrested last night outside Finocchios for his loud and presumably accurate guesses concerning middle-aged Iowans stepping down from a tour bus and their back-home sexual practices with barnyard animals. I may be prejudiced, but Jerusalem's got my vote for poet laureate of the City...

"So," Ded said to Beulah, "Jerusalem was then chosen as San Francisco's poet laureate?"

"No. San Francisco has no official poet laureate. But that didn't stop Tharmas running with the Herb Caen column, thereafter proclaiming Ickey as San Francisco Poet Laureate in all press releases, event posters, and published collections. Other poets didn't accept it, but the public took it as writ."

Ded put the framed column down and picked up a small, well-used hashish pipe he spotted lying nearby. "Have any of Jerusalem's things been removed from the house since his death?"

Beulah thought back. "Only the financial accounts for the Urthon Spectre Trust. In a wide book. Ickey had brought them home after meeting with Urizen the Monday before the New York trip."

Monday, October 10th. The same day the policy was taken out on Jerusalem's life. Also, the same day the poet was sad and behaving oddly in the back of the hearse.

"What happened to them?"

"I gave them to Tharmas the morning we got back from the airport. He accompanied me home to make sure I was okay. Since he was Ickey's business manager and also handled the trust's investments, I thought he should have them."

"Did Jerusalem normally bring the trust's financial accounts home?"

"I don't remember him ever doing it before."

Ded lifted his fingers from the hash pipe, thinking about Tharmas Luvah—the manager of the dead poet's business and money, the friend of the tiny, red-headed prostitute, the proposed razor-wire practical joker, the sole beneficiary under Beulah's will, and according to Ickey's father, Los, none other than Satan Incarnate.

"I'd like to meet Tharmas. Could you introduce me?"

Beulah brightened. "Sure. He's having a pre-parade Halloween party tonight at his place on Russian Hill. I was going to ask if you wanted to go."

Ded was not a party person. For him, standing around with a drink in his hand, trying to make small talk with complete strangers against a background of loud music and raucous voices was a real strain. He never knew what to say, what expression to maintain, or how to react to personal revelations. He always broke conversations off prematurely, so as not to be a burden to those forced to talk to him. Then, he'd slink off to the bathroom to read.

"Sounds great," Ded responded, unable to pass up the chance to quiz the elusive business manager. "My office has set up an appointment for me at five this evening with Bacon Urizen at his law office in the city. I could meet you after that."

"Adam and I will be glad to take you to Bacon's office," Beulah offered, smiling as though she meant it. "Then, when you're done, we'll drive you up to the party."

"Thanks," Ded said, not used to such consideration. He cleared his throat and looked around at the other piles. "Do you have any photographs of Jerusalem?"

Beulah shook her head. "No. Ickey didn't like photographs of himself. He said they always made him look like somebody else."

Beulah raised her index finger to her temple. "I do have something, though." She glided over to the other side of the room and came back with a life-sized plaster cast of a handsome face, looking much as she had, at lunch, described Jerusalem's face.

"Ickey's death mask," she announced, handing it to Ded.

Ded surveyed the chalky, white mask. The eyes and the mouth were closed, the face peaceful. Like the sleeping God. Before the cast had been made, there must have been some postmortem adjustments to the expression Jerusalem had worn in the toilet cubicle. Unlike that terror-distorted face, Ded found this one had a certain familiarity about it.

"I had the undertaker cast it," Beulah explained, "to remind me of the physical Ickey."

Must've taken some restraint to stop at the face, Ded observed to himself, recalling the vivid description of the rest of Jerusalem's body Beulah had given at lunch.

"I don't think Ickey would have approved," Beulah said, a little ill at ease. "I haven't even had the face painted to make it look lifelike."

Ded looked down at the chalk-white mask. "So, you haven't," he confirmed, not at all displeased.

"Ickey told me once that in medieval times, statues of saints were radiantly painted to look full of life."

Ded recalled the painted and clothed statues he himself had seen in a Mexican cathedral. At the time, he had thought they appeared to be vaguely sacrilegious, almost as though the more real a statue looked, the less saint-like it could be.

Beulah reached out for the mask. "Now, our statues have become nothing more than bleached, dishonored skeletons, empty of everything but the whisper of death."

Ded dutifully handed her the plaster cast.

"A mere memory," Beulah grinned without joy, holding the mask high above her head with both hands.

She then lowered the mask, crossed her arms over it, and pressed its face to her chest, the straight nose nestling in her caftan-covered cleavage.

In a spontaneous act of empathy, Ded inhaled a long, deep breath through his nostrils.

"I'll leave you to get on with your work," Beulah murmured and floated out of the room like a meadow nymph clasping the moon.

⁂

Ded spent the next few hours looking through the piles in the various rooms.

Most of the books he found were old and heavy, and appeared to be in Latin, Greek, or Hebrew. The few in English ranged from a massive volume entitled *The Hermetic and Alchemical Writings of Aureolus Philippus Theophrastus Bombast of Hohenheim, Called Paracelsus the Great* (born 1493 A.D., died 1541 A.D.) to a tract published in 1641 A.D. by John Milton entitled *Of Reformation Touching Church Discipline in England.*

Thumbing through one volume, Ded noticed scribbles in the

margins that were arguments for and against the adjacent text, accompanied by a plethora of exclamation points. He compared the handwriting with that in Jerusalem's spiral notebook. It seemed identical. Another tome contained similar scribblings. Apparently, Jerusalem had not only read these ponderous books but had taken their contents seriously.

In all of the piles, Ded found no pictures of Jerusalem, just as Beulah predicted. But he did find many *by* him, mostly drawings of people involved in conflict, agony, or death. Like the picture of the fallen Urizen, they were drawn with thin, precise lines in a monumental style, making the characters appear massively solid, yet strangely, at the same time, almost weightless.

By the end of his search, Ded discovered something else. Despite all of Beulah's talk about the memory of Jerusalem being preserved in the highest level of God's consciousness, Jerusalem himself seemed to have been exceedingly concerned with preserving his own memories in a much more concrete form—by bronzing them like baby shoes, each with a little memorial inscription.

Among the hundred-plus bronzed items Ded uncovered were: a used condom (First love. The Whore, Baghdad-by-the-Bay.); a proctologist's rubber glove shaped in a one-fingered, obscene gesture (Greetings from your government. The Army Induction Center, Oakland, California.); a small, flattened piece of broccoli (Whence came the truth that all things must pass. The driveway, Lambeth.); and a large, partly squashed lump of dog shit (Price paid for fixing my eyes on the heavens. Ghirardelli Square.). Each bronze had a different date inscribed on the bottom, the latest being for the broccoli, October 10th, 1977

In the light of Jerusalem's erudite metaphysics, heavy-duty reading, and monumental drawings, the inferences to be drawn from these various bronzed items were, to say the least, confusing.

Or as Ded put it so elegantly to himself: *You wouldn't think someone reading a 17th-century tract entitled* Of Reformation Touching Church Discipline in England *would be into preserving dog poop for posterity.*

Placing the dog poop back down, Ded saw something that filled out the picture. At the bottom of the pile was a yellowed matchbook, its matches all gone. Printed on its cover was "Little Joe's," with a Columbus Avenue[4] address.

No wonder the death mask looked familiar! Ded thought.

On his last visit to San Francisco, Little Joe's was the eatery where Ded had met that idiot poet declaiming to his fellows. On that night, four years before, Ded had not only seen and heard, but also spoken to Ickey Jerusalem himself.

❧

The main feature of Little Joe's was a long, fifteen-seat lunch counter stretching from the window to the back. Ded had been sitting at this crowded counter, eating that night's special of veal, risotto, and chard fried in olive oil and capers. On the other side of the counter stood the joint's one scowling waitress and two singing Italian cooks, carrying on their work with all the melodrama of an ill-mannered, economy version of a Verdi opera. The unkempt Jerusalem and his friends had been sitting immediately behind Ded at one of the small round tables crammed up against the wall.

After Jerusalem made his statement about "the permanent, living reality," and after Ded turned to discover (to his surprise) that no one was laughing, the poet continued. "A great poet has the vision to see with perfect clarity what he wants to see."

Ded rolled his eyes.

"The great poet's poems," Jerusalem proclaimed grandly, "express the ultimate reality of fulfilled desire and unbounded freedom."

At that, Ded could not restrain himself. "Like Ferlinghetti's poem about the pigeon statues for generals?"

The group of poets turned to face him.

---

4 Little Joe's later moved from Columbus Avenue to Broadway.

"Ferlinghetti?" Jerusalem said, his surprised face breaking into a smile.

"Ferlinghetti!?" he repeated, puffs of pre-laughter exiting through his nostrils.

"Ferlinghetti!!?" His broad shoulders shook.

"Ferlinghetti!!!?" Jerusalem threw his head back and guffawed loudly, insanely, with a noise not unlike a suction pump clogged with chard.

Ded tried to ignore him.

A few minutes later, however, the poet was still laughing and, the claims adjuster was distressed to note, the rest of Little Joe's had joined in.

Ded decided it was time to leave.

What really gets me, he fumed as he strode down Columbus Avenue, *are those two Italian cooks and that scowling waitress. I can't believe they've read even a single one of Ferlinghetti's poems.*

Ded might have taken a different view of the mockery he'd suffered at Little Joe's if he had he been aware that several years later, the guffawing poet would die a horrible, suffocating death in an airplane toilet, and that he, Ded, would end up rummaging through the dead man's most personal effects and communing with his stunningly sensuous girlfriend.

Around three-thirty in the afternoon, Ded flagged down Adam Ghostflea as he was passing to ask if he could use a phone. Ded was scheduled to call the purser and he also wanted to give Inspector O'Nadir some marching orders.

Ghostflea led Ded through a door in the living room into the large, attached tower, the ground floor of which was what Ded took to be the master bedroom, lit by a single, good-sized, sash window facing the garden. Ghostflea led him up narrow stairs through the bedroom's very high ceiling and into Jerusalem's spacious study. The study itself had no ceiling other than the underside of the tower's peaked roof. The room was surrounded on four sides with three-foot-high wainscoting, and above that, running up to the eaves, leaded light windows divided into small, diamond-shaped panes, affording a spectacular 360-degree view over the surrounding treetops. From the ground, Ded had not realized Lambeth was set at the very top of the hill.

In the center of the room was a wooden desk—more like an immense table—with colossal, square, fluted legs. Spying, among other things on the desk, a red phone, Ded sat down in the comfortable, swivel chair and began making his calls.

He rang the purser first, but there was no answer. Then, he dialed O'Nadir's office on the off chance he'd be in on a Saturday.

"Great you called, Dr. Deadly," the inspector said through expressive chewing of his gum. "I was afraid you'd lost my number. I got through to the New York hotel's cleaning outfit, Angel Cleaners. They said they would check who was on duty the day Urizen's cleaning was done and get back to me so we can compare the staff's prints against those on the plastic bag."

"When they get back to you," Ded said, "could you have them check their customer records against the names of the other first-class passengers? So we can tell if anyone else got a plastic bag?"

"Sure," O'Nadir replied.

"Did Angel Cleaners give you the number for the tag?"

"Oh, yeah. I've got it somewhere here." The sound of O'Nadir skimming through a file came over the line. "Yep, here it is."

Ded took out his loose-leaf notepad and fumbled in his pocket for his pen before remembering it was still back in the hotel room. He picked up a ballpoint from the desk and wrote the number down as O'Nadir read it out in the manner of someone who had never gotten along with the numerical side of life.

"Anything more?" Ded asked.

"Nope."

Ded took this as his cue to fill O'Nadir in on everything he had learned or that had happened to him in the 24 hours since they'd talked at the Hall of Justice, and then to ask the inspector to undertake a few chores, given that Ded was going to be tied up for the rest of the day at Bacon Urizen's office and then at Tharmas Luvah's Halloween party: call the Marin County Sheriff's office to get someone to dig the bullet out of the Mount Tamalpais amphitheater stage for analysis; check with the airline if anyone with a relationship to Jerusalem was on the plane in business or economy, in case they'd slipped into first class to kill Jerusalem; and follow up with the purser on what he'd seen on the plane.

"Wow," O'Nadir commented when Ded had finished. "While I've done nothing more than make a call to the cleaners, you've been on a tear. Halloween party invites. Pint-sized prostitutes. Rabid seeing-eye dogs. Dead-eye gunshots. Central-Valley Okies. Cannibalistic funerals. Razor-wire traps. Jacked-up hearses. Sleeping gods' shrunken minds. Armadillo orgies. Scrawled warning notes. And now here you are, holed up at home with Ickey Jerusalem's lovely personal assistant. Who knows what could happen next?"

"It's strictly business," Ded stated for the record.

O'Nadir laughed. "Naturally, Dr. Deadly."

Ded hung up on the chortling inspector and tapped the blunt end of the ballpoint on his chin, thinking about O'Nadir's ongoing discussions with the cleaners. Even if they located a worker with suede gloves, that still didn't explain the glove prints all over the cubicle. Somebody on the flight was wearing gloves. But who?

As Ded went through the passengers, there flashed into his mind two gloved hands raised above him as he cowered on the steps outside the Holiday Inn. *Adam Ghostflea!*

Ded rested the top of the pen on his lip. *But what motive could Ghostflea have had to murder Jerusalem?*

Looking up in thought, he noticed that the underside of the slanted ceiling had a large rectangle darker than the surrounding wood, as though something mounted there had been removed. A picture? A mirror?

Returning his eyes to the desk, Ded spotted a clear tape dispenser next to the phone. He patted his lower left jacket pocket containing the gardening gloves. They were really too bulky to carry around, plus he didn't feel good about depriving Beulah of protection against the razor wire while gardening. He laid down the two gloves, palm sides up. Then, he carefully stuck strips of tape on each glove finger and thumb, and across each palm. When he was done, he laid two evidence bags flat, one to the left and one to the right, and then removed the strips of tape and stuck them down in the position they were on the respective glove.

Putting the tape-covered evidence bags in his lower left jacket pocket, Ded noticed the message light was blinking on an answering machine on the other side of the phone. The message must have come in during the funeral and Beulah had not yet been in the study, or if she had, could not see the blinking light. It wasn't proper, Ded knew, but he couldn't resist. He turned the volume down and pressed the "play" button. That morning's date and time were announced, and then the pleasant, upper-crust, New York voice of a young woman came on. "Hi. This is Gwen. Just a quick confirmation I've got my ticket to Grand Cayman and will meet you Monday afternoon around three-thirty at the American Airlines first-class lounge at SFO. See you then."

Ded reset the message so the light would start blinking again. *Beulah is meeting some young woman at the airport Monday afternoon? Why? Is this Gwen a sighted accomplice of some sort? Why would she and Beulah be flying to the Cayman Islands?*

Having played the message without authorization, he couldn't ask Beulah who Gwen was. He'd have to wait until the woman's name came up from another source. In the meantime, he'd figure out a way to keep a watch on Beulah on Monday evening.

Ded glanced down at the leather desk-protector pad on which was resting a single sheet of narrow-lined paper. He rotated the paper. At the top were the handwritten letters "RWB" followed by a ten-digit number and a question mark. Midway down the paper were three unlabeled, hand-drawn vertical columns. In the left and middle columns were recent dates and three-digit numbers, respectively. In the right column, a mix of larger numbers were all carried out to two decimal points. The handwriting looked similar to Jerusalem's.

Ded copied the top number in his notepad, along with a sampling of the entries. He then slipped his notepad and the ballpoint into his inside jacket pocket. *Tonight, at Tharmas Luvah's, I'll see if I can get a peek at the trust's financials and find out where these numbers might fit.*

As Ded rose to his feet, he noticed a small wastepaper basket on the floor at the end of the desk behind a massive square leg. It was a typical wastepaper basket in shape, with a wide, round mouth at the top and cylindrical sides tapering to a smaller, round, flat bottom. However, instead of being made of plastic, wood, metal, or wicker, it was made of strips of formerly molten glass, frozen in the act of whirling around the vortex of a tornado. Through the clear glass, Ded could make out a couple of items.

Sliding his swivel chair over, he tilted the wastebasket with one hand. With the other, he reached in and pulled out a hollow, pristine, plastic figurine of a red-haired, bucked-tooth boy turning into a donkey. It wasn't Bottom but rather Lampwick, from the Disney movie, Pinocchio, which Ded has seen as a boy. He pinched the figurine's glued-on, single-feathered bowler hat between his thumb and forefinger, examined the hole in the bottom to make sure the figurine was empty, and then slipped it into an evidence bag. He put the bag into the lower right outside pocket of his jacket.

Still standing, he reached back into the vortex and pulled out the only other thing there: a crumpled piece of paper. He delicately uncrumpled the paper, taking care to touch only the corners, and stretched it mostly flat on the desktop. It was a note composed of individual letters of different sizes pasted from various publications.

Mr. Jerusalem,

> Despite what your poetry may say, it is not proper to have sex with someone to whom you are not married, no matter how long the relationship has been going on, nor how long you expect it to continue. Since you clearly are not willing to do the right thing, I have vowed to kill you, and should I discover anyone else has taken your place, I will kill them as well.
> There is no escape.
> N.

Jesus, Ded thought. A *death-threat from a religious nut who was upset that Jerusalem was having sex with Beulah out of wedlock?* The claims adjuster studied the note. *Strange. There are so many unmarried people having sex, why pick Jerusalem? Could it be one of the fundamentalists among his family and acquaintances in Eden? Or maybe the note writer has a relationship with Beulah?*

Ded went through the list of people he'd encountered so far in his investigation. No one in Jerusalem's coterie or family had the initial "N". Outside that group, the purser's middle name was Nebuchadnezzar, and O'Nadir's name had a capital "N" after the "O"; however, neither of those two people would likely go by the initial "N" nor qualify as a religious nut.

Whoever "N" was, the poet apparently hadn't taken the threat seriously, given that he'd wadded the note up and thrown it in the trash.

Ghostflea's small head popped above the study floor from the stairs below. It was time to go to San Francisco for Ded's meeting with Jerusalem's lawyer, followed by the Halloween party at the apartment of his business manager.

Folding together the opposing top and bottom corners of the death threat, Ded was able to fit it into another evidence bag. He inserted the bag under the back cover of his copy of the poetry anthology and gently closed the book to avoid destroying any prints. Then, picking up the book and the pair of gloves, he followed the sturdy, leprous Ghostflea down the stairs to meet Beulah. After a brief detour by Ded to return the gardening gloves to the shed, they all got into the hearse.

As luck would have it, Mr. Dead-Meat Fangs Who Loves Eating Fly Zippers had been given the night off, his loving mistress concerned he'd had such a tough day barking all the way home after the attack of the rubber tires. As they now headed to San Francisco, the dog's fortuitous absence allowed Ded the luxury of focusing his grimaces and cringes solely on the foul-mouthed, cross-eyed incarnation of reckless endangerment to whom his local transportation needs had become involuntarily linked.

PART THREE

CHAPTER 15

FALLEN VS. UNFALLEN CHAINS

Below the dark, polished Bank of America tower was a barren plaza, deep in shadow. On the right side of the plaza was an enormous, cold, black, hard-edged lump of modern sculpture. What the sculptor intended his work to represent no one knew; the people of San Francisco, however, universally referred to it as the "Banker's Heart."

Agreeing to meet Beulah and Ghostflea later at the Banker's Heart, Ded exited the hearse, entered the building through the lobby, and took the express elevator to the top business floor where Urizen & Fallen, Bacon Urizen's law firm, had its offices.

As Ded stepped off the elevator, his ears popped from the altitude. He thought back on the thousands of airplane takeoffs he had experienced. Going up had always been easy. They popped every time, without him even thinking about it. That said, the ease with which his body adjusted to the reduction in cabin pressure in a climbing plane tended to create problems of its own, at least, regarding orifices other than his ears.

It was one thing for his *eardrums* to pop, but quite another for—

He paused, trying to blot out the memory of the totally amazed look of his seatmate after the takeoff from Tokyo.

Ded turned to the large, oak doors of Bacon Urizen's office, located at one end of the elevator bank. Until now, he hadn't thought about the odors of high-rise offices. Lofty offices like Urizen's undoubtedly had the highest status of any in modern society, yet logically, based on their altitude, they correspondingly had one of the highest incidences of flatulence, a means of bodily expression not normally associated with the promotion of social prestige.

The people working up here, Ded mused, *must wonder after a while whether it's really worth it.*

Ded opened the door to Urizen & Fallen and froze, overwhelmed. Not, as he would have expected entering a den of legal minds, by claustrophobia; nor, given his immediately previous revelation with respect to high-rise offices, by flatulophobia. Instead, in an entirely new departure for Ded, by acrophobia.

The entire far, northern wall of the reception area seemed to have been blown away, opening the inside to the outside in a breathtaking, unobstructed view of the Bay—Telegraph Hill, Russian Hill, Alcatraz, Angel Island, Belvedere, Sausalito, the Marin Headlands, and the Golden Gate Bridge.

Accepting the receptionist's cold assurances there was a window in place, Ded let go of the doorknob and cautiously approached the edge. The view from Mount Tamalpais had been higher and more panoramic, but it had not had the dramatic shift from a closed interior to a boundless exterior provided by floor-to-ceiling windows.

Feeling unprotected, naked, and afraid of falling, he backed away and formally announced himself to the receptionist, who was seated at a long desk against the beige-tapestried left wall. Ded's voice broke as he gave Urizen's name.

"Just a moment," the receptionist said, lifting her phone.

Noticing a telescope on a tripod near the wall of windows, Ded sidled over, trying to maintain as casual an air as he could in the face of the chasm yawning before him. Bending, he peered into the lens. It was focused on a bedroom in the Holiday Inn, four short blocks away.

Ded removed his eye from the lens in disgust. *Somebody at this exalted firm is a voyeur.*

He glanced at the receptionist, who was still busy on the phone, then tried the telescope's dials to see if he could increase the magnification.

He couldn't. The previous pervert had already set it to maximum.

Ded took off his glasses and peeked into the lens again to get a better view. He adjusted the focus. The bed, running parallel to the wide window, was neatly made. At its foot was an open, empty garment bag. On top of the bag was a small suitcase, as though casually left there by its owner hurrying out that morning.

Jesus, Ded thought, thunderstruck. *That's my room!*

"Mr. Urizen can see you directly," the receptionist announced.

Ded raised his eye from the telescope. *Had Bacon Urizen been peering into my room? If so, why?*

He followed the receptionist through a door on the right into a broad, north-south corridor with empty (it being Saturday) secretaries' desks outside lawyers' offices. *Maybe it was Urizen who sent the vertically challenged prostitute with the warning message, and so he had simply used the telescope to confirm she had fulfilled her mission.*

The receptionist opened the first door, which led into Urizen's huge, northeast corner office with its expanse of polished parquet flooring. Backed up against the north window was a credenza, a throne-like swivel chair, and a massive mahogany desk. Facing the desk from the opposite side was a smaller, wood and leather chair. The rest of the office on the right was taken up with a conversation area consisting of a six-legged couch, several easy chairs, and a shag-pile throw rug. Apart from the lounging area was a large, round table surrounded by swivel chairs.

The obese lawyer was already standing, the pudgy fingers of his left hand resting on the near edge of his desk to keep his body from toppling over. Bacon Urizen drew back his enormous, bald head and focused a questioning monocle on Ded, as though studying up close a lower life form previously seen from afar.

Ded glanced reflexively at the window behind Urizen's desk. It was the same ceiling-to-floor type as those in the reception area, with the same view, but without the telescope. *Christ!* Ded thought. *Was Urizen watching me last night during my four minutes and fifty-five seconds of free video?* Ded's room lights had been off, but the bright light from the porn movie might have made everything visible.

The senior partner proffered a limp right hand. "Mr. Smith?" Something in the tone of his exceptionally deep voice suggested he had, in fact, been watching.

"Yes, that's right," Ded replied, camouflaging his disquiet by striding forward to give the lawyer's hand an inappropriately firm shake.

"How do you—" The strong downstroke with which Ded began his shake yanked the bachelor attorney off his center of gravity. "—do?"

Urizen gasped, snatching his hand back to keep upright.

Unaware he had pulled Urizen off balance, Ded assumed the lawyer's sudden recoil was due to where the man had seen that strong downstroke before.

Ded stared at his guilty hand, hanging alone in the air, and tried to think what to say. "Awfully high up here, isn't it?" he stammered, motioning at the view.

Urizen, his balance and composure regained, gave Ded a mocking smile. "Nothing ever gets by you, does it, Mr. Smith?"

Ded bobbed his head noncommittally. Feigning nonchalance, he edged closer to the window to look down at his room. *No,* he decided, after craning his head this way and then that. *The downward angle of view is too steep.*

Through that telescope in reception, Urizen might have been able to see the back of the prone Ded's naked lower legs across the bed, with the soles of his feet towards the window, but not see the rest of his body beyond the bed, creating a span from just above his knees on the edge of the mattress to a yard out, where his chest was being supported by the stretched straps of the hotel's collapsible suitcase-stand, his hand towel positioned just right on the floor beneath the body bridge, as he strained to lift his head to view, just past the watch timer on his raised left wrist, the fascinating images on the TV screen near the door.

Assured his dignity was intact (or more precisely, assured his dignity appeared to others intact), Ded turned back to the task at hand. From his interrogation at the airport, he knew Urizen could be difficult. To get the information he needed, he would have to work on establishing rapport.

Ded smiled with excess friendliness at the overweight patrician. "I hear the Bank of America tower is the tallest building floorwise in San Francisco."

Urizen did not reply. However, from the lawyer's general demeanor, the insurance investigator could tell the man was not amazed by this revelation.

Unsure what to say next, Ded looked back out the window and surveyed the rolling hills of the city. If he looked hard enough, they appeared to move. "I wonder what will happen when the earthquake comes."

"I suppose," Urizen said with a worn-out sigh, "you would then be prattling on about how the Bank of America tower was now the *longest* building floorwise in San Francisco. Don't you think?"

Ded edged back from the window.

Urizen wearily pivoted his great bulk around to take in the view. "We have an office pool to predict the exact spot we will land. Perhaps you'd like to put in a bet?"

"Not if I have to be present to collect."

Ded fastened his gaze on the Golden Gate in the distance. The sun was setting. The evening fog was oozing under the bridge into the Bay like a giant cotton amoeba, smothering everything in its path. Ded watched it, transfixed by the eeriness of the sight.

Urizen stepped carefully around the front of his desk and stood next to Ded, aspirating deeply. "Often, the fog swallows the whole earth below in an endless sea of white, leaving me up here alone, basking in the sun."

Ded swiveled his head toward Urizen. It was the first time he had heard the lawyer say something that didn't include a question.

"It must be good for your tan," Ded declared. In his rush to seize the opportunity to establish rapport, the words ran out of his mouth, bypassing his brain.

The lawyer tentatively raised his right hand and touched the top of his large head. His hairless scalp, like the rest of his skin, was the color of whey.

Appearing to lose the strength to stand, Urizen limped farther around his desk to the throne-like chair behind it, eased himself into the seat, and with his stomach resting gratefully on his lap, exhaled.

In a tiny, glass vase on the desk was a single white rose, so pale it appeared almost sick.

Urizen motioned for Ded to take the wood and leather chair at the front of the desk. "The tinted windows block any chance of that," he replied to Ded's tanning comment. "Which, between us, is a good thing. Clients don't trust an attorney with a tan. Makes them think he spends an excessive amount of time away from his law books. The only way for an attorney to appear authoritative is to develop an appropriate bar pallor."

Ded sat and crossed his legs. "Yes, a lawyer definitely needs a *bar* pallor," he agreed, emphasizing the word "bar" to show he appreciated the pun. "But you don't want to go so far you fade away like Sir Joshua Reynolds's paintings."

Urizen gazed through his monocle at Ded. "I don't know why Miss Vala used that quotation at the funeral. Mr. Jerusalem *hated* Reynolds. The poem was meant to be ironic. As usual, she was so intent on mouthing her idol's words, she missed their substance."

He frowned and looked down at his trousers, as though remembering a recent indignity. "Lord, save me from blind followers," he prayed.

In the awkward silence that followed, Ded noticed a small, framed drawing on a polished hardwood credenza behind Urizen's chair. It was drawn in the same style as the picture of God bifurcating reality, and showed a cherub emerging from a large egg.

"One of Ickey Jerusalem's drawings?" Ded asked, gesturing with his head.

"No, mine," Urizen answered without looking. "When I was young. At boarding school. Won me the student art prize."

The former prize-winner stared impassively at the claims adjuster. Then, with great effort, he swiveled his heavy chair 180 degrees to face the drawing on the credenza, lurched down, and opened the cabinet doors beneath. "Drink?"

"Some water, thanks," Ded said.

Urizen glanced partly back. "A man after my own heart."

A moment later, Urizen brought his body around, each hand holding a glass filled with water and a few cubes of ice. He gave one to Ded and lifted the other in a listless toast. "Although, I don't think mine is a heart you'd want to go after."

Ded assessed him with a quizzical eye.

"My heart. It's failing." Glumly, Urizen opened his arms to draw attention to his physique. "Once, I had a strong body, a full head of hair, and a ruddy complexion. Now, I have high blood pressure, elevated cholesterol, blocked arteries, squeaky valves, shortness of breath, coldness in my extremities, and perpetual angina. My diet is restricted. I'm not supposed to drink alcohol. I'm not supposed to exercise. I'm not supposed to get excited. I'm not supposed to have sex. I'm pallid. I'm bald. I'm fat."

"No, certainly not," Ded objected, feeling a heartfelt expression of sympathy was required. "Pleasantly plump, maybe. But fat? No, no, no."

From Urizen's scowl, Ded could tell he was not used to receiving such sincere expressions of sympathy.

The San Francisco Brahmin took a sip of water as if to wash from his memory the description of himself as pleasantly plump. "Well, Mr. Smith, although I answered all the questions you asked me at the airport security office last week, I know I was a little short with you. I was angry about being kept overlong at baggage claim at that time of night and then forced to walk up a broken escalator. I apologize for my behavior. Ask me whatever further questions you want, and I'll try to answer to the best of my ability."

"Thank you," Ded said, taken aback by the lawyer's sudden willingness to talk. *That pleasantly plump stuff really did the trick.* "Let me start with something I didn't know during the interview but do now. A little under two weeks before Ickey Jerusalem died, the Urthon Spectre Trust took out with my company a twenty-million-dollar policy on his life."

Urizen leaned back in his throne, stroking his sallow pate with his palm. "Yes. I arranged it."

"And you designated Beulah Vala as beneficiary?"

"That was Mr. Jerusalem's wish."

"Did Beulah know about the policy?"

"I do not think so. Mr. Jerusalem said he wanted to keep it secret from not just her but everyone else."

So, Ded thought, *unless somebody slipped up, when Beulah said she didn't know about the policy, she was telling the truth, and Tharmas Luvah didn't know about it either. Meaning the policy couldn't have been a motive for either of them to murder Jerusalem. Of course, that doesn't mean that either of them couldn't have had another motive.*

"Did Jerusalem have a will?"

"Yes, to handle everything he had outside of the investments in the Urthon Spectre Trust—his house, his hearse, his sailboat, his personal effects. After various, specific bequests, the residual beneficiary is his oldest brother, Theo, if he's alive. Otherwise, in order of birth, each of his surviving brothers."

"I understand the trust's default beneficiary, unless Jerusalem modified it, is the same as you've just described for the will."

Urizen sighed. "Monday morning, I'll be reading Mr. Jerusalem's bequests. He specified that anyone who wanted could attend. So, you're welcome to come along, if you want. It begins here, at ten."

Ded nodded his acceptance of the invitation. "I understand from Beulah Vala that you and Jerusalem talked on the plane about some changes to his trust and will. Would they have affected the beneficiary designation?"

Urizen interlocked his pudgy fingers awkwardly behind his head, elbows out. "You understand, I am sure, that is information I cannot give you, as any communications Mr. Jerusalem and I might have had are subject to attorney-client privilege?"

Ded considered pushing the point but decided against it. "In any case, you didn't make the changes?"

Urizen lowered his hands to his lap. "No. Mr. Jerusalem had made his request at lunch in New York, the day we left. There hadn't been time."

Ded finished off his water. "From the urgency of Jerusalem's requests, plus the new insurance policy on his life, one might conclude he was afraid he didn't have long to live."

Urizen looked at Ded's glass, empty except for the two ice cubes at the bottom. "More water?"

"No thanks," Ded replied.

Urizen rotated his chair to refill his glass from the cabinet, came back around, raised his glass in a mechanical toast, and took a sip. "When Mr. Jerusalem first took up with Beulah Vala, he gave up alcohol and drugs. But six months ago, I don't know why, he started using them again. Heavily. Fortunately, he only indulged in private at Lambeth, so there were no embarrassing public antics to worry about. But unfortunately, for me, at least, whenever I had to go to his house, he obliged me to join him in his drinking. He'd literally force the stuff on me. Flask-shaped bottles of sweetened wine one would get rolling winos outside the Greyhound Bus Station. Names like Night Train Express. Thunderbird. Ripple. Not the type of bouquet I was interested in dying for."

Urizen took another sip, this time to cleanse his palate. "And then there was the hashish smoking."

Ripple and hashish? Ded thought. *No wonder Jerusalem couldn't look at the sun without seeing the Heavenly Host.*

"And the dancing," Urizen continued. "Leaping about the room like an epileptic on hot coals, hooting in time to the music. It wasn't the kind of thing a man in my condition should've been doing."

He lay back in his chair. "Plus, the continual sex with Miss Vala."

Surprise tinged with jealousy surged up through Ded's chest. "You had sex with Beulah Vala?"

"No," Urizen replied somberly. "That was something Jerusalem wanted to do by himself. I'd have been dead for sure."

Relieved, Ded suppressed his jealousy and marched his mind back to the picture of the poet that Urizen had just been painting. "From your description, it sounds like Jerusalem had some sort of death wish."

"That's what Dr. Ulro thought. One day, when I was at Lambeth, he'd come by to give Mr. Jerusalem his annual checkup and started chastising him, telling him if he didn't want to shorten his lifespan considerably, he would have to stop drinking, smoking, dancing, and making love, or at least confine himself to one such activity at a time."

"What did Jerusalem say to that?"

"He said, 'The road of excess leads to the palace of wisdom.'"

"Which meant?"

"I assume," Urizen answered, gazing at his huge stomach, seemingly so pregnant yet so absent of life, "that the road of restraint leads to the palace of ignorance."

"Which means?"

Urizen looked up, slightly impatient at having to explain such an obvious point. "Since Mr. Jerusalem believed the true reality could be grasped only by the unfettered, creative imagination breaking through the prison walls of the objective world, it is obvious from his little epigram he believed he would be more likely to generate that creativity if he lived his life to the extreme, completely free from any restraint."

Although Ded did not feel this was as obvious as Urizen did, he could see where it was leading. "So, you think Jerusalem, in an attempt to reach the palace of wisdom last week in the plane, had decided to inflict on himself the most extreme experience available to a living being?"

Urizen shrugged that it was possible.

Ded thought this over before going back to pick up on something Urizen had said. "You said you saw Dr. Ulro chastising Jerusalem about his lifestyle. Are you aware of their name-calling match that occurred in Ulro's office before the trip to New York?"

"No. But then, name-calling was not that unusual between them. Particularly on Mr. Jerusalem's part. He had a whole slew of slurs when it came to the good doctor. Although, his favorite in the last few months, I found slightly exaggerated."

"What was that?"

Urizen smiled dryly. "Satan Incarnate."

Ded's mind flashed back to what Dr. Ulro had said in the airport security interview room about the expression on the corpse—that it looked as though Jerusalem had at last come face to face with Satan Incarnate. "You don't think the name fits Dr. Ulro?"

"Not really. The Dr. Ulro I know has always been a person of the highest moral virtue." He spoke the last three words with a touch of mockery.

"'A person of the highest moral virtue,'" Ded quoted, thinking about the death-threat note Ickey had received. "Is that a euphemism for 'religious nut'?"

Urizen raised his free eyebrow at Ded. "Not at all. I understand that following the death of his parents, Mr. Ulro, as he then was, toyed some with fundamentalism. But after studying evolution in college, he gave up the fire and brimstone to become an atheist." Urizen finished his drink. "Let it never be said that Dr. Bromion Ulro is not a man of great philosophical depth."

Ded looked at the two ice cubes melting at the bottom of his empty glass, pondering the red-headed hooker's warning to him to beware of the doctor. "You can't think of any reason why Dr. Ulro would have wanted Jerusalem dead?"

"What?" Urizen exclaimed. "Are you suggesting Mr. Jerusalem's death wasn't suicide?"

"Just trying to cover all the bases."

"Apart from the puerile name calling," Urizen scoffed, "I know of nothing that would suggest Dr. Ulro would or could kill Mr. Jerusalem."

Which means, Ded thought, *Urizen wasn't the one who sent the hooker to give me the warning.*

"Do you think, Mr. Urizen," Ded asked, "you could introduce me to Dr. Ulro? My office has been unable to get through to him."

"I think it's better if you get someone else to introduce you."

"Why's that?"

"Mr. Smith, did anyone ever enlighten you on why doctors hate lawyers?"

Ded indicated no one ever had and he was interested in learning. This was in part because he might glean important information about Dr. Ulro, with whom Ded still didn't have an appointment, and in part because he suspected Urizen might end up inadvertently revealing useful tidbits about himself.

"Most people think it's because lawyers are always suing doctors for malpractice or trying to make fools of them on the stand, or that lawyers go to school for half the number of years doctors do to make roughly the same amount of money. But those are all mere rationalizations. The real cause is that doctors and lawyers have entirely opposing views of the world."

"In what way?"

"Doctors tend to be absolutists, while lawyers tend to be questioners."

Puzzled, Ded encouraged Urizen to explain further.

"Let's start with doctors. Doctors are convinced their work is helping mankind. After all, they heal the sick. Likewise, they are convinced there is a truth, and all they need to do is find it. In college, they memorize reams of chemical and biological truths. In medical school, they scribble down more complex truths promulgated by their god-like professors, and then regurgitate those truths on the exam. Later, they go to work in hierarchical residency hospitals, in which every person has his place, from the egotistical top surgeon down to the humble guy who empties the bedpans. The result is that doctors develop a very low tolerance of ambiguity, the ability to stand a situation which has not been resolved. This not only makes them terrible negotiators, but more importantly, often drives them to find truth where none exists, producing rigid and ideological views on politics, society, morality, everything—all of these being absolutist traits that describe Dr. Ulro to a T."

"And lawyers?"

"Lawyers, on the other hand, are merely hired gladiators whose goal is not to find the truth but to find interpretations of the law that will benefit their client. They learn some law, sure, but most of their education is in how to see all sides of any issue, spotting and exploiting where the meaning is ambiguous or the laws conflict, so as to allow questions to be raised. As for respecting authority, on the first day of law school, the professor says, 'Look at this Supreme Court decision. Isn't this stupid?' From there, a lawyer learns how to tear down an opponent's arguments in order to promote those that help the client. Eventually, lawyers come to believe that not only is truth irrelevant but, in fact, there *is* no single truth. Needless to say, lawyers have a very high tolerance for ambiguity. This makes them not only excellent negotiators, but also much more tolerant on politics, society, morality, etcetera."

"All of the latter being 'questioner' traits which describe you to a T?"

Bacon Urizen smiled in agreement.

"If you can't introduce me to Dr. Ulro," Ded said, "can you recommend somebody who can?"

"You might try Tharmas Luvah, Mr. Jerusalem's business manager. I think he's on better terms. Last week, when I was sleeping on the plane, the sound of Dr. Ulro's distinctively high-pitched voice woke me up. Surprised he was on the flight, I looked back towards the spiral staircase and saw him and Mr. Luvah talking."

"What about?" This was the first Ded had heard about Tharmas Luvah and Dr. Ulro conferring on the flight.

"I don't know. I couldn't hear. They were too far away. After confirming it was indeed the doctor, I went back to sleep."

I'll have to ask Tharmas Luvah about this tonight when I see him, Ded thought.

But first, Ded had several more questions to ask of Urizen.

CHAPTER 16

HEARING THE PUPPETEER'S VOICE

Ded watched as Urizen waddled back to his desk, having taken a benign-prostatic-hyperplasian bathroom break. The lawyer settled into his chair and gave Ded the nod to continue.

"When did Ickey Jerusalem choose you as his lawyer?"

"He didn't choose me as his lawyer. Los, his father, hired me to keep the boy out of the draft after his son moved to San Francisco following his graduation from Oxford."

"Did you succeed?"

Urizen nodded.

"How?"

"Psychological grounds."

"Based on what evidence?"

"He was having conversations with his dead brother, Orc. The draft board's doctors found them most disconcerting." Urizen gave Ded a conspiratorial look. "Particularly during the rectal exam."

Ded returned the lawyer's look as best he could. "I've heard Jerusalem's mother wanted him to enlist. Didn't she resist your efforts to keep him out?"

"Oh, yes. Enith threatened to tell the examiners it was all a fraud. Apparently, she'd talked to the dead Orc herself and ascertained he'd had no conversations with Ickey for months. However, while she was still asleep in her San Francisco hotel on the morning of the hearing, Los was able to sneak a life-sized, stuffed rhinoceros into her bathroom."

Urizen steepled his fingers, recalling the moment. "Unaware, Enith staggered out of bed, trudged to her bathroom, opened the door, and—" He raised his eyebrows. "Enith is not what you would consider an excitable woman." He sucked in his lips. "The audiotape of the trumpeting bull elephant was what tipped the balance."

Deadpan, the attorney inspected the ends of his steepled fingers. "A couple of hours after the appointment at the Oakland Induction Center, Los caught up with Enith on Highway 99 at the Eden exit. She was still running. Had forgotten completely about the draft."

Urizen leaned back in his chair, the recollection of his minor victory over Enith appearing to restore some of his strength.

"I assume Ickey Jerusalem was grateful for your help?" Ded said.

"In the context of Mr. Jerusalem, I don't know if 'grateful' is a word that has much meaning. Shortly after his Uncle Urthon died, when Mr. Jerusalem attained the requisite age of 25, he gained full power over the trust, including the right to amend any of the provisions and call for income and capital at will. He exercised his new powers to remove Los as trustee and appoint me in his stead. Not because he was grateful but rather because Mr. Jerusalem wanted someone in charge who was not his intellectual inferior." Urizen's self-assessment was given as a matter of course, with only the slightest degree of pomposity.

"So, Jerusalem respected your intelligence?"

"No. He *recognized* my intelligence. Given we viewed reality in such different ways, he could have no more respect for my intelligence than I could for his."

"Different ways? You mean, like doctors versus lawyers?"

"No. To Mr. Jerusalem, both doctors and lawyers, despite being respectively absolutists and questioners, view the world from the same, sorry realm."

Urizen leaned forward to put his open hand near the single white rose on his desk. "Take this rose."

Ded focused on the flower, while unconsciously pushing his thighs together.

"Mr. Jerusalem would supposedly reach out with his creative imagination to pierce the veil of the rose and unify his mind with a part of the rose's true reality existing in the highest level of God's consciousness—say, the Virgin Mary, in all her purity and beauty, or perhaps Death himself, sickly and pale."

Ded squirmed a bit in his seat. He had this part down pat. "While you and Dr. Ulro remain stuck in the mid-level, shrunken consciousness of the sleeping God, that is, humanity's consciousness, condemned to see the rose as a separate physical object."

"No," Urizen said, although impressed with Ded's knowledge, "much worse than that. The way Dr. Ulro and I think about the rose takes us even further from the highest level, down into the lowest level of God's consciousness."

Ded squeezed his hands together on his lap, recalling he had failed to ask Beulah to explain this lowest level.

"If Dr. Ulro and I were asked to describe the rose precisely, we'd do so by using our reason to analyze it from a variety of points of view—its shape, its height, its width, its color, its softness, and so on, usually by reference to some abstract, lowest-common-denominator measuring rod, such as centimeters, spectral wavelength, or milligrams of pressure per square millimeter, allowing us to compare the rose accurately with anything else in the world we wished."

Ded felt uncomfortable. Not because of what Urizen was saying, but because he had, almost out of the blue, become aware of a large, if belated, air pressure equalization on the verge of occurring through one of his orifices, and in a manner extremely unlikely to raise his standing in polite society.

"And it doesn't stop there," the lawyer went on in his resonant bass voice. "For the doctor and I then use those comparisons to develop abstract formulae and theories to describe the relations between the measurements."

No doubt about it, Ded sweated. *It's a huge one. We're talking kilograms per square millimeter here, at least. I haven't got a chance in hell of keeping it in.*

"While the fall from the highest level to the mid-level reduced God's consciousness to that which can be perceived by the five senses," the lecturing lawyer declared, oblivious to his listener's distress, "our fallen reason now reduces God's—that is, *our*—consciousness even further…"

Ded nodded with pretend interest as the irresistible pressure inside approached the limit of his control.

"…condemning us to experience life only secondhand, through self-created, lifeless abstractions…"

The peculiar, high-pitched staccato of Ded's control giving way lasted for a full nine seconds, sounding to all the world like the distressed barking of an imaginary spider ensconced inside the claims adjuster's underpants.

During the first second, Urizen's non-monocled eyebrow lifted, followed in later seconds by Urizen's other eyebrow gradually lifting to boot, until, as the sound came to a sickly conclusion at the end of the ninth second, the lawyer's monocle popped from his eye, leaving behind a facial expression that was the nonverbal equivalent of *What in Christ's name was that?*

Oh, how embarrassing, Ded moaned to himself. *Bacon Urizen is giving me a brilliant lecture on the lowest level of God's consciousness and the only comment I can make is a sound like a barking spider.*

Ded briefly considered telling Urizen it was the lawyer's fault for not having taken an office on a lower floor, but lacking the chutzpah to carry it off, he instead took the path of least resistance, pretending nothing untoward had occurred.

Urizen replaced his monocle and peered at Ded. At this altitude, the lawyer was doubtless used to discreet silent-but-deadlies. But a nine-second barking spider was another matter altogether.

No repetition occurring, the lawyer shrugged and returned to his exposition. "…moving us as far as possible from the rose's highest-level reality…"

Urizen stopped and crinkled his nose, seemingly analyzing and comparing a new, powerfully physical attribute of his guest's breach of etiquette that had, at that very moment, begun imprinting itself on one of his senses.

Ded held his breath, concerned he was on the brink of being ejected from the lawyer's office for conduct unbecoming a philosopher.

But Urizen made no comment, unphilosophical odors, even powerful ones, apparently being a common occurrence in his office. Instead, the heavyweight mouthpiece, instinctively tucking his head against his neck to get away from the smell, soldiered on, speaking out of what appeared (due to his now-squashed double chin) to be the top of his three mouths. "…leaving us trapped between…"

Urizen exhaled and inhaled snappily through his mouth. "…the abstract descriptions below, through which Dr. Ulro and I perceive the world…"

Another, shallower, exhale-inhale. "…and the abstract theories above, we construct from those descriptions…"

Exhale-inhale. "…locking us up inside our own self-created Hell…"

A deep breath. "…the abode of that part of God's consciousness Mr. Jerusalem called, 'Satan Incarnate.'"

Ded nodded as he repeated Urizen's last thirteen words at a leisurely pace, both to emphasize that when it came to understanding this three-levels stuff, there were no flies on him, and also to buy as much time as possible for the embarrassing evidence of his boo-boo to dissipate.

In the interlude, though, he couldn't help asking himself, *So, does this mean Dr. Ulro and Bacon Urizen are joint Satan Incarnates?*

❧

Urizen held in the remainder of his breath for a few more seconds, exhaled audibly, and then tested the air with several hesitant nasal intakes. Deciding that, while not all that pleasant, the smell was no longer as life-threatening as it had first appeared, he continued his lecture. "Of course, Dr. Ulro and I were not alone. When God's consciousness shrank into the mid-level human consciousness, not only were there humans with sufficient creative imagination to occasionally pierce the physical world, there were also humans with sufficient reasoning capacity to analyze the physical world as a collection of abstractions and then fit those abstractions into complex theories."

"I understand now why Jerusalem recognized but did not respect your intelligence," Ded said, privately discouraged by the rapidly expanding list of Satan Incarnates. "You and your ilk from the lowest level were spreading abstract thinking throughout the mid-level, making it more difficult for anybody to glimpse the highest level."

"Worse than that," Urizen said. "Whenever in the mid-level someone with creative imagination did manage through his artistry to unite the sleeping God's consciousness with such a glimpse, Satan immediately hid it from the sleeping God's view in a web of abstractions."

"Could you give me an example?"

"Let's say the uniting is through a poem. Before the ink has dried, literature professors spring up from Hell and begin explaining the meaning of the poem, analyzing the details of its construction, boxing the piece into a particular poetic movement, issuing rules to others on how it should be read, and so on, until eventually, the poet's holistic glimpse of God's infinite and eternal creative imagination can no longer be directly experienced by the reader. While claiming to be enhancing the glimpse, the literature professors are, in fact, doing the exact opposite. Not because they are evil, but because, being slaves to reason, they are able to take in visions only as a collection of abstractions to fit into theories."

"I see," Ded said. For he did see. At least, based on the internal logic of Jerusalem's ideas. But since Ded did not accept that the universe was the mind of God, he didn't understand what was so bad about looking at things through abstractions and theories. Those were a much better way of understanding what was happening than being trapped inside the experience itself.

"Interestingly," Urizen continued, "Mr. Jerusalem portrayed Satan Incarnate in Hell as being upside down, as though having been cast in headfirst at the Fall. Satan, however, still thinks he is right-side up, and thus, his constructed theories 'above' his head are the highest possible attainment, rather than merely the deepest part of Hell. At the same time, he views everyone and everything else as mere abstractions far 'below' his feet. Humans standing right-side up in the mid-level seem, from the inverted Satan's viewpoint at the lowest level, to have their feet in the air and their heads buried in the physical world, and the highest level of God's consciousness is, to Satan, so far 'below' these 'buried' human heads, it's become nothing more than a distant, unseen specter."

Ded nodded. Although he didn't personally know any literature professors, he found Urizen's description of them as upside down in Hell uncannily satisfying.

"Of course," Urizen continued, "Mr. Jerusalem's tripartite-consciousness metaphysics is total hogwash, failing to bear up under even the most superficial of analyses. However, since he was my client, I didn't feel I could point this out to him directly. Accordingly, using my lawyer's questioner skills, I'd play the ingénue, continually making 'innocent' queries designed to cause him to doubt his ideas."

Urizen's voice assumed a guileless tone, as though talking to Jerusalem. "Isn't the shrunken consciousness of the sleeping God not only separated from the physical world but is itself divided into several billion human consciousnesses? So, if you, one of those consciousnesses, reaches out to pierce the objective veil and unite the true reality of the rose with your divine creative imagination in order to see, say, the Virgin Mary, in all her purity and beauty, everybody else's consciousness remains unchanged?

"If that's true, then what happens when another of those billions of other human consciousnesses uses its creative imagination in the same way? Is it unable to get through the veil and see the Virgin Mary because that specific true reality is already stuck to your head?

"What if that other human consciousness sees instead in the white rose the image of Death, sickly and pale? Is that allowed because that specific reality of the rose is not yet stuck to your head?

"What I'm struggling with, Mr. Jerusalem, and so perhaps you can help me understand, is how do you tell the difference between uniting with an object's true reality with your subjective mind's creative imagination, and simply using the normal, associative creativity of one's brain to imagine, solely in your head, whatever you might about an object you happen to be viewing?"

Urizen took on a look of quiet satisfaction. "Mr. Jerusalem would try to answer, but never clearly and explicitly enough that I would not be able to find tiny, ambiguous interstices in his logic, through which I could then draw my analytical razor, slicing his arguments ever thinner, until they became a tissue of meaningless distinctions."

The lawyer shook his head with a glimmer of regret. "Despite Mr. Jerusalem being so much more youthful, healthy, and robust than me, he'd invariably end up wracked with doubt and fall into a deep, almost suicidal depression lasting for several days."

Ded perked up at this unexpected coda. "When was the last time your 'innocent' questioning resulted in Ickey Jerusalem falling into a deep, almost suicidal depression?"

Urizen peered up to the left, as though trying to remember, although Ded got the feeling the memory was already present in his consciousness. "Monday, October 10th."

The olfactory remnants of Ded's gaseous indiscretion having at last faded from the room, the life insurance investigator had one more set of questions for the lawyer. "Have you read Ickey Jerusalem's epic poems just published as part of the anthology?"

Urizen glanced at his watch as though he had another appointment. "I haven't read them yet, but from what I've heard, they're all the same. Brilliantly logical elaborations on his absurd parable of the sleeping God."

"Do you think Jerusalem genuinely believed in that parable?"

Urizen angled toward his window. The sun had set. The fog, which earlier had begun to crawl under the Golden Gate Bridge, now covered everything below the Bank of America tower. The moon shone in the clear, night sky.

"On July 4th last year, the Bicentennial, I was working late. The moon and the fog were just like this." Urizen peered down at the sea of cotton as though waiting for something to appear. "Suddenly, a tiny ball of fire shot out of the fog from where Alcatraz was buried. Reaching its apogee in the moonlight, the ball exploded into a multicolored crystal clarity and then quickly faded. A moment later, the phenomenon repeated. And then again. Somewhere on that prison island beneath the gloom, someone was sending up rockets of celebration." Urizen swiveled back to face Ded. "I was likely the only person in the world who could see."

He looked Ded straight in the eyes. "To me, Mr. Jerusalem's poems were like those rockets, and Mr. Jerusalem himself was like the fog below. I didn't have to see what was happening on Alcatraz to appreciate the show."

Urizen's intercom buzzed and the receptionist's voice came over the line. "Mr. Ijim to see you, sir."

"Fine," he told her. "I'm finishing with Mr. Smith."

Ded got out of his seat. "Is that Cousin Ijim? The gigantic man who carried you on his back out of the amphitheater?"

"Yes," Urizen answered, struggling up from his chair. "I'm helping him with a retirement community he's developing on Ferrous Peak."

"The trust is investing?"

"Certainly not." The medicine-ball-shaped attorney was now ushering Ded to the door. "To ensure that the trust's assets are used only for the benefit of the beneficiary, investments connected with other family members are strictly prohibited. Mr. Ijim is an entirely separate client."

"What's the retirement community called?" Ded asked, feeling an irrational need to prolong the interview.

Urizen opened the door and shook Ded's hand as he simultaneously drew him out of the office. "Golden Sun City."

Cousin Ijim was lumbering across the secretaries' corridor, the receptionist scurrying behind. He was dressed in lumberjack clothes and wore the face of a man terrorized by demons. "Urizen, you fiend, hold thy glib and eloquent tongue."

"Come in, come in," Urizen said, stepping back so Cousin Ijim could duck under the door's lintel.

"They're after me," Cousin Ijim lamented, "and soon, they'll be after you, too."

"Don't worry," Urizen replied, "I've—"

Urizen shut the door, cutting off the rest of the sentence.

Ded held the elevator door open to let a short, skinny, Filipina cleaning woman carrying a mop and bucket join him. He pushed the button for the street level. As the elevator began its descent, Ded reviewed what he had learned about Ickey Jerusalem. It was all such a jumble of weird theories, contradictory behavior, and confusing and ambiguous pronouncements, he couldn't ever hope to figure out what was going on in the poet's mind that night in the plane.

The only way I could ever know for sure is to talk directly to Ickey Jerusalem, he mused. *And that's impossible.*

Ded touched his ears. Despite the pressure increasing with the drop, they were not popping as they should. But then, as he had learned from his years of air travel, going down was always much tougher than going up. Conveniently, he had garnered a wealth of techniques to deal with the problem.

He swallowed.

Nothing happened.

He swallowed again, this time with great exaggeration.

Nothing.

He swallowed once more, this time following it with a forced yawn.

Still nothing.

He swallowed and yawned, adding a simultaneous tug at both his earlobes.

His ears remained stubbornly unpopped, the pressure becoming increasingly unpleasant.

With renewed effort, Ded swallowed, yawned, tugged at his earlobes, and this time, stuck out his tongue as far as it would go.

Out of the corner of his eye, he noticed the Filipina cleaning woman backing into the far corner of the car, holding her mop out like a crucifix against the evil one.

Ded grimaced apologetically at the woman and turned away. There was only one hope. The Valsalva maneuver. It had never failed.

Ded took a deep breath, closed his mouth, pinched his nose, and blew against his cheeks with gradually increasing pressure.

When the elevator at last reached the ground floor, Ded turned to the opening door, his eyes focused on his pinched nose, his cheeks the size of cantaloupes, his face a deep, oxygen-starved purple, and his ears, despite everything, unpopped.

The cleaning woman, still warding him off with her upraised mop, edged out of the elevator. Once clear, she stopped, made a sudden threatening motion with the mop so as to put him off balance, and took off in a run to the safety of housekeeping, her bucket banging noisily against the side of her leg.

Ded released his nose and exhaled. Suffering from a slight, hypoxic wooziness, he stumbled through the lobby and out into the dark, fog-shrouded plaza, heading for the Banker's Heart. His ears felt like they had corks driven into them. His pinch-bruised nose was filling with mucus. The fog was so thick, he could hardly see a thing. He felt disoriented, cut off from reality.

Just then, he saw a robed man coming toward him out of the mist. His feet seemed to be floating an inch or two above the ground. He had a large head. Prominent eyebrows. A straight nose. A sma—

"Jesus Christ," Ded gasped as the man drew closer and the claims adjuster could see him distinctly. "It's Ickey Jerusalem!"

"What do you think?" the man asked in a voice that was more angelic than human. His small lips barely moved, if at all. His wide-set eyes were closed.

Ded attempted a few incoherent beginnings of an answer, looking into the fog, trying to figure out what to say.

And then, Ded's ears popped. He tentatively lowered his eyes back to the mystically serene countenance of Ickey Jerusalem. "Beulah?"

"You like it?" Her voice came from behind the face. "It's my costume for Tharmas's party tonight. We're supposed to go as the person we most admire."

Ded's pulse rate dropped to double figures. Beulah, her hair piled back out of sight, was wearing Jerusalem's death mask, painted to look real.

"It's ideal for you," Ded said. *After all, there aren't that many people who can wear a mask with closed eyes.* He examined the detailing on the eyebrows, painted in all likelihood by her chauffeur. "Aren't you afraid, though, it might offend someone?"

"Why?" Beulah asked.

"I mean, Jerusalem has been dead for only a week."

"But Ickey's not dead," Beulah objected sweetly. "He's merely left the mid-level of the subject and object to—"

"I know, I know," Ded interrupted. "To enter the highest level of God's consciousness where everyone sits around in airline toilet cubicles with their pants puddling at their ankles, their heads stuck in plastic bags, and their faces fixed in silent screams."

There was a long pause during which Ded regretted his testiness. Why couldn't he let Beulah know he was fascinated by her ideas?

"However you characterize Ickey's final transformation," Beulah proclaimed quietly from behind the plaster cast, "there is no way it could ever make wearing his likeness offensive." She moved the mask to the side and revealed her face, giving the figure the appearance of now having two heads, one male and one female. "Perhaps you could explain why you think it would."

Ded stood for some time, looking from the eternal serenity of the dead poet's face to the infinite innocence of Beulah's, and back again.

"I'm not sure I can," he had to admit. "I'm not sure I can."

Suddenly, a husky, masculine voice seemed to burst from the frozen-lipped death mask. "Miss Vala is still alive! Miss Vala is still alive! So, nobody's going to be offended by *my* costume."

From behind Beulah, Adam Ghostflea stepped sideways into view. He was wearing a strawberry-blond woman's wig, a billowing, cut-off peasant's blouse, and a low-slung, brown suede micro-skirt.

While there was no question whom Ghostflea most admired, his minimalist costume did nothing to lessen the impact of the exposed areas of his body—his cracked, ruddy-red skin; his He-Man legs, arms, and torso; his too-small, sloping-back head; his pointed, gold-tipped eye teeth; his scrawny red tongue wriggling from his mouth; and his bulging, burning, crossed eyes.

Still, Ded was not offended by Ghostflea's outfit. Having suffered from unattractiveness all of his life, the claims adjuster felt a deep empathy for the man. It wasn't the chauffeur's fault he looked as he did. Or that he adored an unattainable mistress. It was downright unfair.

CHAPTER 17

THE LIGHT FLICKERING FROM THE SIDE

Embedded in the grid pattern of streets imposed on San Francisco's hills, Jones Street ran up the back of Russian Hill, crossed Green Street at the crest, and headed straight down the front of Russian Hill, first crossing Union Street a block below, where the evening fog bank usually began, and then continuing across ten more parallel streets until it reached the edge of the Bay. The segment of Jones Street between Green and Union was one of the steepest in San Francisco, so steep that steps had been cut into the sidewalk.

Off the middle of the steep segment of Jones Street, running ninety degrees to the right, was a gently winding, concrete pathway called Macondray Lane. An ivy-covered archway marked its entrance. On the downhill side of the lane was a wall of small, three- and four-story townhouses and apartment buildings, one including the apartment belonging to Tharmas Luvah, Jerusalem's business manager. On the uphill side was a steep, rocky slope, overgrown with a riot of ferns and flowers, that harbored birds, squirrels, and even a few raccoons.

Although the lane provided adequate space for walking, it was much too narrow for a car.

Which may help explain Ded's astonishment when Adam Ghostflea drove the hearse into it.

Ghostflea's decision to turn into Macondray Lane may have had something to do with the speed at which the hearse had been traveling. A few moments before the turn, a serene Beulah and a terrified Ded were sitting in the back seat as the hearse raced up the back of Russian Hill at a speed far over the legal limit and came to Green Street at the crest. At that point, Jones Street dropped away so sharply down to Union Street that the hearse had, to the horror of the agog Ded, launched into space. As Ghostflea couldn't have seen anything before him but the hood and the sky, he must have concluded he had at last reached the edge of the earth.

Ded watched the chauffeur grip the steering wheel of the falling hearse while looking stoically from side to side, as if waiting for the infamous world-supporting stack of planet-sized turtles to come into view.

By the time the front of the hearse had dropped sufficiently for Ghostflea to realize the turtles were for another day, the vehicle had been accelerating at a rate of 32 feet per second per second for over three seconds and was just touching down opposite the entrance to the lane. At that point, it was either zip rightwards into the lane at 75 miles an hour, or after ten downhill, fog-bound blocks, fly off a pier at Fisherman's Wharf at 210. Ghostflea had reasonably chosen the lane.

A normal person would have recognized the hearse was not going to fit when the hood demolished the ivy-covered archway.

"Christ," Ded cried, slapping his palms onto his forehead.

Fifty feet later, driving with the downhill wheels on the pathway and the uphill wheels about four feet from horizontal amid the ferns and flowers, Ghostflea seemed to sense something was not right. Removing his foot from the gas and following up with much desperate stamping, Ghostflea was finally able to locate the brake pedal and bring the hearse to a stop, right before an open-mouthed, upright raccoon.

Once Ded had recovered enough to shakily open the hearse door, he helped Beulah out on the downhill side—quite sensible, given the topography, since their exit was not only assisted by gravity but also accomplishable without having to machete their way through a jungle.

Fortuitously, there were no other people in Macondray Lane. Who knows what they would have thought at the sight of a bewigged, mini-skirted, bug-eyed Ghostflea crawling out of the driver's window on the elevated side. The grating string of Anglo-Saxon epithets he was muttering was particularly unsettling. Finally emerging, scratched and rumpled, from the undergrowth near the front of the vehicle, he leapt up and delivered a flying kick to the grill—clearly breaking character in his attempted portrayal of the admired Miss Vala.

Beulah took Ded's arm. "Do you see the high-rise on Green Street?" she asked.

Ded peered up past the foliage to a twenty-story structure overlooking the lane, lit against the moonless night by the various lights of its apartments. "Yes," he answered.

"Bacon Urizen has the penthouse."

Ded focused on the top floor. Light was coming through the windows. A balcony ran the length of the apartment. He noted that although Urizen's building had fewer floors than the Bank of America tower, its location on top of Russian Hill provided the lawyer with a much higher view of the Bay than that of Urizen & Fallen.

৵

Ded, Beulah, and Ghostflea were buzzed into Tharmas Luvah's Macondray Lane building. They took the two flights of stairs to his floor. As they approached his apartment, they heard the sounds of the party. Ded rang the doorbell. Beulah adjusted Ickey Jerusalem's death mask.

Still concerned about the obvious bad taste of Beulah's costume,

Ded prepared for the inevitable shocked reaction of Jerusalem's business manager.

The door opened. Standing there with his arms open wide in greeting was a figure wearing a robe similar to Beulah's. The face, though, was of a much more widely admired man than even Ickey Jerusalem.

The false beard and the crown of thorns gave him away.

The figure beamed at the new arrivals. "Welcome to the house of the Lord," he said in a voice resonating through his nose.

Ded struggled for an appropriately polite response as the greeter's eyes moved to Beulah.

"Jesus Christ!" Jesus Christ cried in camp surprise, the crown of thorns slipping askew over an eyebrow. "How blasphemous can yuh get?!"

"Do you think so, Tharmas?" Beulah hesitated. She recognized the business manager's voice, but being blind, could not see what he was wearing.

"Oh, it's *yuh*, Beulah," Tharmas said, relieved. He readjusted his headpiece. "No. No. Your costume ain't blasphemous, dear. Not for yuh. After all, Ickey was without question the guy yuh most admired."

Tharmas Luvah removed his eyes from the disturbingly lifelike death mask and examined the body-built, bewigged, miniskirted figure next to Beulah. "Goodness gracious, Ghostflea. Who woulda thought the person yuh most admire is a tranny?"

Ghostflea's bug eyes flared up in anger. "Miss Vala is not a—"

"Don't worry, dear," Tharmas cut him off. "Your secret is safe with me. Although I'm not sure it'll be safe with anyone else who sees yuh tonight."

Having dispatched with the chauffeur, Tharmas focused on Ded's plain suit and tie. "Oh, what a great gag," he exclaimed, clapping. "Yuh came as yourself."

"Just conforming to the party invitation," Ded said in his defense.

Beulah felt for Ded's arm. "Tharmas, this is Ded Smith, the claims adjuster from Ickey's life insurance company."

"Pleased to meet yuh," Tharmas grinned broadly.

It was the first time Ded had ever shaken hands with someone dressed as Jesus. He was surprised to see the outfit included suede gloves.

Perhaps they cover his stigmata.

~

Tharmas's apartment had a large, natural-wood living room, the north wall of which consisted of a multitude of French doors that opened onto a huge, natural-wood deck overlooking the Bay—or more precisely, the evening fog blanket, the edge of which was lapping at the four-story buildings lining the north side of Union Street a half-block below. In the moonless night, the fog glowed eerily from the building, street, and marine-navigation lights buried underneath.

Not one of the party's guests, crowded throughout the living room and the deck, appeared to conform to the conventional managerial and financial types Ded had expected to find. Half looked like Madame Tussauds wax figures on their night off and the other half like escapees from Hieronymus Bosch's painting, *The Garden of Earthly Delights*.

One man (at least, that was Ded's best guess) came gliding by on roller skates with twenty yards of paisley silk wrapped around his torso and legs, several pounds of mascara on his eyes, a pair of antennae bouncing on his head, and on his swept-back arms, giant, flapping butterfly wings. As he curtsied gracefully to Ded, the claims adjuster noticed that, unusual for a butterfly, the man had a penis for a nose.

Needless to say, whom this man most admired was a complete and utter mystery.

Tharmas Luvah put his hand on Ded's back—in a rather overly familiar manner, Ded felt—and while Beulah and Ghostflea went to get refreshments, guided the life insurance investigator across the room.

"I'd like yuh to meet my date for the evening," Tharmas said, presenting an attractive young woman dressed as a plate of spaghetti.

The gigantic plate was fixed around her waist like the rings of

Saturn and piled high with white plastic tubing, on top of which had been poured several gallons of Bolognese sauce. In the middle, in front, resting on the ersatz spaghetti, were her two colossal naked breasts, painted to look like meatballs.

Tharmas gave Ded a knowing smile and flitted off.

To be frank, Ded did not have much practice in making small talk with women dressed as plates of spaghetti, especially ones with such enormous meatballs. He stood dumbly for some time, casting about for an opening line.

"You come here often?" he inquired at last.

The young woman looked at him vacantly, her mouth hanging open, a fleck of drool on her lower lip. She appeared to be on some kind of drug.

Ded tried again, pasting his lips into his cheeriest smile. "When did you first meet Tharmas Luvah?"

The woman showed a glimmer of response, looking hazily at the ceiling as though trying to remember. "About a year ago," she began haltingly. "I…" She hesitated. "No… No, it was yesterday."

"Yes, darn," Ded observed, "time certainly goes slowly when you're having fun."

The woman's face went blank.

Ded looked at her breasts. They seemed bored.

"Nice weather, isn't it?" Ded addressed her nipples.

"Hey!" The woman glared in a manner that would have been profoundly terrifying had she been dressed as something other than a dish of pasta. "Are you staring at my tits?"

"Good gracious, no," Ded replied. "I think they're staring at me."

This reply seemed to satisfy her. Leastwise, as far as Ded could tell. From that moment, apart from remaining upright, the woman did not register a single overt sign of life.

"Beulah says yuh'd like to ask me about Ickey," Tharmas oozed as he came up. "I know I shoulda returned the calls from your company, but something inside me wants to avoid dealing with his death. I've come around, though. As Ickey's friend and business manager, getting this resolved is more important than sticking my head in the sand. Or, for that matter, making the same old small talk at yet another party." He put his gloved hand on Ded's shoulder. "Would yuh like to come into my study?"

Ded grabbed a drink and a sandwich from Ghostflea, who had arrived with a piled-high platter. Leaving the cross-eyed "tranny" staring dumbfounded at the two giant globes of brown meat on the ersatz spaghetti, Ded let Tharmas usher him down a long hallway, far away from the strain of forced socializing.

CHAPTER 18

THE BODY TURNED AROUND

In Tharmas Luvah's natural-wood study, the curtains were drawn and the lights were low. Except for occasional, distant laughing or shrieking coming from the party, it was quiet. The room was a mess. Boxes, files, letters, and the detritus of paperwork were piled in every corner and on every surface. The business manager cleared the seats of two leather easy chairs in the corner, sat down in one, and directed Ded to sit in the other. They scooted the chairs to face each other.

In a beaten-brass frame up above Tharmas's seat was a drawing done in the same fine-line style as Ickey Jerusalem's Urizen picture over the fireplace in his Oakland Hills house. This one, rather than portraying God bifurcating reality, showed the full-frontal view of a nude, muscular young man, standing on one leg with his other leg extending back and to the side, his arms spread wide, palms out in exultation. His electrified, curly hair radiated outwards. Rays of light emanated from his head and torso. At the bottom of the picture, winging away from the viewer through the young man's legs, just below his miniscule cock and balls, was a giant bat. A plaque on the bottom of the frame read "Glad Day."

Ded recalled the couplet on the loose page from Jerusalem's pocket about the bat leaving the brain that won't believe. He examined the creature more closely. Odd. It had the wings of a bat, but the body of a moth.

Hanging above the picture, like an abstract Christmas tree, was a Lebanese Maronite crucifix, its multiple crossarms shortening as they approached the top.

Ded dropped his eyes and watched through his thick glasses as the Jesus-costumed Tharmas took from a pocket in his robe some cigarette papers and a small pouch, then began rolling a joint.

Behold, Ded couldn't help smirking, *the son of God.*

He looked back up at the light-radiating young man in the picture above Tharmas. *And who's he? The* Sun *of God?*

Tharmas licked the edge of the cigarette paper with his oversized, sensuous tongue, tucked the joint between his lips, lit the end, and took a long, deep drag. Holding the smoke in his lungs, he offered Ded the joint.

Ded demurred. Someone resolutely against Sicilian Illusions was likewise not open to the drug-induced kind. Or, at least, that was how Ded rationalized it. In fact, this was the first time anyone had offered him drugs, let alone while he was on the job, so he hadn't had the opportunity to formulate anything other than the safest response.

As the business manager took several more deep drags, Ded took a bite of his sandwich and tried to make out, underneath the robe, the clip-on beard, and the crown of thorns, the real Tharmas Luvah. Early thirties. Thin but muscular. Middle Eastern-looking. Curly black hair. Dark eyes. Sunken cheeks. Pointed goatee, the tip of which Ded could see peeking out from under the clip-on beard.

Who knows, Ded mused. *Perhaps much the way the real Jesus looked.*

Ded tried to picture the real Jesus walking through the Holy Land. Bringing the Word of God to man. Performing miracles with loaves and fish, and the odd cadaver. Traipsing across large bodies of water. Getting betrayed for thirty pieces of silver. Hanging in agony on the cross. Bleeding from his crown of thorns and the wound in his side. Fading like a dying sun. Voluntarily suffering a martyr's death to save all mankind from sin.

What would He have thought if He'd known that two thousand years later, He would be someone's idea of a good Halloween costume?

Ded washed his bite of sandwich down with his drink. On the other hand, what would Jesus have thought if He'd had even an inkling of the industry He was creating? Not just Maronites, but Roman Catholics, Greek Orthodoxes, Russian Orthodoxes, Nestorians, Coptics, Lutherans, Calvinists, Zwinglians, Presbyterians, Anglicans, Episcopalians, Methodists, Baptists, Pentecostals, Mormons, Swedenborgians, Moravians, Moonies, and more. All the thousands of branches, sects, and sub-sects of Christianity, each claiming in great seriousness to read something different into the Messiah's short, garbled, and—to Ded, at least—singularly unimpressive ministry.

Ded hadn't had much religious education. But he'd had, in any event, enough curiosity to sit down and read the four Gospels from beginning to end. After which he had come to the opinion they didn't make any sense. Once you cut through the magic tricks and hallucinations, all you're left with is an illiterate Jewish carpenter spouting a few ambiguous parables and half-baked *non sequiturs* to a motley collection of misfits, and then, "Up on the cross you go, boy," He's gone.

It just wasn't the way a well-organized Creator of the Universe ought to go about starting a religion. A real God, if He existed, would have come out of the sky with all trumpets blaring, and then and there laid down exactly what He wanted everyone to do. "You do this, this, and this, and it's eternity in the Elysian Fields. Or that, that, and that, and it's 'Hello, Beulah, North Dakota.'"

According to a pocketbook history of Christianity Ded had once read, the year before Jesus died, nine other men had declared themselves to be the Messiah and were summarily crucified on Calvary Hill for their pains.

In that light, it seemed to Ded that Pontius Pilate had most likely sentenced Jesus to death for being a bore.

The fact that of all the messiahs crucified during that year, it was Jesus who hit the jackpot and had a worldwide religion based on him had little to do, Ded was convinced, with the substance of Jesus's ministry and a lot to do with the salesmanship of his followers three hundred years later. Although they then made up less than five percent of the population of Rome, they were nonetheless able to edge out Mithraism, Manichaeism, and all the other offbeat religions vying for Emperor Constantine's ear by promising him life everlasting if he signed on the dotted line. Thanks to a loophole in the consumer protection laws concerning unverifiable promises, the Christians assumed the power of the State and from that took over much of the Western world.

Since the prisoners in the Cave so desperately needed the illusion of meaning, it was only natural to Ded that from time to time, someone arose to cast the necessary flickering shadows. The one and only qualification appeared to be an ability to cast them in so nebulous and mysterious a manner that anyone could read into them anything he wanted. Jesus clearly won the brass ring in His day. But He wasn't all that special.

Based on what Ded had seen in the last day-and-a-half, the prize could just as easily have gone to Ickey Jerusalem.

Tharmas stared at his joint, releasing his breath in a sigh as pleasure at last swept up through his body into his brain. Ded, seeing Tharmas's increasingly vacant look, became concerned if he waited any longer to ask his questions, it might be too late.

He leaned forward in his chair. "So, I take it, Tharmas, Jesus is the person you most admire?"

Tharmas, startled by Ded's voice, looked up, his consciousness taking in the question with an apparent two-second delay. As the second of those seconds expired, a beneficent, Christ-like smile surfaced. "Insofar as Jesus's teachings have removed any limits on who or what I can fuck, yeah, yeah, He is."

Ded sat there for a moment, unable to come up with a follow-up question, the answer to which wasn't going to open up a whole new area of Biblical interpretation he really didn't have time now to get into.

Tharmas could be joking. Or, given the Christian injunction to love thy neighbor as thyself, perhaps his statement was simply another example of the dangerous ambiguity inherent in even the most innocuous of Jesus's pronouncements.

"Women," Tharmas sighed, staring dreamily into the air. "Men… sheep… Great Danes… penguins… Chihuahuas… halibut…" With his free hand, he absently adjusted his crown of thorns. "Easy chairs…"

He stroked the armrest of Ded's chair and fell silent with a faraway, contented look, as though reliving some pleasurable experience that even someone with Ded's widened perspective would find hard to imagine.

"Uh, right," Ded said. "I think, yes, I would have to agree that, for you, as far as sexual intercourse goes, the limits have definitely been removed."

Tharmas, still locked in his reverie, did not respond. From the way he was gazing at Ded's armrest, it was plain that if he wasn't snapped out of it, Tharmas would soon provide an explicit demonstration of the unimaginable.

"Tharmas!" Ded barked.

The business manager blinked, seemingly unable to recall where he was. "Tharmas?" he repeated uncertainly. With his strong nasal twang, it came out sounding like Thomas, his real name according to Los.

"When did you first meet Jerusalem?" Ded asked, trying to hold the man's attention.

Tharmas perked up at the mention of the dead poet. "Eight years ago." He leaned conspiratorially. "Right after I sold my hippie paraphernalia business. It'd been a real money-spinner, but low-class thugs were replacing the middle-class kids. So, I was looking for the next thing. Ickey was in a similar position. He'd just been left a fortune and had taken a bus to North Beach to get away from the fog and think about his future as a poet. We sat next to each other at breakfast at Mama's on Washington Square. I gave him the pitch and he made me his business manager. The best decision he ever made."

"Why?"

"It was me who opened him up, yuh know." Tharmas put his gloved knuckles back-to-back and pulled something imaginary apart.

Unsure what the something was, Ded mimicked Tharmas's motions.

Tharmas sat back and nodded to confirm that, *yeah*, that was what he had done to Ickey. "Yuh shoulda seen him when I first met him. Terrorized by the desire to be a credit to his parents. Ground down from living in the fog belt with Brom and Rahab. Exhausted by his boring routine in the engraving shop. Locked up inside his 'shell of duty'—his words—to the point he'd quit writing poems. Well, I shattered that shell forever."

"How?"

"Convinced him to move to North Beach. Yeah, I introduced him to a life unrestrained by rules of convention, a life full of freedom, of joy. Exposed him to psychedelic hippies, radical lesbians, anti-war activists, ghetto rioters. Overwhelmed him with new experiences, new info, new people. Opened up his self so wide it disappeared, swallowed up, he told me, by the ability of his creative imagination to take in any thing, any time, any way, any where, no matter what."

Yep, Ded thought, *I can see why Ickey's father described Tharmas as Satan.*

The business manager nodded again. "If not for me, Ickey never woulda become the poet he was."

"Wasn't Beulah also instrumental in nurturing Jerusalem's poetic genius?" Ded asked, feeling defensive and faintly argumentative on her behalf.

"Ah, Beulah." Tharmas laid his head back on his chair, closing his eyes. "Beulah, the blind. Like a raw diamond buried beneath the earth. That's how Ickey described her." He took on a poet's posturing. "Clothed in a rugged covering but open all within… Holding in her hallowed center the heavens of bright eternity."

Then he slumped back into himself. "Whatever the hell that means."

Tharmas drew in more marijuana smoke and leisurely let it out. "What Ickey needed was an opening outward." He brought his head forward until his dark eyes were level with Ded's. "Something Beulah couldn't give him."

Ded looked away, making a production of finishing his sandwich. The image of Beulah as a buried diamond illuminated his mind. After swallowing the last bite, he asked, "So, Tharmas, do you often play practical jokes on Beulah?"

"What? I never play practical jokes. I think they're fuckin' stupid."

"So, the razor wire wasn't a joke?"

"Razor wire? Where?"

"Just joking." Ded swiftly exited the subject, having been unable to get a response that might lead somewhere.

Tharmas's eyes softened. "I introduced them, yuh know. He'd come over from Lambeth on one of his few visits, and I took him to dinner at Little Joe's, where he used to hang out. Afterwards, we walked to a nude wrestling place on Broadway for a drink. Beulah was there, dispatching opponents left and right. Ickey asked me who she was. I gave him her name. Told him how she'd lost her sight in Golden Gate Park after reading his poem on some LSD blotting paper." Tharmas sighed. "Naturally, Ickey had to take her in. As he took in everything I gave him." The business manager picked absently at a spot on the palm of his left glove. "All as fodder for his poems."

He raised his dark, challenging eyes to Ded. "I wasn't no poet. I didn't have Ickey's skill. But I think Ickey realized that in my own chaotic way, I was as creative as him."

"Was that before or after he took your accounts home to study?" Ded inquired, hoping to catch the business manager off-guard.

It took Tharmas a moment to understand the implication of Ded's question. When he did, his response was to burst out laughing. "I was Ickey's dealmaker—publishing, readings, investments, that kinda thing—not his bookkeeper."

"But didn't you remove his financial accounts from his house after you got back from the airport with Beulah?"

"Technically, they weren't Ickey's accounts. They're the accounts of the Urthon Spectre Trust. And they weren't the originals, just copies. I took them from Lambeth merely to give to Urizen. As he's the trustee, I thought he'd want them back, even though I assumed he woulda just passed them on to his co-founding partner who manages the trust's day-to-day accounting and other operations." Tharmas contemplated the burning reefer butt between his gloved fingers. "Milton Fallen." His face became serious. "Now, there's a really dangerous mind."

Tharmas took another draw on what was left of the joint. Ded could tell the business manager was beginning to drift on cannabis clouds, and soon he wouldn't be of much help.

"Why didn't you talk to Jerusalem during the flight?" Ded interjected, trying to keep Tharmas with him.

Tharmas raised an eyebrow. "After what he'd told me the day we arrived in New York?"

"What was that?"

"He said when we got back to San Francisco, he wouldn't need a business manager no more."

"He fired you?"

"More like the job was being fired from me."

Ded adjusted his glasses. "Did he give a reason?"

"No. He said I'd find out soon enough. And he was right. I did." Tharmas began morosely stroking the wiry filaments of his false beard with the leather-covered thumb of his joint-holding hand.

"Why wouldn't he need a business manager once he got back to San Francisco?"

Tharmas gave Ded a peculiar look. "He was committing suicide before we got there."

"Oh, yes." Ded had almost forgotten, his attention diverted by speculation on whether Jerusalem's perfunctory dismissal of the very business manager—who, at least in the manager's own eyes, had made Jerusalem such a success—would have made that manager angry enough to kill.

Tharmas took a final puff on the butt, tapped it out on his long tongue, and placed it back in his pouch. "If I'd paid just a little more attention, I coulda saved his life."

Ded reached into his inside jacket pocket and drew out his notepad. He leafed through the pages until he found the entry he wanted. "Can you tell me what you and Dr. Bromion Ulro talked about on the plane?"

"Brom," Tharmas began. Then he seemed to think better of it. "Nothing much. Each of us asked what the other was doing on the flight and gave a brief answer. I asked Brom how his family was getting along. He told me to go fuck myself."

"What did you say to that?"

"I told him I'd love to, but every time I'd tried it in the past, my dong was always pointing in the wrong direction."

"Was that the end of the conversation?"

"No. He said he was surprised there was a direction my dong didn't point."

Tharmas made a minimal gesture suggestive of throwing up his hands. "I decided it wasn't worth continuing our little chat."

"I take it Dr. Ulro doesn't like you."

"Let's just say the good doctor doesn't like to see convention flouted. Particularly where dong-pointing is concerned."

Ded skimmed his page of notes. "Dr. Ulro and Jerusalem had an argument on the Thursday before the flight to New York. Do you know what it was about?"

"An argument? No. But if there was one, it was likely another replay of the same old offense from years ago."

"You mean the cuckolding of Theo, Jerusalem's brother, by Brom?"

"Shit, no. Something much more interesting than that. The cuckolding of Brom by Ickey."

This was news. "Jerusalem had an affair with Rahab Oothoon?" Ded wrote "Rahab + Jerusalem!" and underlined it twice.

Tharmas nodded.

"How serious was it?" Ded asked, wondering if this could be the dark, secret love in the sick-rose poem.

"It began casually enough after Ickey moved into their house in the Sunset District. Rahab discovered he was still a virgin and couldn't resist the challenge. But it went further than she'd expected. Ickey turned out to be fantastic in bed. I figure Ickey was porking her fairly regularly the whole time he lived with them. Brom found out and hit the ceiling. In the end, though, Rahab went back to Brom."

This is what was missing from Beulah's telling of the story, Ded realized. *Jerusalem had an affair with Rahab. Which explains why Dr. Ulro hated Ickey, and also why Jerusalem's brother, Theo, Rahab's ex-husband, might have hated Ickey, too.*

"Tharmas, my home office has struck out with the doctor. Do you know anyone who could get me an appointment with him?"

"Nope. I don't think I know nobody nowhere on good terms with Brom. I mean, we're talking about a guy with all the charm of a dog fart. He might appear harmless from afar, but once yuh've been up close, it ain't an experience yuh'd want to repeat. I'll tell yuh what, though. Me and him belong to the Three Heavens Country Club in Marin. I haven't been for a couple months, but I think Brom still spends almost every weekend there. Maybe I can arrange to sneak yuh in. Say, around eleven tomorrow morning? I'd take yuh myself, but I'm supposed to see Beulah at her house in the East Bay."

"That would be great," Ded said, while he wondered what Tharmas could want from Beulah. *Is he going to try another practical joke? Or…?*

Ded felt a twinge of jealousy

The Halloween Jesus Christ, hunched over in concentration, began rolling himself another joint.

"Apart from the beard and the crown of thorns," Ded asked, "do you see any similarity between you and Jesus?"

Tharmas sealed the cigarette paper with his tongue. "Well, both of us are really into knowledge by immediate perception. It's what I do naturally, yuh know. And what I, after opening Ickey up to the world, taught him how to do."

"I don't remember anything in the Bible about Jesus being into something called 'knowledge by immediate perception.'"

Tharmas lit his fresh joint, took a deep hit, and let out the smoke. "Not in so many words. But that's how He taught."

"How He taught?"

Tharmas took another long drag. His speech was slowing now, and his movements were becoming even more languid. "Through parables."

Tharmas eased the smoke out of his lungs. His eyes were once again acquiring that faraway look. Ded stretched his lips. "Let me get this straight. By parables you mean stories, like Aesop's fables?"

"Y-e-a-h." Tharmas drew out the word as if luxuriating in the positive feel of his answer. "But with no one-line moral at the end."

"Why no moral?"

Tharmas gesticulated with his joint. "As Ickey said later, after he understood it all, trying to sum up a parable in a moral is like trying to explain the meaning of a poem." While the business manager spoke, his attention became increasingly wrapped up in the intensity of what he was quoting. "Yuh end up reducing a complex reality to a least-common-denominator generalization, which, though easy to put into your pocket and carry off, contains only part of that reality."

Tharmas nodded, as though to say to himself, *Yeah, that's right, that's it,* and took yet another strong drag through his phony beard.

"Could you give me an illustration?"

Tharmas exhaled through his down-curving nose. "I can give yuh two. Two separate parables, which Ickey used later to make the point."

Holding his joint between his index finger and his thumb, he raised the middle finger of the same gloved hand. "Parable One." He smacked his lips in exaggerated preparation. "Once upon a time, a tiny worm was born on the petals of a beautiful rose growing on top of a high garden wall." Tharmas held his smoldering joint as though it was a worm and touched the mouth-end down on the palm of his other hand.

Rose? Ded thought. *Worm?* The image of the two caterpillars on the front of Tharmas's VW bus came to mind.

"The worm, without a thought to what it was doing, began eating the petals of the rose." Tharmas moved the joint around his palm to represent the worm eating the rose, but it looked to Ded more like a miniature dirt bike on the International Glove Circuit.

"As it devoured the life of the rose, the worm grew larger and larger." The moving joint slowed as the gloved hand contorted with the ebbing of the rose's life force.

"Until, at last, the rose died. And the worm, no longer having nothing to cling to, fell down over the side of the wall." The gloved hand crumbled and the joint, still held between Tharmas's thumb and index finger, traced a slow arc to the planked floor. "Landing on the surface of a hot, dry, concrete parking lot." Bending over his knees, Tharmas sent the joint limping around the floor. "The worm crawled across the barren land, this way and that, but there wasn't no food, no water, only jagged pebbles and searing heat. The worm began to shrivel.

"Oh, where is my beautiful rose?" Tharmas lamented on behalf of the dying worm in a sort of oral, Stanislavski-method-acting interpretation of Betty Boop. "Oh, the delicious taste. The soft texture. The cool morning dew on its petals. Oh. Oh. Oh."

The joint rolled over on the floor and died. Not an Academy-Award-winning performance, but then, when your leading actor is a saliva-glued cylinder of paper stuffed with dried weed, your expectations mustn't start all that high.

Tharmas lifted his joint and found it had gone out. "Moral of the story?"

Ded thought about it. Even Aesop would have had difficulty with this one.

"Absence makes the heart grow fonder," Tharmas proclaimed.

Yeah, I guess so, Ded thought, although it seemed a long and involved way to make such an obvious point.

Tharmas relit his joint, took a drag, and then exhaled. "Parable Two. The same worm on the same rose. Only this time when it falls, bloated from the dead flower, it lands not in a parking lot but on the soft, moist, inviting carcass of a gigantic bat that moments before had become disoriented in the sun and crashed into the ground at the foot of the wall."

The joint bounced up and down on the floor. "Oh, boy!" Tharmas was Betty Boop again. "Dead bat!" The ecstatic joint buried its damp mouth-end in the imaginary carcass, while Tharmas, now the narrator, concluded, "And the worm spent the rest of its life feeding on the bat, never once thinking about the rose."

Tharmas held his joint up near his temple. "Moral of the story?"

Ded didn't even try.

Tharmas took a drag on the joint. "Out of sight, out of mind."

Tharmas sat back. Then, a moment later, seeming to remember the point, he sat forward again. "Did yuh notice anything about the two morals?"

"Yes," Ded said after a quick think. "Each contradicts the other.'"

"Right. And why's that?" Tharmas didn't wait for Ded's answer. "Because as Ickey said, each one-line moral is just a thin shadow of its parable's complex reality, a tiny part of the truth." Tharmas was back in his sermon-repeating mode, speaking with the vehemence of the converted. "Within the parables themselves, there ain't no contradiction. In one, out of sight *is* out of mind. In the other, the opposite."

Ded was not so easily convinced. "There's another possibility," he said. "Perhaps the reason the morals contradict each other is simply that they are not generalized enough. Refine the moral to 'You will miss what you used to have unless you find something better' and *voilà,* the contradiction disappears."

"Sure, that specific contradiction disappears," Tharmas agreed, his face convoluted with focus, "but then, so does most of the meaning of the moral. Plus, it don't completely solve the problem. Say the worm finds something better but still misses the rose out of homesickness, or habit, or general schmaltziness. What's your new moral then? 'Yuh'll miss what yuh used to have unless yuh don't miss what yuh used to have?' That's a moral that don't allow no contradictions, but only because it ain't conveying no meaning."

Tharmas held his joint up, preparatory to one final drag. "The only way to avoid contradictions *and* at the same time have full meaning is to ditch the moral and do as I do, gain knowledge of the world by immediate perception."

"So, you're saying you're the one responsible for Ickey's ability to unite his mind with the true reality through his poetry."

"Not in so many words. As I ain't got no proper education, I find it difficult to make heads or tails out of a lot of Ickey's poems. Sure, I've learned to repeat the key phrases, but that don't mean I understand them. And all that metaphysical stuff about God's shrunken consciousness reaching out with the creative imagination to unite with the true reality, it hurts my head. So, if Ickey followed my way of seeing the world, that wouldn't guarantee he'd ever see the true reality. But at least he'd no longer be heading off in the wrong direction, toward the abstractions of Hell, the abode of the upside-down Satan. And more important, when the true reality *did* arrive, he'd be facing the right way, towards the highest level of God's consciousness, able to gain knowledge of that reality by immediate perception, which, by automatically avoiding any analysis, would deny Satan any openings to smother the glimpse in abstractions."

Ded closed his eyes as he tried to abstract out the meaning from Tharmas's words. Was this what Ickey Jerusalem had meant when he told Beulah the thing itself is always more powerfully poetic than its symbol? Was this the reason Ded found Jesus Christ and Ickey Jerusalem so incomprehensible? Because—like Urizen, the upside-down Satan Incarnate, analyzing the white rose—Ded had been trying to understand their message in the wrong way, from the level of an abstract, explicit generalization, where only a small part of the reality was filtering through?

Ded opened his myopic eyes to find Tharmas waiting. "To understand what truly happened to Ickey Jerusalem last week, I've got to get inside his mind, find out what he was thinking. I've been trying to learn about his metaphysics in the hope I could deduce—"

There was a knock at the door. A man entered, elegantly attired from head to toe in a half-ton of peacock feathers and inflated condoms.

"Excuse me, Jesus," the man said, peering out through the forest of unnatural excrescences that seemed to have taken root on his face and body.

The man's eyes and his prim, if now muffled voice triggered in Ded a faint *déjà vu*.

"Excuse me, Jesus," the man repeated, "but your cross is ready."

Tharmas rose. The befeathered, becondomed man glanced nervously at Ded, turned, and hurried out.

"A cross?" Ded asked as he stood. "Carrying things a little far, aren't you?"

"Just down to the big Halloween parade on Polk Street,[5]" Tharmas replied cheerfully. "It's not that heavy. Particularly since I'll be dragging one end on the ground. Do it every year."

Tharmas walked to the door, stepped into the hallway, and then turned back to Ded. "Yuh ain't never going to deduce your way into

---

5 In 1979, two years after this scene, the Halloween parade was moved from Polk Street to the Castro district, which had become a major center of gay culture.

Ickey's mind. Despite what it says in most detective stories, real knowledge ain't by deduction, but by immediate perception." Tharmas drew himself up as though delivering the Sermon on the Mount. "Verily, I say unto thee: Christ addresses himself to the man, not his reason.

"Think about it," he smiled enigmatically, and then left.

ঌ

Alone, Ded thought about it. Trying to know someone by immediate perception sounded a lot easier to accomplish than its more sophisticated cousin, writing a poem to unite with the true reality. But even then, how was he going to gain such knowledge of someone who was dead? Whose only mortal remains were, at that moment, working their way through the lower intestines of some funeral attendees and Mount Tamalpais squirrels? What was Ded supposed to do, hang around selected toilets and trees, hoping to take in some passing number twos by immediate perception? Or, since a tiny part of those remains was surely moving through himself, ensure that the next time he sat down on the throne, he kept looking down between his legs, ready, at a split-second's notice, to take the plop in by immediate perception before it hit the water?

Despairing, Ded tucked his notepad in his inside jacket pocket. As he did so, he brushed Jerusalem's spiral notebook. Ded drew it out and opened it to the top page, the one containing the poem Jerusalem had supposedly written just before his death.

Perhaps I should read it again—not to break it down into its parts to abstract out its meaning, but rather, to read it as Jerusalem might have intended, as a perfect unity, as a totality, by immediate perception.

Feeling a bit foolish, Ded stared at the entire poem, attempting to take it all in at once.

After about a minute of perceiving little more than the relative fuzzy shapes of the two stanzas and the occasional punctuation mark or phrase that caught his eye, Ded decided, that, perfect unity or not, Jerusalem must have intended for his readers to at least be allowed to read the words one by one.

The key, he assumed, was to take in each word without analyzing it first—something he could not remember ever having done.

Taking a deep breath and switching his analytical powers to *off*, he began reading the poem, trying as best he could to directly absorb its meaning.

The Sick Rose
O Rose thou art sick.
The invisible worm,
That flies in the night
In the howling storm:
Has found out thy bed
Of crimson joy:
And ~~her~~his dark secret love
Does thy life destroy.

To Ded's surprise, as he finished the poem, he thought he could feel slightly beyond the limit of his consciousness (was it really there or was he fooling himself?) an undefined sense of what Jerusalem must have been thinking: a sense of unease, of betrayal. But by whom? Bromion Ulro? Tharmas Luvah? Bacon Urizen? Adam Ghostflea? Beulah Vala? Or even by Jerusalem himself?

Try as he might, Ded was unable to achieve any greater clarity. However, for the first time since encountering Jerusalem's metaphysics, he had a glimmer of comprehension.

Ded's leather-bound anthology of Jerusalem's poetry currently lay on the floor of the hearse's back seat. Maybe, if he sat down and read through the poems using Tharmas's technique, there was a chance he could grow the undefined feeling he had into complete understanding.

To be sure, the chance was slim. But given that the poems were the only direct link he had to Jerusalem's mind, it was worth a shot.

Slipping the poet's notebook back into his pocket, Ded stood up to leave Tharmas's office. As he faced the door, he recollected the man in the peacock feathers and condoms calling Tharmas to the cross.

The eyes and the voice, Ded realized. *No wonder they triggered* déjà vu. *It was the purser!*

CHAPTER 19

THE GLARE OF THE FLAMES

Ded and Beulah stood at the entrance to Macondray Lane, waving goodbye to Tharmas as he headed down Jones toward Union Street with a large, wooden cross hooked over his right shoulder. Given the steepness of Jones, Tharmas didn't need to drag the cross at all. In fact, from the way the business manager was soon skidding and fishtailing down the sidewalk, his main effort was put into trying to hold the cross back. Before he reached Union Street, where the evening fog bank began, he had broken into an unchristlike, sandals-flapping, downhill run in a frantic attempt to avoid being crushed.

Neither Beulah nor Ded had wanted to go to the parade. She was tired from a long, momentous day, and he, although curious about the spectacle, was also tired. More importantly, something in Beulah's manner encouraged him to stick with her, if he could.

"Interesting guy," Ded commented.

Beulah agreed with a blind nod as Tharmas shot across Union Street (where he should have turned left) and continued down the hill in the direction of the Bay, his plate-of-pasta date and the excrescences-sprouting purser bouncing after him, crying, "Whoa! Whoa! Whoa!" as they all disappeared into the fog.

The symbolism inherent in a cross pushing Jesus down the hill was something even a fundamentalist atheist like Ded could appreciate. The symbolism inherent in his two companions following behind, on the other hand, was, unquestionably, lost on all but the most devout Christians.

How fortunate it is for Christianity, Ded thought, *that the real Jesus Christ had to carry his cross only* uphill*—and without having to share the top billing with a set of Brobdingnagian boobs masquerading as meatballs and a five-and-a-half-foot-tall porcupine of peacock feathers and inflated condoms.*

"Damn," Ded muttered. He had forgotten to ask the business manager what he was doing with the flaming-red-haired prostitute at the funeral.

He made a mental note to ask next time he saw Tharmas—and equally, if not more importantly, to find out what the purser was doing at the party and whether it related to the coat the purser had hung in the closet.

Beulah finally took off Jerusalem's death mask. She shook out her hair. Then, Ded escorted her back into Macondray Lane. He could see Adam Ghostflea, dressed in his Beulah-Vala costume, standing under a streetlight by the hearse, which was still parked with its left wheels on the path and its right wheels four feet higher, hidden in the foliage covering the steep side of the hill.

"Let's hope," Ded said as he helped Beulah step over the demolished ivy-covered archway, "Ghostflea can back out in a less damaging—"

Before he could finish what he was saying, something whizzed past Ded's head and demolished a plant pot on the porch of a house to the left. A split second later came the muffled gun report and the sound of a near-simultaneous reloading mechanism.

"Bullet!" Ded cried and hauled Beulah uphill to the protection of a large tree above the foot of the fallen arch. He peeked around the tree.

He didn't see anything until his eyes reached Urizen's penthouse apartment. The light from its windows made a silhouette of an extremely large person, perhaps the lawyer, leaning over the railing. Ded couldn't see if the person had a rifle in his hand.

Schuupp! A bullet struck the center of the tree trunk about a foot from his head.

Ded drew back into the shadow of the trunk.

"What's happening?" Beulah asked in bewilderment.

"Somebody's shooting at us from Urizen's apartment building," he explained. "It's too dangerous to walk from here to the hearse." Ded looked at the standing, oblivious chauffeur. "Ghostflea! Hey!"

The chauffeur looked up, his skinny tongue slithering out of his fanged mouth.

Ded gestured with his arm. "Back the car up to here."

Ghostflea sucked his tongue in and nodded. Not wanting to fight his way up the steep slope through the ferns and flowers to get to the British-side driver's door, he decided to enter through the downhill passenger's side. He dropped into a squat and waddled on his haunches along the overhanging vehicle until he was beneath the left front passenger door. Reaching over his head, he grabbed hold of the door handle and leaned back, preparing to give it a hard tug.

Ded, wanting to say something, leaned out, inadvertently putting his forehead beyond the shelter of the tree. *Schuupp!* A bullet took a bite out of the trunk inches above his head.

He jumped back to safety and checked Beulah to make sure she was still protected.

Almost immediately, Ded heard the click of the hearse door opening. Taking care this time, he looked towards the hearse just as Ghostflea, losing his overhead support, spun onto his back as the edge of the fifty pounds of hinged-door metal he was gripping swung down upon him.

For a moment, the chauffeur lay on his back, his left hand and midsection pinned under the edge of the newly opened door, his naked legs and free right arm squirming in the air like those of an exotic, mud-red insect caught in a trap.

His performance failing to entice anyone to come to his aid, Ghostflea humphed and squeezed himself aftward from under the door edge. Once clear, he stood up, his head now inside the car, brushed himself off, straightened his Beulah-Vala wig, grabbed the steering wheel with his outstretched right hand, and clambered, with a lot of slipping and sliding, onto the side-sloping front passenger's seat, eventually bringing his feet up into the footwell. Taking a breath, he reached down with his left hand to pull the door up. Grunting and groaning, he got it halfway off the ground before losing his grip. The fifty pounds of metal swung back against the pavement with a whack. Ghostflea spat out something abusive.

"Good God, man," Ded moaned, shaking his hands hopelessly in front of his face, inadvertently putting them beyond the protection afforded by the tree from the uphill marksman. A bullet whizzed between his unprotected fingers.

After a few seconds of rest, the chauffeur tried again to lift the door. And then again. And then again, going through the same routine each time—except, that is, for his croaking profanity, which became increasingly elaborate and vituperative.

This went on for some time. Indeed, it probably would have gone on all night, had not a middle-aged woman in a bathrobe come out of the nearest house, growling about needing "to get some goddamn fucking sleep," squatted down, and used her shoulder to summarily push the door shut.

Sourly refusing to acknowledge the woman's assistance, or, for that matter, even glance in her direction, Ghostflea started the hearse and revved the engine. A moment later, the vehicle shot backwards in Beulah and Ded's general direction.

"Christ," Ded exclaimed, jumping back as the dead center of the hearse's rear bumper collided with the tree.

Schuupp! A bullet creased the Jones Street side of the tree, about waist high, burning a track along the back side of the life insurance investigator's now exposed belt.

Ded cupped his hands and called to Ghostflea. "Go forward and then back to here and stop." He pointed to the fallen archway.

Ghostflea drove forward and then backed up, once again into the tree.

Ded waved his arms wildly, pointing at the downhill side. "No! No! Here! Here!"

The third time was the charm. The chauffeur stopped the hearse so that the tree protected the passenger door. Ded opened it, ushered Beulah into the footwell, crawled in himself, and slammed the door shut.

"Let's get out of here," he ordered, with a protective arm around Beulah.

Ghostflea put the hearse in gear, stepped on the gas, and raced the vehicle not backwards toward Jones Street, but forward, returning into the lamp-lit Macondray Lane to the sounds of whizzing bullets, softened gun firings, reloading clicks, and lead smashing into brick. Strangely, none of the lead struck the hearse. It was as though the shooter had been so surprised by the sudden reappearance of the vehicle, he'd lost control of his gun.

"No, back it out," Ded yelled. "Back it out! Onto Jones Street!"

Which, when Ghostflea eventually got the hearse into reverse, was exactly what he did.

A few minutes later, the hearse turned off Jones Street onto Union and headed downtown. The vehicle was now shielded from Urizen's high-rise by a wall of four-story apartment buildings. Ded helped Beulah up onto the back seat, made sure she was okay, and then took his own seat. He was shaking. Beulah, as usual, didn't seem bothered at all.

Without asking, Ded grabbed the car phone and dialed O'Nadir at home. The inspector answered after the third ring with a gruff "Yeah?" A television program blared in the background.

"Sorry to bother you but I've got something urgent. A few minutes ago, on Macondray Lane, someone started shooting at Beulah Vala and me."

"Jesus. You think this is connected to the potshot at the funeral?"

"Yeah. This time, the shots looked like they came from the top of the big high-rise above the Lane. Where Bacon Urizen's penthouse is. I could see someone big leaning over his railing but couldn't tell if he had a gun."

"I'll get some beat cops to talk to Urizen, assuming he's there, and see if they can search his place for a weapon. Then, they can go to Macondray Lane, set up the crime scene tape, and station someone to let residents in and out."

"Everything took place on the Jones-Street-side half of the Lane. So, your forensics people only need to cover that area. Tell them to look for a bullethole about head high in the middle of the big tree near the fallen archway, on the side facing the high-rise. I heard one go in. Might still be identifiable."

"Got it. Where are you now?"

"With Beulah Vala. Her chauffeur is going to drop me off at my hotel."

"Any idea why Urizen would want to kill you or Miss Vala?"

"None whatsoever. I met with him earlier and he gave no hint he would do such a thing. By the way, since you and I last talked, I've uncovered more interesting info. But it's late, you're at home with your family, nothing's pressing, and frankly, I'm a little shattered. I'll ring you first thing in the morning and fill you in."

"Okay, look forward to your call," O'Nadir said. "Meanwhile, I hope you enjoy the rest of your evening with your very own PER-sonal assistant."

"I don't know wha—"

O'Nadir hung up with a salacious giggle.

Replacing the handset, Ded looked out the window as the hearse descended into the shroud of fog. He stared into the murkiness for some time.

Realizing there was nothing to see, he shifted his attention to Beulah, who, holding Jerusalem's death mask in her lap and wearing her dark glasses, was now reclining in her seat with her flowing, reddish-blond hair wreathing her lovely face, lost in another world, a secret, inner world to which Ded had only the palest hope of ever being admitted. What was going on in that interesting mind of hers?

Perhaps if?

Switching his analytical powers to *off*, as he had done earlier when reading Jerusalem's poem, he adjusted his high-powered spectacles, leaned toward Beulah, and willed himself to take her in by immediate perception.

Instantly, his efforts were rewarded with a menagerie of feelings welling up inside, butterfly-netted glimpses of the varied wonders of Beulah's inner world: Imaginative receptivity. Passive pleasure. Gently erotic imagery. Transient intimations of infinity and eternity not yet hammered into definite form.

Beulah, perhaps drawn by the magnetism of Ded's perceiving, rolled her head on the back of her seat and seemed to fix her face on his.

Ded drew back, unnerved by the sudden sense that she was now perceiving him in the same manner as he was perceiving her.

"Beulah," he said, concealing his emotions behind a façade of professionalism while repeating O'Nadir's last question to him, "Do you have any idea why Bacon Urizen would have wanted to kill you?"

Beulah rolled her head back and forth to indicate she did not.

"What about Tharmas Luvah?" Ded asked, thinking about the razor wire and the business manager's disparaging remarks about her.

She rolled her head again. "He's my oldest friend in San Francisco. As you know, he was with me in the rose garden when I beheld the Heavenly Host in the sky."

She pressed her head into the back of the seat, appearing to relive the warmth of the sunlight.

Ded shivered. "Why did Tharmas wait so long before telling Jerusalem you were blinded by his poem?"

"I don't know. I think he was afraid of the effect it might have had on Ickey. Ickey was already in a bad way. Being promoted as poet laureate by his business manager had set him up for attacks. Other poets started cold shouldering him. Critics, savaging his work. One in particular, an English professor at UCSF, made fun of his Anglicisms, old-fashioned phrasing, initial-capitalizing nouns, and eccentric spelling. Pointed out how he was violating all the rules of proper poetry. Labelled him a lightweight. Ickey was devastated. He lost his confidence. He started giving readings only when he was totally stoned and drunk. Fairly quickly, he developed writer's block. That's why he decided to move to the Oakland Hills—to get away. But that didn't solve anything. Divorcing himself from the world also divorced him from his sources of inspiration. His writer's block continued. As did his emotional turmoil. And the drinking and drugs. Fortunately, as I indicated earlier, his eventually learning about my being blinded by his poem, far from devastating him further, led to the inspiration for his parable of the sleeping God, and from that, to the writing of his epic poetry."

"I see why Tharmas would have been hesitant to tell Jerusalem one of his poems had caused someone to be blinded," Ded concurred, although he couldn't keep himself from considering what other reasons the business manager might have had to keep Beulah to himself. "Can you tell me if you and Tharmas were ever lovers?"

Beulah tilted her head back to Ded. "No. He tried, naturally. But there was something about him. We were so similar, so close, so made for each other, or perhaps from each other, I felt taking him as a lover would've been too much like masturbation."

Her use of such a coarse word caused Ded to cough reflexively—a close observer might even have said "guiltily."

"I hadn't thought of Tharmas as being that much like you."

"That's because he has so much more energy than me. An infinite pool of unconscious energy. While I merely simmer, Tharmas boils, exploding, as Ickey described it, through the lid of conventional behavior with the uncontrolled power of chaos." Beulah lifted her innocent eyebrows. "Ickey said he had never met anyone as free from the petty fetters of conformity, or as dedicated to pursuing a life full of joy, unrestrained by the chains of religion, society, or morality."

For a moment, Ded said nothing. The description of how free Tharmas was in his actions was making Ded feel cramped, limited, and inadequate, as though… well, to tell the truth, as though he was hopelessly lacking in a broadened perspective.

"I noticed Tharmas was wearing suede gloves tonight," Ded mentioned, trying to direct the conversation to that which he had been employed to investigate. He needed to determine who had left suede glove prints on Jerusalem's toilet as well as the cleaning bag.

"He wears them all the time," Beulah confirmed. "Protects him from doorknob germs."

"Doorknob germs?!" Ded thought back to the Disney goat pinching the interview room doorknob with a handkerchief. Tharmas must not have been wearing gloves that night.

"Oh, not just on doorknobs," Beulah replied, in case Ded thought Tharmas might be narrow-minded in his fears. "They're also on handshakes, used soap, toilet seats, that sort of thing."

"Gosh," Ded said, "it's nice to know there's at least one thing that can fetter the uncontrolled power of chaos."

"There are many things which can fetter the power of chaos," Beulah said, "but only a few which can incorporate it into form."

Ded sighed. It was like carrying on a conversation with Bartlett's Quotations. He debated whether to risk asking Beulah what she meant. He was tired of being constantly embarrassed by his lack of understanding.

"It took Ickey," Beulah explained helpfully in her junior instructress voice, "to incorporate Tharmas's power, his infinite pool of unconscious energy, into form."

Ded couldn't stop himself. "Through poetry?"

Beulah hummed in the affirmative.

Despite himself, Ded puffed up his chest. The right answer had come to him at once—by what could only be described as immediate perception. That Tharmas had intimated the same thing less than a half hour before was beside the point.

Ickey's poetry incorporated Tharmas's energy into form. Ded savored the idea.

"Jerusalem must have found it tough when he got to Tharmas's sex life," he observed.

Beulah acknowledged Ded's observation with a smile.

Ded shook his head. "I don't think I've ever encountered anything so formless. I'm amazed only his hands were covered in suede."

"He does tend to be indiscriminate."

"*Tend* to be?" Ded spluttered. While mildly disapproving of Tharmas's behavior, he couldn't help feeling a touch of envy—at least, at the business manager's ability with women.

In the three-and-a-half years of traveling since Harriet left him, the sad and lonely Ded had managed only one encounter: a female Sumo wrestler who for some unknown reason took a fancy to him as he sat in the audience of her Ginza show. Ded thought nothing of it until two o'clock in the morning, when he awoke in his hotel room to find himself being sexually molested by a beer belly in pigtails. Once he realized who it was, he figured, *Oh, well, I guess beggars can't be choosers,* and with a sigh, rolled the willing wrestler over onto her back and climbed on top to consummate the relationship—such as it was. Unfortunately, the lady's Sumo stomach was so massive, Ded's operative organ had been unable to reach.

Talk about feelings of inadequacy, Ded shuddered as he sat in the back seat of the hearse. *Jesus Christ!* He returned his gaze to Beulah, wondering if she could sense his failure to measure up. "What about Jerusalem? Was he promiscuous, too?"

A romantic glow came over Beulah. "No, Ickey felt only by focusing intensely on one woman could he obtain any depth of experience."

Ded thought this over. He couldn't really say that focusing intensely on the female Sumo wrestler had produced a deep experience. In fact, it hadn't even produced a shallow one.

He shuddered once again at the memory. He understood the lady had been frustrated. But pointing at his penis and laughing hysterically had been totally uncalled for.

"It's true," Ded said, forcing his attention away from his inadequacies and back to his interviewee, "the more someone spreads himself thin, the more he loses his depth of feeling."

After all, isn't that what the infinitely broadened perspective of my Grand Unifying Theory has done? Widened me so much that I no longer feel deeply about anything?

He looked into Beulah's pink, innocent face. "The only way to experience anything deeply," he said, a hint of sadness in his voice, "is to put your blinders on."

"Blinders?" Beulah asked. She must have detected Ded's change in mood because she reached over with her dainty hand and touched his forearm.

The whole right side of Ded's body went limp.

"Blinders to keep you from putting things in perspective," Ded elaborated, struggling to keep his perspective. "To keep you from expanding your field of view."

Beulah slid over on the seat and put her head on his shoulder. The feel of her flowing, reddish-blond hair electrified his cheek.

"You see, the wider your field of view," Ded labored on, "the lower your emotional reaction…"

Beulah's fingertips glided down the length of his forearm, coming to rest on his upturned palm.

"…until your field of view becomes so open that it encompasses everything," Ded staggered on, "and you see, at last, the meaningless black void…"

Beulah lifted her lips up to Ded until they were less than an inch from his.

"...and, and," Ded floundered, looking for the end of the sentence, "you lose any feelings you may ever have had."

As he gazed through his Coke-bottle bottom lenses into Beulah's dark glasses, the form of her body seemed to dissolve around the periphery of his vision, leaving nothing but her substance. When she finally spoke, it was with a tenderness that closed around him:

To see a World in a Grain of Sand
And a Heaven in a Wild Flower
Hold Infinity in the palm of your hand
And Eternity in an hour

Ded listened raptly, imagining he could see fairies of light breaking through her words, escaping to freedom.

"After God fell asleep," Beulah breathed delicately on his lips, "and space and time were separated, man could see infinity and eternity only as something which extended indefinitely... an amorphous black void without end... and so, without meaning, like twin Medusas turning everyone who looked upon them to stone."

Beulah stroked Ded's palm with a touch that was almost not there.

"True infinity and eternity," she whispered, "exist only in the here and now, when the imagination perceives... creates... loves." She spoke the last word extraordinarily slowly.

Ded did not try to analyze the logic of what she was saying. He knew she was addressing herself to the man, not his reason. He understood with the totality of his being—as Ickey Jerusalem must have understood. He could feel the bitterness, the loneliness, the pride, the fear, the envy, and the boredom draining from his body into the pool of her existence.

Gently, oh, so gently, he bent down, and kissed her on the mouth.

And for the most infinitesimal of eternities, he felt space and time unite.

ﻌ

Beulah's lips tasted like roses.

At least, what Ded assumed roses tasted like. His experience of flower-eating was fairly limited.

Ded's analytical mind clicked back on, lifting him out of the delightful Sicilian Illusion into which he had fallen. *To tell the truth,* he reasoned, *unless you're the type who likes to drink perfume, roses can't be all that delicious. Nowhere near as delicious as carrots.*

But then, it must be hard to feel romantic about a woman whose lips taste like carrots.

ﻌ

The hearse stopped, and so did the kiss. Beulah sat up straight and Ded looked beyond her, through the window. They had arrived at Lambeth, Ickey Jerusalem's house in the Oakland Hills.

"I thought we were going to my hotel," Ded protested feebly. "I may have to meet with Dr. Ulro tomorrow at his country club."

"Adam can take you. Although he's my lifeline to the world, I won't need him. I always spend Sundays working in my garden."

"Uh, okay, I guess," Ded gave in meekly.

"Now, come," Beulah murmured, drawing him out of the hearse. "For love is the door to the imaginative world."

"Yes, of course," Ded stammered as he grabbed his copy of Jerusalem's poems from the floor. "Although I can't say I've ever quite thought of it in that way before."

Meanwhile, he was thinking, *I mustn't forget to check for razor wire before going through the front door.*

ﻌ

Boy, was Beulah right about that imaginative world stuff.

Her inventive foreplay, perhaps as compensation for her blindness, was greater than anything Ded had ever dreamt possible.

And her sense of touch. *My God.*

Framed against the red, satin sheets of Beulah's bed, her body was as perfect as he had imagined. The monumental twin domes of her mothering breasts, calling him home to suckle. Her athletic hips, swiveling lasciviously on the fulcrum of her wasp waist. Her long, thin limbs, moving sinuously over every inch of his flesh.

And her eyes. *My God, her eyes.*

At first, when Beulah climbed into bed and removed her dark glasses, she kept her eyes demurely closed. But later, as foreplay drove her in a burst of passion to reach up, wrap her legs around Ded's waist, and pull him down into the center of her being, she had thrown her eyelids wide open, revealing at last what she had been hiding all this time.

Her eyes were hauntingly beautiful, almost holy. Perfect, immaculate whites surrounding sky-blue irises, in turn surrounding the infinite, black void of her pupils. And never fixed on one spot, but moving aimlessly, often in different directions. Hers were the eyes of a martyred saint being burned at the stake. Or, perhaps more appropriately, being impaled on it.

And then there was the way Beulah kept howling at the top of her lungs. Ded found it dismaying, really. Not merely because of what she was howling (Deeper! Deeper! Come on, Ickey, quit fooling around! Put it in deeper!), but also because her bedroom window was wide open. It was clear Ded was not the only one who could hear her. From the back yard, near Adam Ghostflea's cabin, came the sounds of Scofield bouncing off the wire-mesh walls of his cage and barking wildly.

What with Beulah's arms and legs roving randomly over Ded's body, her pelvis rotating in every possible direction around his manhood, her eyeballs meandering about independently in their sockets in front of his spectacles-befogged face, her erect nipples squashing gradually across his chest toward opposite points of the compass, and her deafening screams ricocheting off the walls to assault his ears from a hundred different angles—not to mention her hyperkinetic dog barking in the back yard like Cerberus at the gates of Hell—it was not surprising Ded soon became disoriented. Struggling in the midst of Beulah's passion, he started to lose track of soul and body. Of space and time. Of reason and emotion. Energy and form. Subject and object.

"What's happening?" he cried out at one point. "Am I on top? Or am I on the bottom? Am I inside of you? Or are you inside of me?"

To Ded, it seemed the two of them were no longer separate. They were uniting. They were merging. They were coming together.

Which, indeed, is exactly what they did.

৵

Ded lay on his back in the bed, studying the ceiling through his 800-diopter glasses. While it was too corny to say he had felt the earth move, he had certainly found himself placing the occasional bet on exactly which spot he was going to land.

Beulah was lying next to him on her side, her dark glasses back on, her long, strawberry-blond hair caressing his arm. She drew a lazy finger down and around his chest.

"The body," she recited, "is but the part of the soul that can be perceived by the five senses."

"As you can tell, that's the part I've sold to the devil."

Beulah laughed. "You can't sell to the devil that which is already his." She leaned over to kiss his chest.

"I can't?" Ded wondered what freakish attraction his body held for this wonderful woman. He thought back to Beulah's lunchtime description of Jerusalem's physique. Broad shoulders. Powerful arms. A sinewy chest. By comparison, Ded's body must have felt like an anorexic wearing a wetsuit made of flab.

He gazed down at his body. *I'm damn lucky her bizarre beliefs allow her to perceive so much more than is there.*

Still, her sleeping with him was so contrary to what one would have expected, she just had to have an ulterior motive. Perhaps, trying to turn his head, so he wouldn't notice the evidence tying her to Jerusalem's death.

"Beulah," Ded said, "can you tell me why you've chosen to seduce *me*, of all people?"

"It's very straightforward, really," she said breezily. "Up until this evening, Ickey was the only person I'd ever slept with. This morning, at the funeral, when I realized he'd left my life for good, I was overcome with a deep loneliness. I didn't want to spend tonight alone. Fortunately, there you were. A discreet stranger, who, in the short time we'd been together, I'd grown to trust. Even better, you were someone guaranteed to leave in a few days, after your job was done. Ideal, really. At least compared to my limited alternatives. The rough-skinned, fanged Adam Ghostflea? The overweight, infirm Bacon Urizen? The shallow, conformist, and married Brom Ulro? And the too-much-like-masturbation Tharmas Luvah?"

Goodness, Ded marveled, *am I really the second person Beulah has ever slept with?*

To Ded, Beulah's professed loneliness rang true. For hadn't she called him by Jerusalem's first name during their lovemaking (in the process, raising an issue regarding Ded's comparatively inadequate dimensions)? As for an ulterior motive, she was not pretending to be looking for a long-term relationship. And while she had tried to convert him to Jerusalem's point of view, she had not once tried to steer the investigation away from herself. Nor had she, in fact, expressed any interest whatsoever in what he or O'Nadir might be uncovering.

The most that could be said is that during the just-finished lovemaking, Ded had perhaps fooled himself into perceiving in Beulah so much more than there was. But then, it was possible the "much more" was actually there.

Ded was overcome with the desire to find out. "Tell me about yourself, Beulah. Where are you from? What was your family like? That sort of thing."

"Sure," she answered chirpily, as though happy he'd asked, and proceeded to give him the whole story.

Beulah, now 23½ years old, was born and raised in Orlando, Florida. When she was only seven, her father, who worked as Tarzan wrestling alligators at Jungle World, disappeared without a trace. Beulah's mother, suspecting a *ménage à trois* (Jane and Cheetah had disappeared at the same time), reacted by giving up on life, retiring to her clear-plastic-covered, La-Z-Boy recliner to watch TV, chain-smoke Virginia Slims, and grow increasingly blobulous, leaving Beulah to take on the responsibility for cooking, cleaning, and generally running the household. The seven-year-old fulfilled her new role with her customary cheerfulness and efficiency.

Beulah had worshipped her father, but she refused to allow his disappearance to disturb her equanimity. However, perhaps as a sign of what was going on inside, she started sucking her thumb, a practice that soon led to bucked teeth.

When she reached puberty, the comments from boys about her newly oversized breasts caused her such embarrassment that she took to wearing her mother's muumuus to hide her figure, which served only to create the mistaken impression she, too, was horrendously fat.

Beulah spent little time with others over the years—at first, due to the pressures of her household duties, and later, due to her fellow classmates rejecting her as a bucktoothed, ugly fat girl. Apart from her mother, her only real friend was an uncle in the military, stationed overseas, who occasionally spent his leave at the house, horsing around with her. When she was a sophomore in high school, her uncle, an Army Explosive Ordnance Disposal specialist, was killed trying to disarm a bomb planted by the Baader-Meinhof Gang at the U.S. Embassy in Bonn.

Thereafter, Beulah spent most of her free time caring for the vegetables and flowers in a little garden in her back yard.

Graduating from high school with a diligent B average, she went on to study landscape gardening at a local junior college while continuing to nurse her mother (who was now dying of lung cancer) and holding down a job tending the hydroponically grown marijuana plants in the non-chemical-products division of a drug-dealing operation founded by a local hippie. Beulah had such a green thumb, she doubled his production, earning his eternal gratitude.

After Mrs. Vala had breathed her last tortured breath, Beulah sold the TV and her mother's bed, clothes, and wedding ring, and used the proceeds to get braces for her misaligned teeth.

A year after that, upon graduating from junior college and having the final tightening of her braces, Beulah disposed of everything else in the house except a framed picture of her father, quit her job, and hitchhiked to the other side of the United States to take up a landscape gardening job in San Francisco's Golden Gate Park.

It was there—shortly after the removal of her braces by a Haight-Ashbury dentist and the replacement of her muumuu with a halter top and a micro-skirt—that she lost her eyesight staring at God.

❧

Ded now understood why Beulah earlier had described herself as unattractive. She'd gone blind so soon after becoming beautiful, she still saw herself as her high school classmates had seen her.

"And now," Beulah said. "How about you? Tell me how you became a life insurance investigator."

Goodness, Ded thought. Nobody had asked him about himself *ever*, other than Harriet. He realized how much he missed these post-coital exchanges of life stories.

So, he let her have it.

❧

In college, Ded had been a highly intelligent student of sociology. However, with little experience of the world, he lacked judgment, and so tended to follow any idea to its logical conclusion without being able to recognize when he had crossed into absurdity.

Unfortunately, he crossed into absurdity most often during exams. By graduation, his grades were so bad, going on to graduate school was out of the question—even in sociology. And so, instead, he took the first job he was offered: a claims adjuster in the Buffalo headquarters of the Olympian Life Insurance Company. Not as a traveling claims adjuster, because the company already had one, which they considered more than enough. Instead, he started as just another bureaucrat sitting at a desk, communicating with the outside world by checking boxes on triplicate forms.

Not all that different from sociology, he consoled himself.

Occasionally, Ded found outlets for his sociological interests, mainly in the form of tightly reasoned memos to his boss, which pointed out inappropriate, normative content in the language of the company's contracts of insurance.

"One need only look at the title 'Whole Life Policy' to see what I mean."

Then, three years later, shortly after Ded's wife, Harriet, announced her intention of filling their house with children, the company's sole traveling claims adjuster was sucked out of an airliner's emergency exit door at 35,000 feet and smashed, entirely coincidentally, through the roof of the Multi-Ethnic Folk Dancing Club.

As one would expect in a municipality known for its traditional social values, the other desk-bound Buffalo claims adjusters, already having houses filled with children, had no desire to travel outside the city. As a result, not long after yet another of Ded's chiding memos to his boss, this time on the logical contradictions in the phrase "death benefit," Ded was transferred into the traveling adjuster's vacancy, with his boss's ambiguous recommendation that he should best utilize his talents by following to the last detail the example of his predecessor.

~

Ded looked up from his soliloquy and noticed Beulah's eyes had glazed over.

He liked to hear himself talk as much as anybody else. But he had a broad enough perspective to know that when his monologue had caused the eyes of a blind person to glaze over, it was time to stop. He removed his glasses, slipped down in the bed, and set about regaining Beulah's interest by wagging his tongue in an entirely different manner.

A half hour later, following a further bout of extravagant intercourse, the two of them both lay back in another state of post-sex exhaustion.

"Are you married, Ded?"

"Kind of late to ask me that," the life insurance investigator joked. "But no, I'm not. I'm divorced."

"What happened?"

Ded launched into the whole dismal tale, a tale he had never told anyone.

~

When Ded took the job of traveling claims adjuster, he was a fairly provincial person, having never been beyond the Buffalo city limits. All at once, with no time to adjust, he became a full-scale business traveler, jetting off to New York City, Chicago, Boca Raton, San Francisco, London, Jerusalem, Bangkok, and wherever else the Olympian Life Insurance Company sent him.

Ded loved it. Something about being a modern-day road warrior—zooming around the world alone, armed with nothing but an under-the-seat case and a garment bag, living by his wits in continually changing locations—struck a chord, resonating with his very being in a drug-like rush of euphoria.

"I think you've become addicted to traveling," Harriet commented during one of his weekly pass-throughs to pick up a clean set of underwear and some freshly ironed shirts.

"Addicted, hell," he giggled. "I've overdosed."

His wife put down her iron. "I'm serious. It's not just because you're gone most of the time. Even when you're here, your mind seems to be somewhere else."

"It's North Dakota all over again," Ded explained. "You know, the guy who was unable to imagine himself anywhere other than where he was."

"Yes, I remember."

"Well, for me, it's the direct opposite. Look at my life now. Hopping from community to community. Cut off from my own. At each stop, reaching out over yet another subculture, bringing it back into my mind, analyzing it, organizing it, categorizing it, reducing it to simple pro-and-con symbols on a sheet of paper, all in preparation for that necessary, final judgment, and then flying off again before the bonds of community ensnare me. My perspective is growing by leaps and bounds. My mind—unable to keep track of where I was yesterday versus where I'm going tomorrow, or what time it is there versus what time it is here—is becoming like a fourth-dimensional version of one of those modern art… What do they call it? Cubist paintings? A jumble of perspectives so wide and all-encompassing, that in the opposite of the North Dakota hometown booster, I can imagine myself everywhere other than where I am."

Harriet pondered his words. "Well," she said in a small voice, resuming her ironing, "that certainly explains why we don't see you at Thursday night folk dancing anymore."

Ded put his hand on her shoulder, eager to make her understand, but not knowing how to do it without hurting her feelings.

She did not look up from her ironing. Only later did Ded realize what she had taken from the conversation: in her husband's eyes, she was now a frumpy small-town housewife, and thus, lest she lose him for good, she would have to throw off the shackles of her limited upbringing and become a modern woman.

The next time Ded arrived home, Harriet announced she had gone back on the pill and was firmly set on raising her status above that of a mere housewife.

Since Ded spent so much time away from home widening his perspective, he depended on his wife to be his anchor to the world.

Therefore, at the back of his mind, he was a little uneasy about any course of action which might set that anchor free. But believing strongly that everyone should try to widen his or her perspective, and motivated by his love for Harriet, over the next few years, he did what he could to support her in her attempts at self-improvement.

She felt ill-traveled? Ded spent his limited vacations rushing about in airplanes with her in order to confirm, as he saw it, famous places indeed looked like their photographs.

She felt educationally inadequate? He arranged for her to take courses at Erie Community College, despite her ignoring his advice that the three courses she chose—*Modern American Astrology, Math for Cashiers*, and *Home Cat Photography*—were unlikely to rocket her into the local intelligentsia.

She felt socially inferior? Despite Ded himself seeing all status seeking as meaningless, he borrowed heavily to fund her purchases of expensive china and silverware, so she could give her fish sticks and Pop-Tarts a touch of class.

She felt culturally inferior? On weekends when he was in town, he accompanied her to operas, poetry readings, and *avant-garde* plays he never would have attended on his own. "Here's a play you might like, dear," he would say, after looking through the Saturday listings. "Consists primarily of two naked people haranguing each other elliptically while doing unmentionable things to a beagle with a fork. I bet that's got a lot of critical acclaim."

She felt sexually inexperienced? He acquiesced to her having affairs.

Whatever she wanted, he went along with.

In their eighth year of marriage, she called him one morning from the bed of her current lover to say she was no longer going to put up with Ded oppressing her. She wanted to be free.

Ded had no choice but to accede to her wishes.

He gave her their home and began his life of perpetual business travel.

ᨒ

"Sad," Beulah commented. Unlike his exposition on life at the Olympian Life Insurance headquarters, the story of Ded's divorce had her fully engrossed. Pulsing with empathy she rolled over on top of him, and with incredible control of her private parts, enveloped him once more in her love.

If only, Ded thought as he was submerged in pleasure, *my dear Harriet, when setting out to become a modern woman, had forgotten about trying to move up into various higher status boxes and instead allowed herself to develop into a unique, fully integrated human being like Beulah.*

If there was anyone who was the absolute opposite of the small town in North Dakota bearing her name, it was the woman enveloping him now.

ᨒ

That was how it went for most of the night. Ded and Beulah would make fantastic love, she would ask him about himself, and he, thrilled that a woman was showing interest, would launch into a lengthy exposition until she either was overcome with empathy or had demonstrably lost interest—such as whenever he started going on about his Grand Unifying Theory and rather quickly her jaw was hanging slack or she was snoring loudly—and they would make love again.

As the night wore on, Ded's strength began to wane. Although he desired Beulah as much as when he had started, he was finding it increasingly difficult to gather together the necessary passion to unite with her yet another time.

The effect of their lovemaking on Beulah, on the other hand, was the opposite. With each coupling, she became stronger, wilder, more abandoned in her lust.

Things came to a head around four in the morning. As Ded valiantly rallied his body to enter Beulah one last time, she began reciting the most extraordinary of verses:

And if the Babe is born a Boy
He's given to a Woman Old
Who nails him down upon a rock
Catches his Shrieks in Cups of gold

She binds iron thorns around his head
She pierces both his hands & feet
She cuts his heart out at his side
To make it feel both cold & heat

Her fingers number every Nerve
Just as a Miser counts his gold
She lives upon his shrieks & cries
And She grows young as he grows old

Till he becomes a bleeding youth
And she becomes a Virgin bright
Then he rends up his Manacles
And binds her down for his delight

He plants himself in all her Nerves
Just as a Husbandman his mould
And She becomes his dwelling place
And Garden fruitful Seventy fold

If Beulah had stopped there, it might have been okay. But she didn't. Her recitation went on and on, relating how the woman continued to get younger and younger while the man got older and older, declining into an aged shadow, to be at last driven out of his house and condemned to wander the countryside, looking for young maidens to turn into old hags, so he might once again become a baby and get re-nailed to the rock.

If this jolly tale was intended to encourage Ded in his endeavors, it failed miserably. He already felt as though his body had aged seventy years since he'd climbed into bed. He did not need to hear any talk implying Beulah might throw him out of the house for nonperformance. His manhood began to wither.

Ded reached for his anthology of Jerusalem's poetry lying by the bed and began urgently leafing through the pages, searching for an antidote.

"Aha!" he cried when his eyes caught the dramatic words. He read them out, as loudly as he could:

> Bring me my Bow of burning gold:
> Bring me my Arrows of desire:
> Bring me my Spear: O clouds, unfold!
> Bring me my Chariot of fire!

The effect was phenomenal. Not just on his manhood, which hardened into a rhinoceros horn of lust and charged through Beulah's ecstatic southern gate. Not just on Beulah, who whooped "Hooray!" and began reciting full-blast yet another disturbing verse:

> The Grave shrieks with delight, & shakes
> Her hollow womb, & clasps the solid stem:
> Her bosom swells with wild desire:
> And milk & blood & glandous wine
> In rivers rush & shout & dance,
> On mountain, dale and plain.

(Good God, Ded thought.)

But there was also the effect of the chariot-of-fire poem on Scofield, who, plainly a poetry lover, ripped open the wire mesh of his cage with his teeth, and barking like there was no tomorrow, dashed into the yard and bounded in through the bedroom window.

Amazingly, although for the next five minutes Ded continued walloping Beulah with his pelvis, the dog did not bite him. The reason, no question about it, was that Scofield had become too involved in subjecting Ded's bare behind to frantic, sexual indignities of his own.

Although Ded had to admit that the repeated goosing by a dog's dick did add a new dimension to his stroke, he couldn't help wondering, as the last great orgasm came over him, whether he was, upon reflection, failing to keep the proper distance between himself and those he was supposed to be investigating.

PART FOUR

CHAPTER 20

FIRE BLINDNESS

Ded woke on his back, the sun streaming through the open window onto the bed. The window box held a profusion of flowers. Birds sang in the poplar trees. Beulah slept, her head resting on Ded's right shoulder. Scofield was also asleep, *his* head resting on Ded's *left* shoulder. The dog appeared to be smiling.

Gingerly, Ded moved his left arm down to reach the anthology of Jerusalem's poetry resting on his groin. Scofield stirred, vibrated his lower lip, twitched his back legs, and sighed. What the dog was dreaming about, Ded did not want to know.

Holding the anthology overhead, Ded brought his right hand up and began looking through the index under "Beulah." He was curious to read what the poet had written about his personal assistant. Ded picked out an entry and turned to a line at the end of stanza in a long poem:

> Such is a Vision of the lamentation of Beulah over Ololon

Ololon? Ded was puzzled. He hadn't run across that name before. A tender swelling rose in his chest at the thought of the sleeping Beulah lamenting anything. Looking for the cause of her possible unhappiness, his eyes moved up to the middle of the stanza:

> … the Rose still sleeps
> None dare to wake her…

Beulah stirred in her sleep, nuzzling against him. *A rose,* Ded agreed, not daring to wake her. *Yes. Yes.*

> … soon she bursts her crimson curtaind bed
> And comes forth in the majesty of beauty; every Flower,
> The Pink, the Jessamine, the Wall-flower, the Carnation,
> The Jonquil, the mild Lilly opes her heavens! every Tree,
> And Flower & Herb soon fill the air with an innumerable Dance
> Yet all in order sweet & lovely. Men are sick with love!

Ded lay the book on his chest. *Men are sick with love.* It was true. The rose wasn't sick—*he* was. He was sick. Sick with love. Such was the vision of his very own lamentation.

Ded twisted his head and kissed Beulah gently on the forehead.

There was a whimper on his left. It was Scofield. Still asleep on Ded's other shoulder, the dog was offering his forehead with a blissful, expectant expression.

Ded winced. *In your dreams, dog.*

Suddenly claustrophobic, Ded slid up to the bed's headboard, allowing the two extra heads on his shoulders to slip onto the pillows. Then, leaving Beulah and Scofield deep in slumber, he picked up the anthology of poems, got out of bed, put on his glasses, and walked to the bedroom window to take in the view.

Above was the sun in a cloudless, blue sky. Ahead, in the garden, surrounded by coils of razor wire, was every tree, flower, and herb described in the poem. And directly below the window, in the barren mud of the flowerbed, were two distinct shoe prints pointed houseward.

Was someone standing here last night? Ded gasped. *If so, who? The religious nut who wrote the death threat? Now looking to kill the person who had taken Jerusalem's place in Beulah's bed? Standing there, waiting for Beulah's vicious dog to leave so he could crawl in through the window and snuff out my life?*

Ded studied the prints. One heel had a cross and the other had a groove down its middle from the back to the front, giving it the unmistakable appearance of a backwards cloven hoof. Not unlike the hoof Ded would have expected to be made by the upside-down Satan.

Anxiety flooding into his mind, Ded quickly dressed, then left to find the kitchen for some coffee. On the way, he passed what appeared to be a closet-sized guest bedroom with a single, monastic window near the ceiling. The bedclothes were a mess, as though the guest had just left. *Has someone been staying here?* Ded wondered. *Were they here last night?*

At the back of the house, the kitchen was empty. Ded opened a cupboard to search for coffee. Inside, he found a bag of shelled walnuts, a big bar of cooking chocolate, a packet of Life Savers mints, and several jars of wild cherry jam and ground aniseed.

As a girl, Beulah cooked for her mother. There's no reason she couldn't still cook after losing her sight. Just has to be more careful, I guess.

As he closed the cupboard to open another, something at the end of the counter caught his eye: Adam Ghostflea's suede chauffeur gloves.

If the chauffeur had come into the kitchen at any point last night, he would have heard everything.

Ded picked up the gloves and stuffed them into his jacket pocket.

"Find what you wanted?"

Ded whirled about. Beulah was standing in the door, her bathrobe hanging open, her dark glasses on, stretching her arms sleepily over her head.

"I thought you were asleep," Ded stammered.

"I was, until someone gave me a tender kiss on the forehead."

"Must've been Scofield," Ded said with pretended gruffness.

Beulah smiled and floated in the direction of Ded's voice with her arms raised before her. She gave him a hug. "It was a nice kiss," she cooed.

Ded started to hug her back, but she pushed away. She went over to another cupboard and pulled down a coffee can.

"I couldn't help myself," he admitted. "You were so lovely, lying there in the morning light."

"You're sweet." Beulah waved him off as she fitted the filter on the drip.

Morning light, midnight darkness, Ded reflected. *It's all the same to her.*

He wanted to take her in his arms and hold her to him, but he didn't have the courage.

❧

A short time later, they sat down to their coffee and toast. He should have been starving after last night's efforts, yet Ded wasn't hungry at all. He remained immobile in his chair, watching Beulah eat, anxious questions running through his head. *Was I really just a convenient stop gap for her loneliness? The least worst of her rather limited potential sex partners? Expected now to quietly move on out of her life?*

After a few minutes of this, Ded couldn't bear it anymore. "Beulah, I don't want you to feel last night was just some kind of cheap fling. I like you a lot. And I want very much to see you again."

"Sure," Beulah declared cheerfully, "anytime."

Taken literally, her words could not have been more positive. But Ded was no longer reading merely literally. He wanted to hear from her something deeper, something richer, something that wasn't there.

He played with his knife. "Beulah?" She was devouring the last of her toast. "Beulah, do you like me?"

"Sure." She licked the crumbs from her lower lip. "You're an awfully nice guy."

"I mean—"

Beulah held up her hand. She drained her coffee, patted her mouth with her napkin, rose, and came around to Ded's side of the table. She took his head in her hands and spoke:

> He who bends to himself a joy
> Doth the winged life destroy
> But he who kisses the joy as it flies
> Lives in eternity's sunrise.

Then, she kissed him on the forehead. "I'm going back to sleep. Have a nice day."

∽

Ded sat alone for some time after Beulah left, contemplating the fathomless black pool of coffee in his cup.

Despite the impeccable logic of his Grand Unifying Theory, it wasn't working at the moment. In fact, he wondered if it had ever really worked. Although he had volubly claimed the protection of his ultra-widened perspective ever since the Miami-to-L.A. red-eye three years ago, he still suffered increasingly powerful attacks of emptiness, loneliness, claustrophobia, and despair.

One joyful, poetry-infused night with Beulah had been all it took to make those terrible feelings disappear completely.

And now, in a flash, they had reappeared with a vengeance.

Adam Ghostflea poked his undersized head around the kitchen door. "Miss Vala says she'll spend the day working in her garden. Scofield will protect her. I'm to take you to the hotel and any other place you want to go. Are you ready?"

Picking up his anthology, Ded nodded, stood, walked to the sink, and poured his coffee down the drain.

༄

In the back of the hearse, sealed inside his own subjective self, Ded brooded on his abstractions. *What I felt was only* a *chemically based bonding response*, he kept trying to assure himself. *Nothing more. It shouldn't be taken seriously. Beulah obviously isn't taking it seriously.*

༄

Behind the wheel, Adam Ghostflea was uttering guttural curses about Scofield having eaten his gloves.

The hearse was coasting down the rounded face of the Oakland Hills on a long, curving highway that was empty of traffic. Peering out at the limitless view, Ded couldn't help feeling like a tiny fly perched on the descending rim of a colossal, slowly turning cogwheel. Helpless. Passive. Uncomprehending.

Ded tried to get control of his emotions. *Beulah might have had an innocent reason for going to bed with me, but she's still a major suspect, if only because she was sitting next to Jerusalem on the plane. But what motive she could have had for murder isn't clear. She apparently didn't know about the life insurance policy, and even if she did, I don't see her giving up her life with Jerusalem just to get the $20-million payout. She worships Jerusalem's metaphysics. And except for the fact Jerusalem spent most of his time tied up in his poetry, he seemed to provide for her every need.*

Whatever reason for murder might exist, Ded made an oath to himself, *I can't let my feelings get in the way of uncovering it.*

At the bottom of the hill, the highway, settling onto stilts, headed straight across the flatness of Oakland toward the Bay, and then curved right to run parallel to the shore. Through the clear Sunday morning air, Ded could see San Francisco across the water, the hulking, dark Bank of America tower jutting out of its center.

Ded thought of Bacon Urizen, sitting up in his office alone, gazing out over the Bay. God in his Heaven.

Or was it his Hell?

The same place Ded was now.

Ded slid open the glass divider separating him from the driver. "Ghostflea, would you happen to know why Jerusalem wanted Urizen to amend the Urthon Spectre Trust?"

Ghostflea spun his pop-eyed head around to face Ded, his skinny, flaccid tongue lagging behind. "He did not want Mr. Urizen to be his executioner."

"What?"

"In New York, in the back seat of the limo, he told Mr. Urizen he would not be his executioner."

Ded brought his eyebrows together. "Are you sure Jerusalem didn't say 'executor'? Under the will?"

"Executor, yes. And trustee. Mr. Jerusalem told Mr. Urizen he would not be his trustee anymore."

"Why not?"

"Mr. Jerusalem didn't say,"

"Did he say who he wanted as a replacement?"

"Not when I was around."

"Interesting," Ded said, closing the glass divider. He may have felt like hell, but his curiosity was suddenly alive and kicking.

As Ded pulled his loose-leaf notepad out of his inside jacket pocket to record the info about the change of executor and trustee, the top corner of its cover got caught in the wire spiral across the top of Jerusalem's notebook in the same pocket, pulling the notebook out. Jerusalem's notebook hit the floor, disgorging a photograph formerly hidden between the last page and the bottom cover.

Ded picked up the photograph. It was a formal, waist-upwards picture of an attractive but prim young woman who was conservatively dressed and wearing a tie. On the back was printed "Gwendolyn Heva," and stamped below was the name and the New York City address of what Ded assumed to be the photographer's studio, "Poppins & Partners."

Jesus, Ded thought, *is this the "Gwen" Beulah might be meeting at the airport tomorrow? If so, why was her picture in Jerusalem's notebook? Was Jerusalem in on the meeting as well?*

He thought it through. *Or was Gwen's message on the answering machine yesterday not for Beulah, but for Jerusalem? From the photographer's studio address and her accent, Miss Heva appears to live in New York and thus when she left the message, could have been unaware the poet had died. Had Jerusalem met her at his book launch and invited her to join him two weeks later for an illicit island getaway?*

Ded made a mental note to find out what flight Miss Heva would be coming in on, and then, after slipping the photograph into a clear evidence bag, put the bag into his suit jacket pocket.

ஒ

At the hotel, Adam Ghostflea stayed downstairs to trade expletives with the doorman over who should pay for the large, porcelain flower planter shattered by the hearse. According to Ghostflea, the hotel was at fault for placing the planter where automobile traffic could hit it. According to the doorman, the hotel had been entirely reasonable in its assumption that automobile traffic would not reach the top of the entryway steps. Nor, for that matter, that a jacked-up hearse would come roaring through the double doors and into the lobby.

Ded checked for messages at reception. There was a note from Tharmas asking Ded to call as soon as possible, and a large envelope from Inspector O'Nadir along with several phone messages from him.

Ded took the elevator up to his floor and then let himself into his room. He needed a shower, a shave, and a change of clothes. But first, he had to talk to his ex-wife. He looked at his watch. It was midday in Buffalo.

Ded had not spoken to Harriet since he'd left town after she filed for the divorce. Why it was so urgent to talk to her now, he couldn't say. Perhaps it was a result of his having, the night before, discussed with someone for the first time how he'd lost her. Or perhaps due to how he was feeling now, after Beulah's brush-off at breakfast. Whatever it was, he felt an insatiable curiosity about how his ex-wife's life was going.

By this time, she's most likely become a fully liberated, modern woman. Ded prepared himself as he dialed her number. *Who knows what she'll find offensive?*

To Ded's surprise, Harriet seemed genuinely pleased to hear from him, and after asking how he was ("Adequate," he lied), she launched into a monologue on her life post-divorce.

To make a long story short: she had found Jesus. Ded was not aware Jesus had been lost, but for the sake of the conversation, did not disclose this to Harriet. Her discovery of the Son of God had a lot to do with a charismatic Pentecostal whom she had met at a bus stop on the day of the final decree, and whom, a few days later, she married. For the last three years, she had spent much of her time praying to Jesus (although for what, she didn't say). Not that she slavishly followed all the religious beliefs of her new husband. For instance, she refused to speak in tongues, a practice she described as "hopelessly low-class." She also had a differing textual interpretation of the Bible as to whether the Almighty had decreed that toilet seats should be left up or down.

First and foremost, despite her close relationship with the Son of God, her life was more than merely religion. At one point, she mentioned a daytime TV soap opera. At another, an oldies-but-goldies radio station. A little later, she actually launched into ramblingly enthusiastic praise for bowling and several other similarly useless pursuits.

From all this, Ded understood Harriet had returned to the Cave. Far from having become a fully liberated, modern woman like Beulah, she had refastened her blinders and chains, and become once again totally gripped by the shadows on the wall.

Which made the last thing she said to him right before the call ended all the more illogical.

"You know, Ded," she confided, "I don't think I've ever felt so totally free."

Ded stared at the hung-up phone. Curiously, despite her statement's illogicality, he understood it totally—not by conscious analysis but by immediate perception.

ꕥ

Ded called Tharmas, who picked up on the fourth ring.

"I'm loaning my car to someone today," Tharmas informed Ded. "So, I can't go over to see Beulah. If yuh've got a car, I can take yuh to the country club. Make it easier for me to sneak yuh in."

"Adam Ghostflea is chauffeuring me around today, so I can swing by in maybe an hour to pick you up."

"Fab. Even if the doctor ain't at the country club, it's still a nice thing to do on the Sabbath. I've been ringing Beulah to let her know I can't come, but she ain't picking up."

"I think she's outside tending her garden," Ded said.

After he hung up with Tharmas, Ded turned his attention to the envelope. Scrawled across the face was a note from O'Nadir: "Call after you've read this. I've John Doe'd it, but with your fantastic logical powers, you should be able to figure out who it is."

ꕥ

Sworn statement of John Doe, 7:33 a.m., Sunday, October 30th, 1977.

First, let me say that while I write this statement, I am still suffering from unwanted flashback hallucinations intruding into my thoughts. When they occur, I stop until they pass, and then continue writing. Therefore, hopefully, what you are reading here should be a true and fair account of what happened, unaffected by any remnants of the drugs in my system.

Last night, after returning from work, I made supper and then sat down to read the files of some cases I was working on. Around 8:30 p.m., reception rang to say they had a package for me. I told them to bring it up.

The package was a white, rectangular box, a little over a foot square and six inches high. It was bound with a red ribbon and had a white card stuck to the top with a note handwritten in block letters that read: "BELATED HAPPY BIRTHDAY, FROM ORC." The letters were squared off at the top and bottom, as though inscribed between two parallel rulers. A few letters overlapped in places. Only later did I realize this must have been a technique to camouflage the handwriting.

My birthday had, in fact, been Friday, St. Jude's day, although as is true every year, I held no celebrations, and no one sent me anything. To receive a gift was highly unusual, and a gift from Ickey Jerusalem's dead brother, I have to admit, was unique.

Sitting on the couch that faces the sliding doors to my balcony, I opened the box. Inside, I found a single red rose with its thornless stem stuck through a cork in a water-filled laboratory tube made of what appeared to be frosted glass. Next to the rose was a pocket cassette player affixed with a small square of paper. "PLAY ME FIRST" had been written in the same overlapping lettering as the note on the outside of the box.

Curious, I pressed "Play." A husky voice, either a woman imitating a man or a man imitating a woman (I couldn't be sure), gave instructions. "Take the tube in both your hands, contemplate the rose's beauty, and you shall find what's coming to you."

While a brief, bored humming came from the tape, I picked up the tube to look at the rose and felt a graininess on my fingertips. Then, the voice began reciting a poem.

> Howling & Wailing fly the souls from Urizen's strong hand
> For from the hand of Urizen the myriads fall like stars
> Into their own appointed places driven back by the winds
> The naked warriors rush together down to the sea shores
> They are become like wintry flocks like forests stripd of leaves
> The Kings & Princes of the Earth cry with a feeble cry
> Driven on the unproducing sands & on the hardend rocks

And all the while the flames of Orc follow the ventrous feet
Of Urizen & all the while the Trump of Tharmas sounds
Weeping & wailing fly the souls from Urizen's strong hand

As the poem was recited, I held the tube in my left hand, lifted my strengthening right hand before my face, its back side towards me, and soon saw howling and wailing souls flying from my palm. They went through the closed sliding doors without breaking the glass, then into the night, followed thereafter by a myriad of stars blasted from my hand by powerful winds. Then, naked Philistine warriors were rushing after them, as though running from the giant jawbone of an ass, streaming down to huddle like the trees of a stripped forest on a beach that had arisen between a levitating Macondray Lane and the downhill Union Street buildings, at the far edge of which lapped the infinite, glowing fog of the Bay. On the beach's unproducing sands and hardened rocks, I could discern kings and princes of the earth, crying feebly.

Back in my penthouse, the flaming body of Ickey Jerusalem, pretending to be his dead brother, Orc, rolled about my now-massive feet on the carpet, stimulating monstrous vents above my toes to disgorge millions of tons of clay, burying the Jerusalem/Orc, before running out and over the balcony, and smothering Macondray Lane and the beach beyond, stopping only at the fog's edge.

My left hand shot into the air, and releasing its grip, sent the tube-mounted rose in an arc up and backwards, crashing down to the floor behind the couch. From the shattered, tubular vase, the rose rapidly expanded to fill the back two thirds of my living room as the space itself morphed into an iridescent, brightly multicolored cave. While immense, soft, perfumed petals began to crowd against me, Tharmas Luvah exploded from the giant rose's center, blowing a massive foghorn of plenty, out of which there machine-gunned a stream of white roses that were instantly sliced by an infinite number of razors into spinning, angular pieces—themselves soon transformed into fluffy white lambs—before dissolving into yet more streaming, ghostly souls heading down to submerge themselves beneath the mud.

When the horn was at last empty, there boomed an irresistible command, more mighty than I had ever heard before, urging me, "Fly! Fly! Fly after the weeping-and-wailing, fleeing souls! Fly after them, Bacon Urizen, the all-powerful, conqueror of the universe!"

I turned to the sliding door through which all the ghostlike souls and whatever else had streamed. Feeling utterly invincible, I rose purposively to my feet and strode toward the balcony.

The next thing I knew, I was sitting on my bottom, on the carpet.

"Open the sliding glass door!" Tharmas's horn ordered. "Open the sliding door, Bacon Urizen! And fly after the dead souls! The universe is yours for the taking!"

I struggled again to my feet, slid open the door, and lumbered out with my arms outstretched like a dragon's wings, ready to fly, fly, fly!

But my glorious takeoff failed when my what-I-assumed-all-conquering belly hit the balcony's railing.

Gazing into the moonless night and then over the broad expanse of clay reaching to the lucent, earth-blanketing fog, I leaned onto the metal barrier. I began flapping my arms while pathetically whimpering, "Fly! Fly! Fly!"

To my frustration, the barrier was just high enough that I couldn't lever myself over it. Beating my winglike arms with an even greater determination, I strained to lift my bulk onto my tiptoes, eventually shifting sufficient of my abdominal weight onto the railing. Leaning forward, I began pivoting over, like a great, bloated seesaw, my head end accelerating downwards.

As I approached the point of no return, a great weight fell without warning onto the backs of my knees, driving my elevated legs down and the top half of my body up, flipping me off the railing and into the apartment, sprawling me onto the floor. There, I lay on my back, still weakly flapping my arms and moaning, "Fly! Fly! Come on, fly!"

Unbeknownst to me, someone with a spare key to my penthouse

had let themselves in, seen what I was attempting, and used their own body as a hard counterweight to save the day.

Once I was safe on the floor, the rescuer turned off the cassette player. Noticing the powder on the shards of the tube and on my fingers, they soaked my hands in bowls of water and toweled them clean to stop the drug from continuing to flow into my system. Then, gradually, they began talking me down, leaving only when, less than half an hour later, reception rang to say the police were coming up. The door was left open for them to enter.

I can state for the record I have no idea who could have sent me such a package.

While you will have to try to find out who, could you please do so in a manner that, to the extent possible, keeps everything quiet, at least, until you have solved the case? As the senior partner in trust and estates, the last thing I want is to find my name plastered over the tabloid press accompanied by wild speculations about my professional and personal life.

~

"Well, well, Dr. Deadly," O'Nadir said, smugly nudging the life insurance investigator through the phone. "Not in your room last night or this morning. Get a nice Halloween treat, did you?"

"Got something, all right." Ded played along, suppressing the uninvited emotions triggered by the inspector's inquiry. "Only, I'm not sure whether it was a treat or a trick."

O'Nadir sniggered lewdly, and then, masculine protocol having been properly observed, asked, "What do you think of the sworn statement?"

"I take it the officers who arrived were the beat cops you'd sent in response to the shots fired at Beulah and me last night?"

"Yep. One officer searched the apartment for firearms but found nothing. The other called an ambulance to take Urizen to the UCSF Hospital overdose unit. This morning, after Urizen had somewhat recovered, I got his statement."

"What was on the glass tube?"

"According to Urizen's blood tests and the forensics examination of the tube shards, pure LSD crystals. Very powerful stuff. One gram of LSD crystals can make ten thousand hits. A single thumbprint, maybe one hundred hits. Plus, by getting into the body through the skin, the hallucinogen goes straight into the bloodstream, bypassing digestion."

"Fingerprints?"

"Apart from Urizen's, there were glove prints on the box and the tape player. We'll have to wait until tomorrow for identification. That's the soonest our UC academic can look at them."

"Do we know who saved him?"

"Urizen won't say, other than it was a friend. Claims the identity is not relevant."

"Did reception see anyone coming up or down?"

"No. But apparently the apartment key can be used in the elevator to go to and from the penthouse and the garage without stopping in between. There's also a back stairway, so the friend could have come and gone with no one else seeing."

"The friend could be Cousin Ijim," Ded suggested. "One of the names I asked you to check against the economy class manifest when that airline's department opens on Monday. He's a giant of a man. Carried Urizen up the steps of the amphitheater after the funeral and also appeared unannounced at Urizen's office as my interview was ending yesterday."

"Given you've already encountered at the Holiday Inn the smallest female involved in the case, Deadly, maybe it would round out things if I left to you, as well, the largest male."

"Sure," Ded said. "Got any other leads?"

"Just the description of the person who delivered the package. The guard couldn't tell by voice or body movements whether it was a man or a woman, but from what he could see, the deliverer was covered from head to toe with a half-ton of peacock feathers and inflated condoms."

"Jesus," Ded exclaimed, "that's the purser. I saw him dressed up like that at Tharmas Luvah's Halloween party last night."

"May explain why he didn't reply to the message I left after you asked me to call him. I guess we'll have to do a full-court press to bring him in, and Tharmas Luvah besides. For all we know, he could have sent the purser to do the dirty deed."

"And killed Ickey Jerusalem, too," Ded added. "In New York, before the flight back, Jerusalem fired him as his business manager."

"That may fit with something else," the inspector said. "Do you remember you asked me to find out from Angel Cleaners who else in Jerusalem's party had cleaning done?"

"Yep."

"Well, they just got back to me. Only one other person. Tharmas Luvah."

"Hmm," Ded said. "If the purser was working with Tharmas to attack Urizen, it's possible he was also working with him to kill Jerusalem. It's a shot in the dark, but perhaps you can find out from the airline why those first-class stewardesses didn't show up the night of the flight."

"Will do."

"In the meantime, don't worry about talking to Tharmas Luvah. I'm picking him up to go to the Three Heavens Country Club in Marin, to meet Dr. Bromion Ulro. Ulro, you might be interested to know, hates Bacon Urizen—although the doctor appears to hate everybody on an equal opportunity basis. Hopefully, before the day's out, I'll have been able to ferret out some answers."

"Sounds good," O'Nadir said. "When you get to Macondray Lane to pick up Luvah, you'll see my forensic guys there looking for slugs from the shots last night. Tell Ben I said for him to let you through the crime scene tape."

"Great. I'll take the opportunity to give him the evidence I've gathered so far."

Ded then quickly outlined the new evidence he had gathered since they'd last talked as well as crucial information garnered in his latest encounters with Urizen, Luvah, and Beulah—leaving out his lovemaking with latter. *It having,* he decided, *absolutely no bearing on the case.*

⁂

After finishing his *toilette,* Ded went downstairs, climbed into the hearse, and told Ghostflea to head to Tharmas Luvah's apartment. "And, for Christ's sake," he added, "drive carefully."

Ghostflea took Ded's admonition to heart. Deliberately, without hitting a thing, he executed a perfect five-point turn in the hotel's lobby and drove the hearse back down the entryway stairs like an understated version of a monster truck.

At the bottom, continuing at a snail's pace, he inched out of the driveway and headed up Kearney Street and then diagonally up Columbus Avenue toward the Union Street turn for Russian Hill, eventually arriving at his destination without having created a single untoward automotive incident—apart, obviously, from the eleven-block-long tailback of madly honking drivers, who, Ghostflea complained irritably to Ded, had "no fucking appreciation whatsoever of careful driving."

When Ded looked back at the honking drivers, he couldn't help but wonder whether one of them was the marksman who had nearly killed him twice, or perhaps the religious nut, a cleaning bag in his hand, biding his time as he stalked his current prey.

The life insurance claims adjuster compressed his body lower on his seat to make himself less visible.

⁂

After handing Ben the bagged evidence with instructions to check for not only fingerprints but also foreign substances, Ded walked up Macondray Lane and collected Tharmas Luvah.

In the daylight, without his false beard and crown of thorns, the business manager no longer bore much resemblance to Jesus. Instead, with his posture now stooped, his curly black hair unkempt, his dark eyes sleepless and brooding, his sunken cheeks covered in stubble, and his goatee fully exposed and scraggly, he could just as easily have been mistaken for Judas Iscariot the morning after.

"Was that Robert N. William I saw at your party?" Ded asked as they walked to the hearse that was waiting, sensibly, at the entrance to the Lane. "Decked out in all the condoms and peacock feathers?"

"Yeah. The purser on the flight. Turns out we got a lot in common."

"Did you send him out last night to deliver a package?"

"Nope."

"Where's he now?"

"Driving my VW bus. After the parade ended in the usual tear gas and rioting, and my plate-of-spaghetti date went off with some visiting Swedes who wanted to play with her meatballs, Robert decided to spend the night at my place. This morning, about half an hour before yuh arrived, he said he needed to get to the airport in time for an important meeting, so I gave him the keys and pointed out where it was parked—as always, at the Taylor Street end of the lane, behind the illegal cones I use to keep everyone out when it ain't there."

"Did he say a meeting or a flight?"

Tharmas looked stricken. "I hope not a flight. I need my wheels back."

Ded ducked under the crime scene tape at the Jones Street end of the lane and rushed to the hearse, Tharmas Luvah following behind. Entering the vehicle, Ded grabbed the car phone and rang O'Nadir. "It's possible the purser is fleeing the state, if not the country. He's heading to the airport in Luvah's hippie VW bus. It's painted on the left side with a picture of a winged, goatlike devil above a winged blond woman, and on the right a naked man floating above a dead Eve wrapped in a snake. On the back, there's an androgynous contortionist running sideways while facing away, and on the front, two caterpillars on a leaf. Vanity license plate LUV TREE."

"I'm on it," O'Nadir replied. "I assume the purser's no longer wearing his Halloween costume?"

Ded read the descriptive hands of the now-concerned business manager, who had slid in next to him, close enough to have overheard O'Nadir's assumption. "No," Ded relayed. "A flight uniform he'd worn before coming to Tharmas Luvah's and dressing up for the party."

O'Nadir hung up to start sending out the all-points bulletin.

"Good God," Tharmas said. "What's Robert done?"

"Can't say. We'll know more when we find him."

Tharmas let out a long whistle of consternation. He then took from his pocket a plastic bag of weed and a pack of cigarette papers, and rolled a morning joint, using his Moray-eel tongue to seal the paper. "New batch. Been pre-cooked in an oven for an hour. Ready to blow your head off."

Ded smiled noncommittally, and after sliding the partition open, told Ghostflea to take them to Dr. Ulro's country club in Marin. "And you needn't drive as slowly as you did from the hotel," the life insurance investigator advised. "We'd like to get there before Thanksgiving."

As Ded closed the glass divider, Tharmas looked up from his completed doobie. "Now yuh got some idea why Ickey fired him."

"Fired him?" Ded asked. "When?"

"In New York, the morning before the red-eye back to San Francisco. Ghostflea had made a real mess of the limo rental. He'd never driven an American car with its steering wheel on the left side. Ickey gave him thirty days to find another job."

"But Jerusalem had employed him since moving to the East Bay. He would've noticed Ghostflea couldn't drive long before that. Even with the steering wheel on the English side."

Tharmas held the unlit joint in his hand. "That last couple of weeks before he died, Ickey seemed to be looking at things with new eyes. Firing Ghostflea. Firing me. I can't explain it. But his whole attitude seemed different."

"And he didn't tell you what was on his mind?"

"Nope. But it wasn't me who he spent most of his time talking to."

"Who was that, then?"

Tharmas pursed his lips, stretched them wide, and pursed them again. "His dead brother, Orc."

It was all Ded could do to keep his jaw from falling open.

"Over the last six months," Tharmas said, "the number of times I overheard Ickey jabbering with Orc increased exponentially. But in the final two weeks of his life, the mood of the conversations abruptly changed. Although I could hear only one side, Ickey seemed, for the first time, to be enjoying them."

I've got to find out what caused that change, Ded thought. *But how?*

"Say," Tharmas noted, smiling proudly, "I couldn't help but hear yuh describe my VW bus on the phone. Sounded like yuh've seen it."

"Yes. Up on Mount Tamalpais, before the funeral. Couldn't make head nor tails out of the pictures."

"Me, neither," Tharmas admitted, lighting his joint, taking a long drag. "Who in the hell are those two caterpillars? And that splayed *Furious Desires*, bi guy, pushing from behind? And the Great Red Dragon? And the blond woman, supposedly clothed in the sun. What sun? Where? And what's the story with the newest picture, the one with the wimpy Satan guy floating above the dead Eve wrapped in the snake? Even by immediate perception, I ain't got no clue."

He took another hit and then offered the joint to Ded. As before, the claims adjuster refused. This time, though, it was a considered decision. The business manager let the smoke out between his lips.

"To tell the truth, the only picture of his I ever really liked was 'Glad Day.' A naked young guy standing on his left leg with arms open wide, rays of light spiking out in all directions, and a giant bat flying through his legs. Really cool. Yuh probably saw it hanging in my office yesterday evening. Ickey painted it when he first moved to North Beach and kept it in his office there, and later, in the Oakland Hills. Strangely, the Friday before we left for New York, he suddenly showed up at Macondray Lane with the painting, saying he had no more use for it."

Ded entered a moment of intense cogitation, first recalling the same-sized dark rectangle he had seen on the slanted ceiling of Jerualem's home office and then trying to figure out why Jerusalem might have decided he no longer had any use for the painting.

As Ded surfaced at the end of the moment, still stumped, he found himself absently staring at the business manager's orangey-red, short-sleeved shirt (apparently the same one he'd been wearing at the funeral) and noticed for the first time, stitched on the left pocket, a bright, flaming-red Chinese dragon.

An image popped into Ded's mind.

"At the funeral yesterday, Tharmas, an extremely short woman stood next to you. With flaming-red hair. Who was she?"

Tharmas's eyes lit up. "Oh, her." He smiled mischievously. "I'll tell yuh what. Rather than waste your time giving yuh the dope, why don't I simply introduce yuh to her so yuh can get everything from the horse's mouth? Let me check later today to see if she's around."

"That would be great."

If the redhead was indeed the hyper-compact harlot, Ded figured he could handle that particular mouth with a little more dignity than he had at the Holiday Inn. Not being naked would help, as would his current depleted state, thanks to a night with Beulah.

Tharmas took another pull on his joint.

Ded choose his next words with care. "Tharmas, I don't want you to take this the wrong way, but you don't seem like someone a prudent person would select to handle his business affairs."

Tharmas smiled a serpent's smile. "Luckily, Ickey wasn't no prudent person. That's why he chose me. Because I ain't no prudent person, neither. When I make investment decisions, I never bother with things like 'balanced diversification,' 'numerical analysis,' or 'financial ratios.' My method is to simply take in the proposed investment by immediate perception. If I see an innumerable company of the Heavenly Host crying, 'Holy, Holy, Holy is the Lord God Almighty,' I invest. If not, I leave the money in T-bills."

"Have you been successful?"

Tharmas shrugged. "I think so."

"You don't know?"

"Yuh'd have to ask Bacon Urizen. As I said last night, he keeps the books."

"But didn't anybody ever say anything to you about how you were doing?"

"No. Well, about six months ago, Ickey did say he wanted me to stop making investments for a while. But I don't think it had anything to do with my performance."

"Who made investments after that?"

"No one, as far as I know. I don't think Urizen did. He's so conservative, he keeps all his own money in cash. The whole time I've been business manager, he brought me only one investment to look at, and that was one the trust wasn't allowed to invest in anyway, because of a no-relatives clause. Cousin Ijim's development on Ferrous Peak. Urizen was hot for it for himself because it required only a guarantee, no cash. I checked it out, but despite the name 'Golden Sun City,' the Heavenly Host just wasn't there."

Tharmas studied the palms of his gloved hands.

Ded gestured toward the gloves. "You always wear those?"

"Almost always."

"Why didn't you have them on when Inspector O'Nadir interviewed you at the airport?"

"I took them off when my fingerprints were taken, and then, as I was washing the ink off, the security officer hauled me out for the interview. I had to go back for my gloves."

Tharmas's goateed face was open and honest, like that of a used-car salesman on late-night TV, although one with a definite morning-after tinge.

Ded, having got through the major questions he'd had for Tharmas, relaxed a bit. "How was the parade?"

"Hard to say." Tharmas drew his palm back over his hair. "Something about dressing up like Jesus and dragging a cross down the street seems to bring the weirdos outta the woodwork."

Ded hummed his agreement.

"One guy thought he was Simon of Cyrene. Kept coming up and trying to carry my cross for me. Others kept begging me for a miracle. The same thing happens every year."

Tharmas, holding the reefer, touched Ded's arm with his free hand. "The spookiest are the beady-eyed spectators—and there are a lot of them—who come up and tell me in barely controlled voices that I'm gonna roast in hell for what I am doing. Invariably, a few threaten to stone me to death right there. Their faces were so filled with hatred."

"Must have been devout Christians," Ded ventured.

Tharmas parked his joint between his lips. "Two thousand years ago," he declared, the end of his joint flapping, "those same people woulda shouted their hatred at the real Jesus for ignoring Nobodaddy's righteous laws."

"*Nobodaddy*?" Ded tried to recollect where he had heard the name.

"The Old Testament God. A version of Satan."

"The Old Testament God was Satan?"

"Yep. Yuh know how Ickey said Satan tries to keep humanity from the creative imagination by reducing experiences to abstractions, like Aesop's one-line morals we discussed, and then by producing from those abstractions even more abstract theories, like the literary critics analyzing Ickey's poetry?"

Ded nodded.

"Well, Satan don't stop at abstract descriptions and theories. Whenever he can, he turns them into rules yuh gotta follow. In the case of the Old Testament, page after page of thou-shalt-not, righteous laws about worship, food, sex, clothing, family, everything—which, if yuh don't go along with, yuh get the jealous, vengeful, angry, all-powerful Nobodaddy on your case something fierce, but which, if yuh do go along with, means yuh have to bottle up your imagination or, even better, stamp it out altogether." Tharmas took the joint out of his mouth and nodded at Ded as though to say this was something he understood instinctively, passionately. "Ickey called Nobodaddy's righteous laws the 'Tree of Mystery.'"

Ded's ears perked up. *Dr. Bromion Ulro! "The fruit of the Tree of Mystery" was what Jerusalem accused the doctor of being during their argument. And Nobodaddy was Ulro's nickname in high school during his free-love-hating, fundamentalist phase. And… and… the initial for Nobodaddy is "N," the signature on the death threat.*

The business manager continued his thought. "Jesus, like Ickey, came into this world to free our creative imagination from the Tree of Mystery, but got crucified on it instead."

CHAPTER 21

THE DANCING SHADOW PUPPETS

Back when Ded was still married, he and Harriet were invited to a country club by a couple they had met. Not wanting to expose to ridicule his pale, skinny body upon which direct sunlight had not fallen for years, Ded conveniently left his swimming gear at home. He failed, however, to consider the resourcefulness of his wife. In short order, Ded found himself standing by the pool trying to look as suave as he could while wearing a pair of borrowed, oversized swimming briefs.

The problem with the briefs was not merely that the waist was so big that Ded had to cinch it up with his left hand, but also that the leg openings were so big that Ded had to hold them down with his right hand to keep his private parts from being exposed—an occurrence which, when it happened, tended to impede conversation.

When the club's activity director announced a "splash dance" competition in the shallow end of the pool, Ded tried to beat a hasty retreat to the changing rooms, but Harriet, not having noticed his difficulties, had other ideas. As he desperately held on to the top and the bottom of his swimming briefs, his spouse, chattering about how they had to learn to live life to the fullest, dragged him by the arm to the pool and pushed him in.

"Whoopee!" she cried as she jumped in after him.

Ded could have scrambled out and run away. All in all, however, he found he was better off in the pool. With his lower half underwater, there was considerably less danger his diminutive penis would be observed peeking from under his billowing briefs and waving at passersby.

Ded's understanding of the activity director's sketchy instructions on splash dancing was that the nine competing couples were supposed to stand in the waist-high water and when the music came on, dance about, making splashes. The winners would be the couple whose splashes were the biggest. Therefore, at the first sounds of the rock-and-roll beat, Ded closed his eyes, spread his knees to keep his trunks up, and began clomping from side to side, slapping the water with both arms like a windmill gone berserk.

About five seconds later, the music stopped.

"Hey, you," the activity director barked.

"Who? Me?" Ded said, shaking the droplets off his glasses.

"Yes, you," the activity director confirmed. "Out of the pool."

Ded took the steps out of the pool, holding his swimming trunks in the two-handed, protective position. He could not imagine how anyone could have been making bigger splashes than he.

Harriet followed him out, slapping first one and then the other side of her head to knock the water out of her ears.

The rock music started again. Ded glanced back towards the pool. The other couples were dancing, as plainly they had been doing before, in a smooth, elegant manner, making sophisticated, tiny splashes that were exquisitely synchronized with the beat.

Looking around the concrete apron, Ded was startled to see that although he was no longer participating in the contest, it was at him that most of the spectators were staring.

It did not take long before the couple who had invited them suggested that, given the circumstances, it was understandable if Ded and his uncomprehending wife wanted to leave.

ര

Ded doubted that country clubs had any kind of information exchange. Nonetheless, he thought it was interesting that from the splash-dancing experience many years earlier up to Tharmas's invitation, he had never once been invited to a country club anywhere in the world.

ര

Dr. Bromion Ulro's country club, the Three Heavens, was on the northeast edge of the Marin County neighborhood of Terra Linda. To enter the grounds the hearse drove between two gigantic Corinthian columns jointly supporting a classical pediment with bas reliefs of gamboling satyrs and nymphs. The vehicle then meandered down a long, tree-lined drive with golf course on either side for as far as the eye could see. After passing by innumerable, fenced-in tennis courts, it arrived at a parking lot in front of a massive, two-story, classical Roman building with rows of identical Corinthian columns on the outside.

The three occupants of the elevated hearse made their way gingerly down to the ground and began walking towards a ten-foot-square opening between two of the columns, below a Roman lettered sign, THE BATHS.

The desk clerk, dressed in a toga, watched them approach. Ded, in his thick glasses, wore an ill-fitting black suit, a pure-white shirt, a gray paisley tie, and policeman's black clodhoppers. The unshaven, uncombed, goateed Tharmas was dressed in his wrinkled orangey-red shirt with its stitched dragon over the pocket, excessively baggy, bell-bottomed pants, and holey tennis shoes. Ghostflea had gone casual in tight, mud-colored trousers covered with five-pointed, gold shooting stars and a drip-dry T-shirt sporting a picture of a large acorn surrounded by thorns. The combination of the chauffeur's crossed, bulging eyes and his reconnoitering, tube-like tongue gave the impression he was looking for a fresh bowl of blood to sip.

For some reason, the desk clerk did not appear to think they were members.

"Do you gentlemen need help?" he inquired in a tone indicating the answer was definitely *yes*.

Tharmas leaned on the counter. "Is Brom Ulro here today?"

"Are you a member, sir?"

Tharmas gave him a plastic card.

The desk clerk compared the card with the club member's list. A moment later, he looked up, his visage caught uncomfortably between disbelief and obsequiousness. He handed the card back to Tharmas. "I believe Dr. Ulro is out by the pool, Sir. He was there a half hour ago when I last looked."

Not splash dancing, I hope, Ded thought as he signed the proffered guest register.

❧

The Olympic-sized pool was beyond the back door of reception. A broad, mosaic, cobblestone apron surrounded it on four sides. Surrounding that was a continuous porch fronted with more two-story columns supporting its roof and backed with plastered walls through which were punched one-story-high barrel vaults heading back into the distance. The façade of each vault had a semicircular window filling the arch above and an enormous wooden door set in the brick screen below. Each door was labelled with something the members might need. Exercise. Recreation. Beauty. Steam. Sauna. Cool Dip. Massage. Lockers. Showers. Toilets. Cafe. Bar.

There were forty or fifty people in or around the pool. Protected from the wind by the ring of walls, most of them lay luxuriating in the sun, wrapped up in themselves, their bodies trim, tanned, and well-groomed. Even their bathing suits exuded style and taste.

Ded felt like a sociologist stumbling upon a new village. But, in this case, standing there in his thick glasses and off-the-rack suit, he couldn't help feeling the person who had no idea what was really going on was him.

Tharmas pointed out Dr. Ulro. Dressed in immaculate tennis whites, he was sitting at a circular, canopied table with two young boys. From thirty-feet away, the doctor looked exactly like a male model. The straight, blond hair. The perfect teeth. The even tan. The flat stomach. And the supercilious expression.

Ded followed Ghostflea and Tharmas as they threaded through the poolside tables.

As they got closer, Dr. Ulro began to look less like a male model and more like someone made up to look like a male model from thirty feet away. All the physical deceptions Ded had noticed in the airport interview room came into focus. The toupée. The false teeth. The tanning dye. The abdominal girdle's shape beneath his tennis shirt.

Only the supercilious expression was real.

The doctor, his large hands gripping his knees, was talking to someone in the water.

"Looks like she's in," Tharmas said ironically, gesturing toward the pool.

Ded looked as directed and saw that the "someone" in the pool was the short, roly-poly, orange-freckled prostitute from the Holiday Inn!

She was lounging on an inflated scarlet dragon that matched her flaming-red hair. Her fleshy contours overflowed from a tight, shiny purple, low-and-high-cut one-piece bathing suit. As at the Holiday Inn, she was covered with imitation gold, precious stones, and pearls set in a myriad of anklets, rings, bracelets, arm bands, necklaces, earrings, barrettes, and an elaborate sequined headband with the mysterious sunburst broach in the middle of the ancient script.

"Rahab!" Tharmas greeted the woman as he knelt at the pool's edge.

Jesus, Ded thought. *The prostitute is Rahab Oothoon? The current wife of Dr. Bromion Ulro? The hippie ex-wife of Theo Jerusalem? The fog-belt cohabitant who took Ickey Jerusalem's virginity?*

"Tharmas!" The woman flashed her dark eyes back with all the sexual innuendo she could muster. She extended her hand. Tharmas took it and kissed it. She extended her other hand. Tharmas took that and kissed it, too. Holding both her hands, Tharmas drew the floating dragon closer and kissed her a third time, on the lips, a long, lingering kiss of which Dr. Ulro discernibly did not approve.

Still holding Tharmas's gloved hands, Rahab rolled off the dragon and into the water. The sudden disparity between Tharmas's precarious balance and the weight of Rahab's ornaments almost pulled the business manager into the pool. Luckily, he had had the foresight to hook his leg around a water-volleyball post. Straining and grunting, he managed to hoist Rahab's plump form up onto the cobblestone apron. She stood there, glittering in the sunlight, then dried herself sensuously with a large towel, draped it around her shoulders, turned a bistro chair at the table so it faced the new guests, and clambered onto it like an overweight child. She pulled her tent-like towel around her, hiding most of her body except for her abbreviated legs dangling below the knee, unable to reach the ground. On the table to her left was a large Bloody Mary.

"Brom," Tharmas wheezed as he put a gloved palm on the doctor's shoulder. "We missed yuh at the funeral yesterday."

Dr. Ulro continued looking straight ahead, clearly unhappy about this invasion of his highly organized space. "I had a medical conference in L.A. the last few days," he said dismissively in his breakneck, squeaky, Central-Valley voice. "Got back this morning, too late for the funeral."

Ded sniffed. There was that antiseptic smell he'd detected during the airport interview—and somewhere else. *Where?*

Dr. Ulro gestured mechanically toward the two young boys sitting next to him before continuing in his ridiculously rapid falsetto. "I was hoping to spend quality time today with Hand and Hyle. They see so little of their father."

"Quite nice, then, ain't it," Tharmas said, still breathing heavily, "that they get to see so much of *yuh*."

The spotted butterball that was Dr. Ulro's wife suppressed a laugh.

Ded scrutinized the boys. They were twins. About eight-years old. Both grave, neat, and polite. With mussed up, curly hair, prominent eyebrows, wide-set eyes, straight noses, small mouths, and diminutive chins.

Dr. Ulro pointedly studied Tharmas's unshaven face and rumpled clothes. "Went a little overboard celebrating Ickey's death, did you?" He raised a manicured hand to stop Tharmas's reply. "You don't have to tell me what the funeral was like. I can guess."

He opened his tanned arms like the gates of a canal lock, composed his thoughts, and proceeded to give, in his castrato monotone, an impromptu funeral oration audible only to those around the table.

"Dear friends, Ickey Jerusalem, through the exercise of his creative imagination, has at last united subject and object, soul and body, emotion and reason, energy and form, hot and cold, left and right, Laurel and Hardy, and anything else which with your limited vision you might've thought were separate, and thereby metamorphosed himself into eternity and infinity, which, thanks to careful redefinition, have nothing at all to do with time and space, and so has become one with God. The fact he appears to be lying here before you on the ground, deader than a doornail, merely shows how much creative imagination you lack."

Not a bad summary, Ded reckoned.

"Right?" Dr. Ulro dared.

Tharmas did not answer.

"Who gave the oration?" Dr. Ulro demanded. "Miss Blind Obedience? Did she mention anything about radio waves from the sun controlling her brain? Maybe she read that letter from her psychotherapist that used to be pinned to the front of her blouse." He assumed the dry formality of psychotherapy and intoned, "To whom it may concern: Beulah Vala is sane and should not be placed in an institution, so long as she follows the treatment I have prescribed. Yours, Illegible."

Dr. Ulro's neatly trimmed eyebrows took on a mock quizzicality. "What was that treatment, anyway, Luvah? Do you remember? Something about spending quality time each day worshipping a giant broccoli?"

Again, Tharmas did not rise to the bait.

"Whatever it was, from the few times I've seen her since, I'd say she's given up worshiping broccoli in favor of the ritual sacrifice of pant zippers to Tyrannosaurus Rex, the seeing-eye dog." Dr. Ulro bent and made a show of looking under the table. "Poor ol' Scolie's still around, isn't he? Or—" he pointed at Adam Ghostflea "—has Sloppalong Catastrophe here finally run him over with the hearse?"

Ghostflea recoiled from the polished nail of the doctor's index finger.

"Or maybe," Dr. Ulro continued his relentless, high-register *tour d'offence*, "poor ol' Scolie, having had his canine beliefs thoroughly questioned by that bald-headed blimp, Bacon Urizen, has decided to enter a tantric monastery and spend the rest of his life performing a nirvana-like humping of the yoga master's naked lower leg."

The doctor turned to Ded, taking a special interest in his black suit and shoes. "Ah. The undertaker. The cop who interviewed me the night of Ickey's death."

"Ded Smith," Tharmas said. "He's not a cop. He's an insurance claims adjuster. He wants to talk to yuh about Ickey's death."

The doctor's chubby little wife looked up from her Bloody Mary as though noticing Ded for the first time. Glancing familiarly at his crotch, she flashed him a seductive, tomato-tinted smile.

Dr. Ulro's blue eyes had not moved from Ded. "Sorry, Mr. Smith, but I'm not interested in learning anything more about the subject."

"I thought perhaps I could learn a few things from you," Ded countered politely.

Dr. Ulro's eyes narrowed. "You'll have to stand in line, I'm afraid."

Tharmas patted his pockets as though looking for something that clearly wasn't there. "Fuck me, Ded," he apologized. "I brought yuh over here to meet the good doctor and forgot the fucking pieces of smoked glass to hold in front of your eyes."

"Now, now." Dr. Ulro gave his index finger a stylistic wag at the business manager. "Remember what the prophet, Ickey, wrote. 'Humility is only Doubt, And does the Sun & Moon blot out.' We wouldn't want that to happen, would we? I mean, think about it. No sun. No moon. It'd be most inconvenient. You'd have to carry a flashlight with you every time you went outside."

"Dr. Ulro," Ded tried, "my questions—"

"Mr. Smith," the doctor interrupted, "if I've said anything to insult you, please believe me, I meant it."

Ded held his tongue and looked to Tharmas for help.

Tharmas concentrated for a moment and then moved behind Rahab's chair. His face took on an earnest veneer as he prepared to boom forth. "Of course, Doctor, I gotta respect your opinion as a medical man. But I don't agree with your advice on the best way to have sex with a chicken."

The doctor blanched and glanced furtively at the nearby tables. Several people had turned their heads in his direction.

"It's obvious yuh've had much more experience at this than me, Doctor," the business manager continued in a clarion tone, "but arguing for holding the bird by its wings is plain wrong."

More heads turned, and some people began to whisper and point.

"You held a chicken by the wings, Daddy?" one twin asked. "Why did you do that?"

"Shhh!" Dr. Ulro silenced him. Rahab was snickering.

"See, if yuh instead hold the chicken by its *neck*, it'll be able to flap its wings." Tharmas moved his elbows up and down to demonstrate. "Guaranteed to produce, I think, a much more feel-good experience for your pecker."

Twenty to thirty eavesdroppers swiveled their heads in unison to see how the doctor would respond.

Dr. Ulro, stony-faced, did not reply.

"Sex between a man and a chicken is unnatural," an elderly lady at a nearby table said, clearly having given the matter considerable thought.

"That's exactly what the chicken said," Tharmas declared and began flitting under and over the neighboring tables, flapping his elbows and squawking like an excited hen.

Ded leaned over to Dr. Ulro. "Would you like to talk about Ickey Jerusalem's death?"

"Okay, okay," the doctor conceded defeat.

Ded signaled to Tharmas, who stopped dead.

"Chicken Tourette's syndrome," Tharmas said to the couple on whose table he had just been trying to lay an egg. "Tragedy of my life."

ර

After Dr. Ulro had sent Hand and Hyle off to play ping pong in the rec room, Ghostflea and Ded pulled up chairs and sat at the table. Tharmas squatted on the ground near Rahab's swinging feet.

"Doctor," Ded began, "you and Jerusalem grew up together in Eden, in the Central Valley?"

The Ken-doll-like Dr. Ulro surveyed the next-door tables to see if anyone had overheard Ded's question. Deciding no one had, he gave a minimalist nod in reply.

"Can you dig it, dude?" the wrapped-up Rahab interjected with a startling combination of lilting lewdness and hippie slang. "For my old man, Eden is a good place to be *from*."

Dr. Ulro gave no visible sign his wife had spoken.

"Am I correct, Doctor, you and Ickey Jerusalem were close while growing up?"

"No," Dr. Ulro replied in a calculated, if rapid and high-pitched, tone. "I mean, I knew him, obviously. But not well. Ickey tended to keep to himself. And then there was the difference in our backgrounds."

"Difference in backgrounds?"

"Ickey's parents were Okies."

"Oklahomans who fled the Dust Bowl during the Depression?"

Dr. Ulro indicated yes.

"In Eden," Rahab volunteered lasciviously, holding her Bloody Mary in her hands as she wiped a blood-red mustache from her upper lip with her tongue, "it was awfully important to be able to tell who was an Okie and who was not. Wasn't it, babe?"

Dr. Ulro did a slow burn.

"Amazing, just amazing," Tharmas effervesced. He bent down to kiss Rahab's brightly painted toenails with an excess of reverence. "'Her whole Life is an Epigram smack smooth & nobly pend,'" he said, plainly quoting one of Jerusalem's poems, "'Platted quite neat to catch applause with a sliding noose at the end.'"

Rahab covered the beginnings of a titter with a straight face.

Ded wanted to ask where the doctor's parents—the town slut and town drunk—ranked in Eden's pecking order, but saw nothing to be gained. Instead, he asked, "After Jerusalem graduated from Oxford, Doctor, he lived with you and Mrs. Ulro in San Francisco?"

"Yes, while I was going to medical school."

"Before we got hitched," his wife added, crunching a piece of cucumber she'd plucked from her drink.

Dr. Ulro shot her a frown at this unnecessary revelation and then, equally as fast, shifted his manikin face back into neutral. "Los asked me to take Ickey in. He was having a difficult time adjusting to the world."

The manikin face shifted again, this time into what the doctor probably considered a look of human concern. "Although we had never been close, I believed I could help."

"What was his problem?"

"He thought he wanted to be a poet." Dr. Ulro folded his gargantuan hands on his lap. "But he didn't have the first idea how to go about it. No plans, no schedule, no to-do list. Kept wandering the house, the back of his hand slapped to his forehead, crying, 'Woe! Woe! Woe!' and then running off to his room to scribble out a few pathetic poems. *Songs of Experience*, he called the collection." The doctor looked at his hands. "As though he'd had any experience worth singing about."

"He had some, for sure," Rahab said suggestively.

Ded turned to Rahab. "You liked Jerusalem's poetry?"

"I got off on the mucho creative way he united opposites," she said with a titillating wink. "The crazy way he could make time and space seem like one big high."

Dr. Ulro snorted. "Seem like an *eternity* and an *infinity*, you mean. Some of the stuff he wrote after he got past those dippy *Songs of Experience*. Good God. Endless, turgid, labyrinthine, stream-of-consciousness meanderings, as convoluted as they were unintelligible. I remember telling him if he was going to insist on poetry, he should learn to stick to the short stuff. The witty maxims. The rhyming couplets. The light verses. Those are the things that sell, not just to the women's magazines, but—if he was really good—to posterity. A hundred years after a poet dies, the only people who ever read his long poems are those who have to—college professors, literature students, literary critics. The real immortality is in the short pieces. Those are what people'll put in their anthologies, use in their everyday speech, and list in their dictionaries of quotations."

The doctor scrutinized the fingernails on his right hand. "Of course, I eventually pointed out that if he *really* wanted to do something useful, he should give up poetry altogether. Which, by the end of his three years with us, was precisely what he'd done. Under my tutelage, he soon came to see that being a poet wasn't a proper job. Not like working at an engraving shop. He began to get his life in order, and started thinking about making that contribution to society his father had always wanted him to make."

Dr. Ulro looked up from his fingernails, caught sight of Ghostflea's confused, bulging eyes staring at him, and briefly lost his train of thought. "But then," he continued after a few stutters, "that damned

Uncle Urthon died, and this gold-digging, former hippie-trinket-seller here—" Ulro jerked his thumb toward Tharmas. "—latched onto his prey, and Ickey fell into the degeneracy of North Beach."

Tharmas grinned triumphantly. "And he became an overnight success as a poet."

Dr. Ulro narrowed his venomous eyes at Tharmas. "Only because he'd followed my advice about switching to the short stuff."

"Right." Tharmas nodded sarcastically.

The doctor turned from Tharmas with a well-rehearsed look of exasperation. "Needless to say, Ickey couldn't leave well enough alone. After five years on North Beach, he suffered delusions of grandeur and retreated to the Oakland Hills, where, several months later, when his famous vision of the sleeping God was triggered by his encounter with Miss B.O., he reverted to the pretentious, unintelligible interminability he'd played around with in earlier days. Epic poems, he now called them. As though that excused their inability to communicate."

"So, you've read Ickey's recent poems?" Ded asked.

"A few. I got some drafts from Theo a few weeks ago."

"Jerusalem's brother?" Ded turned back to Rahab, who, still covered by the towel, had placed both of her feet up onto the chair seat to inspect the toenails Tharmas had kissed. "Weren't you and Theo married once?"

"Once."

"And yet Theo still is on good terms with your husband?"

"Why shouldn't he be?" Dr. Ulro broke in. "Theo threw Rahab out. A couple of months later, when I entered the University of San Francisco for my pre-med studies, I found her wandering around the Haight-Ashbury. I took her in. Cared for her."

"A sperm burglar had hit the jackpot," Rahab disclosed, dropping her eyes.

"Was it Theo's?" Ded pressed, remembering Beulah's intimation that Ulro and Rahab had been lovers from almost the day she'd married Theo.

Rahab caught Dr. Ulro's fleeting look. She looked down again without answering.

"Where's the child now?" Ded asked.

The doctor answered. "She was stillborn."

"Tirzah," Rahab murmured, having lowered her feet. She fiddled with a ruby teardrop necklace. "That was the name we gave her."

Both the doctor and his wife went silent.

Rahab's lower lip began to tremble. She slumped in her chair, weighed down with sadness—her red hair, her countenance, her shoulders, her breasts, her stomach, her baby-fat legs—all drooping so gloomily Ded found himself imagining, against his better judgment, the severely depressed expression on her towel-hidden nether regions.

"The baby was a goddamned mutant," Tharmas barged in with the explanation for Ded's benefit. "Had five heads." The business manager raised his balled right hand, nails facing his nose, and, one by one, straightened his fingers and then his thumb so as to emphasize the number. "It was considered fairly unusual at the time."

Ded looked askance at Tharmas.

"Rahab told me all about it," the business manager said. "What was even weirder was that each head had a different sense organ. One had the eyes. Another the nose. Another the ears. Another the tongue. Another the lips."

Ded searched the Ulros for confirmation, but they kept their faces averted.

"Since each sense organ was connected to a different brain," the business manager continued, now addressing several of the adjacent club members who were listening, aghast, "who knows what Tirzah woulda made of the outside world if she'd lived." He wrinkled his brow meditatively. "My guess is, since she had both a female and a male sex organ positioned just-right in her crotch, her interest in the outside world woulda been pretty limited."

❧

Dr. Ulro raised his azure eyes to Ded. "Do you think we could continue this inquiry somewhere else, Mr. Smith? Someplace where we might have more privacy?"

"How about a game of golf?" Tharmas suggested. "Ded and yuh could share a cart."

Dr. Ulro's eyes had not left Ded. "I think I'd prefer the clubhouse bar."

"Now that yuh mention it, so would I," Tharmas said. "I don't feel like doing my chicken imitation where I might get hit by golf balls."

The clubhouse bar immediately lost its attractiveness to Dr. Ulro. He unwillingly left with Tharmas and Ghostflea to arrange a tee-off time.

Oblivious to the doctor's nervous backward glances at his wife, Ded promised to join them after he talked to Rahab Oothoon.

CHAPTER 22

THE PUPPETEER

Ded switched chairs so he could face Mrs. Ulro head-on, steeling himself against a replay of the sexual aggressiveness she had exhibited at the Holiday Inn. After his night with Beulah, Ded wasn't interested in mere meretricious lust. What he had experienced with the blind personal assistant was a much more complete coupling, one that had generated in him an unusual, obligatory loyalty he did not want to breech, notwithstanding Beulah's breakfast indications of non-attachment and his own reaffirmed resolve to uncover any grudges against Jerusalem that Beulah might be hiding.

Ded could only hope that in a public place like the pool area, the doctor's wife would behave with some propriety.

"Mrs. Ulro," Ded began.

"Rahab," she said, fixing him with an insolent stare as she lay back in her chair and spread her thick legs, cracking open her terrycloth tent. "Oothoon."

Ded glanced around the pool. Because of the angle of view through the narrow opening in Rahab's towel tent, no one else could see.

"Those dudes won't help you," Rahab said. "They may look elegantly moral, sipping their chilled white wine, not letting a single swear word pass their lips. But in the evenings, at the get-togethers in their homes, they're the first to throw their keys into the swap bowl."

She cocked her head toward a thirty-something woman in a bathrobe being led into a private massage chamber by a young, bodybuilder masseur wearing nothing but a loin cloth.

Goodness, Ded realized. *The person who has no idea what is really going on in this village is definitely me.*

Rahab put her hands on her knees and stared hard at Ded.

Despite the claims adjuster's loyalty to Beulah, he could feel an enemy collaborator stirring in his boxer shorts. If Rahab now opened her kimono, Ded would likely encounter an embarrassing intra-body difference of opinion. Ded focused his mind's eye for a moment on Beulah, with her radiating glow of unformed wonder, of hope, of faith, and of mercy, his abiding suspicions of her momentarily suppressed. Regrounded, he popped his lids open and redoubled his concentration on the task at hand.

"Don't worry," Rahab said, before he could utter a word. "Only joshing. I'm not going to try to get off with you. Frankly, Daddy-o, you aren't my type."

Ded was relieved, and also a tad insulted. Was he so unattractive among those with eyesight that not even a sex-mad prostitute would sleep with him?

"At the Holiday Inn," he said, "why did you tell me to beware of the doctor?"

"Because, man, I think he bumped off Ickey."

"Why?" Ded asked, surprised at the first forthright accusation of murder he had heard so far.

"The Thursday before Ickey left for his publishing gig in New York, Brom came back from the office, totally flipped. 'That's it,' he told me, 'I won't take Ickey's flouting of convention anymore. He's a dead man.'"

Maybe, Ded mused, *Dr. Ulro* is *the author of the death threat. Not a nut for religion, but for following convention.* "Did he tell you what was said during the argument?"

"I asked, but Brom clammed up. The next thing I knew, he'd booked a round-trip flight to New York for the following week. When I asked why, he mumbled something about a medical conference. For the next few days before he left, he was so uptight, our communication was zilch."

"Did you warn Ickey?"

"For sure. But he didn't seem to fret about it much."

"After Ickey died, why didn't you go to the police with this information?"

"Tried last week. Rang and was put on hold. They wanted to know who I was. I didn't want to tell them. So, I sent an anonymous note. Then, there was a call at the house from your employer, trying to set up an appointment with my old man. They gave your name and where you'd be bunking Friday night. Since the cops were useless, I decided to approach you. I'd serviced some of the hotel staff before. So, it was easy to find your room number and book a room next to yours. I met my clients there and killed two birds with one stone."

Rahab luxuriantly stretched her compact arms, yawned, and then reached into a small, jeweled purse hanging among her many necklaces and pulled out a candy bar in a waterproof wrapper. She unwrapped the candy and gobbled it down. "I love scarfing sweets almost as much as experiencing the big O."

She unpinned her piled-high hair and let it fall sensuously over her body until it reached her waist. In Ded's boxers, the enemy collaborator, taking notice, raised its head.

"Did your husband know what you were doing at the Holiday Inn?"

"I didn't tell Brom specifically, but he knew generally what was going down."

"And… he was okay with that?"

"Sure. It all started at the stillbirth of Tirzah, the fruit of his having knocked me up when I was still Theo's old lady. In the delivery room,

Brom was so freaked out when he saw a five-headed hermaphrodite coming out of me, he swore off sex forever. Apart, that is, from his regularly beating his meat. When I pointed out I still had needs requiring the participation of other parties, his possessive side popped up big-time and made it clear free love was not an option. I told him it was no problem. I'd do the dirty deed only with men who'd pay the going rate."

"Are you saying your highly conventional husband agreed to you becoming a prostitute?"

"It took some headbanging, but in the end, he came around. My pitch played to his rule-bound way of thinking, by moving everything into the proper black-and-white boxes. If I'm being paid for it, how could it be 'free' love? It's merely a business transaction, and in the business transaction box, no love is involved."

"I see," Ded said, impressed by the logic.

"On top of that, I promised to turn over any bread I earned. That way, he could sit not in the box marked 'cuckold' but in a much more complimentary box entitled 'all-conquering pimp dominating his very-own degraded whore.'"

Ded looked at Rahab with entirely new eyes. There was much more to this woman than the mere selling of her body.

"After I stated my position, I hung tough, didn't concede a thing, and let his doctor-like emotional need for quick closure push him my way. To get him over the hump, I agreed my tricks would never include our acquaintances. That way, everyone we knew would think our marriage was as conventional as any other—something much more important to my old man than whether our marriage actually *is* conventional. And as a final sweetener, I offered him the chance, whenever he wanted, to wax his carrot outside any room I happened to be grooving in—something he said he'd done earlier in Eden when his mother was performing her recognized town role."

Yes, Ded had to admit. *This is one impressive lady, living her life on her own, unconventional terms.*

"Between us, the combination of voyeurism and playing the pimp role is what's kept Brom from running off with someone more conventional. No goody-two-shoes can give him that combination."

"Why didn't you just walk away for the freedom to have sex with whomever you wanted?"

"The deal with Brom was great for me. In return for somewhat reining in my sexual appetites, I kept a dependable, soon-to-be-rich doctor who would take care of me without, at that point, my having to tie the knot. Plus, as you might imagine, getting paid by strangers for bonking has, over the years, added a certain spice to my life."

"So, you've kept to the agreement?"

"Yes. Unlike the plastic hypocrites here at Three Heavens, I've avoided sleeping with acquaintances. The ironic thing is none of them would've cared about my sleeping around. But my old man just didn't cotton on. Having moved here from the conservative Eden, he got it in his social climber's head that the Marin County types are the same. He has made so many self-satisfied pronouncements on the subject, none of our acquaintances have ever bothered to straighten him out."

"But what about when Jerusalem was living with you and your husband? Didn't your affair with him violate the payment-only, non-acquaintance clause?"

"Sure. But I couldn't help myself."

"How did Dr. Ulro respond when he found out?"

"Brom freaked out big-time. Called Ickey an immoral ingrate for seducing me, although it was me who'd come on to Ickey. Brom bitched about everything he'd done for Ickey. He'd housed him. Encouraged his employment as an engraver. Advised him on life choices. Eventually, Brom worked himself into such a frenzy, he got out his father's old army gun and took a shot at Ickey. Luckily, he missed completely."

"Does Dr. Ulro still have the gun?"

"No. He threw it away as part of the deal."

"What deal?"

"To save Ickey's life, I agreed to put the kibosh on the charitable side-banging and get hitched to Brom. Since Brom was getting good grease from Los for Ickey to crash with us, he allowed Ickey to stay. To make sure my old man would play it straight after that, I dug the bullet out of the couch and put it on prominent display as a righteous reminder to him of how close he'd come to ending up in the slammer."

Rahab sucked in her lips. "To tell the truth, saving Ickey's life wasn't the only reason I brought down the curtain on our hanky-panky. When Ickey moved in, I was blown away by his poetry. Once I got to know him, though, I could see a poet and his poetry are not at all the same bag. Apart from looking like a hunk and being a natural in bed, he was a drag to live with. Flakey, gnarly, hassling, sometimes on a downer, sometimes unglued, flipping his wig over the smallest stuff, sometimes strung out on this thing or that, and at other times, a complete pantywaist when it came to living life. Brom, on the other hand, set in his rules and his boxes, was the exact opposite. Stable. Solid. Unchanging. Dependable. Standing against the chaos of life. Qualities I soon realized were what I wanted for me, and more importantly, for my unborn sprogs."

"You were pregnant *again*?"

Rahab put her knees down, her stubby lower legs dangling again in the air. "With Hand and Hyle."

"By Jerusalem?"

"Yep."

"How did Ulro feel about Jerusalem fathering Hand and Hyle?"

"Brom was totally laid back about it. After all, despite his mental problems with bonking, he wanted kids in the worst way. And as he said at the time, if you believe that a newborn child is nothing but a blank slate, as he did, then what's important is not who quarries the slate but who does the etching."

"Did Ickey believe that, too?"

"Fortunately not. Otherwise, he wouldn't have been okay with someone else raising his kiddies. Ickey often said a newborn child was a garden, fully planted, with its unique, full potential intact, needing only to be nurtured to grow. So, in the end, Brom got two children he could mold into his image, and Ickey, as the planter, got all the parental kicks of a cuckoo who'd laid an egg in another bird's nest."

"Why didn't you tell me all this at the Holiday Inn?"

"I wanted to, but after I got my first sentence out, I smelled the antiseptic."

"Antiseptic?"

"My husband's got a special surgical antiseptic wash," she explained.

"I know the smell," Ded said. "I encountered it when I interviewed him at the airport and again when I arrived by the pool today—and it must be what I smelled in my hotel room after you left. I thought it had come from you."

"The smell hit me right between the eyes," Rahab said. "Brom was supposed to have gone to L.A., but as soon as I smelled it, I knew he was nearby. Maybe he'd been waxing his carrot outside the room in which I conducted my business with the three guys. All I know is I figured out he was standing in the dark part of the corridor, listening to me ratting him out. I became instantly shitbaked I was now next on his list."

Rahab put an earnest hand on Ded's knee. "Dude, you've got to stop my old man before he offs me."

Ded nodded politely, but despite feeling favorably disposed to Rahab, even respecting her, he wasn't convinced Dr. Ulro had a clear motive for murdering Jerusalem, much less Rahab. Certainly, based on what he'd learned about the doctor, the religious nut scenario was out the window. As was jealousy. And the cuckolding. And the poet's supposed flouting of convention.

Either Dr. Ulro is innocent of Ickey Jerusalem's death, Ded reasoned, *or Rahab Oothoon is not revealing the doctor's true motivations.*

"Mr. Ded Smith?" a voice asked from behind. Ded turned to find the man from reception standing a respectful distance back. "I have a call for you at the front desk from an Inspector O'Nadir."

Ded got up, and after confirming *sotto voce* to Rahab he would keep their conversation confidential "from you know who," headed to the front desk.

ళ

"Since you told me this morning where you were going," O'Nadir jumped right in, "I decided to ring you about some developing news."

"What's happened?"

"We found the VW bus. With the purser, Robert N. William, in it. Parked perpendicular on the Taylor Street end of Macondray Lane, facing out. The purser was sitting in the driver's seat. Stone dead."

"Jesus. How?"

"Garroted from behind with some kind of thin cord. Eyes bulging out. Dashboard kicked to hell by his flailing feet. A real mafia type job."

Ded quivered. He'd seen the purser only twice and talked to him on the phone once, but now found himself horrified by the viciousness of the purser's strangling.

"Time of death?" he asked O'Nadir in a forced, matter-of-fact voice.

"Coroner says around mid-morning."

"That's about when I picked up Tharmas Luvah." There flashed into Ded's mind the image of the hearse pulling up to one end of the Lane while the purser was kicking the dashboard in his death throes at the other. "Any leads?"

"Since my forensics guys were already on Macondray Lane looking for bullets, it didn't take them long to survey the VW bus. It had been washed and waxed recently—"

"Likely for Jerusalem's funeral on Saturday," Ded cut in. "I saw it there, looking pristine."

"—so there weren't a lot of background prints to confuse things. Apart from those of purser, the only others were made by gloves. A set on the outside of the driver's door, another on the steering wheel, and a complete, open-finger, left-hand glove print on one of the double doors on the uphill side, as though someone was using that hand to gain leverage while they lifted the other door. We'll find out tomorrow from our college professor whether the prints are from the same gloves."

"A lot of stuff backed up here because someone won't work weekends," Ded grumbled.

"Well, you know. Academics."

Why was Robert N. William killed? Ded wondered. *To shut him up so he wouldn't tell who'd asked him to deliver the LSD package to Urizen's apartment? So he wouldn't disclose what he'd seen about the coat on the plane? As revenge for the LSD attack on Urizen? A lover's spat with Tharmas?*

O'Nadir continued. "While waiting for the prints, perhaps we should focus on who had the opportunity to do this killing. I know Bacon Urizen was home by then, although given his difficulty climbing the out-of-service escalator at the airport, he would have had to employ the buddy you mentioned for the dirty work. And Tharmas Luvah, who could have done it before he met you for the drive to the country club."

"Adam Ghostflea has been with me since the early morning," Ded reported, "after we left Beulah Vala at her house, without her lifeline to the world. I'd say they're both out of suspicion. And Dr. Ulro was at the country club when we arrived, and had been there for at least a half hour, according to the guy at reception. So, unless he took a helicopter, he couldn't have done the killing. I'll be playing golf with Tharmas and the doctor in a few moments. I'll see what I can find out. In the meantime, let's keep the purser's death quiet."

"Good idea," O'Nadir agreed. "Now, on to the bullets fired at you on Macondray Lane. Most that hit the bricks were smashed up, but Ben managed to remove the one in the tree in near-perfect condition. A 45-caliber slug. All we need to do is find the gun it came from."

"Someone shooting a 45 from the apartment's balcony wouldn't be as accurate as at least the first few shots seemed to be," Ded said. "Plus, the gun report was highly suppressed. There must have been a silencer, and that would have screwed up the aim further."

"I think the shooter wasn't as far away as you thought. Before removing the slug, Ben used a trajectory stick and determined the shot came not from the penthouse, but from the vacant lot on the Macondray Lane side of Green Street, across from the high-rise."

So, if it wasn't Urizen, who was up in his penthouse, drugged, Ded reasoned, *and not Tharmas or the purser, who were heading down Jones Street to the parade, and not Beulah or Ghostflea, who were with me, who could it have been? Cousin Ijim? Except he's likely the friend who rescued Urizen on the balcony. That leaves only one suspect from the list unaccounted for. Dr. Bromion Ulro. But didn't he say earlier he was at a medical conference in L.A. the last few days, so couldn't have been here last night?*

Stumped for the moment, Ded dropped the subject and dutifully began relating to the inspector what he'd learned so far that day from Tharmas, Urizen, and Rahab—in the process, committing O'Nadir to keeping confidential the couple's unusual private arrangements.

"Christ," O'Nadir said. "Who would've thought it?"

CHAPTER 23

THE ORIGIN OF THE SHADOWS

Ded was not looking forward to the golf game. With all the suspicions piling up regarding Tharmas and the doctor, compounded by the garroting of the purser, Ded was concerned for his personal safety. Who knew what either of the two might do if they felt threatened? Beat Ded to death with a 1-wood? Run him over with a golf cart? Drown him in a water hazard?

Equally worrying was that Ded had never before played golf. Once again, he was going to expose his gaucheness at a ritzy country club and suffer a worldwide ban.

Dr. Ulro, Tharmas, and Ghostflea were already gathered at the first tee, the doctor having changed from his tennis whites into his golfing attire.

"We took the liberty of choosing some clubs for you," the doctor said to Ded as he arrived, pointing at a full golf bag on a nearby cart. From the doctor's manner, it was clear he was participating in this whole affair under sufferance.

Dr. Ulro stepped up to the tee. "Okay, let's get this over with."

He proceeded to execute a perfect line drive.

Jesus, Ded sighed.

Tharmas was next, executing an acceptable drive, although with less distance.

He is *a member of the golf club, after all,* Ded figured.

Dr. Ulro turned to Ghostflea, who obediently trudged to the tee.

He can't be all that good at the game, Ded hoped, *given his isolated, homeschooled background and his dubious coordination, as evidenced by his hearse driving.*

Ghostflea put his ball on a tee, limbered up his powerfully built arms, lifted his club back, and swung, connecting with the ball to send it in a straight, if high arc down the fairway. He beamed at Ded and walked over to stand next to him. "My parents' compound had miniature golf. Homemade by my dad. That's where I learned to swing hard. After each hit, I'd spend many hours in the woods looking for the ball. My father often told me he thought I was missing the point of miniature golf."

Ghostflea's face took on a quizzical expression. "What *is* the point of miniature golf?"

Ded didn't answer. He was too busy trying to recall instructions from a golf program he had seen on TV. Something about keeping his eye on the ball, his head down, his feet flat, and following through.

Oh, what the heck. He took the largest wood out of his bag, teed up, addressed the ball, pulled back, and swung with an excellent follow-through. A beautiful shot flew straight and true from the face of his club. Regrettably, the subject of the shot was a large dirt-and-grass divot from his side of the tee. The ball remained standing on its perch.

Refusing to look back at what he assumed were the smirking faces of his golfing companions, Ded tried again. But the same thing happened—although this time, the divot came from the other side of the tee.

Frustrated, embarrassed, and becoming desperate, Ded swung

again, much too fast, with the same result, except this time, the divot hole was in front of the tee.

"Mr. Smith." Dr. Ulro's shrill, sarcastic tone stopped Ded from another attempt. "Perhaps it's your club. Let's try something else." He drew from his bag a driver. Apparently brand new, it was decorated with a red bow, to which was attached a white card. "It's a gift from my wife. A high-tech club that's supposed to make connecting with the ball easier. I have yet to use it."

He removed the bow and card, handed the driver to Ded, and stepped much farther away than before.

Ded addressed the ball one more time. The club seemed heavier in his hands than the previous one.

"Concentrate on the power of your swing," the doctor advised.

Ded brought the driver up over his head, paused to get his concentration, and then swung with all his might. This time, there was no divot. The club whipped down, passed two inches above the ball, and as it followed into the upswing, flew out of Ded's hands to trace a parabolic arc high in the air, then gracefully fell toward a spot on the fairway about forty feet away.

Kaboom!!! The driver hit the grass with a massive explosion that vaporized the club and dug a two-foot deep, four-foot diameter hole in the ground.

"Goodness!" Dr. Ulro exclaimed in falsetto. "I think I need to have a talk with my wife."

"Wow, Ded," Tharmas said. "How in the fuck did yuh do that?"

"I didn't," Ded objected as he came out of the instinctive crouch he'd ducked into when the multifarious pieces of grass and dirt had hit him. He noticed Adam Ghostflea studying his own driver while he slowly swung it back and forth, as though considering launching it into a similar arc.

The course marshal came rushing up in his cart. "What was that?"

"Just a defective club," Dr. Ulro answered calmly.

Amazingly, such was the authority of Dr. Ulro, and the course marshal's fear of bad press for Three Heavens, the marshal, without further comment, left to find the groundsman to fill in the crater.

Just a defective club? Ded raged internally. *I could have been killed!*

Was Rahab trying to kill the doctor, so the club ending up in my hands was nothing more than an accident? Or did Dr. Ulro booby-trap the club to kill me and forge the note to incriminate Rahab?

"Doctor," Ded said, just managing to hide his shock and anger behind a professional veneer, "when did Rahab give you that club?"

"A taxi delivered it to the golf shop some time this morning in a box marked 'Extremely Fragile,' and a member of staff brought it over to me after we secured our tee time."

"Could I see the card?"

The doctor handed him the card with the red bow still attached. Ded held the card at the corners. The message read: "FOR ALL YOU HAVE DONE. LOVE, RAHAB."

The capital letters had been written in the same style as the gift note delivered to Urizen on Saturday night. *Were both gifts from Rahab?* Ded speculated. *Or from Dr. Ulro? Or…?*

"I thought the note looked a little dodgy," Dr. Ulro admitted.

So, you gave the club to me to see what would happen? Ded thought testily.

"I suggest, Doctor," Ded said instead, "as soon as we finish, we determine whether the club was really sent by your wife." Without asking, Ded slipped the card and bow into one of his evidence bags and then tucked the bag with its contents into his lower left jacket pocket. "In the meantime, I think it's best for everyone if I quit playing this game. No reason, though, for you and the others not to continue. I'll ride along in your golf cart, so we can talk. In fact, I'm happy to do the driving."

If only, he added in his mind, *to limit your ability to use the cart as a weapon against me.*

❧

The game did not progress beyond the second hole.

At the end of the first hole, it became evident Ghostflea's chances of completing the course under par were handicapped by his belief (likely arising from his experience missing the point of miniature golf) that the goal of the game was to hit the ball as hard as possible over the green, one side to the other, without ever landing on it. When his score reached 162 and he still had gotten no closer to the first-hole flag, Tharmas and Dr. Ulro decided they might as well putt without him.

"The way he's playing," Tharmas observed, "the green is the safest place for us to be."

When they finished putting, they sat back to watch Ghostflea still hitting his ball back and forth over their heads, his upper lip curled in barely suppressed contempt at the inability of his fellow players to keep their balls out of the hole.

In the end—after the course marshal drove up in his golf cart to inform them that in light of the bitter mood of the twenty-two waiting golfing parties, he could no longer assure Ghostflea's safety—they decided to take the chauffeur to the next hole, making a special point of congratulating him on the magnitude of his score.

❧

The second hole was the killer, protected as it was with doglegs, sand traps, water hazards, and fingers of dense underbrush.

Dr. Ulro, who knew the course well, expertly landed his ball on the green.

Tharmas had less success, his ball ending up in the water, where the business manager lost all his balls trying to hit out.

"I failed to maintain the proper concentration," Tharmas confided to Ded later. "After all, I was up to my armpits in quicksand at the time. And then there was my having to dodge a barrage of golf balls from Ghostflea, who, still at the tee, had decided every time his ball fell into a hazard, he'd write it off and tee up another. If I'd not remembered a *Popular Mechanics* article I read as a boy on how to make pontoon bridges out of fallen trees, I doubt I'd have gotten out alive."

As they gathered at the second-hole green, Dr. Ulro declared himself the game's winner on the basis he was the only one who had any golf balls left. The group agreed there was not much point in continuing the game, a conclusion with which the ever-present course marshal heartily concurred. After discreetly surveying the malevolent army of golfers still backed up behind, they decided it might be best to return to the clubhouse by driving their carts around the remaining sixteen holes.

Tharmas sped off in the first cart with the hefty Ghostflea squeezed in beside him. Ded and Dr. Ulro followed about thirty yards behind.

❧

The doctor sat to Ded's right under the cart's canopy, dressed in his starched golfing outfit and bouncing along with the speeding car. "Okay, Mr. Smith, what were you talking to my wife about?"

Ded, gripping the steering wheel, briefly studied the doctor's sky-blue contact lenses floating on the surface of his dirt-brown irises. "Just trying to find out what she knew."

"About what?"

"I don't reveal to anyone what interviewees tell me unless it's absolutely necessary for my investigation."

"Yes, you don't want to go around ruining people's reputations for no reason."

"No." As a fraught silence settled, Ded decided to change the topic. "Dr. Ulro, you said you were at a medical conference in L.A. Can you give me details? Where the conference was held, where you stayed, how you traveled—that sort of thing."

Despite the doctor's controlled, imitation male-model appearance, Ded could tell Ulro thought it was beneath him to answer questions posed by a mere life insurance claims adjuster.

"The conference was at the Bel Air," the doctor relented with a resigned disdain several staves above the treble clef. "I flew down on the

PSA[6] shuttle Thursday night and back this morning. Since I came here straight from the airport, I've got all the receipts in my locker, including the conference nametag, hotel bill, and flight ticket stubs. If you feel you must be thorough, I can give them to you when we get back."

"Thanks. I'll take you up on that."

If those receipts provide an ironclad alibi, Ded thought, *it'll be difficult to tie the doctor to any of the goings-on in the last few days, including the potshots yesterday.*

"Did you know Ickey Jerusalem was going to be on your plane from New York?"

"No," Dr. Ulro said. "Not until I got up to take a pee. First, I saw Bacon Urizen and Adam Ghostflea sleeping in their seats. Then, I met Tharmas walking down the stairs, as I was about to go up. He told me they were coming back from Ickey's publishing event in New York."

"Did he say anything else?"

"He asked whether Rahab and the twins had left me yet. I answered by suggesting he perform a certain highly graphic if physically impossible act of self-knowledge. It wasn't a long conversation."

"After you finished in the upstairs toilet, Doctor, did you see Tharmas again?"

"No. As I returned to my seat, I didn't see him anywhere around Urizen or Ghostflea."

Ded digested this fact. "Did you happen to notice where Ickey Jerusalem was sitting?"

"No. The last thing I wanted was to make eye contact and find myself involved in yet another palaver about the whole enchilada being nothing more than the mind of an infinitely creative God."

---

6 Pacific Southwest Airlines. A year later, one of its planes, with the company's trademark smile painted under its nose, was caught on camera, its wings on fire, as it plummeted to the ground, killing all onboard. A decade later, after a disgruntled employee purposely crashed a PSA plane, also killing all on board, the airline went out of business.

"You say, 'another palaver'. Was the previous one the argument you had with Jerusalem in your office on Thursday, October 13th?"

The doctor eyed Ded as though wondering from where the claims adjuster had learned about this particular altercation. "Yeah. That was it. Before he came to my office for his checkup, I'd received the drafts of his epic poems from Theo, allowing me to understand what Ickey's new metaphysics was all about. I couldn't resist showing him where he'd gone wrong."

"What did you say?"

Dr. Ulro put on his most reasonable face. "No one, let alone me, doubts the creative imagination exists. Lateral thinking, the psychologists call it. The ability of the brain to associate ideas and images on a suggestive rather than a strictly logical basis. An ability that evolved in man because of its occasional usefulness in solving problems. Although most of the associated ideas and images are worthless, every once in a while, one does point the logical capabilities of the brain toward new solutions which otherwise would remain hidden behind unexamined assumptions."

The doctor glanced at an empty green they were passing, the result of their having backed everybody up at the first hole. "But I said that, to me, what he was doing with this little trick of the brain is the same thing the Navaho Indians do with the chemical reaction of the brain to the active ingredients in the peyote mushroom, or the swami cultists do with the Alpha-wave response of the brain to rhythmic chanting—identify the trick effect with God, embellish it with reams of complex, theological verbiage purporting to explain the entire universe, and then set about forcing into the resulting straightjacket all the rest of human experience, including the 99% to which any fool could see it is not meant to apply."

"Sort of like what modern Christians have done with love," Ded said.

The doctor's countenance appeared puzzled, and then, as understanding sank in, broke into a sinister smile of approval. "Love your enemy, indeed."

❧

By presenting his oft-expressed views about the Christians and love, Ded had demonstrated that on a purely rational basis, he agreed with what Dr. Ulro was saying. The true reality of any experience lay in its scientific cause. The difficulty Ded was having at the moment was that somehow, after his night with Beulah, his understanding was going beyond the purely rational. Purely rational descriptions of reality, such as love as a chemically based bonding response, now seemed too skeletal. Bleached of life. Empty of everything but the whisper of death.

❧

"I told Ickey in no uncertain terms he should forget all his cornball fantasies. Instead, as I'd explained to him for years, if he wanted to get on in this world, he needed to do as I do and just accept things the way they are. Conform to the rules governing our existence. The mechanics of nature. The dictates of convention. When I set out to straighten a nose or tuck a chin, it's the mechanics of nature that are my guide. When I set out to improve my standing in the profession or encourage potential patients to take me seriously, it's the dictates of convention. Only by conforming to those two sets of rules can I acquire sufficient control over the world to achieve freedom, and sufficient material possessions to achieve happiness—a full bank account, a big house, a fast car, a fashionable wife, two beautiful children."

"What did Jerusalem say to that?" Ded asked, while silently wondering whether "fashionable" was really the proper description of Rahab Oothoon.

"He said I was a turd."

"And after that?"

"After that, he began to get personal."

"Like what?"

The doctor peered upwards in malign contemplation. "Let's see. He said I had a vegetable eye. A tin ear. A cement head. He said I worshipped death. That I was the fruit of the Tree of Mystery—whatever that is. He even accused me of being Satan Incarnate."

"Why Satan Incarnate?" Ded asked.

"I asked him what sins he was accusing me of. But all he said was that nowhere in the Bible is Satan accused of sin. Only of unbelief. To which I replied, that seemed a rather low bar to achieving Satanhood."

The doctor clenched his hands into exasperated fists and shook them at either side of his head.

"That was it?" Ded asked.

The doctor rubbed his face with his hands, and when he dropped them, he had relaxed back into his neutral mask. "Pretty much. Ickey stormed out of my office soon after, promising never to return."

Ded had the distinct feeling the doctor was hiding something. But he didn't think pressing him further at the moment would yield any results.

❧

Ded drove the cart up the next rise and onto a paved path bordered by six-inch diameter logs. The smooth path wound through a shady grove of trees toward the eleventh-hole tee.

Now that the ride was less bumpy, Dr. Ulro leaned back, put his feet on the front railing, and sneered up at the cart's canvas canopy. "It's a well-known historical cycle, you know."

"What is?" Ded asked. Driving on the path required less concentration than on the fairway, and he, too, was beginning to relax.

"A civilization begins when its people are hardworking, organized, practical, responsible, respect authority, and know the difference between right and wrong. It gains control over the world. Accumulates material wealth. And then…"

"And then?"

"And then fruitcakes like Ickey Jerusalem come along, preaching artistic fulfillment, pleasure-seeking, moral license, and mysticism…" The doctor's attention seemed to drift. "…having sex with women to whom they are not married… while quoting poetry at the top of their lungs… with the window wide open so everyone can hear… even going so far as to include animals in the act…"

Christ! Ded thought. *Is he talking about Jerusalem? Or about* me*?*

With a look of disgust, the doctor shook his head to bring himself back on course. "And in no time, the powerful civilization collapses into decadence, anarchy, and chaos."

Afraid to ask to whom the doctor might have been referring, but desperately wanting the answer, Ded tried his new method of finding the truth. Rolling his eyes briefly onto the plastic surgeon's profile, he attempted to read him by immediate perception.

He was unsuccessful. Not because there wasn't anything behind the doctor's façade to perceive. Ded didn't get far enough along to tell. Rather, it was because, in trying to take him in by immediate perception, Ded failed to notice the pathway's oncoming sharp left turn.

The front wheels of the speeding cart hit the six-inch-high log border and bounced up and over, bucking Dr. Ulro's feet, which had been resting on the front railing, into space. A split-second later, the back wheels hit the border in the same way, pitching the rest of the doctor's body upwards, driving his head into the canvas canopy. Ded jammed on the brakes, stopping the cart but, sadly, not Dr. Ulro, who continued sailing forward, landing with the back of his knees hooked up over the cart's front railing, his head and shoulders down in the footwell, and unbeknownst to him, his toupée dangling from the ceiling by a clump of hair that had become stuck between the canvas and one of the horizontal roof supports.

For a moment, Dr. Ulro remained in this inverted position, clearly amazed at the speed at which everything had collapsed into anarchy and chaos.

"Sorry," Ded muttered as he straightened his glasses.

Dr. Ulro focused on the blond mobile pirouetting above him.

"Shit!" he cursed, when he realized what it was. Struggling onto the seat, he snatched the toupée and patted it into position.

Dr. Ulro glowered at Ded in what Ded felt was an exceptionally personal way. "That's why it's so important to stop the fruitcakes before they trigger the Apocalypse."

Stop them by killing them? Ded didn't dare speak this follow-up.

But the doctor, putting a few finishing touches on his re-placed wig, answered Ded's unspoken query with a loathing as total as it was high-pitched. "By snuffing them out."

Lost for words, Ded swallowed some air and got out to move the border log aside so he could reverse the cart back onto the path.

❧

About twenty yards up ahead, Tharmas's cart disappeared behind some bushes on the far side of the seventeenth-hole green, where four women golfers were putting. One of the women, who had been watching Tharmas's cart zigzagging up the fairway, made a cackling comment and then bent over, concentrating on her putt. The hole flag lay on the ground.

From behind the bushes, a voice suddenly spake as it were the noise of thunder:

> The beast that thou sawest was, and is not; and shall ascend out of the bottomless pit, and go into perdition: and they that dwell on the earth shall wonder, whose names were not written in the Book of Life from the foundation of the world, when they behold the beast that was, and is not, and yet is.

The four women stared, nonplussed, at the bushes.

"Behold!" Tharmas exalted as his cart broke through the bushes onto the green. "It's me, Jesus Christ, come again!" He leaned out of the moving cart and snatched the hole flag from the ground. "Woe, woe, woe, to the inhabiters of the earth by reason of the voices of the trumpet of the angels, which are yet to sound!" Holding the pole like a lance, his eyes as a flame of fire, he jammed his foot on the accelerator and charged straight at the cackler.

The woman, revealing at least a passing acquaintance with the

Apocalypse from the Book of Revelation, threw down her putter and took off back up the fairway like a bat out of hell—a rather appropriate cliché, given the circumstances.

Tharmas raced back up the fairway in hot pursuit, assailing her with shouts of "Repent! Repent!"—accompanied by encouraging pokes at her rear with his makeshift lance.

"The good life, heh?" The goateed Tharmas winked at Ded and Dr. Ulro as he whizzed past, hot on the heels of the quick and the goosed.

Sitting in the cart's passenger seat, Ghostflea's protruding visual organs looked more misaligned than usual, as though trying to comprehend the rules for this aspect of the game of golf.

"If it's a point a poke," an admiring Ghostflea was saying to Tharmas, "your score'll be astronomical! Sure beats hitting the ball back and forth across the green."

༄

Continuing on his way to the eighteenth-hole fairway, Ded passed the cackler's open-mouthed companions. Beside him in the cart, Dr. Ulro sat equally open-mouthed.

"Doctor?"

Dr. Ulro shut his mouth.

"Doctor?" Ded repeated.

"Tharmas Luvah," the doctor snarled. "There's the real Satan Incarnate." The plastic surgeon's malice-filled eyes surged with a sudden intensity. Powerful. Dark. Menacing. Almost, one might say—but for his accompanying Country-Western, helium-breathing voice—Satanic.

"Another fruitcake that needs to be snuffed out as soon as possible," the doctor hissed to no one in particular.

༄

While negotiating the final pathway into the safe haven of the clubhouse cart return, Ded mulled over what Dr. Ulro's particular version of the pot calling the kettle black might mean.

"Doctor," Ded addressed his passenger as they got out of the cart. "Will you be available tomorrow if I need to ask you a few more questions?"

"If you insist," the doctor grudgingly replied, as though he, in truth, never wanted to talk to Ded again. "I may be available around lunchtime. In the morning, I'll be at Urizen & Fallen."

"For the reading of the bequests?"

"Yes." The doctor's face slipped once again into neutral mode. "According to a letter I received last week from Bacon Urizen, I've been named as a beneficiary."

~

While they all turned their rented clubs in at the clubhouse, Tharmas complained vociferously about having been given only six balls to complete an 18-hole course. "That's less than a third of a ball per hole," he pointed out to the golf clerk, who merely shrugged and returned the business manager's rented clubs to the rack.

Meanwhile, Ded tracked down the staff member who had received the gift club for Dr. Ulro and got a description of the taxi. The guy couldn't remember the company's name, but he said the car had an abnormal orangey-red color.

After that, everyone went back to the main building. Tharmas and Ghostflea, to cadge some food from the luncheon buffet, and Ded and Dr. Ulro, to pick up the doctor's receipts from his locker.

Rahab was nowhere to be found, so they couldn't ask her whether she had sent the exploding club.

After delivering the receipts, Dr. Ulro begged off, saying he had something important to do, and Ded joined the business manager and the chauffeur at the buffet.

CHAPTER 24

BLINDED BY THE LIGHT COMING FROM OUTSIDE

"How about a little run up to the wineries in the Napa Valley?" Tharmas asked, stroking his goatee as they returned to the hearse.

Ded put off answering as they all climbed into the vehicle. He didn't really want to spend the rest of the day with Tharmas. He was becoming confused about his feelings and his beliefs, and the last thing he wanted was to be around someone so chaotic and unpredictable. But then, Ded recognized he had an obligation to continue his investigation into Ickey Jerusalem's death, and he still had to get some answers from the business manager.

"The wineries are okay with me," Ded said, "provided you promise to keep the Beast of Revelations in check while we're there."

Tharmas chuckled. "Sooner murder an infant in its cradle than nurse unacted desires," he announced. Ded assumed it was a quote from an Ickey Jerusalem poem. "But for yuh, Ded, I'll make an exception."

Ded dipped his head in acknowledgment. "I'm sure those who have failed to get their names into the Book of Life will be most grateful. And the mothers of cradled infants as well."

Tharmas pulled open the glass divider to the driver's seat. "To Christian Brothers Winery, Ghostflea." Then, not bothering to close it again, Tharmas lay back, shut his eyes, and let the wind coming through the open passenger windows wash over him.

Ded did the same.

The problem for Ded was, like his feelings and beliefs, the investigation itself was becoming confused. Despite his thinking Dr. Ulro (or was it Tharmas?) was now the number one suspect of Jerusalem's murder, there were still too many other victims, too many other motives, too many other clues, too many other potential killers. Even Ded's newfound by-immediate-perception understanding, which he'd hoped would give a clearer picture of what had happened, had only succeeded in drawing him further from an explicit accusation.

What Ded really wanted to do was to forget about the investigation, forget about Tharmas Luvah, Adam Ghostflea, Dr. Bromion Ulro, Bacon Urizen, and the deceased Robert N. William, and head back up to the Oakland Hills to spend the day in bed with the remaining suspect, Beulah Vala, escaping from the prison of his subjective self by uniting with her amazingly beautiful objective outside. Sure, their unions last night had been nothing more than Sicilian Illusions, but that abstract knowledge now mattered less and less. What mattered was what he felt.

With some effort, Ded brought his mind back to the task at hand. His conversation with Dr. Ulro had generated new questions for Jerusalem's business manager that needed answering.

"Tell me, Tharmas, that night on the plane, where did you go after talking to Dr. Ulro?"

Tharmas, his eyes still shut, broke into a lecherous grin. "I looked around to see what I could pick up."

Ded steeled himself to hear yet another tale of Tharmas's sexual conquests.

ꟹ

Despite spending much of the last three-and-a-half years on airplanes, Ded had never once picked up a woman on a plane.

It was not because he was unattractive to women. That had nothing to do with it.

All right, maybe something to do with it. But certainly not everything.

I mean, logically, Ded often assured himself, *there have to be some female passengers out there who like nerds.*

The real problem, Ded knew, was that he didn't give off the right signals.

I've tried. God knows, I've tried.

How many times had he sat, immobile, beside an indifferent woman, like a rudderless vessel desperate to be rescued by a passing ship, semaphoring awkward, subliminal signals in her direction? But the message always seemed to come out the same: "Man overboard! Abandon ship!"

ꟹ

"And *did* you pick up someone, Tharmas?" Ded asked, not really wanting to be told.

Tharmas snuggled farther back into his seat. "In a way." His massive tongue snaked out between his lips, reached its limit, and then withdrew. "Robert N. William and I got sorta up close and personal in the back row, on the left side of first class."

"What do you mean, up clo—"

The sound of a siren cut through the air. Tharmas and Ded turned to look through the rear window to find a motorcycle policeman tailing the hearse, lights flashing.

The business manager scrunched down in his seat, reached into his pocket, removed his small, highly illegal marijuana bag, scooped out half the contents with his fingers, and thrust it into Ded's hand. "Quick, help me eat this," he ordered before emptying the remainder of the bag into his own mouth.

Adam Ghostflea pulled the hearse to the side of the road. The motorcycle stopped behind. After a frantic moment considering the alternatives, Ded shoved the palmful of shredded weed into his mouth and swallowed it down.

The policeman got off his motorcycle, gathered his gear, strode cockily up to the open front left window, and leaned in to confront the driver.

A few confused seconds later, the policeman straightened up, and still trying to look cocky, strode around the hood to the British hearse's driver's seat.

Ded took a final pick between his teeth with his fingernail to clear any leaf fragments that might have gotten stuck.

The cop leaned into Ghostflea's open window and caught sight of the satanic-looking chauffeur's small, swept-back head with its cracked red skin, bulging eyes, gold-capped eye teeth, and wormlike tongue. "Jesus" he exclaimed, backing rapidly out of the window.

A few steps back, the cop, regaining control, resumed his macho pose as though nothing had happened, although this time at a safer distance.

"Been drinking, have we?" he asked, referring possibly to the chauffeur's appearance, but more likely to the manner in which the hearse had been weaving all over the road.

Ghostflea gave a minute negative indication with his head, clamming up, Ded assumed, due to his previously stated fear of the police.

Tharmas scooted forward to the open partition just behind Ghostflea's head. "The guy drives that way normally," he informed the cop through the front window.

Putting his hand on his gun, the cop motioned for Ghostflea, the meek, to get out of the car.

"The man's a menace," Tharmas declared bitterly to the policeman, shifting to his own open window. "We knew we was taking our lives in our hands with him as our chauffeur, but what could we do? Me and my companion here drew the short straws. We begged to go with the rest of our tour group in the other limo, but twenty-five passengers per vehicle was the absolute limit."

Ded looked out of his side of the hearse. A large, black car with darkened windows glided by, as though to allow its driver time to gawk.

"Actually, it was the two U.S. Marines who first drew the short straws," Tharmas whined. "But after they burst into tears, the group, out of some kinda weird sense of patriotism, let them off the hook."

While the cop prepared the breathalyzer bag for Ghostflea, Tharmas bellyached in great detail about each of the next four rounds of straw drawing, ending respectively, he claimed, in a sudden heart attack, a shitting in the pants, the sale of a three-year-old boy to the highest bidder, and a favorable interpretation of the rules regarding the gluing together of two short straws with a wad of bubble gum to make one long one.

"That decision was a fix," Tharmas griped. "The broad who was doing the gluing promised free sex for anyone who went along."

As Ghostflea blew into the breathalyzer, Tharmas gave a heartbreaking description of the fifth and final drawing, in which Tharmas and Ded, unable to come up with an original excuse, had been bundled by the rest of the tour group, kicking and screaming, into Ghostflea's hearse. Tharmas was now almost weeping. "I kept pleading, 'What about that free sex I was promised?'"

Ghostflea finished blowing in the breathalyzer. The policeman took it back and studied it. There were no traces whatsoever of alcohol.

"Hard to believe, ain't it?" Tharmas said with sympathy.

The cop eyed Tharmas sternly, a myriad of potential violations whirring through his mind. Then, grudgingly, he gave Ghostflea back his license and motioned for him to go.

"Have a nice day!" Tharmas chirped through the window as the hearse pulled away.

The policeman stood by the roadside, watching after them, his hand resting on his gun holster.

Tharmas leaned through the open divide. "Start weaving," he suggested to Ghostflea. "It'll make it harder for him to get a clear shot."

❧

Ded was lifting Ickey Jerusalem's anthology to search for Tharmas's previously quoted murdered baby verse when the bullet hit. There was no sound of broken glass. This was because the shot came not from the rear but from the left. Ded could tell by the barely audible gunshot and by the path of the bullet itself, which entered his open window and knocked the book out of his hand, smashing it against the right door next to Tharmas.

"Jesus!" Ded exclaimed. "What the—"

He turned to the left and caught a glimpse of the formerly gawking black car, parked parallel with the road, about 50 feet back from the verge behind a barbed wire fence. Someone standing on the far side of the car, wearing a blue knit cap, was resting what looked like a short rifle on the roof, aiming straight at Ded.

Ded ducked just before a second bullet whizzed through the open left window and this time, due to the changed angle from the hearse moving on, exited through Ghostflea's open window right behind his providently small head.

By the time Ded sat up again, the hearse had moved around a forested curve in the road, denying the black car the line of sight for a third shot.

"He's gonna have to back up to the gate in the barbed wire fence in order to come after us," said Tharmas, who had not bothered to duck. "So, we got a few moments to lose him."

"Step on it, Ghostflea," Ded said.

Ghostflea, who, at the time of the shooting, had been at the top of second gear, promptly shifted into fifth and put the pedal to the metal. The engine lugged for a few moments before it flooded and died. The hearse rolled to a stop next to a dirt track heading off into the woods on the right.

"Everybody out and push!" Ded ordered. "And Ghostflea, while you're pushing, turn the steering wheel into the track."

Fortunately, the heavy weight of the hearse was more than offset by the track leading gently downhill. In response to their pushing, the vehicle initially picked up speed. Then, as the track reached a level area, it slowed.

With the engine off, Ded could hear the roar of the speeding black car coming up the main road. "Hit the deck," he barked, as the rapidly slowing hearse limped into the forest.

All three dropped behind the bushes and flattened themselves onto the dirt.

The black car rushed by on the main road and then could be heard disappearing into the distance.

If the car's driver had looked hard to the right when he went past, he would have seen the hearse. They could only hope he had been totally focused on the road ahead.

They waited a few minutes to see if the black car would come back. Hearing nothing, they stood up and brushed off the dirt. Ded told Ghostflea to get in, start the engine (which, by now, had drained its excess fuel), and creep back to the main road. There, on Ded's instructions, after looking both ways, Ghostflea turned left and headed in the direction of the country club.

"I've got a longer but safer back way to the winery," Tharmas offered.

"Probably just as safe to be at the winery as anywhere else," Ded said. "Let's do it."

Ded retrieved Jerusalem's anthology from the hearse's carpeted floor. The bullet had pierced the book's cover at the page margin. It was still inside. All Ded had to do was open the book to the bullet and turn the pages thereafter one at a time until it fell out.

He decided to wait until he got back to his hotel.

Ded considered calling O'Nadir on the car phone, but unlike the shooting at Macondray Lane, Ded already had the bullet, and in near perfect condition. The inspector might be able to get the Marin County Sheriff's Office to send somebody out to take plaster casts of the shooter's tire tracks and footprints, assuming the shooter had not brushed them away, but that would likely take hours, if not days, and Ded did not want to interrupt the other parts of his investigation by waiting around to show them precisely where everything had been. Plus, having just swallowed a handful of marijuana, he soon might not be in a sufficient condition to talk to the authorities.

Who could the shooter be? Ded pondered. *Dr. Ulro? Cousin Ijim, on behalf Bacon Urizen? Rahab? Theo? Los? Someone else from Jerusalem's Central-Valley, extended family? Enith? Grandma Enion, maybe?*

Tharmas, Ghostflea, and Ded sat in the tasting room of the Christian Brothers Winery, each with a glass of wine. Ded wasn't certain, but he suspected the marijuana he had swallowed was beginning to take effect. His consciousness seemed to be continually flicking forward, starting each microsecond anew from the last. He was having trouble keeping his concentration.

Tharmas held his glass up to the light and swirled it around. "This wine has got nice legs."

As Ded listened to each syllable being spoken by the business manager, it seemed to lock away in its own separate compartment in time.

Ghostflea looked hard at Tharmas's glass and then looked down into his own with a bewildered expression. "I don't see any legs."

With a mystifying, stroboscopic motion, Ded lifted his glass up to the light and examined it closely. The thin stem reminded him of Beulah's tiny waist, and the spreading outline of the bowl, of her open legs, held high in the air. He brought the glass down and lowered his nose into the opening, inhaling deeply.

"Raw fish," he said, the two words taking an extraordinarily long time to get out.

Tharmas looked over from his wine. "Huh?"

Ghostflea leaned closer to peer suspiciously at Ded's glass.

"Raw fish," Ded repeated, backing his whole being, jerking frame by frame, out of his glass. "The Japanese use it like we use wine."

"You mean they get drunk on it?" Tharmas screwed up his face at the idea of a large, dusty bottle filled with fermented fish.

"They don't get drunk on it," Ded objected, trying to smother a burble of giggles. "They get snobbish about it. Just like we do about our carefully spoiled grape juice."

Ded pulled his rapidly disintegrating attention together around his idea. "The more a refined Japanese person can infer from the appearance, the texture, the aroma, and the taste of a piece of dead fish, the more cultured he is considered to be."

"Interesting," Tharmas said, looking at his wine glass with what Ded thought were new eyes.

"Yes," Ded deadpanned. "But not as interesting as the discerning-palate snobbism of the untouchables in Uttar Pradesh, India, who eat grain gleaned from the excrement of cows."

Tharmas put his glass down on the table with a thump. "Jesus," he winced. "No wonder nobody wants to touch them."

"What?" Ghostflea said huskily. "Raw fish have legs, too?"

Ghostflea was a little behind in the conversation.

Ded, unable to contain himself any longer, broke into a fit of the giggles. Contagious, they passed to Tharmas and then to Ghostflea and back, though, of course, neither of the other two knew what Ded was laughing about.

For quite a while, Ded sat at the table, sniggering over how he'd shown Tharmas that the whole sophisticated wine experience was merely another Sicilian Illusion.

Then, abruptly, he stopped and frowned.

Why did he always take so seriously the task of making other people see nothing was to be taken seriously? Why was he driven to compare, abstract, analyze, and theorize to the point of destroying the immediacy of experience? He was like Nobodaddy, who destroyed Jesus on the Tree of Mystery. Like the night-flying, invisible worm, who destroyed the rose in the poem. Like the person or persons who destroyed Ickey Jerusalem on the plane.

Ded stared into the dark, red wine at the bottom of his glass, the words "destroyed Ickey Jerusalem in the plane" echoing in his head. He tried to recollect what it was he had been thinking when he had begun the train of thought ending with those words, but for the life of him, he couldn't.

Why does everything have to be so goddamn transient? So temporary.

Like his unions with Beulah. If only he hadn't fallen back into reality, he'd never have known they were an illusion. He could have escaped forever from the lonely claustrophobia of his "self."

⁂

They visited several of the Napa Valley wineries, all much the same in decor and offerings, although the later ones seemed to have increasingly less stable floors. In the last winery, this distracting architectural flaw was compounded by high, institutional-pink walls that kept leaning in to look at the top of Ded's head. The three-story wine tanks on either side were breathing in and out like huge, dark red, rubber lungs.

At one point on the guided tour, Ded saw Tharmas perched on top of one of these aspirating tanks, declaiming what Ded assumed to be a Jerusalem poem:

> Tyger Tyger burning bright,
> In the forests of the night;
> What immortal hand or eye,
> Dare frame thy fearful symmetry?

A question whose cosmological significance appeared lost on the small army of security guards clambering up the slippery sides of the tank toward the declaimer.

"Yes!" Ded blurted out, much to his surprise, not to mention that of the seven other people on the winery tour. "What hand, indeed?!"

Shortly afterwards, the faulty concrete floor rose up and smacked Ded on the back of his head. The next thing Ded knew, he was lying on his back, gazing up into Ghostflea's concerned face.

"Good God, Ghostflea," Ded tittered, "you're drunk." Ded could tell from the chauffeur's bulging eyes. For once, they were looking straight at him.

The next thing he knew, management had concluded that Tharmas, Ghostflea, and Ded had had enough to drink, and had tapped security to escort them out of the building.

"The tygers of wrath," Ded kept trying to explain to his accompanying guard, "are so much wiser than the horses of instruction. Can't you see it? The concept is so concrete, I can almost reach out and touch it. Here and now."

❧

Ded did not remember much about the following ride in the hearse, having achieved an amnesiac state that one must see as an example of the merciful way nature deals with those who have lived through the experience of being chauffeured by a gigantic, drunken flea.

The only memory Ded had at the end was of a white, stick-style farmhouse with a large, red barn set amidst several old-root vineyards Ghostflea had roared through when he'd gotten lost looking for the passing lane on the highway. Night had fallen, and the little farmhouse glowed in the moonlight. Ded felt an overwhelming urge to get out, buy the place, marry a local girl, move in, make some kids, and harness his psyche to the heartaches and joys of working the earth. All he needed, he knew, was to put on his blinders.

As the house disappeared behind him, though, he realized it was impossible. There weren't any blinders he could put on that he wouldn't feel obliged to take off right away.

⸙

Tharmas arranged dinner at an elegant restaurant outside of St. Helena with a fancy, foreign-sounding name that Ded never quite caught. "In Vino Varicose" was the closest he could get to it. *Not all that appetizing a name for a restaurant,* he thought as they were seated, but he was too ravenously hungry to care.

Over the next two hours, Ded must have eaten everything on the menu. Twice. No, three times. Now, with the major effects of the marijuana having receded, Ded sat, drunk, his bloated belly straining the limits of his flesh. Across the table, Adam Ghostflea, his true inner personality at last revealed by drink, slept with his head on the white tablecloth. Next to the chauffeur, Tharmas was chattering on about some sexual adventure he'd had with a Slinky-spring toy descending the stairs. "Yuh gotta be damn quick, Ded, I can tell yuh that."

Ded stared through his thick glasses into a snifter of dark red wine, lost in a morass of freely associating ideas and images from which he was vainly trying to find his way out. His newly developed poetic understanding kept offering him brief, partial glimpses of escape, but each time those glimpses, pointing, like Tharmas's dong, in every direction at once, lacked the coherence necessary to resist the centripetal force of his logic, and he found himself being pulled, kicking and screaming, back into his solitary, subjective self.

Let's face it, Ded reasoned morosely, *the only permanent way out allowed by logic is death.*

The image of Ickey Jerusalem, bound and smothered, materialized in his mind.

Perhaps the poet had killed himself after all.

༄

"What's the matter?" Tharmas asked, miffed at Ded's lack of interest in his hard-won Slinky-spring ecstasy.

Ded raised his rheumy eyes. "There's no permanent way out," he slobbered.

"Of what?"

"Of the subjective self, the shrunken consciousness of the sleeping God." Ded was having trouble with all the "s" and "sh" sounds necessary to express Ickey Jerusalem's metaphysics. "Trapped in Hell's web of abstractions."

"But there's a way out," Tharmas said. "Or at least, Ickey said there is."

Ded viewed the business manager through a boozy haze. "If you mean through love or poetry, forget it. Those are only temporary or partial."

"I don't mean those," Tharmas said. "I mean a way Ickey believed would be both permanent and total."

"Which is?" Ded demanded.

"Simple." Tharmas raised his glass. "By waking the sleeping God."

Of course, Ded thought. *Why didn't I think of that? That could have been exactly what the poet was trying to do on the toilet.*

"And how was Jerusalem going to do that?" Ded asked, interested for purposes of both his investigation and his own personal release.

"I dunno. As I told yuh last night, Ickey's metaphysics hurts my head. So, the few times he tried to explain the details of waking the sleeping God, my mind completely shut down."

"Great," Ded slurred sarcastically. Overcome by the apparent hopelessness of ever being able to find the answer he was seeking, he backed away from his glass, stood unsteadily on the seat of his chair, and formed his hands into a megaphone. "Wake up, God!" he shouted with all his might. "Time to get up!"

This brought Tharmas wobbling to his feet. "Yeah, wake up, God!" He climbed onto his chair. "Come on, Big Boy! Rise and shine!"

Roughly thirty other people in the chic restaurant, half-chewed food visible in their mouths, gaped at Ded and Tharmas. One heavyset gentleman at the table behind Ghostflea found the strong emotion evoked by the drunken display hard to contain. "Sit down, you assholes," he growled.

Tharmas, evidencing a truly Christian character, blew the man a kiss off his gloved palm.

The man, who, from his military haircut, Ded took as someone unaccustomed to being blown Christian kisses by another male, leapt out of his seat, lumbered toward their table, grabbed Tharmas's neck with his left hand, and cocked his right fist. "You fucking pervert."

Ded marveled at how the guy could know so much about the business manager merely from grabbing his neck.

It was unlucky for Tharmas that in Mr. Crewcut's scale of social snobbism, fucking perverts seemed to rank only slightly above male ballet dancers.

Ded cringed, waiting for the cocked fist to bust into Tharmas's mouth and shatter its way through a cloud of broken enamel. The man, however, did not swing—not because he had second thoughts about the appropriate way to deal with someone of Tharmas's social standing, but because Adam Ghostflea woke up, saw what was happening, rocketed to his feet, and pinched the man at the base of his neck.

The guy remained standing for the longest time—long enough for Ghostflea to return sleepily to his seat—and then fell to the floor like a ton of poorly wrapped sausages.

Ded, agog, still on his feet on his chair, shifted his gaze between the sleepy Ghostflea and the collapsed body.

Warily, the tuxedoed *maître d'* approached the table.

"Check, please," Tharmas requested matter-of-factly.

The *maître d'* hesitated and then scuttled off to get the bill.

"Enough of this freedom," Tharmas yawned, turning to Ded as though nothing had happened. "Let's go get stuck in the mud."

❧

"So, the pinch you used on Mr. Crewcut was something else your father taught you?" Ded asked Adam Ghostflea, who was holding the left-side passenger door of the hearse open. Tharmas was in the restaurant paying the bill.

"Yesh," the chauffeur replied, slurring the word. He was still drunk. "My father learned it from Kung Fu Master Wu Wu."

Ded, who was still drunk, sat down onto the back seat. "Wu Wu?" It wasn't a name that, in English at least, projected the dignity one associated with a Kung Fu master. It would have been even worse had the master's middle name been the same. *Wu Wu Wu? The mind boggles.*

"Wu Wu was famous," Ghostflea said. "He invented the Touch of Baby Dove."

"What's that?"

"A Kung Fu blow that moves the opponent's nose up onto his forehead." Ghostflea mimed the motion on his own sloping face and forehead.

"Must have made it inconvenient for opponents who wore glasses."

Ghostflea's inebriated popped eyes viewed Ded without understanding.

"Never mind," Ded said. "There's something that's been bothering me. Yesterday morning, when you were attacking the doorman outside the Holiday Inn, why didn't you hit him?"

Ghostflea's look indicated he thought the answer was obvious. "Wu Wu taught that a man is more hurt by losing face than losing his face." The terminal word coming through his sluggish lips sounding almost like *faith.*

"You mean, the doorman was hurt more by being seen to be afraid of blows that did not land?"

The chauffeur bobbed his chin, teetering back and forth with the movements of his head.

"So, if the doorman had not been afraid, you would have clobbered him?"

The chauffeur looked at the ground. "If I'm in danger of losing face, I'd have no choice." Ghostflea closed the passenger door and then clumsily climbed into the driver's seat.

It was a puzzle to Ded how anyone with an unfortunate face like Ghostflea's would have wanted to save it. But then, maybe that assumption was the same mistake Ickey Jerusalem had made a little over a week before when he had given the chauffeur his notice.

CHAPTER 25

FLEEING BACK INSIDE

The mud in which Tharmas intended them to get stuck was to be found in Calistoga, a small town at the northern end of the Napa Valley, famous for its natural hot-spring mud baths that had amazing, curative powers.

After Tharmas paid at reception, the three stripped off their clothes in the locker room, put on white bathrobes, and entered the large, white-washed, concrete-floored bathing room. On the right, seven oversized bathtubs set three feet apart lined the wall. On the left was a row of seven sunken baths filled with steaming mud. Other than a single male attendant, there were no other people there.

Following the attendant's instructions, the men took off their bathrobes and each went to a separate mud bath.

Ded put his glasses on the floor where he could reach them, closed his eyes, entered the bath toes-first, and sank into the primeval ooze until it reached his chin.

It was hot as Hell.

"Just sit and let the mud suck the poisons out of your body," the attendant advised. "I'll be back in a moment."

At first vigilant against Tharmas or someone else sneaking up behind to hold him under the mud, Ded eventually gave himself over to his senses, becoming increasingly passive and detached as the weight of the mud pushed in upon him, sucking out not only his poisons, but also, it seemed, his life, compressing him inexorably into a claustrophobic sleep from which he would awake only if and when the knowledge the poet took to his grave was revealed.

Tharmas stirred in the neighboring bath. "Strange, but this mud here," he noted with a connoisseur's air, "smells exactly like the asshole of a sheep I once knew."

Ded did not respond. He was not listening. His mind was no longer there.

❧

The 747 was tunneling through the night. Ded was inside, sitting in the last row, strapped and immobile, in a middle seat between two passengers. His small suitcase and his garment bag were crammed under his feet, there being no space in the overhead compartment. His seatback was upright, unable to recline because of the rear wall behind.

Feeling hopelessly trapped, Ded looked over the cavernous cabin. All he could see was row after row of passengers, each strapped in his seat and looking straight ahead, away from him. Before the trolleys reached him, the flight attendants had run out of drinks and peanuts. They had run out of meals. The "fasten seat belt" and "toilet occupied" signs had been on during the whole trip. Ded had seen the movie. He had read the in-house magazine. He had heard the audio entertainment. Even the safety lecture and captain's announcements had been recordings he had heard a hundred times. And for the last five hours the man in the aisle seat next to Ded had been explaining the urgent necessity for calendar reform.

Oh, no, Ded groaned, *not Pope Gregory the Thirteenth again.* His seatmate was complaining about the 16th-century change to the calendar in which, with what the man referred to as "typical Catholic incompetence," eleven days had been lost forever.

"For almost a thousand years," the calendarian once more repeated the details, "the West got by with a calendar based on an assumed 365.25-day year, corrected by four-yearly leap years. Sure, the earth actually revolves around the sun in only 365.2425 days, so by Pope Gregory's time, the days and the seasons were slightly out of whack. But did the church say the sensible thing, 'So what? The change has been so slow everyone's gotten used to it.' No, the stupidos, without any consultation whatsoever, went ahead and removed eleven *real* days from that year's calendar, thereby not only depriving everyone of eleven days of pay, but, more importantly, shortening their life span by the same amount. It was downright criminal."

Ded was careful not to make the mistake he had made earlier of quibbling with the calendarian's definition of *real* days. He recalled the man's response with a shudder. "The Spanish Armada, the Treaty of Westphalia, the Declaration of Independence, the storming of the Bastille, the Treaty of Ghent…" For over an hour the man had droned on, relentlessly enumerating everything occurring since the 16th century that had come eleven days too early.

Or was it eleven days too late? Ded wasn't sure.

Ded was on the cusp of being reduced by the tedium and claustrophobia to a blubbering protoplasm. The only thing that had been keeping him sane was the knowledge the flight was scheduled to end—in a mere twenty minutes hence.

The crackle of static came across the public address system. "I'm sorry for the inconvenience," the captain announced, "but we've been instructed by the controller to maintain a holding pattern for an indefinite period."

An indefinite period? Ded tried not to panic, pressing his open hands to either side of his head. His drowning mind searched frantically for something absolute to which to cling. *A 747 carries only about an hour's worth of reserve fuel. If the plane doesn't land during that period, it'll crash.*

He felt better.

At worst, a little over an hour from now, he comforted himself, *KER-SPLOSH! And I'll never have to hear about Pope Gregory again.*

One hour, ten minutes and eleven seconds later, most of which Ded spent hearing about Pope Gregory, the plane touched down and came to a stop. Promising to write his Congressman as soon as possible about the missing days, Ded began to gather up his bags to make his escape from his ponderous seatmate.

"I'm sorry for the inconvenience," the pilot's voice came over the speakers, "but we haven't had a gate assigned yet. We'll have to wait on the runway."

"What next?" Ded groaned.

"And to conserve fuel," the pilot went on, "we'll be turning off the air conditioning and the main lighting."

Ded cursed himself for having opened his big mouth.

The lights went out. The whole plane fell quiet. Even the loquacious calendarian buttoned his lip.

Ded sat in the dark, feeling the inside of the plane grow as hot and stuffy as a coffin. *It can't take that long to get a gate assigned.*

But it could. Two hours later, the plane pulled into a gate.

Streaming with sweat, on the verge of hysteria, Ded grabbed his bags. "I've got to get out of here," he said under his breath. "I've got to get out of here!"

"I'm sorry for the inconvenience," the pilot's voice came on again, "but they seem to be having some difficulty operating the jetway. Please remain in your seats until the maintenance crew has had a chance to fix it."

As a dedicated student of travel statistics, Ded was fully aware that failure to get the jetway out to the plane after an interminable flight was the leading cause of passenger suicides. *Whatever you do,* he tried to reason with his panicking self, *don't kill yourself now. You're going to need all your strength to fight your way out of here.*

With a total act of will, Ded remained sitting, wedged in his center seat, crammed with his bags, at the rear of the crowded aircraft, letting one phrase repeat in his head. *You're not trapped. You're not trapped. You're not trapped.*

Forty-five minutes later, at the bump of the jetway against the aircraft, a cheer went up near the front. Everyone jumped out of their seats. Everyone, that was, except the calendarian, who continued to block Ded's access to the aisle.

"As we're at the back of the plane, there's no reason to stand up before it empties," he informed Ded. "True, I might get a few seconds' head start on retrieving my carry on from the overhead locker, but such a small amount of time is neither here nor there, given the flight is already eleven days off schedule."

Ded stood up, bending to keep from bumping his head on the overhead luggage compartment, and after a lengthy exertion, managed to wrestle his small suitcase and his garment bag up from between his legs.

"Excuse me, excuse me," he jabbered as he stepped over his seatmate and fell into the aisle. Ded crawled to his feet. The way was packed.

"I'm sorry for the inconvenience," the pilot said over the public address, "but we seem to be having some difficulty getting the door open."

That was it. Ded took leave of his senses. "Let me out!" he screamed. "Let me out!"

Holding a bag in each hand, he pushed through the other passengers toward the front, stumbling over barricades of suitcases and paper shopping bags, reeling before the gauntlet of shoulders, hips, and elbows that were trying to impede his progress. "Let me out! Let me out! Let me out!"

The aisle was infinitely long. His battle up it, an eternity. He felt like a salmon trying to swim through a narrow spillway filled with dying fish. Only pure will kept him going.

At last, as he was about to abandon all hope, he reached the front of the economy class cabin, where a stewardess stood with her back to him, watching the door. A quiet rattle could be heard from outside of the plane. With a WHOOSH, the door opened. Ded took a step forward.

"Just a moment," a stewardess said, still facing away as she lifted the back of her arm to block him. "You'll have to let the first- and business-class passengers off first."

"You can't do this," Ded whimpered to the back of the stewardess's head. "I'm a free man."

Impervious, she kept Ded blockaded with her arm held up like an angel of the Lord guarding the pearly gates. "Free man? An airline passenger? Don't make me laugh."

"At least look at me while you're blocking my way," Ded begged, tears rolling down his face. "Can't you?"

The stewardess lowered her arm and turned, revealing her face. She was blind.

More than that, she was Beulah!

She smiled. Her naked gaze, which at first roved aimlessly, fixed on Ded, and he felt himself drawn irresistibly toward her. As his face got closer to hers, her eyes seemed to merge into a single, burning, eternal, infinite sun, and the tube of the airplane fell away, like cast-off blinders, from his field of vision. His claustrophobia dissolved into a feeling of freedom. The black void of his heart began filling with love; the pale specter of his mind, with life. His subjective self blossomed outwards, transforming purposelessness into meaning, until, like the highest level of God's consciousness, it encompassed the entire universe.

Ded opened his mouth to speak and it filled, as if by a miracle, with hot, mineralized mud.

ఆ

"Yuh're not supposed to *eat* it," Tharmas chided with feigned disgust as Ded came spluttering awake. "Yuh don't know where that stuff's been."

Ded sat up, spitting. From the taste, he had a pretty good idea. No wonder it smelled like the asshole of a sheep.

He got to his feet. From his nose on down was a solid coat of dark brown mud.

"Those untouchables in the Uttar Pradesh ain't got nothing on yuh," Tharmas said.

Ded turned as the attendant came through the door. The man stopped and examined the sorrowful sight standing before him. The skinny bowed legs. The arms held out a few inches from the body. All but the upper half of the head covered in a viscous brown ooze.

"Had enough, have we?"

Ded confirmed forlornly with his head.

"Perhaps you should wash," the attendant said, motioning to a shower in the corner.

"Yes," Ded agreed through the viscous coating over his mouth. "Otherwise, my future social life will be even more limited than it already is."

Ded climbed out of the mud bath and clomped to the shower like the *Creature from the Black Lagoon*. It took a lot of vigorous scrubbing under the torrential spray to remove his thick, alien skin and rejoin the human race.

By the time Ded had turned off the water, the attendant had fetched a stack of fresh towels. "How did you like the mud bath, then?"

"I hate to say it," Ded answered, "but the whole experience has left a bad taste in my mouth."

"I'm very sorry, sir. Next time you come, we'll supply you with a snorkel."

The attendant put the towels down and led Ded to a tub filled with clear, hot water. "Direct from the spring," he boasted.

As the attendant went over see to Tharmas and Ghostflea, Ded climbed into the tub and eased himself down until he was floating in the simmering water.

ꟹ

Ded's mind drifted back to Beulah. He could see her eyes in the reflections of the overhead lights dancing on the surface of his bath. And feel her long, rosy-golden hair in the gentle liquid ripples caressing his body.

"So beautiful," he murmured. "So wonderfully beautiful."

He felt as though he wanted to float there forever, contemplating his love.

His heavy eyelids fell closed and he once again saw the stewardess

Beulah's roving eyes fix on his, merging into a single, burning, eternal, infinite sun. Once again, the tube of the airplane fell away, like blinders, from his field of vision. Once again, his subjective self blossomed outwards, transforming purposelessness into meaning, until, like the highest level of God's consciousness, it encompassed the entire universe.

Only this time, when the smoke cleared, the entire encompassed universe was nothing more than the white, stick-style farmhouse with its large red barn in the middle of vineyards.

Sitting on the porch in a simple cotton frock, a barefoot Beulah looked out over the vines. At her feet tumbled a gaggle of happy, bespectacled children. And beside her, in an old rocking chair was Ded himself.

The Ded on the porch stood and spread his arms wide toward the ripening grapes. "The permanent way out," he exulted, "is not to put your blinders *on*, but, instead, to take them *off*. That's the only way you'll ever wake the sleeping God."

Ded's eyelids flew open. He sat up in his tub. *Broadening your perspective is the only way to wake the sleeping God?*

It didn't make any sense. *Sicilian Illusions exist only because people limit their perspective.*

Had Jerusalem found a way to do the impossible? Ded would have to ask Beulah, the next time he saw her.

Peering down into the clear, warm water of his bath, he thought he could make out a glimmer of hope.

Perhaps it wasn't Hell he was in.

It was Purgatory.

CHAPTER 26

GLIMPSES OUT OF THE MOUTH

The door to Ded's hotel room was ajar. Overcome by a sense of uneasiness, the claims adjuster hesitated, taking a deep breath before he pushed the door fully open and stepped in.

The place was a mess. The bed was torn apart. His garment bag and small suitcase were ripped open. Clothes, toiletries, and papers were everywhere.

Ded considered vacating the premises until he was able to get O'Nadir's forensics guys in to look for prints. But it was too late at night for such a disruption. Instead, he would touch as little as possible until morning. Since whoever had ransacked the room likely left prints of one sort or another on almost everything in it, the delay shouldn't make much difference.

Anyway, glancing around, Ded could see that nothing significant was missing. Whatever the intruder had been looking for apparently hadn't been found.

Ded closed the door and fastened the lock and chain. Then, as during his first night, he dragged the too-short chair inches from the doorknob and balanced his small suitcase against the door on the top of the seatback.

He went to the window. Sperm-shaped drops of rain slithered across the glass. In the darkness outside, he could see the Bank of America tower. All of its lights were out except those at its top, in the offices of Urizen & Fallen. He closed the curtains.

He had slept on the ride back from Calistoga. As a result, he already could feel the beginnings of a wine hangover, exacerbated by a slight unreality to his perceptions generated by trace remains of marijuana still in his system.

Let's hope God doesn't feel like this when He wakes up from His *long slumber,* Ded grumbled. *Or He might say, "Fuck it," and go right back to sleep.*

With a sigh, he set about removing the bullet lodged in his Ickey Jerusalem anthology by pulling open the relevant pages, one by one.

Slipping the bullet into yet another evidence bag, he noticed his message light was on and checked with the hotel operator. Inspector O'Nadir had called. Ded immediately rang him at home.

"Jesus," O'Nadir complained groggily in a whisper so as not to wake his wife, "do you know what time it is?"

"Please forgive me," Ded said. "I seem to have lost track of time."

"It's almost midnight."

"Goodness, is it?" Ded's tone changed to one of urgent concern. "You better hurry up and tell me why you called before you turn back into a pumpkin."

O'Nadir sighed. "Just a moment." A few seconds later, he picked up an extension in another room and began riffling through some notes.

"Before you give me your stuff," Ded said, "let me fill you in on what's happened since we spoke this afternoon." He then described the exploding golf club, Dr. Ulro wanting to kill all the fruitcakes, the doctor's travel receipts, the shots at the hearse, Ghostflea pinching Mr. Crewcut at the base of his neck, etc., ending with: "I've been invited to the reading of the bequests tomorrow morning at ten, at Urizen's office. You want to come?"

"Should I?"

"I think so. I've got more bagged evidence to give you. Plus, there's a set of fingerprints we don't have but I'd like you to take from one of the attendees."

"I'll bring my kit," O'Nadir said.

"I wouldn't like to raise any suspicions. Can you take the prints without the subject knowing?"

"I've got just the thing." The inspector made a note. "What about the Ulros and the exploding golf club? Should I bring 'em in?"

"Since I had an interview with each of them this afternoon, I'm probably the best person to follow up. But you can talk to them yourself after the reading of the bequests, which I'm sure both will be attending. I'd appreciate it, though, if you restricted your questions to the exploding driver and didn't get into their peculiar personal arrangements."

"No problem," the inspector answered. "Anything else?"

"Could you check which taxi companies have an orangey-red livery? And then check which of those made a delivery to the Three Heavens Country Club this morning? Hopefully, we can find out where the exploding golf club came from. And see if the perpetrator used the taxi company for anything else."

"You got it," O'Nadir said after writing all his tasks down. "Now, I have a few things for you. First, the Marin County sheriff's office recovered the slug from the Mount Tamalpais amphitheater stage. They'll courier it over, first thing tomorrow morning." O'Nadir was speaking in a monotone, as though reading from his notes.

"Second, I talked to Angel Cleaners in New York. Their bagging process is done by machine. When their employees put the bagged clothes into the delivery box, they usually grasp the wire hanger and let the clothes fold as they are lowered—though, occasionally, they'll fold the bag with their hands. None of the employees wear gloves, so that can't explain the glove prints all over the bag."

O'Nadir's voice became more natural. "I plan to ask the NYPD tomorrow to take fingerprints of the cleaners' employees. Based on their past practices, though, it'll take at least a week for the prints to arrive here in San Francisco."

"Since we're only looking for someone with especially large handprints," Ded suggested, "why don't you call the cleaners back and see if any of their employees fit that description?"

"I'll call them in the morning." O'Nadir paused to make a note. "Oh, you asked me to track down the two missing flight attendants. Turns out they and the purser were staying at the same New York hotel as Ickey Jerusalem's party. I haven't been able to talk to them, but given the lower level of confidentiality regarding staff than passengers, the airline was able to tell me that both stewardesses showed up at the New-York-to-San-Francisco red-eye the day *after* Jerusalem's flight, claiming to have received a message at the hotel postponing their work slot until then. If the two stewardesses had followed company rules requiring them to immediately ring back to confirm receipt of any such messages, the airline would've had time to correct the error."

"When will you be able to talk to the flight attendants?"

"One is in the Far East and one is in Europe. I left messages for them to call me collect."

Ded yawned. "That's it?"

"Yep. Where are you now?"

"The hotel."

"Sleeping alone tonight, are we?"

"Whether I'm sleeping alone or not," Ded humored him, "depends solely on how wide my perspective is."

"From what I hear," O'Nadir leered, "it's not how wide your perspective is, but how you use it."

"You're a real philosopher, O'Nadir, for a cave dweller. See you at the reading of the bequests."

Ded was about to put the receiver down when he caught a glimpse of the mess around him. "Oh, one other thing. When I was out today, someone ransacked my room. You might want to send Ben and his guys over tomorrow to see if the culprit left any fingerprints. I'll alert the hotel not to clean the room."

Ded gave O'Nadir his room number and then, after enduring the inspector's vulgar comments about what else Ben might find in Ded's uncleaned hotel room, hung up.

Ded brushed his teeth, took off his clothes, climbed into the queen-sized bed, and sat back against the headboard. He surveyed the empty, unused portions of the mattress around him. *No doubt about it,* he brooded. *Tonight, I* am *sleeping alone.*

To cheer himself up, he imagined Beulah lying in the space next to him, her pure, unblemished skin, stippling with the air-conditioned chill.

God, what he wouldn't have given right then to hold her in his arms, and to have her hold him in hers. Not for sex. But—yes, he was not embarrassed to admit it—for love. Wondrous love. Eternal and infinite love in which—

He reached over and took the anthology of Jerusalem's poetry off the nightstand, consulted the index for "love" (fortunately, the bullet hole was confined to the margin), opened it at the first poem referenced, and in a rapture, mouthed the words:

Love and harmony combine
And around our souls intwine,
While thy branches mix with mine,
And our roots together join.

Joys upon our branches sit,
Chirping loud, and singing sweet;
Like gentle streams beneath our feet
Innocence and virtue meet.

Ded sighed. He looked down, noticing his high priest was

becoming a little pompous, evidencing a budding interest in entering by a secret place.

He grabbed the phone by his bed and dialed.

A sleepy voice answered after the fifth ring. "Yes?"

"Love is the door to the imaginative world," the claims adjuster recited, lingering on every word.

"Ded?" Beulah guessed, speaking his name with all the cheery innocence of an awakening homecoming queen.

"Love is the door to the imaginative world," Ded repeated. "And, God, am I hot to enter yours."

Beulah made a long, sensuous sound, as though stretching languidly on her bed. "Okay, here I am."

"Yes, and here I am, at the hotel without a car."

"Oh," Beulah cooed disappointedly. "So, what do you want to do?"

"What I want to do," Ded murmured, "is unite our beings in the eternity of love. Lose ourselves in embraces that…" He found the verse again in Jerusalem's book of poems right before the pompous high priest. "…are Comminglings from the Head even to the Feet." He put the book down. "But as that's not possible, I was thinking that if Jerusalem could reach out with his poetic mind to unite with the sun ninety million miles away, maybe you could do the same for little old me not that far across the Bay."

In his mind's eye, Ded saw Beulah smiling.

"Lie back," she whispered. "Lay the phone by your ear. Close your eyes. Clear your mind of all other thoughts but me."

Ded did as she directed.

"Imagine I'm standing over you, straddling your waist, looking down on you from towering heights, wearing absolutely nothing."

Ded pictured her as described, with one minor exception: she had her dark glasses on.

Beulah paused to gather her words around her and then began, her whisper now slow, sultry, and highly charged with sexual energy. "My rosy blond hair billows dreamily over my baby pink shoulders and strokes my breasts… My breasts, firm and full, heave erotically, their rose-petal nipples straining vainly for lips to suck them dry."

Ded felt his already half-flaccid, inflatable rocket stirring.

Beulah inhaled and let out a long, sensuous breath. "My delicate, innocent fingers rise to the top of my head, pause, and then begin traveling silkily down my long, luxurious tresses… down over my breasts… down my hips… over into the inside of my thighs… and then, gently… hesitantly… upwards… until they join at the fleshy entrance to my being."

Ded's inflating rocket rolled around to the right on its way toward the full-point position.

Beulah's voice deepened. "Now, my fingers, soft as the bosom of a dove, begin stroking, tangentially at first and then more directly, the tiny gatekeeper above the entrance to my being. In response, my gatekeeper begins to swell… my stroking becomes harder… until my gatekeeper snaps to complete attention and my breath becomes heavier. My cheeks, my breasts, and the insides of my thighs begin to blush with passion. My entrance, pulsing with living blood, begins to open."

Ded's rocket was now on its launch pad, aimed directly at the heavens above.

"Below me," Beulah went on huskily, "you manhood is swollen… hard… like petrified stone… waiting."

Ded curled his right hand and moved it downwards.

"I descend… little by little… into a squat… pulling apart with my fingers the moist mouth of my cave… parting the pulpy apple… the sweetest fruit that the worm feeds on… the worm seventy inches long, lasting for sixty winters."

Ded opened his eyes and looked down at what he was about to grasp in his hand. Was she talking about him?

"I take your manhood up inside of me," Beulah groaned.

Ded closed his eyes again. In a single, languorous stroke, he mimicked her taking him up inside.

"My hair, my arms, and my legs envelop you. My breasts press firmly over your face… my nipples squirm into your mouth… and like a baby, you suck for the milk of my love, as my hungry, lower lips begin to suck for the cream of your existence."

Ded's tongue blocked his mouth, and his fist, stroking in a slow, sucking tempo, became more insistent in its upward movements.

"Utterly surrounded by my physical being… unable to speak… unable to see… unable to hear… unable to breathe… unable to move… you feel yourself disappearing… helpless… up inside me."

Ded clung on with both hands. *HoIy, holy, holy, lord God Almighty!*

"Come," Beulah rasped. "Give yourself up… come… come… that's it… come… come… oh… yes… come… come! Come! COME! OH, YES! COME! COME!! COME!!!"

Beulah went silent.

She must've come, Ded concluded.

He knew *he* had.

Ded lay there, his exhausted hands curled tenderly around his deflating rocket.

"Did you come?" Beulah asked, reverting to her normal, chirpy schoolgirl voice.

"Either that," Ded breathed, "or my pecker is involved in some kind of conspiracy to cover the upper half of my body with a milky glue."

"Glad to see I haven't lost my touch," Beulah yawned.

"Can I return the favor?" Ded asked chivalrously, though he lacked the necessary poetic imagination to do the job as well as she had.

"That's sweet, but no. If you don't mind, I'm going back to sleep. See you tomorrow at Bacon's office."

"You won't be able to miss me," Ded said. "Just look for the guy with the bedsheets stuck to his chest."

ര

Ded took a shower and then dried off, rearranged the sheets to provide the largest area of nonstick surface possible, and got back into bed. Jerusalem's anthology was still open, lying near the headboard.

He picked it up. On top of the phrase "a pompous High Priest" sat a random, self-satisfied glop from Ded's eponymous donor, gradually turning brown.

Ded wiped the glop off with the edge of the sheet, returned the anthology to the nightstand, put his glasses next to the book, turned out the lights, and lay back down.

He felt drained. Empty. As though nothing of him remained but his body. Another meaningless, temporary Sicilian Illusion at an end.

Shit, he suddenly realized, *I was so hot to have phone sex, I failed to ask Beulah about how to wake the sleeping God. Where were my priorities?*

He lay there, depressed, figuratively kicking himself.

You know, Ded mused moments later as he felt himself irresistibly retreating into slumber, *that part near the end, about being utterly surrounded by Beulah, unable to speak, unable to see, unable to hear, unable to breathe, unable to move, feeling myself disappearing, helpless, up inside was erotic as hell, but also, now I think about it, somewhat frightening.*

Ded wondered if Ickey Jerusalem ever felt the same way.

Then, a thought struck him. *On the plane, Beulah could have overpowered Jerusalem if she'd been making love to him.*

Once again, Ded was trapped in the crowded plane. Only this time, it was much worse. He was locked in the toilet. Sitting on the seat. Covered from his head to his feet in heavy, brown, malodorous mud. He was unable to move, in part, due to the weight of the mud, but, much more oppressively, due to the embrace of a mysterious, six-foot-tall broccoli "tree" in the cubicle with him. It was planted on his lap, entwining its innumerable roots around his body, searching for nourishment in his coat of sludge.

Affixed to the broccoli's trunklike stalk, immediately below its green broccoli Afro, Ded could see a one-foot-diameter, golden disk. Etched on this faux sun, in the same thin-line style as Jerusalem's engravings, was not the Heavenly Host but a beaming happy face, reminiscent of the gingerbread man at the funeral, though with a few minor differences. The chin had a "V" for a goatee, for one thing. The two dot eyes, rather than sitting directly under the hyphen eyebrows, were crossed, close together, and covered with a single, large monocle. On the forehead was a white headband on which was drawn not Babylonian script but the image of a small serpent entwined around a vertical staff—the universal symbol of a medical doctor.

"I beg your pardon," Ded said to the gargantuan green vegetable as politely as he could, "but this toilet is taken."

As the broccoli bent its golden happy face toward Ded, the clear glass monocle darkened into opacity. The blinded broccoli then reached up with two of its longer roots, pulled a large foil packet from its brain-like green top, tore it open, removed a gigantic clear-plastic condom, and in an act of utter contempt, pulled the thing down over Ded's head.

Reflexively holding his breath, Ded whipped his head from side to side, then up and down, trying to shake the condom off. He attempted to free his arms. He wriggled. He squirmed. He kicked the door with his feet. But he was too tightly bound by the grasp of the broccoli's roots.

Unable to hold his breath any longer, he let it out in a single exhalation. The diaphanous plastic lifted from the surface of his lips. But as soon as he tried to draw another breath, the plastic came back against his mouth, sealing it shut.

Ded sucked and sucked and sucked, but no air could get in. Madly, he tried to bite a hole in the condom, but the smooth, transparent film provided nothing for his snapping teeth to catch onto. His eyes widened in terror.

Air! he screamed silently. *I need air!*

He went wild, great spasms of desperation powering every inch of his body against his bonds in repeated, fruitless attempts to gain release, until, with the life force draining from his suffocating body, he was reduced to an exhausted, quivering palsy, staring helplessly upwards in a wordless plea for mercy from the sightless happy face towering above.

A black rim appeared around Ded's disk-fixed field of view and expanded inwards, contracting his perspective, narrower and narrower, into an evermore constricted tunnel, until all he could see was a tiny pinpoint of light, glistening off the golden face.

The light held on for the longest of moments and then went out.

Ded sat up in his bed, gasping for breath, sweating from head to toe.

God, what a nightmare.

Once his terror subsided, he switched on the lamp, put on his glasses, noted the 2:30 a.m. time on the nightstand clock, plumped up the pillows on the headboard, and leaned back on them, sitting up to study his face in the mirror on the opposite wall. The dream, he was sure, had been a message from his subconscious mind. Something about Ickey Jerusalem's death.

Ded reached for his notepad and wrote down what he remembered. The giant broccoli was almost certainly the Tree of Mystery—unable to see the true reality, and reaching out with its cold roots to squeeze the life out of Ickey Jerusalem. But beyond that? The happy face had symbols representing Tharmas, Ghostflea, Urizen, Dr. Ulro, and with the monocle becoming opaque, Beulah. Had they all been in it together?

Ded took the anthology of Jerusalem's poetry from the nightstand and looked in the index. When he didn't find what he wanted, he closed the book with a disgruntled book-clap-punctuated whoosh of air. There wasn't a single poem about broccoli.

Then, a new thought occurred to him. The morning after, in the bedroom at Lambeth, he had found poems about Beulah referenced in the index. Were there poems about the other suspects as well? He reopened the anthology. Right there in the index where the word "broccoli" should have been was the name "Bromion," followed by a long list of page numbers.

Ded scanned farther up the page, past Beulah. There was Bacon.

He flipped through the other pages of the index, finding more names: Tharmas, Ulro, Urizen, Vala, Adam, Robert, Luvah, and William. The name Ghostflea wasn't in the index, but there was reference to "The Ghost of a Flea."

All the suspects in Jerusalem's coterie were mentioned in his anthology, some of them, judging by the long lists of page references, many times. Even more interestingly, the references seemed congregated in the last section of the book, the one containing the poet's most recent work.

Ded began skimming the latter part of the anthology. He noticed it also contained Jerusalem's engravings, including those Ded had already seen as well as many others. "The Ghost of a Flea" was such an image, clearly modeled on Adam Ghostflea. "Robert" and "William," were separate, homoerotic engravings—although, given the commonality of those names, their appearance as titles of engravings could have been a coincidence, unless Jerusalem somehow knew the purser before the flight.

As for the poems, they were not at all like the ones Ded had read before. They were of monumental length, going on forbiddingly for page after page in loose, eccentrically punctuated free verse, and filled with obscure, capitalized terms: The Garment of War. The Starry Eight. The Mundane Shell. The White Couch. The Polybus. The Vortex. The Veil of Mystery. The Bread of Ages. The Circle of Destiny. The Oak of Weeping. The Chain of Jealousy. The Woof of Six Thousand Years.

The Woof of Six Thousand Years? Ded scratched his head. What the hell was that? The half-life of Scofield's halitosis?

He read more closely. The Woof reference was in a poem about Milton, the author of the 17th-century tract about church discipline Ded had found at Lambeth. According to the poem, Milton had dropped out of the sky one day and taken up residence among the seven bones in Jerusalem's left ankle.

Jerusalem must have been hitting the Ripple and hashish heavily before writing that one.

Unfortunately, the characters in the poems were so abstract, they seemed to have little to say about the reality of their human counterparts. Each of the suspects appeared to have been transformed into a monumentalized archetype, a representation of one or another basic philosophical idea. These archetypes engaged in human behavior, like weeping, frowning, or howling, but it was done with such melodrama, Ded found it hard to feel any empathy for them, despite his newly developed poetic understanding. Whenever a character spoke, it was in the monologue of a bombastic didact, staking out a rigid point of view.

After a few hours of poem reading, Ded, faced with the length, the obscurity, and the abstract didacticism of Jerusalem's work, decided life was too short and gave up.

Before closing the book, though, he turned one last time to the index, where, as he had already noticed in passing, there was mention not merely of the suspects but also of others in Jerusalem's coterie. Enion. Los. Rahab. Oothoon. Hand and Hyle. Some had their names lengthened: Enith*armon*, Theo*tormon*, Ozo*th*, Soth*a*, *An*tamon, Rin*trah*, and Palam*abron*. Changed, sure, but in one form or other, they were all there, even Jerusalem's dead brother, Orc.

Orc. Didn't Tharmas say Jerusalem spent a lot of time talking to Orc?

Perhaps the relevant poems would throw some light on what the two of them might have been discussing.

Despite a natural hesitancy about returning to the poetic morass from which he had just extracted himself, Ded decided to give it one more chance.

Over the next couple of hours, despite plowing valiantly through every reference to Orc—there were more for him than anyone other than Jesus—Ded failed to find a single note of any conversation with Ickey Jerusalem. What he did find, however, pieced together from the often conflicting Orc poems, was much more important. Something that might at last let Ded understand what was going on inside Jerusalem's mind that night on the plane. Something that might simultaneously allow Ded to make his own Beulah-inspired Sicilian Illusions permanent.

It was another parable. Laying out, for all to see, exactly how to wake the sleeping God.

Since Ded was doing the piecing-together, the Orc parable ended up somewhat shorn of its poetic imagery and emotional power. Thus, what Ded was able to see, as he lay in his bed in the Holiday Inn, was only a small part of the truth the parable contained.

But that part was sufficient, when combined with what he had learned so far, for him to employ his exceptional detective skills to grasp the key meaning.

The parable begins with the story now well-known to Ded. After God falls asleep, the good guys—poets and other artists with sufficient residual imagination—start piercing the physical world to capture partial glimpses of the omnipotent creativity at the highest level of God's consciousness. Since the good guys' minds, as everything else, are just part of God's infinitely imaginative mind, the glimpses, if left alone, would burn as a beacon forever in the shrunken consciousness of the sleeping God. However, the glimpses are not left alone. The baddies, slaves to reason, ensnare each of the glimpses in a web of abstractions and pull it down into Hell, to be hidden from the sleeping God's consciousness behind a theoretical façade, supposedly bringing humanity closer to the fully awake God, but in fact, doing the exact opposite.

In the Orc parable, the good guys are represented by an innocent, freedom-loving, passionate youth called Orc. The baddies are represented by an experienced, tyrannous, highly rational senior citizen called Urizen. As the parable progresses, Orc and Urizen keep reappearing to do battle in a myriad of guises—everything from a finger-painting, nursery student being chastised by a neatness-obsessed teacher to a poet being analyzed into nothingness by literary critics to Jesus being crucified by Nobodaddy's righteous laws.

At the end of each battle, Urizen kills Orc, turning him into yet another serpent hanging on a barren tree. Immediately afterwards, Orc is reincarnated into another form.

Gradually, it becomes clear that Orc and Urizen are facets of the same person, Orc flipping upside down and morphing into Urizen as each cycle ages. For instance, shortly following Jesus's crucifixion by Nobodaddy, Orc appears in the form of the early Christian visionaries, experiencing directly and totally Christ's love. Soon, however, the Christian Church thus created begins, under the influence of the Urizen part of Orc's nature, abstracting, theorizing, ritualizing, and institutionalizing, until—while still paying lip service to Christ's love—the Church turns into its exact opposite: an inescapable, totalitarian tyranny requiring absolute obedience in action and even thought, and condemning to eternal hellfire those who don't obey—a hyper-abstract New Testament form of the Old Testament Tree of Mystery from which Jesus intended to free humanity.

However, all is not lost. Each time a cycle repeats, Orc's newly created permanent glimpses of the *un*fallen world accumulate in the consciousness of the sleeping God in a form Jerusalem calls—for comic relief, presumably—Golgonooza. At the same time, Urizen's abstract camouflage of those glimpses accumulates in Hell (like Satan and everything else, merely a part of God's overall mind) in a form Jerusalem calls the Consolidation of Error—an ever-larger and more repressive web of abstractions, eventually separating humanity not only from love, but also, as result of the various cycles, from joy, from beauty, from community, from nobility, from more and more of what it means to be truly human.

When a sufficient number of Orc's glimpses have accumulated in Golgonooza to produce a complete picture of the fully conscious God's omnipotent imagination, and that picture has been totally camouflaged by Urizen's abstract Consolidation of Error, Urizen appears in his final form as Satan Incarnate, along with a character called Rahab, as the Whore of Babylon. They do the dirty deed together, whereupon the Consolidation of Error vanishes. The sleeping God can now see Golgonooza's complete picture of the fully conscious God's mind. Recognizing who He really is, the sleeping God awakes, allowing His formerly shrunken consciousness (powered by the simultaneous reappearance of Orc, in his final incarnation as the Jesus of the Second Coming) to rapidly expand in an apocalypse of fire, reuniting with the hitherto hidden part of His mind and obliterating all the illusory bifurcations of the fallen world.

ↀ

Whew! Ded thought when he finished parsing it all out. *So,* that's *the meaning of the words spoken at the end of my airplane dream at the mud baths. The permanent way out was to take the blinders off. In the case of the sleeping God, the blinders of the Consolidation of Error. Causing Him to awake.*

Is that what Jerusalem was attempting in the toilet?

Ded looked slowly around the room. As far as he could see, the old bifurcations still existed. The Apocalypse had not yet occurred.

Perhaps, Golgonooza wasn't yet complete, Ded speculated. *Beulah did say it would take a whole lot of poems to unite life and death. Or maybe Golgonooza* was *complete, but the trigger didn't present itself. After all, there are no reports of Rahab having been on the flight, never mind Urizen banging her there. And even if the two managed to get it on, while not the sort of asymmetric coupling most people would want to watch, it's hard to see the entire physical universe vanishing in disgust.*

Ded sat bolt upright with an alternative thought. *On the other hand, is it possible Jerusalem discovered a* different *trigger? Something weird he could do while sitting on the toilet that would destroy the Consolidation of Error? And then, before he could finish the job, Satan Incarnate jumped him?*

Ded paused to stare across the room at his face in the mirror.

What the hell am I talking about?

Is this what I'm going to put in my report to the home office?

The answer, of course, was no. Still, Ded couldn't help but marvel at what a long way he had come in the last two days. So long that for the first time, he was beginning to think he might not be able to find the route back to the person he had been. Or even if he could find the route, whether he would have any desire to follow it.

He glanced at the window. Morning light peeked from behind the curtain. In a few more hours, Ickey Jerusalem's bequests were to be read out.

Ded closed the anthology.

If Satan Incarnate did jump Jerusalem, then he is likely also the killer. Dr. Ulro, who often appears Satanic, talked about killing the fruitcakes before they triggered the Apocalypse, but based on the Orc cycle, I'd say the prime suspect is now none other than the person whose most recent incarnation is described in the Orc poems as Satan Incarnate.

This morning, at the reading of the bequests, I'll have a chance to find out what Bacon Urizen has to say for himself.

❧

Ded got out of bed, went to the curtains, and threw them open to the early morning light. He looked up at Urizen's office on the top of the Bank of America tower.

Instantly, a line of bullet holes at eye height appeared from left to right in the glass.

Ded dove to the floor. *Christ, someone is shooting at me from up there. Like in the movie.*

He felt his chest. He hadn't been hit.

But how's that possible?

The fine, white dust falling from above gave him his answer. The shooter had not been up on the high-rise but someplace down below his window. The bullets had entered the hardened safety glass at eye height but gone straight over his head into the ceiling.

Ded came to his feet to the left of the window and peered around the curtain. On the flat roof of a three-story building on Commercial Street (was it the Wing Fat Ho grocery store?), he could see the back of someone wearing a blue knit cap. The figure ducked down into an elevated stairwell compartment while holding behind by the handle, in a naked fist, a flat, rectangular canvas bag.

Ded pulled the curtains closed, his heart pounding.

PART FIVE

CHAPTER 27

THE SHADOWS ON THE GROUND

Carrying the anthology of Ickey Jerusalem's poetry under one arm, Ded opened the door to Urizen & Fallen. Once again, the unbounded view through the wall of glass on the far side of reception stopped him in his tracks. He stood in the doorway, feeling the irresistible pull of infinity sucking him out into space. This time, though, he was not afraid. On the contrary, he was filled with an overpowering desire to step forward, put his weight on his leading leg, extend his other leg back and to one side, spread his arms with hands palms-out, like the naked young man in the picture on Tharmas's home office wall, and with rays of light emanating from his head and torso, lift off the floor and soar straight through the window into the glory of the great unknown.

Swiftly tying this desire down with the bonds of duty, Ded stepped inside and let the door close behind him.

He was late. It had taken some time making his way from the hotel, having to hug the walls and doorways of the buildings so any rooftop shooter would find it difficult to take proper aim.

The receptionist's desk was empty. The only person in the waiting area was a man huddled in a corner chair as far from the window as possible. He was pretending to read a newspaper, holding it open two inches from his face like a shield against the unknown.

Although the man's features were hidden, Ded could tell who he was from the disheveled suit and the sound of gum being chewed.

"Missing our basement office, are we?" Ded asked.

O'Nadir rotated the paper shield away so he could make eye contact. "The newsprint is a little small, that's all."

Mildly euphoric from his unacted desire, Ded strode over and looked out the window.

"It's something that gives life in the Bay Area a certain immediacy. Something that concentrates the mind on the present."

"What's that?" O'Nadir asked suspiciously, having rotated the newspaper back to its original protective position.

"The knowledge that at any moment, an earthquake might occur, and everything will come crashing to the ground."

O'Nadir put his gum chewing on hold. He lowered his newspaper, revealing a pair of tightly shut eyes. "The Bank of America tower will not come crashing to the ground," he said, more in hope than prediction. "I've read how they designed it. Lots of steel. Flexible joints. Plenty of give. So, when an earthquake comes, the building will wave from side to side."

O'Nadir rocked his body in demonstration. It seemed to comfort him.

With a resigned if pleasurable sigh, Ded turned from the window. "Your fingerprint stuff inside your briefcase?"

"No. Outside." O'Nadir's eyes remained fixed on the claims adjuster as he spoke. "The surface has been cleaned and treated. I'll sit on one side of the intended subject and you'll sit on the other. At the appropriate moment, I'll ask him to pass the briefcase to you. As long as we can get him to grab it cleanly, we'll have his prints."

"Very clever."

"Who's the subject?"

Ded looked around to make sure the reception area was still empty. "Tharmas Luvah."

O'Nadir blinked at Ded. "I took his fingerprints at the airport."

"With his gloves on?"

"Well, no. But then, he wasn't wearing any."

Ded "uh-huhed" in a manner indicating he was not at all surprised. He then pulled from his jacket pocket two evidence bags—one with the note and ribbon from the exploding golf club, and the other with the bullet removed from his anthology—and gave them to the inspector.

O'Nadir set his newspaper aside and slipped both bags inside the briefcase, taking care to touch only the latch and the handle. "Thanks. I'll have Ben give these items priority." He snapped the case shut.

"Speaking of Ben," Ded added, "when he goes to my hotel room today for the ransacker's fingerprints, he might take a look at the several bullet holes in the window and the slugs in the ceiling. Assuming they are again 45-caliber, were shot from quite a distance, and hit the glass first, the slugs are unlikely to be buried all that deep. Happened around seven-thirty this morning. Some kind of machine-gun attack, I think."

"Jesus," O'Nadir said. "Poor old Ben doesn't have much of a chance to sit around watching his hand grow when you're in town. Oh, that reminds me, I spoke to the UC Berkeley criminologist. He's got to teach some classes this morning, so he won't show up until the afternoon to review the various glove prints."

"Any other news?"

"I called Angel Cleaners again in New York. There's one person with large hands on their staff. A Tongan guy. Worked for them for the last fifteen years. He said he'd be happy to give his prints to the New York Police Department if we wanted."

Ded tugged at his earlobe. "If he's happy to give his prints to the police, he must be a legal resident. When we've finished here, why don't you call the cleaners back and find out where the guy got his green card? Since he's from the South Pacific, he could have entered the country in San Francisco, so his fingerprints could be on file with the local Immigration and Naturalization Service[7] office."

O'Nadir concentrated a moment as he committed this task to memory. Then, his face brightened. "Oh, trying to track down the two stewardesses this morning, I spoke to another flight attendant at the airport. She said she was in Jerusalem's New York hotel at the same time as the stewardesses. The night before the flight, they all spent a few hours drinking in the cocktail lounge with the purser and—get this—*Tharmas Luvah*. Although she left early to go to bed, around noon the following day, when she was at check-out, she saw Luvah leaving with his bags. The two stewardesses were not with him."

"Luvah never mentioned to me that he got to know the purser before the flight," Ded said. "He—"

"Mr. Smith?"

Ded and O'Nadir looked to find the receptionist had returned. It was the same haughty woman who had been there when Ded had visited Urizen on Saturday evening.

"Mr. Smith?" she asked again primly, recognizing him from his previous visit.

Ded genuflected his face.

"And Mr.—?"

"Inspector O'Nadir."

"Inspector O'Nadir," she echoed. "Could you come this way, please?"

She led them to the same door from reception Ded had used on

7 In March 1, 2003, most of the INS's functions were transferred to three new entities–U.S. Citizenship and Immigration Services (USCIS), U.S. Immigration and Customs Enforcement (ICE), and U.S. Customs and Border Protection (CBP)–within the newly created Department of Homeland Security (DHS), as part of a major government reorganization following the September 11 attacks of 2001.

Saturday. Now, without his attention taken up by the telescope focused on his hotel room window, Ded noticed to the right of the door a large portrait of a gaunt, white-haired man with thin lips and a steely gaze. A gold plaque at the bottom read "Milton Fallen."

Ded stopped. "Miss?"

The receptionist turned and came back to where he and O'Nadir stood before the painting.

"Is this the man who keeps the accounts of the Urthon Spectre Trust?" Ded asked, wondering if there also might be some connection with the Milton in the poem, the one who fell from the sky and took up residence in Jerusalem's ankle.

"*Was*," the receptionist corrected as she looked at the picture. "Sadly, Mr. Fallen passed on, exactly three weeks ago today."

She lowered her eyes respectfully. O'Nadir and Ded did the same, Ded noting to himself that the date of Fallen's death was Monday, October 10th, not only the date the trust took out the insurance policy on Jerusalem's life naming Beulah as the beneficiary but also the date the poet was severely depressed by Urizen's "ingénue" questions, took the trust's financial books home, and acted so oddly in the back of the hearse.

"How did Mr. Fallen die?" Ded asked.

"Old age, mainly," she answered. "He'd become quite elderly and infirm, although he still came to the office every day. His body may have been frail, but his mind was as ordered as it had been on the day he founded the firm. 'Like a well-kept filing cabinet' was how Mr. Urizen often described him. Clean. Neat. Not a thought out of place. It happened at the annual partners' dinner, during the dessert course. Mr. Fallen was explaining double-entry bookkeeping to the senior partners at his table when he began making horrible choking sounds. The partners, assuming this was his throat-clearing preface to some humorous anecdote about credit and debits, sat back, prepared to laugh. Before anyone realized what was happening, Mr. Fallen had buried his face in the Baked Alaska."

The receptionist ushered Ded and O'Nadir through the door. In the secretaries' corridor was the sound of myriad low voices. Most of the desks were filled. The one before the door to Urizen's corner office, however, was empty. The receptionist opened the door and directed Ded and O'Nadir in. Bacon Urizen was not there, but almost everyone else was, sitting on the miscellaneous seating Ded had previously seen, now rearranged in two rows facing the lawyer's desk.

Leading from the doorway, parallel to and about six-feet back from Urizen's desk on Ded's left, was a short row of five swivel chairs. They were all empty except for the third, where the goateed Tharmas Luvah was seated, unshaven, ungroomed, and still in yesterday's clothes.

Behind the swivel chairs was a longer row of seating, anchored closest to Ded by the large couch. Perched on the near end were Ickey Jerusalem's mother and father, Los and Enith, dressed in their best polyester. On the far end sat Jerusalem's brother, Theo. Beside him, a sniveling Grandma Enion was engaged in coating her grandson's supportive shoulder with a multimedia array of tears, drool, and snot.

Beyond the couch, the row extended towards the East-Bay window in a disorganized clutch of easy chairs containing the others: a sullen Dr. Ulro, his good looks slightly marred by the edge of his toupée rising up as he leaned away from Grandma Enion and toward the empty chair beside him, which Ded assumed was reserved for his wife, Rahab Oothoon; a definitely hung-over Adam Ghostflea in the same star-, acorn-, and thorn-picturing clothes he'd worn the day before; and next to Adam, nearest the window, Beulah Vala, wearing her Sunday best—a wide-brimmed, straw hat; a tan, linen blazer; a bright, pastel dress; tiny, white, suede gloves; and floral-rimmed dark glasses. Scofield lay at her feet, growling at nothing in particular.

His imagination having been boosted even further by the night's phone sex, his resulting wild dreams, and his in-depth readings of Ickey Jerusalem's epic poetry, Ded wanted nothing more than to reach out then and there and entangle every part of his mind with Beulah's. But he recalled how, at the previous morning-after, in the kitchen at

Lambeth, Beulah had unexpectedly become so distant. If the same thing happened now, he was not sure he could take it.

As Ded and O'Nadir stepped into the room, Scofield suddenly sniffed, lifted his head, and turned toward the door. Catching sight of Ded, he came to his feet and began wagging his tail excitedly, a look of adoration on his face.

Christ. Ded remembered the unrequested familiarities the dog had forced on him Saturday night in Beulah's bed. He averted his eyes and sat in the first-row semicircle's empty fourth chair, between Tharmas on his left and the empty fifth chair on his right. He deposited the Jerusalem anthology under his seat.

Scofield whimpered and then was quiet. When Ded glanced over, he saw the dog had rested his chin on his paws once more, but still had his soulful, lovesick eyes gazing hopefully in the claims adjuster's direction.

O'Nadir took the second chair in the first row so that Tharmas was now sitting between him and Ded.

"Just the guy I wanted to talk to," Tharmas greeted O'Nadir, his eyes flashing a greater interest in the inspector than the inspector was prepared to accept.

O'Nadir shifted leftwards on his chair, angling his body to face Tharmas more directly but at a greater distance.

"Hoofing it here today from my place," Tharmas explained, "I saw that my VW bus was not in its Taylor Street parking place off Macondray Lane. I take it yuh haven't found Robert N. William?"

"We found him," O'Nadir said.

"Did he do what yuh thought he did?"

"Can't say yet."

"Right. I'm sure yuh'll let me know. Meanwhile, can I have my VW back?"

"It's at an evidence lockup at the station. I'll see what I can do."

Looking back over his right shoulder, Ded noticed that all the other people in the room, including, it appeared, even the sightless Beulah, were now staring at something at the front.

Ded followed their line of sight. Resting next to the now-yellowing white rose on Urizen's desk was a large, brass frame containing a life-sized photograph of Ickey Jerusalem's face. The poet was looking straight into the camera. His curly hair blazed out from the edges of his forehead. The full lips of his small mouth were twisted. His prominent eyebrows were awry. His wide-set eyes had just the right amount of strabismus to make him look like some kind of deranged murderer about to explain the logic of his crime.

"*Not* a good picture," Ded said under his breath to Tharmas.

"Ickey always looked awful in photos," the business manager said out of the side of his mouth. "That's why he dodged them if he could. Yuh shoulda seen his passport picture. Unbelievable. Last year, when we flew to England, the immigration officer took one look at it, shook his head, whistled, and gave the passport back, saying, 'I'm sorry, but I don't think we can allow someone who looks like this into the country.'"

"Did he let you guys through?"

"Only after Ickey agreed to draw dark glasses and a beard on the photo." Tharmas tugged at the end of his goatee with his gloved fingers. "Strange, really, because Ickey, in person, in three dimensions, in motion, was a handsome guy. Urizen once described him as looking like Apollo himself." The business manager screwed up his face. "Whoever Apollo is."

Ded recalled once again Beulah's passionately tactile description on the porch at Lambeth, while watching the warm, midday sun begin its long afternoon fall into the sea. He wondered whether there was any significance in the ugliness of Jerusalem in photos and his handsomeness in person.

Ded peeked at the pink-skinned Beulah by the window, so lovely, so serene, so innocent—as she had been Sunday morning in bed, the still sleeping rose that none dared to wake.

He started. *The still sleeping rose—w*as there a connection, poetic or otherwise, with the still sleeping God?

Ded picked up his anthology of Ickey Jerusalem's poetry from under his seat and looked in the index under "rose." There were only two entries, both of which he had already read. The poem near the beginning of the book about the rose that was sleeping, and the poem at the end about the rose that was sick. Nothing in between.

Closing the book and resting it on his thigh, Ded turned back toward Beulah. The morning sun was beginning to rise from its hiding place behind her hat. Below, through the wall of glass, was the hazy view to the east: The Bay Bridge, Yerba Buena Island, Treasure Island, Berkeley, the Oakland Hills, and Mount Diablo.

Ded lowered his eyes to the polished parquet floor behind Scofield. Beulah's chair was on casters. He checked out the other chairs in the room. They were on casters as well. So was the couch.

Poor O'Nadir, Ded noted wryly. *When the earthquake comes and the building starts to wave side to side, we're all going to roll out the window.* He pictured the group, eyes fixed on Jerusalem's grinning photograph, hands gripping their armrests, sliding in perfect synchronization across the room and out through the glass, all too mesmerized by the face of the poet to notice.

For a moment, the group hung in midair, supported by the power of the poet's gaze.

Before any of them could fall, out of the blue came the soaring, radiating figure of Ded himself. He swept them all up into his spread-wide arms to carry them off into the glory of the great unknown.

"Like being in an airplane, isn't it?" Los, sitting on the couch to the right and behind, had noticed Ded's preoccupied stare and intervened in his Oklahoman accent.

Expressing agreement, Ded swiveled to face Jerusalem's stocky father.

"So far above humankind," Enith observed enigmatically. "So close to God."

Los took off his polyester coat, wrapped it around Enith's thin shoulders, and put his callused index finger to her lips. "Just the opposite, dear. The farther above humankind you go, the farther from God you will be. Because the only place the Holy Spirit can be found is in humans."

"Aeeiiiiiiiiii!!!" Grandma Enion wailed from the other end of the couch, presumably not at all pleased with Los's news about the location of the Holy Spirit.

Los looked at her with his sad, bloodshot eyes, then turned back to Ded. "The mother of us all," he said in a low voice.

"Is Grandma Enion merely mad," Enith eerily asked the space in front of her face, "or is she a harbinger of the Apocalypse?"

"Ickey could never decide," Los explained to Ded.

The Apocalypse? Ded picked up on the word, bringing to mind its place in the parable of Orc.

Los returned his gaze to Grandma Enion, who, still sobbing, had retreated back into the gooey comfort of Theo's shoulder. "Since Ickey died, she's gotten a lot worse. Yesterday in church, I suspected something wasn't entirely right when she laughed out loud twice during the reading of the Apostles' Creed. And then, in the middle of the sermon about Christ on the boat in the Sea of Galilee, she grabbed her stomach, and claiming she was seasick, began calling for the preacher to bring her a barf bag."

"That's unfortunate," Ded said, assuming some sort of acknowledgment was desired.

"You gotta give the preacher credit," Los said to Ded. "Without missing a beat, he changed the subject of the sermon to how the Lord Jesus had been crucified for the sins of the world, whereupon ol' Grandma turned to the row behind us and wailed, 'It weren't fair! It weren't fair! He hadn't done a damn thing to deserve it!' I think the people didn't much appreciate her editorial comment, though they appeared much more concerned by the fact Grandma hadn't received the barf bag she'd asked for."

Grandma Enion, still leaking from the various orifices above her chin, lifted her head from Theo's shoulder and looked blankly around the room, as though dimly aware someone was talking about her, but not certain where the person was. Unable to locate the source, she gave up and began chewing her tongue contentedly with her toothless gums.

At that moment, Rahab Oothoon entered the office dressed in what appeared to be a dance-hall reflector ball. Her plump, freckled body projected from it in two directions—above her nipples on up, and below her crotch on down. She sashayed over to the empty easy chair next to her husband and eased herself up onto the seat.

The doctor gave her a querying look, but she looked past him, flashing her seductive eyes at Theo, who had followed her progress from the door to her chair.

Ded rolled closer to Los. "As I said at the funeral, I'm so sorry about Ickey's death. But I just realized it must be doubly painful, given you previously lost your son, Orc."

Los nodded appreciatively.

"How did it happen?

Plainly not prepared for such a question, Los nonetheless took it in stride. "It was on Ferrous Peak—"

"Where Cousin Ijim is building his Golden Sun City retirement community?"

"Where he *may* be building it. He's way behind schedule, and over the last few months, some of his loans have been called. He may never get it off the ground." Los stared at the dial on his large, elaborate watch as though calculating exactly how much behind schedule Cousin Ijim was.

"I apologize for interrupting you," Ded said. "You were telling me about Orc."

"Oh, yes. Well, we were on a hunting trip around Easter. I'd invited Ickey, but as usual, he declined. Said he had some rhyming couplets to work on at home. On our third day out, Orc got up before I did, and for reasons unknown, he set off without me. After I woke and found him gone, I figured the best thing was to wait at camp. Otherwise, with both of us moving around, we'd never find each other. But when a late winter storm hit and he hadn't come back, I went out looking for him. Disastrously, the snow covered his tracks. I didn't find him until the following morning."

Los's eyes strayed toward Ickey Jerusalem's picture. "At some point, Orc had caught his foot in a steel bear trap. From the cuts on his fingers, it was clear he'd tried desperately to pull the thing open, but he wasn't strong enough. In the night, when the mountain lions come out, the poor boy crawled up the nearest tree as high as the trap's chain would let him."

A tear came to Los's eye. "I found his body hanging over a lower branch. The mountain lions had torn off both his arms and one of his legs. He was frozen right through to his heart."

"He never should've left home," Enith declared to the ceiling. "He should've stayed down below, like his namesake."

"Namesake?" Ded inquired.

"Orcus," Los explained. "The Roman god of the underworld."

"Of Hell," Enith corrected. "According to the dictionary of first names we got from Woolworths."

"You named your child after the Roman god of Hell?" Ded stammered, trying to fit this in with the Orc of the poems where Orc was the exact opposite of Hell.

"It was that damn Ouija board of hers," Los sighed. "What could I do?"

Ded raised an eyebrow. "Did Ickey's name also come from your wife's Ouija board?"

"No, the board's suggestion there was too creepy. I mean, even Enith balked at the thought of naming her son *Blake*."

"From the Old English, 'blaec.'" Enith's grin was empty. "It means 'the dark one.'"

The dark one? Ded averted his eyes from her uncomfortable gaze and looked at Los. "So where did you get the name 'Ickey'?"

"It's short for Icarus. You know, from the Greek myth."

Ded knew. It was the same Greek myth from which his own name had come. Dedalus had been the designer of the labyrinth of Crete. Everyone knew the tale of how Dedalus tried to escape from the island with his son, Icarus, using wings made of feathers and wax, and how Icarus, overcome with the joys of flying, ignored his father's warnings and soared too high, until the sun melted his wings and he fell to his death in the sea.

Curious, Ded observed. *Our parents read the same myth, but while Ickey's parents named him after the character who died from flying to close to the sun, mine named me after the one who survived—by flying low.* Ded adjusted his glasses. *And even more curious, now that I think about it, is that despite the fact my name comes from the character who lived, it's pronounced "dead."*

Unnerved by the accumulating mix of etymological coincidences and anomalies, Ded gave Los and Enith a nod, spun his chair to point to the front, and rolled back up next to Tharmas.

Now was as good a time as any. "O'Nadir," he said, catching the inspector's eyes. "Could you pass me the briefcase, please?"

Cracking his gum, O'Nadir acknowledged Ded's request, lifted the case by its handle, and handed it to Tharmas. The business manager grabbed it in the middle of the narrow sides, exactly as had been planned, and passed it on to Ded. Ded took the case by the handle and studied it as though considering whether he really needed it. Then, shaking his head, he put it down on the floor at his right, unopened.

Bacon Urizen entered the room, a file folder and a manila envelope under his arm. He looked extremely tired, extremely pale, and much, much older than when Ded had seen him two days ago. But today, there was something different about his expression. His lips had a happy upturn. Like the understated, archaic smile of an early Ancient-Greek sculpture. And he was peering around the room with warm, open eyes, as though he was seeing everything by immediate perception.

Is this the effect of his LSD experience Saturday night? Or something else?

Ploddingly, almost painfully, Bacon Urizen lumbered to the front corner of his desk, set the file folder and manila envelope on it, and paused to stare through his monocle at the picture of Jerusalem. The picture stared back like a clinical photograph in a textbook on undiagnosable psychopathologies.

Urizen shook his enormous bald head and turned to the assembled group. "Ladies and gentlemen." Although his voice was as deep as ever, he was breathing with great difficulty. "In accordance with Mr. Jerusalem's wishes, before reading the will, I have something you probably weren't expecting."

CHAPTER 28

THE REFLECTIONS IN THE WATER

Urizen lifted the manila envelope from his desk, tore open the seal, pulled out a seven-inch, Super-8 film reel, and held it up for all to see. "On May Day this year, Mr. Jerusalem recorded this film to be viewed at the reading of his bequests."

Urizen pressed a button on his desk and two men came into the room—one with a roll-up screen on a tripod, which he installed on the credenza behind Urizen's desk, and the other with small projector, which he set up on the top of the desk. While the second man prepared the reel on the projector, the first took the empty chair closest to the door in Ded's row, positioned it behind the projector, helped Urizen to lower his enormous bulk onto it, and then showed him the machine's on-standby-off three-way rocker switch. The lawyer turned the projector to "standby" as both men went around the room closing curtains and turning off lights. Once they finished and the room was dark, they left the office and Urizen started the reel.

An image flickered onto the screen. Ickey Jerusalem was sitting at his kitchen table in Lambeth, alone, wearing a ripped T-shirt over his well-built upper body. From the angle of view, the recording camera appeared to have been set on the counter—Ded recognized the position from his search for coffee the previous morning. Ded could see the camera's klieg lights reflected in the night-time windows behind Jerusalem.

The moving picture differed from the static photograph of Jerusalem, and yet it still lacked the humanity usually afforded by perceiving the third dimension. As a result, Jerusalem's overall appearance fell into that grey area between Apollo and a deranged murderer. Fortunately, due perhaps to the formality of the occasion, Jerusalem had brushed his normally radiating, curly hair neatly down over his head.

The poet was drinking Ripple straight from the bottle. He clunked the bottle back onto the table. When he spoke in his Central-Valley accent, his speech was slightly slurred, as though from drink:

I saw a chapel all of gold
That none did dare to enter in
And many weeping stood without
Weeping mourning worshipping

I saw a serpent rise between
The white pillars of the door
And he forcd & forcd & forcd
Down the golden hinges tore

And along the pavement sweet
Set with pearls & rubies bright
All his slimy length he drew
Till upon the altar white

Vomiting his poison out
On the bread & on the wine
So I turn'd into a sty

And laid me down among the swine

Jerusalem burped loudly to show his poetic recitation had concluded. **So, my good old subjective self has at last been annihilated, huh? How did it happen? A union in infinite and eternal creativity?**

He picked up a hash pipe, lit it, and drew in a long breath. When Jerusalem spoke again, it was in a strained whisper. **Or was it murder?**

Curious as to their reaction to this insinuation, Ded covertly surveyed Jerusalem's friends and acquaintances, their faces illuminated by the screen. No one seemed notably surprised at the poet's surmise, as though it was the kind of thing they expected him to say.

Jerusalem let his breath out with a rush. **Got tired of your very own Old Testament prophet haranguing you all the time, did you? In the stuck elevator while you're trying to get to your office? On the golf course while trying to sink a putt? On the toilet while trying to recover from the previous night's orgy? In the driveway while trying to polish the hearse? In the bedroom while trying to go to bed?**

Jerusalem took another, gurgling drink. **I'm sorry. But once I saw your reality in the mid-level was a mere reflection of the unfallen God in the mirror of the fallen, I had no choice but to play the Old Testament prophet. How else could I make you see what you really are?** He placed the bottle back on the table. **Mirror images. Without depth and reversed. Each of you but the shallow contrary of a different aspect of the unfallen reality. Each of you with your own peculiar pretense designed to murder my creative imagination.**

Jerusalem paused, as though marshaling for an attack. When he next spoke, it was with a prophet's accusatory timbre.

It began with you, Enith, my mother, with your pretense of infinity, played out in your mysterious trances, lost among the invisible specters of the heavens. While I was still a babe and worshipped you as my whole world, you dipped me into the waters of indefinite space, shrinking my consciousness to the limit of contraction and hardening my exterior against human intimacy,

reducing my creative imagination to an inward-looking armored crustacean, alert only for attack or defense.

Ded looked over at Enith. She did not appear to take umbrage at this accusation, being, as she was, in a trance.

Then it was you, Los, my father, with your pretense of eternity, the supposed lasting contributions to humankind you decreed me to make. You drew my eyes to the steeple clock, and as I froze under its hypnotic, ticking spell, you bound my armored imagination with the chains of duty to the rocks below.

Los lowered his eyes sorrowfully to his elaborate watch. It seemed this accusation was not new.

Then, Brom. Jerusalem's tone hardened. **Brom…**

Dr. Bromion Ulro tensed his already clasped hands.

What are you *not* a pretense of, Brom? From your conventional morality, which parodies the true community of humans, to your absolute acceptance of the fallen world, which parodies the poet's absolute perception of the unfallen God, you are the archetype of someone missing the whole point of life.

The doctor relaxed, noticeably relieved Jerusalem had not accused him of anything serious.

Under the guise of my corporeal friend—oh, mark well my words: "Corporeal Friends are Spiritual Enemies"—you did your best to persuade me to accept my fate. "The rocks are a mercy," you sibilated. "They're the limit of opacity. They keep you from falling through to the chaos below. Cling to them. Conform to them. Worship them. For that is the only way you'll ever be able to survive."

Jerusalem took another protracted suck on his hash pipe, followed by an equally protracted exhalation

Whenever Brom turned pompously away, you, Rahab, a whore's pretense of beauty…

Rahab fiddled with one of the many jewels adorning her neck and nervously swung her stout, freckled legs.

…you would materialize beneath me, tied spread-eagled to the

rocks by the bonds of lust. That's when I discovered that, despite my having been dipped into the waters of indefinite space by my mother, there was a part of my exterior that was not only soft but in the right circumstances could become hardened *in favor* of human intimacy.

"Damn," Enith muttered from the depths of her trance, "I knew I should have held him by the heel."

In my shame, I did the only thing I could. I hid the proud organ up inside you, Rahab, to be clamped forever in the vise of paternity.

Jerusalem paused, tinkling his fingers on the side of his bottle, deciding who was next.

Then, you, Tharmas, with your pretense of freedom, your frantic slipping in and out of images and bodies as though they were mere objects for temporary possession. You, riding the missile of Uncle Urthon's hard-packed millions, swooped down and smashed Rahab and the rocks beneath, casting me into the void where the sudden absence of external pressure caused my creative imagination to explode outwards, and finding no form around which to congeal, to eternally expand into emptiness.

Tharmas's dark frown showed this accusation was not new, either.

Like a drowning man, I frantically reached upwards, towards my nascent metaphysics's disturbing mixture of every possible-to-imagine color, and beheld the reflecting surface of the moon. Grabbing you, Beulah Vala, in my arms, I struggled to pull myself out of the void toward God's meaning. But with your pretense of love, your whole-earth, romantic eroticism cloaked in the language of my poems, you drew me down instead, down into your tranquil garden of gratified desire. I took your glowing, formless wonder for Heaven. But it was only a temporary escape. Each time I tried to grasp your essence in sexual fulfillment, I discovered nothing there and fell back to your garden's soft earth. The more we made love, the deeper my dissipating creative imagination sank into the warm soil of your femininity. I became passive, helpless, and unable to create my epic poems.

Grown old in Love from Seven till Seven times Seven
I oft have wishd for Hell for Ease from Heaven.

Beulah removed her hat and turned her face toward the closed curtain. Ded could not see her expression.

Each time my creative imagination lay exhausted in the open grave of Beulah's garden, trying desperately to pull itself toward the highest level of God's consciousness, you, Adam, with your cross-eyed focus on the abstraction-free concrete here and now, which, due to being confined to the imagination-free five senses, is but a pretense of gaining knowledge by immediate perception...

Ghostflea—who, still suffering from the excesses of the night before, had fallen asleep listening to Jerusalem's endless descriptions of people and concepts—came awake in his seat.

"What? What is Mr. Jerusalem saying?"

...you, Adam, disguised as a worm at one with the earth, you crawled into my ear, burrowed deep into my brain, and began gnawing at my faith in a universal, divine human creativity.

"Not me. I don't crawl anywhere. I drive a hearse."

Jerusalem moved on. **And as I looked up out of the grave again, there was Bacon Urizen, blotting the sun and moon as he peered down. You, Urizen. Your clever, analytical thought processes but a pretense of creativity—the epitome of how the imagination, divorced from nature, turns in on itself, away from synthesis and into the sterility of analysis—you, Bacon:**

...the idiot Questioner who is always questioning,
But never capable of answering; who sits with a sly grin
Silently plotting when to question, like a thief in a cave;
Who publishes doubt & calls it knowledge; whose Science is Despair
Whose pretense to knowledge is Envy, whose whole Science is

To destroy the wisdom of the ages to gratify ravenous Envy;
That rages round him like a Wolf day & night without rest

Urizen, curiously, was nodding and murmuring just loud enough for Ded to hear, "Yes. Yes. What you say is true."

With your lawyer's cross-examination, you began to dissect my creativity, a procedure which, since it necessarily involved killing the specimen, predetermined what you'd find in the end. Not imagination. Not God. Not life. But death.

Urizen fixed his face on the screen, silently begging for mercy.

Jerusalem opened his hands and looked from side to side, as though surveying the audience. **With so many of you out to murder my creative imagination, it's only natural I've had to get away. First, from Eden. Then, from the Sunset District's fog belt. And then, from North Beach into the Oakland Hills. But none of my new homes worked as well as I hoped. Since I need each of you for practical things, you've still ended up impinging on my life. So, I've decided to take further protective measures. Install a soundproof glass partition in the hearse to block out Adam. Move into the guest bedroom at Lambeth so I can sleep apart from Beulah. Get drunk and stoned out of my head whenever I'm to encounter my lawyer, business manager, or doctor, to prevent any kind of meaningful conversation from occurring.**

This is the only way my creative imagination can find the freedom to encompass the world with my vision of the highest level of God's consciousness.

Ded risked a look at Beulah and saw she was still turned away, hiding her face and therefore, her emotional state. *It was Jerusalem who'd been sleeping in that monastic cell of a guest bedroom I saw. Desperately trying to separate himself from her.*

On screen, his hash pipe empty, the poet took in a lungful of clean air and blew it out through flapping lips.

Just because I must escape from your influences, you shouldn't

think I'm angry. After all, you can't help yourselves. Being locked in your selfhoods has naturally destroyed your imaginations and hence forced you all to try to destroy any imagination existing in others. You've sinned, it's true. But only Satan would say that means you should be punished.

Here, Jerusalem took on his poetry reading stance, deepening his voice.

> **In Hell all is Self Righteousness; there is no such thing there as Forgiveness of Sin he who does Forgive Sin is Crucified as an Abettor of Criminals. & he who performs Works of Mercy in Any shape whatever is punishd & if possible, destroyd, not thro Envy or Hatred or Malice but thro Self Righteousness that thinks it does God service which God is Satan.**

This brief oration finished, Jerusalem tipped the bottle back and took a mighty drink. He smacked his lips before continuing. **Punishing a man merely suppresses the imagination. Only through forgiveness of sins can the imaginative power in the sinner be released. That's the message Jesus brought to the world: Only through forgiveness of sins can the imaginative power in the sinner be released.**

Jerusalem sounded almost like he was trying to convince himself. He took another swig from his bottle of Ripple.

So, I hereby forgive you. He was now speaking in double time, almost perfunctorily. **I forgive Beulah for loving me the only way she knew how. I forgive Brom for trying to help me accommodate to the necessities of the fallen world. I forgive Tharmas for trying to open me up to life. I forgive Bacon for trying to reason with me. I forgive my father for trying to teach me a sense of duty. I forgive my mother for trying to inculcate in me a belief in something beyond man. I forgive Adam for having no imagination.**

Ded looked around the room. It did not appear the poet's

forgiveness was releasing any noticeable amount of imaginative power. Ghostflea, having added boredom to his hangover, was simultaneously scratching his thinning scalp hair and swinging his skinny tongue from side to side.

Bacon Urizen, though, was jerking his head up and down, mouthing, "Thank you. Thank you. Thank you."

Jerusalem continued in singsong.

& Throughout all Eternity
I forgive you you forgive me.
As our dear Redeemer said:
This the Wine & this the Bread

Clearly enjoying himself, as soon as Jerusalem finished speaking the last line, he began humming it, tapping out the rhythm on the table with his knuckle. This was followed by a short, absentminded silence.

Oh, the poet said as he came back into the present, **and I forgive you, Rahab, for choosing Brom over me. It was, doubtless, for the best. I mean, let's face it, kids are such a drag on genius.**

At the mention of kids, in the film, a bolt of lightning struck outside, lighting up the kitchen windows behind, startling Jerusalem. The poet's demeanor switched instantly into one of profound depression.

God. God. God. Jerusalem's curses were tinged with guilt and self-pity.

O why was I born with a different face
Why was I not born like the rest of my race
When I look, each one starts! when I speak, I offend
Then I'm silent & passive & lose every Friend

Then my verse I dishonour. My pictures despise
My person degrade & my temper chastise
And the pen is my terror, the pencil my shame

All my Talents I bury, and dead is my Fame

I am either too low or too highly prizd
When Elate I am Envy'd, When Meek I'm despisd

Jerusalem threw the bottle across the room—it landed off-screen with a shattering crash. This was followed by another, more prolonged lull, while everyone waited for Ickey Jerusalem to get to the point.

Anyway, Jerusalem continued, having ostensibly resigned himself to finishing the recording, **given you're watching this now, I must've passed over to the other side, and you've all come here in the hopes I can, at last, give you the answer.**

Ded noticed an uncomfortable shuffling throughout the room.

"Please tell us, Ickey," I hear you asking, "now that you've passed over to the other side, please tell us what we've all been waiting to learn these many years. The one question that has been forever poised, unspoken, on our lips. Tell us, Ickey, please: Who's going to get all your money?"

CHAPTER 29

DING AN SICH—EINS

In the film, Jerusalem leaned back on his chair, causing it to creak. **By all means, I need to answer that important question. But before I do, let me dispose of a few personal possessions under my will.** He brought the front legs of the chair back to the floor, took out a folded sheet of paper from his trouser pocket, and flattened it on the table. **Let's see.**

Jerusalem coughed. **To Adam, I give my hearse. I can't think of anything more suitable poetically for transporting his brain around town. Sorry, Adam.** Jerusalem seemed genuinely apologetic. **It's not your fault. It's mine. If only I'd tried harder, I might have been able to widen your vision beyond the end of your nose.**

Ghostflea, from the bewildered way he stared at the end of his nose (his eyes set as they were, he couldn't help it), was yet to realize he was now the owner of the hearse.

To my father, Los, so desiring of my lasting contributions to mankind—

For every thing exists & not one sigh nor smile nor tear,

One hair nor particle of dust, not one can pass away.

—to Los, I give my bronzed dog turd. In fact, all of my bronzed mementos—the used condom, the proctologist's rubber glove, and the myriad other items too indelicate to hint at here.

Too indelicate? Ded recalled the hundred or so bronzed objects he had seen in the piles at Lambeth, trying to remember if there had been anything more indelicate than the condom and the proctologist's glove. *Broccoli! One of the bronzed objects was a small, flattened piece of broccoli.* Not that indelicate, at least not on its face, but nonetheless a peculiar coincidence—given Ded's suffocation dream the night before. *And its inscription. What was it? "Whence came the truth that all things must pass?" Sounds a little inconsistent to me. But perhaps this is just another example of how poets lack the ability to think clearly and concisely.*

The bronzes froze forever those moments of change in my life, Ickey was saying, **when I achieved certain insights. Of course, freezing moments of change isn't the same as perceiving the eternal in those moments of change. To do that, I wrote poetry.** Jerusalem's voice became tender. **Once you can see the difference, Los, you'll have received the greatest gift from me I could ever give.**

Los dabbed his eyes.

Jerusalem took a moment to review his list. **To Enith,** he said, continuing in the same tender tone, **I give my volumes of grand philosophy, theosophy, and theology, so that through my notes in the margins, you can learn to put your faith in what you see, rather than in what you don't.**

A psychiatrist once asked me whether anyone in my family suffered from mental illness. "No," I replied truthfully. "As far as I can tell, they all seem to enjoy it."

Jerusalem took a sudden, borderline sob of a breath. **In your case, Enith, I now realize I was mistaken. Please forgive me.**

The poet straightened his piece of paper needlessly, appearing to swallow his emotions.

To Grandma Enion, he went on bravely, **sitting by the sea, weaving the tangled web of life, wailing and waiting for the ultimate return of Grandfather Tharmas.** He took a breath. **To Grandma, to use on her loom, I give my box of string too short to save.**

Ded, who had just finished noting the broccoli coincidence in his notepad, touched his ballpoint to his lips and began ruminating on this bequest to Grandma Enion. He could not help but feel it was fraught with meaning far beyond mere comment on the old woman's vacant attic. Weaving the tangled web of life? With string too short to save? While waiting for the ultimate return of her mate from the sea? Jerusalem was definitely talking big-time symbolism here.

Certainly, Grandma Enion herself felt there was more to the bequest than met the eye. "Flush it down the toilet!" she ordered Theo. "Flush it down the toilet before it eats us!"

Urizen quickly put the projector on "standby," in response to her outburst. Theo patted her shoulder.

"Yes, Grandma. Right away, Grandma." Theo's eyes followed her gaze to the front of his shirt, where he noticed for the first time that the last half-hour's worth of the old woman's tears, drool, and snot had coalesced into what appeared to be a huge, pulsating, chartreuse amoeba.

"Holy Jesus!" Theo shrieked, leaping up and slapping at the amoeba with both hands.

As soon as the slapping and exclamations died down, Urizen started the projector again. Jerusalem unfroze and continued his bequeathing, once again with feeling.

To Rahab, in memory of Easter Day when I encountered you in your micro-skirt, picking marigolds in Golden Gate Park. To you, I give my wooden statuette of the Indonesian laughing god with the eighteen-inch phallus.

There I was, walking across the park after my trip to the de Young Museum, where I'd bought the statuette in the gift shop. There you were, my dear, bending over, examining the flowers, with

your pantyless backside in the air, a chubby, minikin silhouette of the continent of Africa, affording me a breathtaking view of the Great Rift Valley.

Jerusalem savored the recollection with a sigh. **I'm sorry about the splinters.**

Ded flinched.

Rahab grinned.

Tharmas nudged his elbow into Ded's side and leaned in for a hawk-beaked whisper. "Musta resulted later that evening in good ol' Brom executing one of the most rapid *coitus interruptuses* in history."

Ded flinched again, this time even harder. In his supercharged imagination, he pictured Dr. Ulro exclaiming, "Jesus Christ!" in his high-pitched Central-Valley voice and shooting back out and up onto his knees in order gingerly to examine his pin-cushioned organ in the lamplight, before raising his hopeless eyes to those of his cackling, peewee wife, lying spread-eagled before him on the bed. "Splinters?" he imagined the doctor moaning. "*Again*?"

But Ded knew the scene wasn't possible. *Before Jerusalem moved in with Dr. Ulro and Rahab at their Sunset District home, didn't the doctor give up sex with her due to the still birth of the five-headed Tirzah?*

Fortunately, after the de-splintering by your gynecologist, we were able to resume our affair. God, you were good. What an imaginative talent for the lewd. Such incredible postures. Repeatedly I was left scuttling around you on my knees, searching for an entrance. "Give me a hint," I kept pleading. "Give me a hint, please!"

Ded realized there was another issue of timing and the laughing god. *According to the bill of sale taped to the base I read at Lambeth, Jerusalem purchased the statuette Easter Day, April 10th, this year. So, six months ago, around when Jerusalem moved into the Lambeth guest bedroom, he started a new affair with Rahab. If Beulah found about it recently, she'd have had a definite motive for murder. Ditto Dr. Ulro.*

And then that thing with the pygmy electric eel from your

home aquarium, Jerusalem went on excitedly**. Absolutely shocking. I couldn't sit down for a week.**

The poet savored the memory for a moment.

So, he continued at last, **to you, my dear, the statuette.**

The stern-faced Dr. Ulro turned mechanically to his glitter-ball wife, not so much with consternation as with curiosity about her reaction. Beholding nothing more than an ambiguous half-smile, he rotated his head to the front of the room where her gaze was fixed on the screen. The doctor took hold of his wife's hand and got up to leave.

To Brom Ulro, Jerusalem began on cue.

The doctor sat back down and released his wife's hand.

Excuse me, I mean Doctor Bromion Ulro. We all know how hard it is for a man who wears a toupée to get respect. Jerusalem switched to nursery-rhyme mode.

> **He *makes* the *Lame* to *walk* we *all* agree**
> **But *then* he *strives* to *blind* those *who* can *see*.**

He waited, counting the next four wordless feet of iambic pentameter, coming in on the fifth with: **Like *me*.**

Jerusalem became solemn. **To you, Brom, I give my drawing of the fallen God bifurcating the appearance of reality. If you look beneath the white hair and beard, you'll notice I modeled him after what I thought you'd look like decades hence.**

Dr. Ulro confusedly gazed at the screen, then dropped his eyes to his large, clasped hands.

To Bacon Urizen. How are you doing, Three Eyes? Still alive? Not too much for you, all this, is it?

Urizen, who was resting his mammoth, feeble frame in the chair in front of his desk behind the projector, adjusted his monocle and peered stoically at the screen as though willing to accept with further great thanks whatever Jerusalem gave him.

Jesus, how such a superior mind could have taken up residence

in such a decrepit body. Fat. Bald. Pallid. Suffering every conceivable physical ailment of age. You could have made a fortune playing the "before" in those TV gym commercials.

Ickey took on the tenor of a hyped-up television pitchman. **Are you like good old Bacon here? Chronically ill? Grotesquely obese? On the verge of catastrophic collapse? Yes? Then waddle your piece-of-shit body on down to the Bowlahoola Health Spa and let us fit you out with a set of our patented, fifty-pound ankle weights and put you through a course of our famous "life challenge" workouts on the parallel bars, the vaulting horse, and the high-diving board.**

"My God," you'll be saying to yourself after just a short time, "I can't believe I'm doing this."

But you weren't always that way, were you, Bacon? When you were young, you were strong, handsome, full of life, and based on your drawings, possessed of great artistic potential. Such distinct, sharp, and wiry bounding lines in your images. So unlike the weak imitation and bungling you see in the imperfect art of today.

And then what did you do? Gave it all up to go into the law. To sit in your office, high above the world, drawing not images but distinctions. Still using the finest of lines, though now not to define the boundaries reason gives to human energy, but rather to slice that human energy into lifeless parts.

Jerusalem dropped the slight remonstration that had developed in his manner, returning to the fondness with which he had begun his address of Urizen. **As my bequest to you, Bacon, I give you one more chance. I give you the instrument through which I produced my greatest nonverbal art: my draftsman's pen. May its attenuated point help you trace, at last, the circumference of God.**

Ironic, Ded thought. *Jerusalem took Urizen's pen in the plane and now is giving him back another.*

As Ded recorded this thought in his notepad, his eye caught the end of the ballpoint with which he was writing. His mouth fell open.

He held the pen out and examined it. Below the clicker, flush with the pen's smooth plastic surface, were two tiny gold initials: BU.

Jerusalem went to the next on his list. **To Tharmas Luvah, with your talent for taking confusion and turning it into chaos, I give, as promised, my sailboat.**

Ded, keeping one ear on the bequest to Tharmas, tried to recall where he had picked up Urizen's pen.

So that you may learn to harness the chaos of the sea and the wind, to give your life direction.

Unable to recall the source of the pen, Ded returned his full attention to the screen.

Remember, Tharmas, once you master your craft, you'll always know where you'll be when your ship comes in.

"Where's that?" Tharmas murmured with a touch of sarcasm, as though at last tipped over the edge by Jerusalem's condescension.

On board, came the answer.

To my brothers, Jerusalem soldiered on, **I give the rest of my personal property, divided among them according to their interests.**

None of Jerusalem's brothers were present aside from Theo, who looked to Ded as though he regretted attending.

To Ozo, my paintings. To Soth, my records and tapes. To Tamon, my figurines. To Theo, the residual beneficiary under both my trust and my will after any specific bequests I might make. Dear old Theo. A "good" man. Who—how does my old couplet go?

> **He has observd the Golden Rule**
> **Till hes become the Golden Fool**

To you, Theo, I give my cow horns. Wear them with pride. You earned them.

Theo scowled at Jerusalem's picture, not at all happy with either the specific bequest or the characterization of himself, especially since the source of both had admitted in the film he'd slept with Theo's wife.

The poet finished off his bequests to the rest of his brothers in quick succession, leaving his high school megaphone to Rint, his art books to Palam, and so on, until most of the items Ded remembered from the various piles on the floor at Lambeth were gone.

Jerusalem took another drag from his pipe. When he continued, it was with a profound fatigue.

And now, having disposed of all my personal property, I get to the last bequest. My real estate.

> **There is from Great Eternity a mild & pleasant rest**
> **Namd Beulah a soft Moony Universe feminine, lovely**
> **Pure, mild & Gentle, given in Mercy to those who sleep**

Fighting back an exhausted yawn, Jerusalem forced himself to continue. **To Beulah I give Lambeth. My house. High in the hills. Covered with the untrammeled vine of life. A solid, well-built structure to shelter her from harsh reality.**

I apologize, Beulah, that after all my previous bequests, the house will be empty. But then, so was your love.

As empty as your womb—Jerusalem choked with emotion—**after Ololon.**

The lamentation of Beulah over Ololon, Ded remembered from the sleeping-rose poem he had read Sunday morning at Lambeth. Beulah was still facing away, except now her shoulders shook from soundless sobs.

Ickey Jerusalem was crying as well, his right palm over his eyes. Bucking up, he removed his hand and stared straight into the camera.

"And now, to Ded Smith," Ded half-expected Jerusalem to say. But then, that would have been absurd. Though the poet and the claims adjuster had conversed at Little Joe's four years before, neither had known the other's name.

And now, a newly determined Jerusalem announced, **the money.**

Everyone shifted forward in anticipation.

Los has often expressed concern I've not shown proper thanks to God for the money Uncle Urthon left me. And he's right. I haven't. Why should I?

> **Since all the Riches of this World**
> **May be gifts from the Devil and Earthly Kings**
> **I should suspect that I worshipd the Devil**
> **If I thankd my God for Worldly things.**

And of all worldly things, money is the worst. Money is the root of all evil. Money reduces the abundance and variety of life to a single, lowest-common-denominator definition of worth: price. Money, that consensus of mediocrities, has become the sole medium through which people relate to one another, the sole cement which holds society together. No longer only a means, money has become an end in itself, the pure abstraction of happiness through possession, the invisible web binding man's imagination to the rocks.

"Damn. If that's honestly the way you feel," I can hear you saying, "why keep it? Why don't you get rid of it? Give it all away?"

Jerusalem stared long and hard at his unseen audience. **What do you think I am? An imbecile? If money is the root of all evil, then the last thing I want to do is spread it around.**

Can't you see? The money in the trust is like a fabulous but cursed diamond. I don't want to be responsible for passing a curse on to anyone. Not to my friends. Not to my relations. Not to the poor. Not to the starving in Africa.

I may be dead, Jerusalem summed up, **but I've still got to live with myself.**

Without warning, Jerusalem sneezed. He wiped his nostrils with his list of bequests. **So, I had to come up with a way to dispose of my money that doesn't involve giving it to someone else but still says what I want to say.**

Jerusalem crumpled the paper up and threw it in on the floor. **Stack**

the money around my dead body like a temple, set the whole thing on fire, and mix the resulting ashes into a giant gingerbread cookie to be eaten at my funeral.

Several of those present who had been at the funeral touched their lips at the thought of what fortune might have passed through them.

That was my first idea. But since destroying U.S. legal tender is against the law, I couldn't be sure the trustee would go along with it after I died. So, rather than destroy the money, I had to have the trustee spend it on something that wouldn't leave anything of monetary value behind. Say, transcribing the entire Bible into skywriting. Or composing a pointillist picture of the Golden Sun from different color hats worn by a hundred thousand bald-headed men dog paddling in the Bay. Or constructing in Death Valley a mile-high ice statue of Jesus that, as it melted, would morph into a huge phallus.

Tharmas Luvah bounced his palms together in childlike excitement. "Now we're talking!"

Beside him, O'Nadir blanched at the sacrilege.

Jerusalem acknowledged the brilliance of his imagination with a single *tsk* of his tongue. **Once I sobered up, I realized I was on the wrong track. Spending all my money to leave behind something that would promptly disappear was not really a suitable epitaph for someone like me. I'm a poet. I've spent my life trying to impose a permanent vision on the flux of time. My epitaph should be permanent as well.**

Ergo, refining my previous logic, I decided what I was looking for was an expenditure that would leave behind a statement both permanent but at the same time without monetary value. A definition of the problem which makes the answer obvious.

Everyone was looking at everyone else. From the myriad expressions, it appeared that far from agreeing the answer was obvious, most were unable even to understand Jerusalem's definition of the problem.

Jerusalem gave it to them on a plate. **All the money, you see, is to be spent on my poetry.**

Unfortunately, from the incomprehension on his audience's faces, it seemed the plate he was presenting must have still had its silver heat lid on. **To be spent producing a permanent epitaph etched not in stone or steel or diamond…** The poet figuratively lifted the edge of the lid. **…but in the mind of every human being in the world.** He dropped the lid back down. **Now, how, you ask, do I intend to accomplish this massive job of engraving?**

"Okay," Tharmas spoke to the Ickey Jerusalem on the screen, perhaps miffed at the mile-high phallus not being chosen, "I'll play your silly little game. How do yuh intend to accomplish it?"

Voilà! Jerusalem lifted the imaginary silver lid upwards with a flourish. **The money in the Urthon Spectre Trust will be used to purchase for every household in the world a complete collection of my poems.**

Immediate understanding swept throughout the room. Dr. Ulro grunted in disgust. Beulah's rosebud mouth fell open. Tharmas gently placed his right hand over the right side of his face and looked down. Ghostflea began snoring off-key.

Ded shook his head. *What's the permanent effect of all these books going to be on the four-fifths of the world's population who don't read English?*

Naturally, Jerusalem said, as if in answer to Ded, **it will take time to translate the poems into all the languages of the world. But in the end, almost everyone everywhere will have an equal chance to absorb my inspirations.** Jerusalem's voice grew in enthusiasm. **Everyone everywhere will read my poems. Recite them. Sing them. On the radio. On TV. In schools. In churches. In bars. On buses. In bed. Experiencing my visions, which, when merged into Golgonooza, will make the sum of its visions at last indistinguishable from the totality of the divine reality.**

Given we are now living in the final cycle of history, where our creative imagination has been almost completely suppressed by the upside-down Satan Incarnate's intricate web of abstract rules—of

law, of bureaucracy, of convention, of science, of religion, of pragmatism, of economics, of fashion, of everything—I have no doubt my added glimpses will initially suffer the same fate, ending up camouflaged by Satan inside the Consolidation of Error. However, shortly thereafter, when the Consolidation of Error suddenly vanishes, providing an unobstructed view of the (thanks to me) now perfect Golgonooza, the sleeping God will awake, and in a fiery Apocalypse, His expanding consciousness will reunite with the hidden part of His mind, obliterating all the illusory distinctions like subject and object, time and space, energy and form, emotion and reason, mind and matter, and life and death, which have haunted humankind since the fall, until—

The film abruptly ran out.

Following a moment of private, gum-snapping thought, Inspector O'Nadir rolled his chair behind Tharmas to touch Ded's shoulder. "You think it might be a good idea to stop Ickey Jerusalem's trustee from distributing those poems?"

CHAPTER 30

DING AN SICH—ZWEI

Ded was lost in thought, *So, Jerusalem* was *focused on completing Golgonooza and then causing the Consolidation of Error to disappear, thereby triggering the Apocalypse which he saw as being just around the corner. But as for the identity of the Satan Incarnate who might have jumped him, Jerusalem failed to single out Bacon Urizen. Just the opposite. By accusing his entire coterie of being out to kill his creativity, Jerusalem implied all of them were Satan Incarnate.*

When the reading of the bequests is done, Ded decided, *I've got to find out whether Jerusalem gave anywhere additional descriptions of Satan.*

Ded slapped his hand to his forehead. *Wait! Jerusalem did give one! On the right side of Tharmas's VW bus. The painting,* Satan Exulting over Eve, *done about five months ago. The poet portrayed there the evil one for all to see.*

Ded reviewed what he could remember from his brief viewing Saturday morning of the attractive but wan man with bat wings floating above a supine Eve. Then he methodically compared that image against the people he had met so far during his investigation. *Ghostflea, no. Beulah, no. Urizen, no. Tharmas, no. Los, no. Enith, no. Theo, no. Grandma Enion, definitely no. Rahab? You got to be kidding.*

Ded stroked his chin. *That leaves only one person—Dr. Ulro.*

Ded thought it over. *It's true the doctor is the sole suspect who qualifies as an attractive man in his prime. However, that's only from a distance. And even then, Dr. Ulro's attractiveness mimics the perfection of a smooth, rigid Ken doll, not the supple, characterful human face and body of the floating Satan.*

Maybe rather than focusing on the floating man, Ded concluded, *I should be taking another look at the serpent. Or even Eve. I need to see the painting again.*

Ded turned to O'Nadir, who was patiently waiting for Ded to answer his query about stopping the distribution of the poetry. "How long would it take for you to get me a photo of the painting on the right side of Tharmas's VW bus. From what you said to Tharmas earlier, I understand it's currently at the Hall of Justice's evidence lockup."

"No problem," O'Nadir answered, assuming the answer to his query had been no. "I think forensics has already taken pictures of the entire bus as a record of where the various glove prints were found."

Until he saw the photo, Ded would have to assume that the painting's representation of Satan was purely symbolic—an archetype of the passionless abstractor—and thus no more helpful in identifying who might have jumped Jerusalem than the poet's multiple accusations on his bequest film.

Ded glanced to his left at Tharmas, who was still holding his right hand over the right side of his downcast face. His posture, adopted upon hearing Ickey's announcement about the world-wide distribution of his anthology, appeared to be a disingenuous disguise to shield the business manager's real feelings from the insurance investigator's view.

"Not a single penny for Hand and Hyle," Ded overheard Dr. Ulro say to his wife in his small, birdlike voice. "A baboon would've shown more interest in its offspring."

Ded turned to where they were sitting, on his right, beyond the couch.

"True," Rahab agreed. "But then, baboons are not visionary poets."

Beyond the couple, Beulah was now quietly filling in Ghostflea on what he had missed.

Grandma Enion, under the impression she had been watching some kind of giveaway game show on daytime television, was pestering Theo to tell her what she had won.

"A box of string too short to save," Theo informed her as he wiped at the battered remains of the chartreuse amoeba still clinging heroically to the front of his shirt.

"A box of string too short to save?" Grandma Enion gave Theo a sidelong look and chewed her gums reflectively. "What kind of horseshit is that?"

Urizen had left the projector, turned on the office lights, and was now sitting behind his desk. Ded caught his attention with a raised index finger. "Do you think you'll actually be able to distribute a free copy of Jerusalem's poetry to everybody in the world?"

The worn-out lawyer pressed his pale lips together, opened the folder he had brought with him into his office at the beginning of the meeting, and looked at its contents. "Probably not."

Urizen held up his hand for everyone to be quiet. "I'm afraid I've some rather disturbing news." He hesitated, surveying his attentive audience. "Before our meeting today, I had a look at the money in the Urthon Spectre Trust, and…" He took in a breath. "I'm not sure how to say this, but it appears… it appears Ickey Jerusalem has taken it with him."

The collective expression held by Bacon Urizen's audience was not dissimilar to what one might have seen in the College of Cardinals after the Pope announced some anonymous spelunker had discovered the body of Christ. The stunned silence was followed right away by the stuttered beginnings of half-formed questions emanating from various parts of the room.

"What do you mean?" Los demanded, flabbergasted. Although he had long ago been removed as the trustee, Ded could tell Los still felt a proprietary interest in Uncle Urthon Spectre's bequest.

Urizen closed the folder and drew his pudgy palm wearily over his albino pate. His hand passed down the back of his neck and then slid forward to the front, fingertips breaking contact to the right of his Adam's apple. "About three months ago, Mr. Jerusalem asked me to discreetly liquidate all of his investments and deposit the proceeds in the trust's bank account."

Ded looked at Tharmas. The man's pose had not changed one iota.

"As his trustee," Urizen continued, "I did as he asked. The proceeds came to over one hundred million dollars." He exhaled and sank deeper into his chair. "First thing this morning, preparing for our meeting, I asked the bank to courier over an updated statement. We received it just before the meeting. That's when I discovered everything was gone."

"Gone?" Los exclaimed.

"Gone," Urizen confirmed. "Needless to say, I called the bank. They informed me that on the afternoon of Friday, October 14th, Mr. Jerusalem drew out the total, in cash. Well, all but seventy-three cents."

Los turned somber. "And there are no other assets left, whatsoever?"

"Some real estate limited partnerships that couldn't be liquidated. They are primarily tax shelters with no real value due to very high leverage."

"It's over two weeks since Ickey took the money out," Los said. "How come you just found out now?"

"With the trust assets reduced to cash, there was nothing going on that required close monitoring. We just waited for each monthly statement to see how much interest had been earned. In addition, Milton Fallen, who handled the trust's accounts, died on Monday October 10th, so since then, our attention has been taken up by dealing with other, more pressing administrative loose ends he left behind, plus his funeral the afternoon of Friday, October 14th. Then, from the week beginning Sunday, October 16th, I was in New York. At the end of that week, Mr. Jerusalem died. So, after that, as executor, I've been tied up inventorying Mr. Jerusalem's personal assets and obligations governed by his will."

"Did Jerusalem say why he wanted his investments liquidated?" Ded asked.

"To pay for the worldwide distribution of his poetry."

"You mean, he was planning to die soon?"

"That's not what he said at the time. He told me that having hit on the poetry distribution idea while dictating his bequests, he'd mulled it over for a few months before realizing there was no reason to wait until his death to do it. He intended to start the distribution right after the publication of his collected works in New York. In fact, in pursuance of that goal, I made him an authorized signatory on the trust's account."

Urizen's tired eyes drifted to the back of Jerusalem's picture on his desk. For a moment, no one spoke.

Ded opened his notepad to a clean page. *Let's see,* he thought, remembering a bit of trivia he had learned while engaged in another case. *Two hundred and thirty-three stacked new bills to an inch*. He took a dollar bill out of his wallet and estimated its dimensions. *Two-and-a-half inches by six inches. If the denomination is one hundred dollars—*

Meanwhile, Los scowled at Urizen. "The money must be somewhere. Where have you looked?"

"Nowhere yet. We just discovered it was missing."

Ded finished his calculations. "We're looking for about two cubic yards of hundred-dollar bills," he announced. "Give or take a couple of cubic feet."

O'Nadir blocked out a yard-sized box with his hands. "Should be easy to find."

"Assuming it still exists," Ded observed.

"Yes," Dr. Ulro said. "For all we know, Mr. True Reality decided to mulch it into fertilizer for the Tree of Mystery."

ঌ

"I have a list of addendums further to Mr. Jerusalem's filmed bequests," Urizen said. "Before I read them, I suggest we take a little break. Ghostflea, could you open the curtains, please?"

As the buzz of conversation rose around the room, Ded turned to Tharmas, but the business manager leapt out of his seat and headed to the front of the room. There, he engaged in an intense, confidential colloquy with Urizen.

O'Nadir slipped one seat over to sit beside Ded. "You think it really was Jerusalem who picked up a hundred million dollars from the bank?"

"I assume the bank was careful to check his identity," Ded replied. "And he was a well-known public figure. Someone fastidious at the bank might have tried to call Urizen & Fallen, but most of the firm was likely at Milton Fallen's funeral around then."

O'Nadir grunted and continued in a low voice. "I'm going to find a phone and put Jerusalem's house under surveillance before anybody gets to it. Then I'll call Ben to get the photo you want, have someone pick up this briefcase with its evidence inside-and-out, and send a team over to your room at the Holiday Inn. I've also got to call about that Tongan you and I were talking about. I'll be back in a few minutes."

Ded remained seated as he considered where the disappearance of Ickey Jerusalem's money might fit into his growing assemblage of facts. He lifted Jerusalem's anthology from his left thigh, and looked once again at the index, this time under "money." There were a lot of entries. He chose the latest page reference.

> The accuser of sins by my side does stand
> And he holds my money bag in his hand.

Ded looked up at Jerusalem's photograph, from which the poet grinned demonically. *The accuser of sins? Satan Incarnate? Holds my money bag in his hand? Bacon Urizen?*

The lawyer was still in an earnest conversation with Tharmas. Ded surveyed the room. His gaze, for no particular reason, came to rest on Scofield's glowing eyes.

Instantly, the dog scrambled to his feet and began barking and snarling viciously at Ded. Everyone else fell silent. Beulah grabbed hold of Scofield's harness just as he took off scrabbling across the hardwood floor toward Ded. While the astounded group watched, Beulah was yanked out of her seat and pulled, stumbling, after her seeing-eye dog.

As the beast approached, Ded instinctively threw his hands up to protect his face.

It was the wrong move. Scofield, with a powerful lunge, drove his fanged muzzle into the claims adjuster's groin. Ded cried out, the bloody image of his truncated future sex-life flashing through his mind. So powerful was the image, it took Ded a few seconds to realize that, in fact, Scofield had come over not to bite him, but rather (in the circumstances, perhaps far worse) to *sniff* him—an activity the dog was engaging in with such enthusiasm, wagging his tail like there was no tomorrow, it seemed certain that in only a matter of minutes, Ded would be having carnal relations with one, if not both, of the carnivore's nostrils.

As Ded crossed his legs and tried to twist away, the anthology of Jerusalem's poetry fell to the floor. Glancing back, Ded spotted Los and Enith looking on in amazement.

"I don't know what's gotten into the beast," Ded protested with as much innocence as he could muster. "I've done nothing to encourage such behavior, I swear."

The next time I make love to a woman, Ded silently vowed, *I'm going to make damn sure her dog does not intend to join in.*

Beulah regained her balance (which, given her body's high center of gravity, had seemed in doubt), realigned her floral-rimmed dark glasses, bent down, and began groping sightlessly with her white-gloved hand near Scofield's nose in an attempt to discover the purpose of the dog's social call.

"Ooh!" Ded squealed when she discovered it.

"Is that you, Ded?" Beulah asked.

The faces of the others in the room suggested confusion as to whether the clue to which Beulah was responding was aural or tactile.

"Honestly," Ded asserted for their benefit, "I never would have expected something like this to happen at the reading of a bequest."

Ded lifted Beulah's hand firmly from his groin. "Miss Vala," he stated as formally as he could for the benefit of the onlookers, "your seeing-eye dog seems to have developed an excessive olfactory attachment to the crotch of my trousers." He released her hand, grabbed Scofield's snorfling muzzle, and, though the beast resisted with all its strength, managed to move it a few inches down his thigh.

"Lord knows I'm a tolerant man," he continued loudly, "but there are limits to the sort of behavior one should be expected to accept in a dog."

Indignant, Beulah put her knuckles on her hips. "Are you saying Scofield is impolite?"

"No," Ded replied, recalling Ghostflea's warning about Beulah's inability to tolerate any criticism of her dog, "impolite is not the word that springs to mind." *Uncouth? Gauche? Lacking in the social graces? How do you describe someone who scrabbles across a room on all fours and sticks his nose, uninvited, into your groin?*

"My only concern, Miss Vala," he backpedaled, unable to say what he really thought, "is that in Scofield's eagerness to get to know me, I fear he might injure his delicate nose on my zipper."

"Oh." Beulah seemed mollified, as Ded noticed for the first time a queer fruity smell in the air around her.

"Come here, boy," she commanded, tugging on the dog's harness.

Scofield continued to struggle forward.

"Come here!" Beulah said in a tone like a blow from a rolled-up newspaper.

The dog slunk back.

"Lie down," Beulah ordered.

The dog obediently lay at the foot of the empty chair to Ded's right and looked up at him, whimpering with unrequited love.

Ded took Beulah's delicate arm. "Why don't you sit here?"

He straightened the empty chair on his right and guided her into it. Then, staring hard, he forced the rest of the attendees to avert their eyes and return to whatever private reveries they had been engaged in before the Hound of the Baskervilles had decided to go for the Big Sniff.

Beulah swiveled her chair towards Ded, knocking his briefcase over with her leg. "What's that?" she asked, reaching down and feeling the top.

Ded grabbed the handle and snatched the case away. "Just my briefcase," he answered, putting it behind his chair.

Beulah lifted her exploring hand in Ded's direction and touched the front of his shirt. "Where's the large piece of bed linen you were bragging about on the phone?" she whispered.

"Back in the hotel with most of my chest hairs," Ded whispered back. He looked around to see if anybody was listening. They all seemed to be wrapped up again in their own conversations.

"I had a real nightmare after going to sleep," Ded confided. He described the giant, happy-faced broccoli smothering him with the condom in the airline toilet. "Got any ideas what it might signify?"

"A dream is but the fallen world's parody of a vision," Beulah declared in full kindergarten-teacher mode. "Although the meaning of a *vision* is universal and separate from the person who perceives it, the meaning of a *dream* depends solely on who's dreaming."

"Don't tell me," Ded said. "More thoughts from Chairman Ickey."

"Correct," she answered.

"The guy seems to have created a system to explain everything in the universe."

Beulah gave Ded a forgiving smile. "As Ickey said, 'I must Create a System, or be enslav'd by another Mans.'"

"Perceptive advice," Ded agreed, suddenly irritable. "You should take it."

Beulah's smile continued in its forgiving mode for a moment but then, as the import of the claims adjuster's statement sank in, became confused.

Ded gave her no time to recover. "Tell me, who was Ololon?"

Beulah's confusion disappeared behind a curtain of sadness. She took a deep breath. "The daughter Ickey and I almost had."

"Almost had? Was she stillborn like Rahab's first child, Tirzah?"

"Not stillborn. She was very much alive. She just refused to come out of my womb."

Beulah's head dropped, hiding her moonlike face in her long, strawberry-blond hair. She took another deep breath. "At one point, Ololon's head emerged. But then she opened her eyes, saw Brom, who was handling the delivery, let out a yelp, and fled back up inside me."

"Must've been disconcerting for Dr. Ulro," Ded said woodenly, not knowing how to take such an incredible story.

Beulah sadly agreed. "Try as he could, he couldn't get her to come out again. By the time an OB-GYN came in to perform a cesarean, she was dead."

Beulah cupped her hands, placing them over her nose and mouth. She breathed into them to steady herself. Once calmed, she lowered her hands to her lap. "Ickey said she'd reverted to the state of the unborn imagination and in effect, committed suicide to avoid being born."

"When did this happen?"

"April Fool's Day this year. After that, Ickey never made love to me again." Beulah lowered her head and interlocked her graceful fingers. "He said God had spoken. Sex with me could lead only to the death of his creative imagination."

"What a horrible thing to say," Ded commiserated.

But he was thinking, *Not having had sex for over six months, no wonder she was horny enough to stoop to seducing someone like me.*

He thought back on Beulah saying that the funeral's confirmation Jerusalem was gone had made her feel lonely. *If she'd been isolated from*

Jerusalem in a separate bedroom for over six months without sex, she must have felt lonely long before the funeral.

But also, the investigator in Ded now realized, *if Jerusalem had sworn off intimate relations with Beulah for metaphysical reasons, any attempt by her on the plane to use her sexual skills to lull the poet into a position where she could overpower him would've failed. Jerusalem wouldn't have been interested.*

Beulah raised her head. "For some reason, though, Ickey maintained to his friends the fiction that we were still going to bed ten times a day."

Ded reached over and capped his right palm on her fingers. "Did you know Jerusalem had been carrying on an affair with Rahab since Easter?"

Beulah sighed. "Yes, I knew. He told me before he started. Every Friday afternoon, when Brom was playing golf and Ickey was supposedly sailing, he'd meet up with her instead. Regular as clockwork—although, as Ickey described it, the sex itself was highly *ir*-regular."

"Were you upset?"

"Absolutely not. Ickey did not keep it secret. He told me everything before it began."

"But wasn't he violating his rule that only by focusing intensely on one woman could he obtain any depth of experience?"

"He *was* focusing intensely on one woman—Rahab for sex and me for inspiration. I understood completely that if he wasn't able to sleep with me, he had to get his release with someone, and for that purpose, Rahab was ideal. Good at sex, but with no emotional strings tying him down. For Ickey, it was just pure, physical, unadulterated lust. Plus, Rahab was married with two kids, and as Ickey said in the bequest film, he could never abide children because they 'are such a drag on genius.'"

Ded looked deep into Beulah's fathomless expression, half-hidden behind her dark glasses. He saw no rancor. No jealousy. Only humility, wonder, innocence, beauty, and sadness—infinite and eternal sadness.

But was he seeing what was genuinely there? Or merely projecting what he wanted to see?

I'll have to confirm with Rahab that Beulah approved the new affair before it began. But then, even if Beulah wasn't as tolerant as she claimed, why would she wait six months to seek revenge on Jerusalem?

I'll also need to ask Rahab if and when Dr. Ulro knew about the new affair. After Rahab's previous liaison with Jerusalem, the doctor ended up trying to kill him. This time, the doctor would certainly have made sure he finished the job.

CHAPTER 31

RAISING THE EYES TO THE HEAVENS

Lifting his hand from Beulah's, Ded craned his neck to find where in the room Rahab and Dr. Ulro had gone. But before he could make a move to take his leave of the personal assistant, Tharmas plopped back into the seat to Ded's left and stroked his pointed chin whiskers. "Urizen says without the money, there ain't nothing we can do to fulfill Ickey's last wish."

"If you're talking about what he said on the film," Ded said, "my guess is it wasn't his last wish."

"Why do you say that?"

"If, almost six months after making the film, Jerusalem was still intent on dedicating all his money to the free distribution of his poetry worldwide, he wouldn't have taken the money out of the bank so no one could find it. He would have left it there for his trustee to execute the plan or he would have already paid the printers and distributors to carry it out."

The business manager's tongue snaked out of his mouth, curled upwards at its end, and withdrew post haste into its burrow. "Right."

Inspector O'Nadir returned to the room and sat next to Tharmas. The inspector gave Ded the thumbs-up sign behind Tharmas's back, mouthing, *San Francisco.* Ded deduced he was referring to the Tongan cleaner's port of entry. *Good,* Ded mouthed back. With no further surreptitious signals from the inspector, Ded assumed everything else was in process.

Bacon Urizen announced the end of the break. Once everyone settled down and resumed their seats, he commenced reading the official text of Jerusalem's bequests.

The text didn't reveal much Jerusalem hadn't already said in the film. For what it was worth, Theo was still the residual beneficiary of both the trust and the will. The specific bequests were basically the same, just defined more precisely. The hearse was to be given without gasoline. The pen, without ink. The house, without electricity, gas, sewer, or phone connections. The sailboat, without a sail. The picture of God bifurcating reality, without a frame. The books, without their expensive leather covers. The string, without the box. The bronzes, without their pedestals. The statuette of the Indonesian laughing god with an eighteen-inch phallus, without the god. And so on.

Either Jerusalem was once again making some obscure poetical statement, or he was more parsimonious than Ded would have guessed a dead man would be. After all, what use was an empty picture frame to Jerusalem now? A few gallons of gas? A few drops of ink? A god without its phallus?

As Urizen droned on enumerating Jerusalem's gifts to his brothers, Ded's eyes moved to the dying, white rose on Urizen's desk.

The rose.

Ded reached into his pocket, took out Jerusalem's spiral notebook from the plane, opened the front cover, and reread the poem there.

The Sick Rose

O Rose thou art sick.
The invisible worm,
That flies in the night
In the howling storm:
Has found out thy bed
Of crimson joy:
And ~~her~~his dark secret love
Does thy life destroy.

Wait a minute. He put Jerusalem's notebook on his knee, picked up Jerusalem's anthology from the floor, and thumbed to "The Sick Rose." As he thought, it was the same poem, except the crossed out word "her" in the poet's notebook had been deleted in the anthology.

If "The Sick Rose" was in the anthology published a week before Jerusalem died, he must have written it long before boarding the plane. So, why had Jerusalem been copying the poem again, and marked it with a former correction?

He riffled through the notebook pages following "The Sick Rose." None had any writing on them—at least, on their front sides.

He flipped the notebook over. Through the holes in the cover for the spiral binder wire, he could see thin, ragged strips of the paper edges that were left behind when pages had been torn out. Perhaps the very same pages that had ended up as the scraps in Jerusalem's pocket.

Ded caught the corner of what, until a moment before, he had assumed was the back cover of the notebook. Opening the cover, on what was now the first full page of the notebook, he found, scrawled out in longhand, an entirely new poem!

A wave of expectation mixed with reverence shot through him. This, not "The Sick Rose," must have been the important piece Beulah said Jerusalem had been working on during the flight. Ded began reading.

When Klopstock England defied
Uprose terrible Blake in his pride
For old Nobodaddy aloft
Farted & Belchd & coughd
Then swore a great oath that made heavn quake
And calld aloud to English Blake

There was more to the poem, but Ded paused to get his bearings. Nobodaddy, he knew, was the Old Testament God, from where Dr. Ulro got his nickname. Klopstock was Ickey's Oxford nickname. Blake, the "dark one," was the Ouija board name Los and Enion had rejected for their son. And, according to Beulah, the "English" Ickey was how Jerusalem had described his poetic side.

What Ded had before him, without a doubt, was a bifurcation of Ickey Jerusalem into two parts: a country-hick part challenging a dark poetic part, a bifurcation that so disturbed the Old Testament God, he called out to the poet.

So far, so simple. Ded read on.

Blake was giving his body ease
At Lambeth beneath the poplar trees
From his seat then started he
And turnd himself round three times three
The Moon at that sight blushd scarlet red
The stars threw down their cups & fled
And all the devils that were in hell
Answered with a ninefold yell
Klopstock felt the intripled turn
And all his bowels began to churn
And his bowels turned round three times three
And lockd in his soul with a ninefold key
That from his body it neer could be parted
Till to the last trumpet it was farted

Then again old nobodaddy swore
He neer had seen such a thing before
Since Noah was shut in the ark
Since Eve first chose her hellfire spark
Since twas the fashion to go naked
Since the old anything was created
And in pity he begd him to turn again
And ease poor Klopstocks ninefold pain
From pity then he redend round
And the ninefold Spell unwound

If Blake could do this when he rose up from shite
What might he not do if he sat down to write

Ded lowered the poet's spiral notebook to his thigh, any thought of further interpretation abandoned. *This* was Ickey Jerusalem's last poem? An intimate description of his prowess on the john? Comparing the power of his writings with the power of his bowels?

The poem was so out of character, Ded had a hard time believing Jerusalem had written it. But it was the poet's handwriting, and it was in his notebook. And most persuasive of all, not long after it was written, Jerusalem had ended up in the toilet.

Is this weird poem presenting Jerusalem's different method for triggering the Apocalypse?

Ded rubbed his thumbnail between his two front teeth, then read the final couplet again. He had encountered the British term "shite" once before, in a library dictionary, when, as a bored college student, he had been tracing the etymology of four-letter Anglo-Saxon words. The word, meaning "shit," could be traced all the way back to an Indo-European root meaning that meant "to divide, to cut off, to separate from."

Ded stared at the word. *Was Ickey Jerusalem aware of its etymology? Or had he adopted it while at Oxford as merely another Anglicism?*

Absently, Ded reached down and rubbed his left ankle. Somehow, in the last few moments, it had gone to sleep. In response to the claims adjuster's leftward reach-down, Jerusalem's open spiral notebook, resting on Ded's thigh, dipped headfirst, causing the pages on Ded's side of the spiral wire to slough downwards over the wire. The whole, open notebook then began sliding after the sloughing pages. Reacting quickly, Ded managed to catch the trailing bottom cover (formerly the front) with his free hand before everything passed the point of no return.

Hauling the notebook up by the formerly front cover, he again noticed the "150010/31GHUA843" written on its inside, which he'd suspected earlier of being an offshore bank account number. Studying the letters and digits closely, he focused for the first time on the initials "GH" in the middle. Gwendolyn Heva's initials. Ded removed the initials in his mind and read what was left.

Of course! It all became clear.

He pulled out his loose-leaf notepad, went to a clean page, and wrote the following note:

> Miss Gwendolyn Heva is arriving at SFO at 3 p.m. today on United Airlines flight 843 from NYC. Could you please have Officer Jarvis meet her at the gate and take her to his office so I can talk to her by phone? Tell her that no one will be meeting her in the first-class lounge.

Ded tore out the page and handed it to O'Nadir, putting his index finger to his lips.

O'Nadir read the note and nodded.

Ded recalled Miss Heva's scheduled flight to Grand Cayman. *Had Jerusalem been planning to take the $100 million in his checked luggage to deposit in a Cayman Islands bank? It wouldn't have required more than four large suitcases. And there would've been little danger of discovery.*

Ded knew that although there had been some proposals to tighten airport security earlier in the decade, U.S. international airports still had no X-rays of checked luggage, no Customs inspections upon leaving the country, and no required declarations for the transport of large amounts of money.

At 5 p.m., Ded thought, *I'll see what I can find out from Miss Heva about all this.*

~

At last, Bacon Urizen came to the end of his legalese. He set the pages of the will on his desk. "As it's nearly noon, I've had my secretary make a luncheon reservation at Louie's of Grant Avenue[8], in a private room. We can continue our discussion there."

Urizen gestured toward the wall of windows. "Since it's a nice day, most of you will want to walk. For those of you, like me, who might qualify as the 'before' in a Bowlahoola Health Spa commercial, there is a cab waiting downstairs."

Everyone began gathering their things. Tharmas headed out first. Beulah felt her way to the east window to retrieve her straw hat from her former seat.

O'Nadir got up and took a step toward Ded's chair. "Ben said he already had a photo of the VW painting, so I'm going to ring him now to have it delivered to you at Louie's of Grant Avenue. Meanwhile, I've got to get over to Immigration and Naturalization, and after that, ring Officer Jarvis on meeting Miss H., and then I'll try the airline again about those two stewardesses. I got a feeling they're avoiding me."

O'Nadir, seeming to remember one other thing he had to do, went over to the Ulros, who were getting out of their seats. "When you finish at the restaurant, could you both please come down to the Hall of Justice? I'd like to talk to you about some goings-on at the Three Heavens golf club yesterday."

With reluctance, they both agreed to do so, Dr. Ulro giving the

---

8 The restaurant was a 1970s San Francisco Chinatown landmark that has since fallen, without a trace, into the lowest level of God's consciousness.

proviso that he would have to leave by three-thirty as he had an open clinic between four and five-thirty.

❧

Ded approached Urizen, who was clearing his desk. "Do you think it'd be possible to take a look at the trust's books later today?"

Urizen squinted at Ded through his monocle. "Why?"

"Just curious," Ded lied.

"The books are confidential," Urizen informed him with a touch of his old imperiousness. "Mere curiosity isn't a good enough reason for me to let you examine them, you understand."

"Certainly," Ded agreed. He couldn't let the Urthon Spectre Trust trustee know yet his desire to find a match in the account for the numbers he had found on Jerusalem's desk.

Urizen put some files in his briefcase. "Anyway, don't you think the books are irrelevant now, given the money is no longer there?"

Ded held his tongue. He knew that to bring home the bacon, one sometimes had to be as slippery as a greased pig.

❧

The group exited to the street in two elevators: one for Beulah and Scofield, and one for everyone else.

"I could take it when all you had to worry about was getting bit," Dr. Ulro declared to the others. "But after the four-legged pervert's performance today, I'm damned if I'm going to get into an enclosed space with *him*."

There was hearty agreement throughout the car.

They reached the ground floor in time to see the doors of Beulah's elevator open. Two Japanese businessmen dashed out and raced across the lobby, causing quite a stir, owing partly to their lack of trousers and partly to the way they kept screaming something that sounded like, "Hara-kiri! Hara-kiri! Hara-kiri!"

"Is this the ground floor?" Beulah asked, calling out of the elevator in the general direction of the fleeing businessmen.

Scofield leisurely sauntered out ahead of his mistress, chewing contentedly on the crotches of two well-pressed pants hanging from his lower jaw.

"Really," the girl from Orlando sighed in exasperation when there was no immediate answer to her query about the floor. "The men who ride elevators today are so inconsiderate."

In the confines of the elevator car, Ded thought, *Beulah could not have missed the sounds of Scofield's attack, so her mental blind spot regarding the dog had to be exceptionally powerful to keep her from recognizing what was going on.*

Ded wondered whether this revealed something even broader about Beulah's mind.

&

Outside, Los and Enith climbed into the taxi with Bacon Urizen. They tried to get Grandma Enion to go with them, but no one could figure out how to pry her loose from the fire hydrant.

Which was perhaps just as well. From what Ded could judge, the old woman had entered into a pact with the devil to cover the world in saliva. In the confines of the cab, the results could have been Biblical in their proportions.

Once the taxi left, Grandma Enion unclamped herself from the hydrant and everyone started walking in single file up the hill. Because there was a slight headwind, Ded suggested Grandma be put at the rear on Theo's arm, Ded's unspoken goal being for her to literally cover their tracks, ensuring any shooter attempting to follow would find the slope too slippery to remain upright. Ahead of Grandma Enion and Theo were Dr. Ulro, Ghostflea, Rahab, Ded, and, leading the way, Tharmas.

Aware Rahab was immediately behind him and alone, Ded dropped back to get some answers.

She gave him a welcoming smile as bright as the golden sunburst brooch on her headband framing its stubby, striated, grey phallus.

"Hey, dude, what's up?"

"A few further questions?" Ded murmured.

"Shoot."

"When did your husband find out about your latest affair with Jerusalem?"

Rahab glanced back past Ghostflea to her promenading husband, to make sure he couldn't hear. "Since before it even began, man," she said.

"You gave him advance notice of the affair?"

"It wasn't an affair," Rahab said. "Ickey was paying for the sex. And not only that, on Brom's demand, paying twice the going rate. After I let Brom in on how the non-birth of Ololon had squelched Ickey's humping Beulah, Brom could see Ickey was after nothing more than getting his rocks off. My old man, having given up humping me after the non-birth of Tirzah, totally bought the idea there was no romance in Ickey's actions."

"But wasn't Ickey an acquaintance?"

"For sure, but paying for sex so violated Ickey's high-flown metaphysics, *he* wasn't going to tell anybody. He even kept up the story he was bonking Beulah all day and night. In the end, Ickey's blatant hypocrisy got my old man to go along. Brom even asked me to let Ickey know that he knew what was going down, just so he could hold it over Ickey's head."

"Did Beulah know?"

"Yep. Since she was a friend, I got her approval first. Given the Oothoon business and the pay for play, she gave it the thumbs up."

So, the confirmation of Dr. Ulro's and Beulah's acceptance of the affair six months ago before it began makes it even more unlikely it had anything to do with Jerusalem's murder last week.

"Rahab, since everything was hunky-dory regarding the affair, what did Brom and Jerusalem argue about before the New York trip? You told me at the country club that you didn't know, but given how strongly you feel your husband was the murderer, you must have had a good idea."

Rahab averted her eyes, visibly struggling over whether to reveal what she knew. Coming to a decision, she reluctantly shook her head. "I can't say, man."

Deciding it wasn't worth pushing the point, Ded changed to the other line of questions.

"Did you send your husband a high-tech golf club yesterday?"

"No. I'm not *au fait* enough with golf to know what to get him."

"The gift note was signed by you, and the club subsequently blew up. Luckily, no one was hurt."

"Gnarly," Rahab said, surprised. "Must have been another of my husband's enemies. Look, dude, if I wanted to off my husband, I wouldn't start by plastering my name all over the weapon."

"Fair enough. So you didn't also send a rose powdered with pure LSD to Bacon Urizen on Saturday night? It had the same handwriting on the note."

"Are you putting me on? Why would I send Bacon a rose with acid dust on it? Especially since I'm actually the one who saved Bacon's bacon Saturday night."

"You stopped him from flying off the balcony?"

"Yeah. I'd just come up the garage elevator with the spare key he gave me and bopped into his pad for our weekly rendezvous, when—"

Flabbergasted, Ded cut in. "You'd been having sex with Urizen, too?"

"No. Not really. Bacon couldn't get it up. But we'd been trying. He was strung out on this idea that if only he could pork me, he'd get back his lost youth and everything'd be groovy."

"Did your husband know?"

"Sure. It was the same deal as with Ickey. Double the normal rate and Brom gets to hold the john's blatant hypocrisy over his head. Except in this case, there was a distinct lack of success where consummation's concerned. Well, at least, there was until last night."

"Last night?"

"Yeah. Crazy, huh? When I split from the Three Heavens yesterday, I was so freaked out about what Brom might do, I crashed at Bacon's pad. And we did it. Maybe it was the leftover effects from his acid trip. I mean, he was still dropping in and out of relapse city. Whatever was happening, he found enough imagination for me to turn him on full blast and we did the dirty deed. After that, he seemed to become a totally changed dude."

Urizen has now had sex with Rahab, Ded thought, *as in the Orc cycle's denouement. What's going to happen next?*

"I feel bad about pressing you again, Rahab, but it's really necessary in order to nail your husband. Could you please tell me what Ickey told you about his argument with Brom?"

Rahab's spherical dress glittered in the sun like a revelatory beacon as she flounced her Lilliputian, rotund, bejeweled body from side to side. "The argument," she finally said, "was… was about… about Brom losing—"

"A bunch of crap!" Dr. Ulro, at last noticing Ded and Rahab had been conferring, had barged past Ghostflea to interrupt with this *bon mot*. "That's what it's been this entire morning, a bunch of crap. All that poetical shit on Ickey's film, the half-ass bequests, then the missing hundred million, and now a mandatory luncheon at a restaurant. I'm inclined not to go."

Rahab moved to the left so her husband could come between her and Ded.

"I think it'll be interesting," Ded said. "Everyone who counts in the same room, talking. Something should come up."

Dr. Ulro grunted. His talk of not going to the lunch seemed to have been just a filler, masking his main purpose for butting in: to terminate his wife's private conversation with the life insurance investigator.

Realizing he wasn't going to learn anything more from Rahab at the moment, Ded searched for a gracious way out. Spotting a stooped Tharmas Luvah, trudging along a few steps ahead, lost in his own world, Ded turned back to Rahab and Dr. Ulro. "Excuse me," he said, "I've got to ask Tharmas a few questions."

Hurrying ahead, he reached out and touched the business manager on the shoulder. "What's on your mind, Tharmas?"

The business manager looked up with his dark eyes as Ded fell into step beside him.

"Nothing much. Ickey carting all that money outta the Bank of America, I guess."

"Any idea why he did it?"

Tharmas shrugged, then quoted without feeling, "'Great ends never look at the means but produce them spontaneously.'"

"Do you believe that's true?"

"Ickey did," Tharmas replied. He put his upper lip over his lower lip as he thought further. "Only, now I ain't so sure he was right."

Ded let the business manager dwell on his thoughts for a moment as he tried to find a way to express his next question. In the end, Ded figured he'd simply ask it outright.

"Do you remember meeting two stewardesses at your New York hotel the night before you flew back with Jerusalem?"

"Christ," Tharmas said with a resigned laugh, "they ain't pregnant, too, are they?"

"Too?"

"Every time I go to bed with a woman, she always ends up pregnant. And then the next thing yuh know, she's on my doorstep, speaking glibly about cause and effect." Tharmas moved his palms into an imploring gesture. "They never seem willing to accept it's just a coincidence."

"I don't know, Tharmas, whether the two stewardesses are pregnant. It hadn't even occurred to me you'd gone to bed with them."

"I know it sounds kinda boring, sleeping with stewardesses, but I thought, darn, yuh know, two at once, with full rubber-wear and opposing trapezes." Tharmas drew his upturned palms to below his chest. "One of them had these colossal bazongas, sticking out through circles cut in the rubber." He jiggled his solar-plexus-high, upturned palms for emphasis. "Which added a certain degree of nipple danger when, upside down in mid-trapeze-swing, she started playing Ravel's *Bolero* on the accordion."

Ded said nothing. He had the vague suspicion Tharmas was putting him on. "When did you last see the stewardesses?"

"About midday the following day. After they'd nodded off, completely worn out. I took my bags, put the Do Not Disturb sign on the door, and left the ladies sleeping in my room. I was late for a lunch meeting with the publishers, so I didn't bother to check out. The hotel had an imprint of my credit card."

"Did you leave the stewardesses a message?"

"No, nothing."

"The night before, when you first met them, was the purser, Robert N. William, there?"

"Yeah. He joined us at the bar along with another stewardess."

"So, you got to know the purser before the flight?"

"Yeah, I guess you could say that." Tharmas gave Ded a smile not unlike one would see on a satisfied python digesting his prey.

"Why didn't you say so earlier?"

"Yuh didn't ask."

The group turned onto Grant Avenue, the narrow main street of Chinatown. The sidewalks were teeming with baggy-clothed Chinese immigrants, pushing purposively through, milling about, or standing around, staring, gossiping, bargaining, arguing, and otherwise conversing in their indecipherable tongue.

Tharmas and Ded again dropped into single file, with the business manager in the lead.

Looking around, Ded recalled the sage advice O'Nadir had given four years before when they'd finished the Knife case and were planning to celebrate by going to the afternoon's big Columbus Day parade. "The best place to watch is from Chinatown," the inspector recommended. "The Chinese immigrants are so short, you'll always get an unobstructed view."

Which had turned out to be wholly accurate.

Later that day, as Ded had waited among the Chinatown residents for the baton twirlers and flag-carrying, middle-aged war veterans to march into view, he could have been in a low-flying airplane, looking Godlike from his hermetically sealed heaven as the villagers below scurried about, performing their inscrutable little rituals of life. That combined with having easily solved a difficult case, Ded had felt so far over the heads of the rest of mankind, he was likely the only person alive whose view of the world wasn't being blocked by others.

A few months thereafter, Ded's wife, Harriet, had left him.

ᯅ

Now, here he was, in Chinatown once again. Only this time, looking out over the mass of humanity teeming around him, the feeling that swept over him was not one of superiority but of longing, a deep desire to breach the veneer of sinful pride and connect with his fellow human beings. No longer wanting to lord it over others, what he wanted now was to reach out with his creative imagination to envelop each and every one, by immediate perception, drawing them into his being, merging their marvelous, six-thousand-year-old culture into his own personal Golgonooza.

ᯅ

In front of a shop window displaying an opulent, brocaded silk robe sat an old Chinese panhandler in a tattered suit. Half his teeth were missing. The other half looked like they were about to go. His black hair was snarled. His face was unwashed. Yellow spittle dribbled over the stubble on his chin. Evidently, not a man living up to his full potential.

As Tharmas approached, the panhandler held out an imploring, palsied palm.

"Shit," the business manager muttered as he trudged by, "another imagination looking to be smothered by the pure abstraction of happiness through possession. Ickey Jerusalem, where are yuh when we need yuh?"

Noting that nothing had been dropped in the weighing scale of his hand, the beggar rotated his practiced, imploring look to Ded.

As the panhandler's eyes met his, Ded halted, his weight on his leading foot, his other leg extended back and to one side, his balancing arms spread wide, and his palms out. "'The Princes robes & Beggars rags,'" Ded quoted from Jerusalem's anthology, pivoting to drop a coin into the man's hand, "'are Toadstools on the Misers Bags.'"

The beggar's eyes blinked with incomprehension. And then Ded was off, striding into the great unknown.

Tharmas, stopped, spun around, and peered into Ded's radiating face. "I know that quote."

"To the eye of a miser," Ded grinned, raising his gaze over the business manager's head to the noontime sun, "the golden coin is more beautiful than the Heavenly Host."

Tharmas looked up and beheld the small golden coin, shining brightly in the sky above.

❧

Ded noticed a poster on a nearby brick wall, picturing what looked uncannily like the Asian serpent embroidered on Tharmas's shirt. "1977," the sign announced, "THE CHINESE YEAR OF THE SNAKE."

CHAPTER 32

BLINDED BY THE GOLDEN SUN

When Ded and the others arrived at Louie's of Grant Avenue, Urizen, Los, and Enith were waiting in the cloakroom. With Ghostflea's help, Beulah hung her linen blazer and straw hat on the row of hooks furthest from the door and positioned Scofield underneath them to act as guard dog.

Whether Scofield appreciated the gravity of the mission was unclear. Certainly, it was unorthodox behavior for a guard dog, upon assuming his duties, to promptly engage in the furious licking of his balls.

The group stood for a moment, gazing at the doubled-up canine.

"Must be some special routine he learned at obedience school," Los advised Enith. "You know, to give the impression of nonchalance when faced with great danger."

One by one, most of the gathering turned and drifted out of the cloakroom toward the WAIT HERE TO BE SEATED sign on the far side of the lobby, leaving Tharmas and Ded behind, both still transfixed by Scofield's contortionist's skills.

The business manager sighed enviously. “Wish I could do that.”

“Give it a try,” Ded suggested. “I’m sure the dog would appreciate your help.”

☙

Louie’s elderly Chinese *maître d’* hobbled into the lobby, confirmed the group’s reservation, and then led them upstairs. The old man labored with each step, groaning and cursing under his breath in Chinese as Ded and the others bunched up behind him, not daring to pass.

At the top of the stairs, the *maître d’* stopped to catch his breath and then pointed to a door across the hall. They went in. In the center of the small, private dining room was a large round table. Each place setting had a handleless teacup, an empty bowl, chopsticks, and a small sauce dish. Western utensils for the uninitiated were in an ornate china mug at the center.

Ded helped Beulah into a chair and then sat at her right. He cast his eyes slowly counterclockwise around the table, studying each person in turn—Ghostflea, Urizen, Dr. Ulro, Tharmas, Grandma Enion, Theo, Los, Enith, and the last, on Beulah’s left and sitting as far away from her husband as possible, Rahab Oothoon. A waiter thoughtfully brought a short stack of telephone books for her to sit on, to raise her forearms to table height.

Before Ded had become involved in the investigation, he had known none of these people. Now, after only a few days, he felt he had come to know each of them well, and he realized, to his surprise, despite their all being murder suspects, he really liked them. As he reveled in each one’s peculiar mix of human and poetic attributes, he felt a warmth welling up inside him.

Such was the power of this feeling that Ded even beamed at Dr. Ulro as he came around the table, filling everyone’s cups from the large metal teapot the waitstaff had placed in front of him.

❧

Louie's specialty was *dim sum*—loosely translated as "a little bit of Heaven"—a near-infinite variety of dumplings, egg rolls, eel, chicken feet, and other delicacies. Rather than ordering from a menu, customers took small dishes of what they wanted from various trolleys that were continually wheeled into the room.

As the first set of trolleys arrived and everyone began helping themselves, Ded decided to butt in with the question vexing him most.

"In Jerusalem's bequest film today, Satan Incarnate played a role in the suppression of the creative imagination, eventually leading to the Apocalypse. But it was unclear to me whether Satan Incarnate is an actual person or just an abstract concept."

Everyone looked at everyone else. Then Bacon Urizen, with the *noblesse oblige* of the superior intellect, took up the challenge in his tired sub-baritone. "Both. At the conceptual level, every human who uses their reason to distance themselves from the world is, to that extent, acting as Satan Incarnate. However, Mr. Jerusalem prophesied that among those, one particular human who—although not aware of it until the end of days—had become the embodiment of all that is Satan Incarnate."

"Is that you?" Ded asked. "The Urizen of the Orc cycle?"

"No. Fortunately, Mr. Jerusalem gave specific details of this overarching Satan Incarnate, most of which do not apply to me."

Ded turned to a trolley that had just been wheeled up. He took a small plate of eel for himself, and after a brief consultation, a large white *Bao* bun for Beulah and a dish of garlic prawns for Ghostflea. "And what are those details?"

"Let's see," the lawyer began, studying the approaching trolley through his monocle. "He… I'll use the male pronoun for ease of disposition, although it could just as easily be a she… was born in a place known for its traditional social values."

Ded wrote this first attribute down in his notepad, bringing to mind the memory of Buffalo, New York. Although the city fit the description, Ded paid no attention to this thought, assuming his overactive imagination was simply triggered by Urizen's emphasis on certain words and phrases.

Urizen peeked at the dishes on the lower levels of the trolley. "Raised by a dutiful father and a devout mother."

The image of Buffalo divided, and each half of the split screen in Ded's head zoomed down to focus, on one side, on his dutiful father at his paper-stacked water company office, and on the other, his devout Catholic mother kissing the toe of St. Jude's statue. Entirely natural associations, Ded felt, given Buffalo as the starting point.

The lawyer's uni-spectacled eye caught something on the third level of the trolley. "Spent most of his early life alone in his room. Reducing the world he saw outside to simple abstractions sketched on paper."

Ded saw himself as a child, alone in his room, reducing the world he saw outside to simple abstractions. *There must be many people,* Ded thought, *who spent their childhood alone, sketching stick figures of children playing below their window.*

Ded gauged the reaction of Urizen's audience to the lawyer's exposition. Everyone, except Dr. Ulro, seemed to be exceptionally attentive, quietly bobbing their heads. Or almost everyone. Grandma Enion's attention was occupied with three irregular dumplings on the small dish Theo had placed before her. She examined them as if trying to recall where in her distant past in Eden she had seen them before.

"Theo," she demanded once the connection was made, "what in the hell are these *donkey boogers* doing here?"

Theo, who apparently did not know enough about either *dim sum* or donkeys to rebut her description, gingerly pushed the plate away as though the dumplings were live, miniature hand grenades.

"I heard the Chinese would eat anything, Grandma," he said, "but jumping Jehoshaphat! Donkey boogers?"

Urizen ignored the outburst, chose a small dish of chicken feet from the trolley, lifted up his chopsticks, and returned to pontificating. "He then went on to college."

As Ded wrote this down, his mind drifted to the main building of his alma mater, Buffalo State College.

Urizen artfully picked up a chicken foot with his chopsticks. "There, making few acquaintances and no friends, he was inculcated with a complete, prefabricated world view…"

The Buffalo State College building opened to show Ded as his collegiate self, earnestly beavering away in the Sociology Department as he absorbed its complete, prefabricated world view.

The Ded now beavering away in Louie's Chinese restaurant, jotting the elements of Satan's background in his notepad, naturally noticed the coincidences piling up. How could he not? But he forced himself to wait until he had the full description before making a judgment as to which of the suspects the elements might fit.

"…in which he was taught to believe everything everywhere can be reduced to abstractions on paper, albeit somewhat more complex abstractions than those he had produced in his youth…"

The picture zoomed in on Ded's student desk, on which lay desiccated graphs, pie charts, and scatterplots—sociology's replacements for his youthful stick figures as representations of the world.

"…and from those abstractions, he could see what those wrapped up inside their world could not see."

Ded scratched his head. It was getting very hard to ignore the similarities.

"Am I right so far, Tharmas?" Urizen asked, waving a chopstick-clasped chicken foot.

Tharmas absently dipped his head, his dark, sensuous eyes following the claw, as though lamenting, *Alas, poor Yorick! I knew him well*—the common, if incorrect quote that betrays the reciter as never having read *Hamlet.*

Urizen held the chicken foot before his mouth as he moved into full flow. "Imbued with the fervor of a new convert, he left college for the real world, only to find himself soon packed into a crowd of humans, all the same and extending indefinitely in every direction."

Ded set down his pen, seeing himself in his first Olympian Life Insurance Company job, his desk crammed into the rows and rows of indistinguishable claim adjusters.

Urizen popped the chicken foot in his mouth and chewed it clean. He then placed the bones on his plate.

Ded leaned forward, eager for the exposition to continue.

Urizen pushed his dish away and refocused his eyepiece on Ded. "At the same time, pressed against him, was a young woman. Wrapping her arms around his neck and her legs around his hips, she introduced the young man to lovemaking, and drew him down into the mundane."

The packed life insurance company office morphed into the packed dancefloor of the Multi-Ethnic Folk Dancing Club, where Ded's wife was smothering him in an uncomfortable Bulgarian-dance body hold.

"For the next several years, with his perspective confined by this woman and the others pressing in around him, he lost all interest in reducing to paper anything that had not already been so reduced before he got to it."

In his mind, Ded could see, trapped between the clasping Harriet and himself, hundreds of triplicate claims forms creating an irregular barrier, separating the couple from tip to toe.

"If things had continued in this manner, he would, no doubt ultimately have been able to pass for a normal person. But then…"

Ded, jumping ahead, saw his predecessor at the Olympian Life Insurance Company, being sucked, screaming, through an open airplane door, then falling, arms and legs flailing, until he smashed through the roof of the dancing club, slamming to the ground at Ded's feet.

"…he who preceded him fell from the sky, crashed down, and died, changing the budding Satan's life forever. Stepping onto what was left of the dead one, he freed himself from those who were keeping him down. For the first time in his life, he could see unobstructed in all directions."

Ded saw himself step onto the traveling claims adjuster's corpse, bend his knees, and, holding his arms at either side like wings, jet off into the sky.

Urizen pulled his teacup closer. "A multitude of images, experiences, and insights began flooding into his freshly freed mind, resonating with his being in a drug-like rush of Orc-like euphoria. He tried to make sense of it, giving report after exhilarated report about what he was seeing to those left behind. But he found it hard to keep up. Ultimately, overdosed on the inflow of inputs, he lost track of where he was, and found his jumbled perspectives so wide and all-encompassing, he could imagine himself everywhere other than where he was."

Jesus, Ded thought, reeling at Urizen's accurate description of himself when he had started traveling.

Although still trying to keep an open mind, Ded felt caught in some kind of undertow of images dragging him toward the most patently absurd of conclusions. *True, I was on Jerusalem's flight, but I had nothing to do with his death! At least, nothing that I can remember.*

Urizen raised his cup of Chinese tea to his pale lips, sucked in about a third of the liquid, and sloshed it around in his mouth.

Unsettled, Ded picked up a piece of eel with his fingers, messily removed the spiny backbone, and popped the remaining flesh into his mouth. The taste of a thousand dead mackerel—boiled down into the narrow body of a slithering serpent—poisoned his tongue. He blanched at the overpowering fishiness, and with some effort, swallowed the pulp down. As he did so, he noticed Rahab, sitting on her telephone books on the other side of Beulah, take a plate of eel from the trolley for herself.

The corpulent Urizen straightened his back. "The embryonic-Satan continued for several years in his joyous creativity, stimulated by the multifarious inputs. During this period, however, as his collection of inputs piled up, he began to see connections, and from those connections, he constructed random and disjointed theories into which the incoming inputs could fit, all related to his ability to see what others, with their limited perspective, couldn't."

Ded furrowed his brow. How much longer could he force himself to reserve judgement on the identity of Satan Incarnate? The accumulating facts were overwhelming.

There was a muffled crunch to his left. He glanced over at the jewel-studded Rahab, sensuously masticating an unfilleted piece of eel. She looked up at him and grinned, a minute bone stuck on her eyetooth.

Beulah slid forward and swiveled her ingénue face until her flower-lined dark glasses appeared to peer deep into Ded's soul. "And then, a little over three-and-a-half years ago," she said, taking up from where Urizen left off and replacing the lawyer's bass voice with her girlish, if a little eerie, Florida-sunshine voice, "the proto-Satan's joy was cut short by a highly painful rejection coming out of nowhere, causing him to try to isolate from the source of the pain."

Ded saw himself receiving the phone call from Harriet announcing her desire for a divorce, resulting in him signing everything over to her and taking off on permanent business travel.

"Over the next several months, though, his devastating suffering not only continued but also got worse, and worse, until just when he thought he could no longer stand it, he had a revelation that rapidly brought together all his accumulated ideas into one Grand Unifying Theory, explaining everything in the universe and his part in it."

Grand Unifying Theory? Ded gulped.

"A theory that relieved his pain by distancing himself emotionally from others and his own experiences, so he thereafter related to them solely by comparing, generalizing, categorizing, and abstracting them, reducing their multidimensional humanity to desiccated, paper-thin imprints, and then bringing those imprints back into his mind to be neatly fitted into his theory."

Ded recalled his pain on the Miami-to-L.A. red-eye osmosing from his body as his Grand Unifying Theory had revealed itself.

"Unbeknownst to him, at the moment of his revelation," Beulah continued earnestly, "his whole being instantly inverted, morphing him from Orc into Urizen—the full-blown, upside-down Satan Incarnate. Beneath his chin, a white beard shot out, spreading forward, sideward, and behind, along a horizontal plane, an ever-expanding, intricate system of abstract, interlocking roots, rapidly becoming a solid white screen, to filter out all but the lowest-common-denominator generalizations of his fellow human beings—who, from his inverted point of view, seemed buried headfirst in the physical world 'below'—and to confirm his belief that the feelings and experiences of humankind were mere illusions, shadows on the wall of a cave."

Ded grasped his chin with the eel-scented fingers of his hand. He didn't have a beard, to say nothing of a solid white, horizontal, ever-expanding screen. And he sure as heck wasn't upside down. But he recognized that the screen and the inversion were a metaphor for how he dealt with the world.

Beulah took a deep breath, preparing for what Ded assumed would be another exceedingly long sentence. "Concurrently, his Grand Unifying Theory burst through his scalp from his brain, like flat, black, angular serpents, branching out on the horizontal plane above his head, weaving together into an ever-darker screen..."

Ded touched the top of his head, unable to fathom how this outlandish description might fit him.

"...so, when Satan Incarnate raised his eyes, he saw only blackness, which he mistook for his Grand Unifying Theory's supposedly unobstructed view of reality..."

Ded dropped his hand and his jaw. Beulah, without a doubt, was describing the infinite and eternal black void so key to his discovery of Bottom's error.

"...but which was, in fact, due to Satan's upended state, nothing more than the entrance to the deepest and most light-free pit of Hell."

Ded gulped, realizing how he, during Urizen's Saturday introduction to the idea of the upside-down Satan, had missed the clear application to himself.

Beulah pressed on. "Convinced, nonetheless, he'd found the true meaning of life, he withdrew emotionally into the space between the two inner surfaces of his very own Consolidation of Error—the screen of pure abstraction 'below' and the void of pure theory 'above'—where he could feel safe experiencing life as a mere concept."

Beulah reached blindly with her fingertips to locate Ded's face. Orienting herself from the corners of his thick glasses, she held both white-gloved hands horizontally, palms down, and then placed the left just below his chin and the right just above his head. "Despite the true meaning he thinks he has found," she said, spelling it out in her wraithlike voice, "he is still trapped between the two planes. However free he believes he is, deep inside, he feels isolated, alone, overcome by a suffocating sense of claustrophobia."

It's true I've had such feelings, Ded thought. *And they've recently been getting increasingly worse.* In his hyped-up imagination, Ded found himself transported by the suggestive power of Beulah's voice to the New-York-to-San-Francisco red-eye on which Jerusalem had died. Once more, he sat among the salesmen, overcome with feelings of isolation, loneliness, and suffocating claustrophobia.

"Unconsciously, he tries to escape the only way his relentlessly-pushing-inwards, dual-plane Consolidation of Error will allow." Beulah pressed the back of her lower hand upwards, into Ded's chin. "By pulling the thickening bottom plane up from his chin to increase his distance from the illusions of humanity crowding him from below..." She forced her upper palm down hard onto the crown of Ded's head. "...while pulling the thickening, upper plane down through the top of his head to get closer to the solace of his theory's supposedly unobstructed view of reality."

Ded sat, immobilized, his head squeezed between Beulah's hands, eyes darting from side to side, his frantic mind trying to analyze whether there was anyone else but him at the table who could be said to be trapped between two expanding planes. Ghostflea? Urizen? Ulro? Tharmas? Grandma Enion? Theo? Los? Enith? Rahab? Beulah?

"Naturally," Beulah continued, "the only result of pulling the two surfaces closer is to increase his isolation and claustrophobia." She slid her flat hands until the trailing edges of her little fingers rested on the top and bottom boundaries of Ded's face. "In turn, that causes him to pull the surfaces even closer, in an evermore desperate attempt to escape." She glided her level hands a few inches toward each other along the skin of his face. "Again, and again." She pumped the two surfaces nearer and nearer to each other, approaching the center of Ded's glasses. "Squashing himself further and further down, until, a few years after his revelation…" Almost touching, her hands stopped, leaving only a tiny slit in front of Ded's fearful eyes. "…his head becomes nothing more than the infinitely wide, infinitesimally shallow boundary between the Consolidation of Error's two planes."

Rahab Oothoon pulled in her thoughtful lips, inflating the freckled flesh above and below her mouth. She looked at her husband across the table. "Sounds a lot like you, Brom, wouldn't you say?"

Dr. Ulro, who was in the delicate process of lifting a chicken foot with his chopsticks, unintentionally snapped his fingers and sent the foot spinning through the air, two places to his left, to smack onto the back of Adam Ghostflea's hand at the very moment the chauffeur was shoveling a large prawn into his open mouth with a fork.

Ghostflea studied the distraught claw clinging by its talon-tips to the flap of mud-baked skin between his thumb and index finger. The chauffeur let out a resigned sigh, glad it wasn't a donkey booger. He raised both his frozen hand and his popping eyes inquisitively in the direction from which the chicken-foot had flown.

Dr. Ulro shot daggers at his wife.

Rahab grinned back.

"The next time yuh're gonna use your chopsticks, Brom," Tharmas suggested, "please give us some warning so we can get out our umbrellas."

❧

Ded, his vision narrowed to the slit between Beulah's two hands, paid no attention to the flying claw. Not that he would have been interested. With his overpowering claustrophobia about to cross over into an uncontrolled panic, he was totally concentrated on the trigger that would allow him to escape from between the two surfaces.

"So-o-o-o," Ded said, attempting to sound as casual as his developing hysteria would allow, "perhaps, like it says in the Orc-cycle parable, it's time to have sex with Rahab?"

"Sex with my wife?" Dr. Ulro asked, shocked.

"No," Ded backed off. "Not your wife. In Jerusalem's poems, a fictional Urizen triggers the Apocalypse by having sex with a wholly fictional character called Rahab."

Rahab Oothoon rolled her eyes at a sheepish Bacon Urizen.

Beulah cut in. "The trigger in the poems is not to be taken literally, Brom. It was just an example of something that points up the Consolidation of Error as the exact opposite of God's vision represented in Golgonooza. That what Satan *claims* to be doing is diametrically opposed to what he's *actually* doing. In the case of the Orc poems, pretending to represent love, joy, beauty, community, nobility, and everything else it means to be truly human, while succumbing to the shallow, materialistic, blatant lust of the fictional Rahab. The trigger, though, could be anything that accomplishes that purpose. No matter how small. Any contradiction that Satan's flattened mind struggles manfully to filter and refilter up through the screen of pure abstraction 'below,' trying to produce a conceptual description able to fit precisely into his grand, unifying void of pure theory 'above,' but each time failing in the task, until all at once, Satan comprehends how shallow he, the difference between the two planes, has become, and how that shallowness is the exact opposite of the unlimited freedom promised by his Consolidation of Error.

Drawing in a sudden breath of recognition, he sucks the two

opposing surfaces of the Consolidation of Error through his wafer-thin self, causing them to meet, and like matter and antimatter, to annihilate."

With the excitement of a child, Beulah yanked apart her edgewise hands from in front of Ded's eyes. "Now, with the Consolidation of Error no longer blocking the sleeping God's view, the sleeping God can at last behold, by immediate perception, in all its glory, Golgonooza, the ultimate Consolidation of Truth."

Ded looked down at his dish of eel, up at the peeling white ceiling of Louie's dining room, and then straight into Beulah's opaque glasses. He didn't see anything at all that looked like Golgonooza. Not only that, although Beulah's hands no longer blocked his view, his tormented mind still felt flattened between them.

Perhaps, he speculated hopefully, *it's because the unknown trigger has yet to appear.*

"Shorn of its abstractions," Beulah continued, "Satan's consciousness instantly reunites with the consciousness of the sleeping God, of which it unknowingly has always been a part, and thereby, eternally subordinates its reason to the divine."

Beaming, Beulah now lapsed into what was becoming the standard closing litany. "The sleeping God then awakes, and in a fiery Apocalypse obliterating all the illusory divisions that had seemed so real, His expanding consciousness reunites with His formerly fully conscious mind, until once again, all reality is encompassed in His infinite and eternal creative imagination."

"Spot-on," Urizen agreed, leaning back and stroking his bald head. "Although, I have to say, it's not clear to me why, in such an event, Mr. Jerusalem would've wanted to have all his money in cash."

Urizen glanced at Ded as though the claims adjuster might have the answer.

He didn't.

In truth, Ickey Jerusalem's $100 million dollars was the furthest thing from Ded's mind. Instead, his whole attention was focused on escaping from the two invisible planes still pressing in upon him. First, he tried one direction and then another, but unable to find any way out, he was soon reduced to sitting in his chair, panting in repeated, pathetic attempts to replicate the drawing in of sudden breaths of recognition.

Beulah leaned towards Ded, putting a hand on his sleeve. "In the cloakroom, on the floor," she said, "leaning against the wall underneath my blazer, is my book of Ickey's poems. Could you get it, please?"

"Yes, yes," Ded gasped, welcoming any excuse to leave the table.

ൺ

As Ded entered the cloakroom, Scofield scrambled to his feet, wagging his tail, evidently under the impression Ded was sneaking back for some kind of illicit, cross-species rendezvous.

"N-n-nice dog, n-n-nice dog," Ded murmured as he edged around Scofield, hoping the animal would not take this obviously untrue compliment as an invitation to a bout of mutual rear-end sniffing.

Ded reached down cautiously and took Beulah's anthology of Jerusalem's poetry off the floor. Scofield began to tremble and squeal with emotion, clearly overcome by the belief the claims adjuster was about to read him a love poem.

Ded backed out of range. Scofield, fearing the object of his affections intended to leave, let out a moan of such heart-rending intensity that the claims adjuster stopped dead in his tracks.

He looked around the empty cloakroom. *Oh, what the heck,* he decided. There was no reason not to give the dog a little pleasure.

Ded edged closer to the quivering beast and opened the book at a spot marked with a slip of pink paper. The right-hand page was written in Braille; the left, in regular print. Bending over the dog, he read out in a quiet voice the first stanza to catch his eye.

> God Appears & God is Light
> To those poor Souls who dwell in Night
> But does a Human Form Display
> To those who Dwell in Realms of day

When he finished, he looked at Scofield, now lying on his back, clearly in seventh heaven, his tongue flopping out of his jaws, all four legs waving ecstatically in the air, a full erection conspicuously presented.

This visionary poetry is powerful stuff, Ded observed, returning to the poem. While he hadn't ever seen the poem before, there was something familiar about it. As though someone had once described it to him. Trying to remember who, he read it again.

> God Appears & God is Light
> To those poor Souls who dwell in Night
> But does a Human Form Display
> To those who Dwell in Realms of day

More bifurcation, Ded judged, looking for the poem's universal themes. Or perhaps contradictions. God/Human. Night/Day. Light/Dark. Like the opposing planes pressing down on him.

At this unfortunate simile, the brief distraction afforded to Ded by reading to the dog ended, and he became aware once again of the two huge, oppressive, horizontal planes claustrophobically crushing in on his mind.

Looking up, Ded noticed that the plane "above" was still his Grand Unifying Theory—composed of a broadened perspective, the Cave, and Sicilian Illusions—but looking down, the plane "below," in a peculiar modification of Beulah's description (which perhaps had to do with him being upside down in Hell), had become Ickey Jerusalem's metaphysics—composed of the sleeping God, Satan Incarnate, and Golgonooza.

Ded looked from one to the other, unable to tell which plane was the abstraction and which was the void. All he could tell was that he—the infinitely wide, infinitesimally shallow boundary between—had no hope of escape.

And then, peering straight out through the rapidly diminishing slit between the planes, he saw it. What he'd been looking for. Right there before him. On the opened page of the anthology. In 15-point typeface.

Ded got out his notepad and flicked to the correct place. He compared what was in his notes with what was in the anthology. Manfully struggling to filter and refilter the contradiction he saw through Jerusalem's metaphysics "below" to produce a conceptual description able to fit precisely into Ded's own Grand Unifying Theory "above," he all at once comprehended how shallow the difference between the two had become, and how that shallowness contradicted the unlimited freedom promised by the Consolidation of Error.

Drawing in the sudden breath of recognition, Ded sucked the two planes together through his wafer-thin self, causing them to meet, and like matter and antimatter, to annihilate.

Now, with his view no longer blocked, Ded could at last behold, by immediate perception, the ultimate Consolidation of Truth, revealing at long last, in all its fearful symmetry, exactly who bore the responsibility for Jerusalem's death.

PART SIX

CHAPTER 33

BEYOND THE BURNING GAS BALL

Like the sleeping God awakening, Ded felt an apocalypse of emotions explode in the center of his being.

As much as he longed for its fulfilling wholeness, he still had a job to do in the fallen world. Thus, having been forewarned by Beulah's exposition, Ded instantly shot his web of abstractions all around the underside of his skin to contain the explosion within his being.

Using every ounce of logic at his command, he then drew the abstract web together, compressing the enclosed emotions back down from the size of a man… to the size of a cantaloupe… to that of a pea… to that of a mustard-seed… until it reached the irreducible, geometric point of a tiny, black hole hidden deep within his subjective inside… rendering him once again nothing more, nothing less than the life insurance claims adjuster he'd always been.

Such was the effort involved in pushing forcefully inwards to keep the microscopic apocalyptic ball of emotions compressed, Ded, in an opposite reaction, eased himself outwards, expanding his perspective far beyond his skin, so that, once again, he felt as though he was looking at himself from the outside, watching himself go through the motions, trying to divorce himself from all feeling, except for a certain manic determination to see the case through.

ↂ

Ded took out the ballpoint pen from his pocket. Feeling lightheaded, he touched its clicker to his forehead and closed his eyes. Rather than wanting to spring awake, he was extremely tired, desiring only to retreat further into the security of his own little hell.

While he knew the responsible party, he didn't yet understand the motivation. His job as a life insurance claims adjuster was to figure out the motivation and then put his evidence in a form understandable to those still trapped inside the fallen world.

Until that point, he wasn't going to reveal to anyone what he'd just discovered in the cloakroom.

ↂ

Ded re-entered the dining room and found it in an uproar. The women of the group were still sitting, but Urizen, Tharmas, Ghostflea, Theo, and Los were all standing or kneeling near one end of the table, surrounding Dr. Ulro, who sat dazed on the floor in their midst, his toupée trembling askew on his head like a terrified animal. The Chinese waiters huddled in the opposite corner of the room, apprehensively eyeing the hairpiece, as though at any moment it might attack.

"What happened?" Dr. Ulro asked.

"You choked on a chicken foot," a condescendingly solicitous Urizen answered.

Dr. Ulro tentatively felt his throat with his palm.

Urizen gestured to Ghostflea, who stood nearby. "Fortunately, our friend here was able to grab a toenail and yank it out."

Baffled, Dr. Ulro looked dubiously at his feet, trying to draw the connection between one of his toenails being yanked out and an obstruction flying out of his gullet.

Urizen rested his hand on Tharmas's shoulder. "Mr. Luvah then gave you mouth-to-mouth resuscitation."

The business manager cocked his head shyly to one side, sticking his long, still unsated tongue between his teeth.

The doctor's mouth contorted with disgust.

"Your chair collapsed," Tharmas explained with a touch of drama. "Yuh were knocked out when your head hit the floor."

Dr. Ulro blanched, as though picturing precisely how and with what fervor Tharmas must have been administering mouth-to-mouth resuscitation for the chair to have collapsed.

❧

The elderly Chinese *maître d'* entered behind Ded and hobbled to the table, oblivious to the commotion. Speedily calculating the bill from the number and shape of the dishes used, he wrote out the bill, and left it on the table in a small, stainless steel dish.

Turning to go, the *maître d'* gave a start when he saw Dr. Ulro sitting on the floor. The old man eyeballed him from a few different angles until assured he had taken sufficient stock of the situation. He then stepped painfully forward, drew himself up, and without being asked, proceeded to give the dazed plastic surgeon what appeared to be a stern lecture in Chinese with regard to the San Francisco health inspector's views of customers eating off the floor.

The women continued sitting at the table without paying any attention to what was going on. Beulah seemed deep in thought. Enith was in one of her trances. Grandma Enion was sucking her thumb with delight. And the plump Rahab, perched on her stack of telephone books, picked at crumbs scattered on her plate.

His lecture over, the *maître d'* shuffled out of the room.

Rahab glanced at her chastised husband, his face and his hairpiece competing for first prize in a Most Befuddled contest.

Tharmas, who was standing behind the doctor, looked up and caught her eye. He smiled. Rahab returned the smile with an elusive spin, small chocolate-brown smears at the corners of her mouth.

As Tharmas dropped his attention back to the doctor, Rahab, her heavily made-up eyes still on the business manager, recited so softly Ded suspected only those nearest could hear:

> There is a Smile of Love
> And there is a Smile of Deceit,
> And there is a Smile of Smiles
> In which these two Smiles meet

Beulah swung her head to Rahab. For a millisecond, a look flashed across the sightless woman's beatific face, so fast it was almost subliminal, leaving behind a memory not of its form but of its substance.

It was a look of pure pity.

Ded took his seat on Beulah's right. "Here's your book."

"Thanks," she said absently. He placed the book in her hand, but she didn't open it.

Ded couldn't help but feel he'd been used.

❧

Ghostflea got the doctor a new chair from the corner of the room while Tharmas and Theo helped him to his feet.

Urizen pulled out his checkbook. On its green plastic cover was a picture of an evergreen tree. Underneath were printed the words, "Redwood Bank." The lawyer looked at the bill, wrote out a check, and gave it to a waiter to take to the cashier.

Shortly thereafter, the group split up. Los, Enith, Theo, and Grandma Enion headed off to the bus station to catch the next Greyhound back to Eden. Tharmas Luvah walked up the hill to his place on Macondray Lane, muttering as he left about needing to do some dope. Dr. Ulro, clearly still unnerved by his near-death experience, unsteadily meandered down the street toward where his car was parked, from where, Ded assumed, he would drive to the Hall of Justice, as requested by Inspector O'Nadir for questioning about the exploding golf club.

Ded went to Louie's reception to ask if there was an envelope for him from Ben. There was. But before he could open it, Rahab approached him. Ded thought she looked depressed or perhaps ill. She handed Ded a folded napkin. "Apply your peepers to this when you get a chance. Completes the sentence."

Then, after sharing her plan to drive separately to the Hall of Justice for O'Nadir's interview, she dragged herself away.

The napkin had "Louie's" printed on it. Ded turned it over. On the other side, written in the same childish script as the warning note he had received when he had checked in at the Holiday Inn, were the words, "Hand, Hyle, and me."

Ded tucked the napkin and Ben's unopened envelope inside his anthology of Jerusalem's poems and entered the cloakroom. Scofield was still spaced-out on his back. Four legs in the air. Lolling tongue. Erection.

Adam Ghostflea, straining to avert his eyes from the canine exhibitionism beneath him, was helping Beulah with her blazer and straw hat. Next to them, Bacon Urizen was consciously fixing his attention on a scarf he was taking down from a hook.

Ded took the lawyer aside. "Two cubic yards of hundred-dollar bills is fairly heavy. Did the bank people say what Jerusalem carried it away in?"

The lawyer, worn out from the day's exertions, shook his huge, hairless head.

The investigator turned to Beulah's chauffeur. "Ghostflea, the Friday before you left for New York, did you take Jerusalem to the bank?"

Ghostflea searched his memory before shaking his head *no.*

"Did Jerusalem take the hearse by himself that day?"

Ghostflea searched his memory again. "Yes. Just after lunch."

"Ickey said he had to drop off a picture at Tharmas's," Beulah interjected, smiling serenely. "'Glad Day,' he called it. When we first met, he gave me the etching on which it was based, so I could feel it."

"Ickey told me," Beulah continued, "that after Tharmas's, he had some business to take care of. But he didn't say what."

"Wasn't Friday afternoon the time for his weekly assignation with, well, you know who?"

Beulah lowered her moonlike face. "Yes."

Ded took care to keep his pressurized emotional nanoparticle under total control. "Ghostflea, was there anything in the back of the hearse when Jerusalem returned?"

"No," the chauffeur replied. "Just his windbreaker."

Ded pursed his lips. "So, the money has got to be somewhere other than Jerusalem's house."

"Leaves a lot of places where it could be, don't you think?" Urizen said wearily. He did not seem all that interested in tracking down the missing funds.

"Where's the hearse now?" Ded asked the chauffeur.

"Bank of America's underground parking garage."

"Good, let's start there. Mr. Urizen, do you think Louie's could book us a couple of cabs—one for Beulah and Scofield, and the second for us three?"

CHAPTER 34

THE FAINTEST OF MOONS

On the raised portion of the Bank of America plaza, opposite the Banker's Heart, two gardeners in overalls were replacing the potted flowers. Due to a combination of the building's cold shadow and the high-level winds brought down the face of its 52 stories into the plaza, the petals on the morning's batch had already withered away.

Ded, Ghostflea, Beulah, Scofield (still wobbly from Ded's poem reading), and a reluctant Urizen entered the concourse, then took the elevator down to the basement garage. At the claims adjuster's request, Ghostflea opened the rear hatch of the parked hearse, allowing Ded to look into the storage space behind the leather seats. There was nothing but a yellow windbreaker.

Ded looked under the chassis. He looked under the back seat. He returned to the rear of the hearse and carefully picked over the felt, looking for clues. He lifted the windbreaker out of the way, then levered up the floor of the storage space, exposing the spare wheel. Finding nothing underneath, he laid the floor and the windbreaker back down.

As the life insurance investigator stroked his chin, he noticed his fingers smelled faintly of saltwater. He picked up the windbreaker again and brought it to his nose. It had the same odor. *Although Friday afternoons were when Jerusalem visited Rahab, they were supposed to be for sailing. Had Jerusalem, for once, conformed to his nominal schedule?*

"Jerusalem's sailboat," Ded said, addressing Ghostflea, "the one he bequeathed to Tharmas. Where does he keep it?"

"San Francisco Marina."

"Does the boat have a lot of storage space?"

"I don't know. Mr. Jerusalem always drove himself there."

Ded rolled his head toward Urizen.

"Never seen it," the lawyer said. "Mr. Jerusalem bought it a long time ago."

Ded closed the rear of the hearse, motioned for Ghostflea to put Scofield in his normal front seat, and opened the door to the main passenger compartment.

"Okay," he ordered the others, "let's go take a look for ourselves."

As everyone was quiet on the ride to the marina, Ded took the opportunity to open Ben's envelope. As he studied the photo of *Satan Exulting over Eve,* there suddenly leapt to his eyes that which had been in the painting all along but which, for reasons he would soon be able to explain, he could only now see. The identity of Satan Incarnate was absolutely clear.

Looking up from the photo, Ded saw the back of Ghostflea's small head and remembered at last when and where he had been told about the night/day poem long before he had read it to Scofield. He opened Jerusalem's anthology and, in the light of his now knowing Satan's identity and his having gathered so many necessary facts over the last three days, he carefully reread the poem, spending quite some time parsing it through from different points of view, until he understood how it had ultimately led to Jerusalem's denouement.

All that was missing now were a few odds and ends.

ꟹ

The San Francisco Marina District, one of the few flat areas of the city, was bordered along the water's edge by the football-field-wide, half-mile-long Marina Green. Today, it was populated by Frisbee throwers, kite flyers, and young sunbathers. At the western end of this long stretch of grass was a small, one-story stone building with a Spanish tile roof. On the roof was a yard-high sign: "HARBORMASTER." Beyond a tall chain-link fence running from either side of the building was a maze of floating docks and boats.

For safety, Ded and Urizen left the blind Beulah, the tottering Scofield, and the stumbling Ghostflea on the green near the parking lot and approached the harbormaster's office. There was nobody inside. At the right of a gate in the chain-link fence was a buzzer. Ded pushed it.

A few moments later, a weathered old man in grease-stained coveralls and a scruffy captain's hat with "Harbormaster" emblazoned on it appeared from behind the building. Wiping his hands on a rag, he eyed Urizen and Ded through the wire mesh. "Yeah?"

"We'd like to look at a boat," Ded said.

"Be my guest," the man said, pointing with his thumb to a pair of coin-operated binoculars on the sea wall some distance away, overlooking the shore side of the marina.

Urizen lumbered forward and put his hand on Ded's forearm, giving the claims adjuster a let-me-handle-this look.

"My good man. My name is Bacon Urizen. I am Ickey Jerusalem's lawyer. I would like to inspect his boat."

The old man studied Urizen's pale scalp before dropping his eyes to the bulbous face. "Where's your key?"

"Key?"

"To the gate."

"I don't have one."

The harbormaster held his head first at one angle and then at another, as though trying to see his reflection in Urizen's monocle.

"Then you'll have to ask Ickey Jerusalem to give you his. When he was last here, three Fridays ago, he said nothing about anybody coming to look at his boat."

"Jerusalem was here?" Ded asked, calculating the date as Friday, October 14th, two days before the trip to New York. "Are you sure?"

"Yep," the man said, still squinting at the lawyer's monocle. "It was the day my carburetor broke. Who are you?"

"Ded Smith, claims adjuster for the Olympian Life Insurance Company."

The harbormaster quizzically raised an eyebrow. "Is Jerusalem dead?"

Ded nodded. "When Jerusalem came, was he carrying any large packages?"

The man furrowed his forehead. "Nope."

"Was he alone?"

"He didn't have anybody with him when he arrived." The harbormaster pursed his lips. "But a few minutes after he went off to his boat, another guy showed up at the gate asking whether Jerusalem was inside." The harbormaster gestured toward the floating docks behind him. "Jerusalem's boat ain't visible from here."

"What did the guy look like?"

"Wiry. Dark. Full beard."

"Did you let him in?"

"He didn't seem interested once I told him Jerusalem was here. He wandered off to the sea wall."

Ded turned toward Urizen with a countenance asking who it could have been.

Urizen gave a shrug. He hadn't a clue.

Ded returned to the harbormaster. "You think you could let us in to see Jerusalem's boat?"

The harbormaster stroked the stubble on his chin as he took in Ded's thick glasses, skinny frame, ill-kempt suit, and policeman's shoes, and then Urizen's bald head, monocle, deathly pale complexion, and Goodyear Blimp body.

"Shit," he grunted, "I guess I can stand the embarrassment, if you can."

He opened the gate and motioned for them to follow.

A second later, he stopped and swung around. "Do me a favor, though, will you?" he said in a low voice. "Stay about ten feet behind and pretend you're not with me?"

❧

The harbormaster guided his two charges along the floating piers, past row after row of magnificent sailing crafts that were berthed stern-to, at right angles to the dock. The air filled with the sound of halyards tapping their spars in the brisk afternoon breeze. A couple of times, the harbormaster and Ded had to stop and wait for Urizen to catch up. The corpulent lawyer was having difficulty keeping his balance on the gently rocking walkway.

After about three minutes, they arrived at an elegant 45-foot yacht that looked as though it had been sculpted by the wind from alabaster, mahogany, and brass. Painted in deep blue on its stern was a single capital letter: *C*.

"Is this it?" Ded asked, trying to think whose name began with that letter.

The harbormaster shook his head and motioned in the general direction of a boat just beyond the next berth—a large, black trimaran with a red sail and a gold nameplate on its transom bearing the word *Devil*.

Fits, Ded observed as he approached the boat. *The "dark one."*

"No," the harbormaster snapped impatiently. "There." He pointed to the berth between the yacht and the trimaran.

Ded turned. Floating in the berth, bow outwards, was a grubby, eleven-foot wooden sailing dinghy. Scrawled across its backboard was the name *Icarus*.

"Why did Ickey bother to keep a boat like that here?" Bacon Urizen sniffed as he hobbled up.

"I asked the very same thing," the harbormaster said, eyes on the dinghy. "He said… now, what was it?" His face creased along several lines. "Oh, yeah. He said he didn't want to deprive the poem of its meaning." The man lifted his tattered cap and scratched his head. "Whatever that's supposed to mean."

Ded scanned the trimaran, the yacht, and then the dinghy between. Between the *Devil* and the deep blue *C*.

The harbormaster replaced his cap. "If you ask me, Jerusalem was cruising through the sea of life without the full complement of navigational aids, if you know what I'm saying."

Ded suppressed any residual desire he might have had to apply his creative imagination to Ickey's boat's location. "Did he take the boat out when he was here last?"

"Yeah."

"Where did he go?"

"Onto the Bay." The harbormaster unfurled his arm toward the choppy expanse of water. Ded followed the gesture over the Bay until he spotted the abandoned prison on Alcatraz Island.

A buzzer sounded through multiple dock speakers.

"Damn," the harbormaster cursed. "Someone's at the gate." He pivoted on his heel and hurried away. "I'll see you when you leave."

❧

Jerusalem's berth was separated from the vessels on either side by narrow, perpendicular walkways attached to the dock. The dock-facing stern and the outward-pointing bow of Jerusalem's dinghy were each tied by slack lines to the two walkways.

Careful to maintain his balance in the strong cross-breeze blowing toward the *Devil*, Ded stepped onto the boat and hastily searched it, paying particular attention to the wrapped sail, the Styrofoam floatation compartments in the bow and stern, and the waterproof container fixed under the middle seat, which Ded assumed kept valuables dry while sailing. He checked for lines dangling from the sides that might be attached to underwater parcels.

He found nothing. *Either Jerusalem never had the money on board or he*—Ded looked out onto the Bay—*dumped it overboard?*

His eyes settled on Alcatraz again. *Hid it somewhere?*

Ded glanced at the waterproof container and then up at Urizen, who was leaning, pooped, against a lamppost on the dock. An idea came to him.

"Want to go for a sail?"

The disheveled lawyer gave Ded a sidelong look of disbelief.

"It's a perfect day for it," Ded encouraged him.

"If you want to go sailing, you'll have to go by yourself," Urizen stated firmly. "I'll watch from over there." He pointed to the coin-operated binoculars on the distant seawall.

"Come on," Ded motioned, oozing good-naturedness. "There are some things we need to discuss."

"Like what?" Urizen asked, clamping the lamppost with his fat hands.

The investigator looked him in the eyes. "Like your role as trustee of the Urthon Spectre Trust."

"And why does such a discussion have to be done while sailing?"

"I don't know. Would you feel differently if instead we discuss why you've been paying Rahab Oothoon for sex?"

Urizen's jaw dropped.

Ded beamed broadly. "Come on, humor me."

Urizen stood some time, as though weighing his options. "Do you know how to sail?"

"Of course," Ded assured him. "I had to learn for one of my investigations."

Which was true.

Ded neglected to add he had not been sailing since. After his first set of lessons, he'd lost interest. The result, possibly, of his having to spend most of his subsequent weekends moonlighting at the local McDonald's in order to pay for the school's sunken dinghy.

⸙

Gingerly, Urizen put his right foot into the stern. The dinghy dipped slightly to the starboard side and then stopped when the starboard lines went taut. Urizen brought his left foot in and shifted his considerable weight to the left. The port side of the dinghy bobbed sharply in the water to the limit of the port lines. Overreacting, Urizen rapidly moved his weight back onto his right foot. The boat pitched to the right. Urizen threw his overweight arms in the air in an attempt to keep his balance and leaned again to his left, causing the boat to pitch back double-quick in that direction.

Ded knew then that taking Urizen out for a sail was not the best idea. It was just that thereafter the lawyer managed to stay on his feet for such a long time, a good 45 seconds at least, flailing his arms, teeter-tottering violently back and forth on the rocking vessel, emitting desperate little bleats, that, well, in the end, when the man at last collapsed in a heap in the bottom of the boat, it seemed unfair not to reward him with a cruise.

"Apart from needing a little work on your sea legs," Ded commended the panting Urizen, "I can see you've got a real talent for this sort of thing."

The attorney glowered back.

Ded took off his policeman's shoes, put his socks inside, and wedged the shoes between the forward Styrofoam float compartment and the side of the boat. He then took out his wallet, his loose-leaf notepad, Jerusalem's spiral notebook, and the poetry anthology, and placed them in the waterproof container.

Urizen, who had struggled up onto his elbow, was now looking worriedly at Ded.

"Just in case we get splashed by a wave," Ded said to reassure him. "Maybe you should do the same."

Urizen reluctantly handed over his wallet and checkbook. Ded placed his body between the lawyer and the waterproof container, and before he stashed the lawyer's belongings, quickly compared the contents of the checkbook with something in his own notepad.

His hunch confirmed, Ded locked up the items, and made sure the container was securely fastened. He then set about unwrapping the sail and threading it onto the mast. Urizen, who had finally managed to sit upright on the rear seat, peered up anxiously at the *Devil* and the deep blue *C*.

Once the final sail slide was threaded in, Ded grabbed the halyard and pulling down, raised the mainsail. The Dacron immediately caught the wind. The sailboat slid smartly sideways about two-and-a-half feet, until the mooring ropes at the bow and the stern went taut, whereupon the boat, due to the combination of the crosswind blowing against the sail and the boom still being tied tightly to the tiller, heeled more than 45-degrees, smashing the upper part of its mast into the trimaran next door.

"Release the boom!" Ded cried to his one-man crew.

"Release it yourself," Urizen cried back. "I'm getting the hell out of here." He wobbled to his feet, turned around, put his foot onto the 45-degree-angled rear seat, and with a mighty effort, stepped over the stern toward the dock less than two feet away.

Unhappily, Bacon Urizen seemed unaware of Newton's Third Law of Motion. But then, as any of Urizen's fellow lawyers could have told him, ignorance of the law is no excuse.

As the attorney stepped outwards in one direction, the sailboat slid back in an equal and (apart from the distorting effect of the stretched mooring lines tied to the walkway on the windward side of the boat) nearly opposite direction. The result was that his leading foot came down not on the dock but in the water, followed by the leg to which the foot was attached. The rest of his body indubitably would have been next, had not the lawyer been quick-thinking enough to catch the edge of the dock with his chin and two hands. He clung there with one foot hooked over the back of the dinghy and the other underwater, like an overweight suspension bridge trolling for sharks.

"Don't panic," Ded shouted, leaping up. "There's nothing to worry about."

From Urizen's plaintive gasps, Ded got the impression the attorney was not convinced of the truth of this statement.

Sensing it was best not to alarm Urizen with any sudden movements, Ded assumed an air of exaggerated casualness and sauntered the short length of the heeled boat toward the stern. Once there, he released the boom, righting the sailboat, rocking it from side to side under Urizen's clinging ankle.

Ded patted the whimpering lawyer's heel. "We'll have you back up in a jiffy."

But this prediction was a tad optimistic. Urizen weighed more than a small whale. Worse, he was ticklish, so every time Ded tried to hook his hand under the back of Urizen's belt, the lawyer started flopping around uncontrollably. At one point, a frustrated Ded actually considered using a gaff hook to land him.

Eventually, by levering against the back of the stern and pulling hard on Urizen's dry leg, Ded was able, at some danger to his sacroiliac, to force the dinghy far enough underneath Urizen's thigh to allow the man to rise into a sideward sitting position that straddled the backboard, from where, after spending a few seconds squealing at the unacceptable pressure of the wooden bulwark's edge on his private parts, he fell into the boat.

"There," Ded cooed. "That wasn't so bad, was it?"

Urizen sat on the uncomfortable inner ribbing of the hull, jaw slack, eyes glazed, holding his heart with one hand and his testicles with the other.

Although Ded was hurt by Urizen's failure to thank him, he felt, in light of the difficulties the lawyer had experienced so far, his self-centeredness was forgivable.

❧

Ded helped Urizen crawl to the bow of the boat, out of the way. After checking that the centerboard was locked down, he untied the bow and stern lines that were positioning the dinghy between the two narrow dividers. Satisfied everything was ready to go, he sat down at the rear, holding the tiller in one hand and the main sheet in the other, as the wind pushed the boat into the hull of the *Devil.* Using his foot against the black hull, he maneuvered the dinghy forward, scraping a long, bobbing line of paint off the big, black trimaran with a sound reminiscent of a fingernail scraping across a blackboard.

Urizen cringed at the writing on the wall.

The moving finger writes, Ded observed despite himself, *and having writ, moves on.*

With a final shove of his foot, he pushed the sailboat free from the trimaran. "Get thee behind me, Satan!" he cried, as from the tiny, black hole of his emotions an infinity of massless particles of nihilism shot out in all directions through the subatomic pinpricks in his compressed web of abstractions and inflated the emptiness of his being.

Urizen rolled his eyes hopelessly heavenwards.

Once out in the channel between the floating docks, Ded experimented with the sails and the tiller until he got some control over the boat. Then, focusing on a line of directional buoys, he pointed the prow toward the exit from the marina.

A mere twenty-two minutes and thirteen collisions with parked (and one or two fleeing) yachts later, they were out in the Bay.

"Piece of cake," Ded declared. "I knew it would come back to me eventually."

Urizen, facing away from Ded, did not comment.

The wind was much stronger and the waves were much higher in the Bay than in the marina. The boat whipped along, crashing into the swells, casting spray over the bow.

While Ded had found Ghostflea's driving terrifying, his reaction to the terrifying seas was the exact opposite. Now, in his post-Golgonooza, Apocalypse-compressing self, pierced by the cruel knowledge gained in Louie's cloakroom, Ded was elevated into a Nietzschean-*Übermensch,* laughing-at-danger state of mind.

"Fun, isn't it?" he yelled to Urizen over the noise of the gale.

Urizen rotated in his seat to stare coldly at Ded through a monocle obscured by droplets of salt water. "Fun" was apparently not a word the haughty lawyer would use to describe the experience of sailing through raging waters in an unstable dinghy, dressed in a business suit, with an incompetent at the tiller.

Ded laughed maniacally. To the Nietzschean *Übermensch,* trivial matters such as an incompetent at the tiller were not even worthy of recognition.

Catching sight of Alcatraz, Ded eased out the sail, and changed his heading to run downwind, toward the island. The boat stabilized. With the wind astern, the sailing became much quieter.

Ded leaned closer to Bacon Urizen and addressed him with the excessive politeness Superman would employ when toying with a cornered master criminal. "Could I ask you a few questions, please?"

Urizen gazed contemptuously at *Icarus's* self-appointed captain.

"Good," Ded said. "Why, on Monday, October 10th, did the trust take out an insurance policy on Jerusalem's life naming Beulah as the beneficiary?"

"Why do you think?" Urizen snapped, his annoyance overcoming his trepidation. "If you'd been told to convert all the trust's assets to cash and discovered a three-year-old, twenty-million-dollar policy that had not only a death benefit but also an investment component, wouldn't you have cashed that policy in and replaced it with a cheaper one that had only the death benefit?"

Ded straightened up. "So, the recent Olympian Life Insurance Company policy on Jerusalem's life has the same noninvestment, life-insurance terms as that taken out three years before?"

"Bingo," Urizen fired back.

The put-down inherent in the lawyer's one-word reply bounced harmlessly off the impervious force field of Ded's nihilism. Calmly, the claims adjuster took aim from another direction. "And Jerusalem knew nothing about the replacement?"

Angry, Urizen reloaded and took another shot. "Do you really think a visionary poet like Mr. Jerusalem would involve himself in the financial details of his trust?"

Ded took the hit without even blinking, inserted his words one-by-one into his semi-automatic clip, and let her rip. "Then why on the same date, did Jerusalem take the trust's financial books home?"

Urizen tensed, although it was unclear whether this was because Ded's question had hit its mark or because the Buffalo-bred skipper, noticing the strong current in the Bay pulling him off his Alcatraz course, had suddenly reached out and sheeted in the mainsail, causing the dinghy to heel sharply to leeward.

Ded held the sail in and blasted his opponent again. "Do you think his taking the books home had anything to do with why he wanted to remove you as trustee?"

Urizen nervously shifted toward the now upraised, windward side of the boat. "Who said he wanted to remove me as trustee?" he protested, his bass voice cracking into a baritone.

Ded ignored the feeble *riposte*. "Do you know who was to be your successor?"

Urizen stared anxiously at the lowered, leeward side. "Haven't you heard about client confidences? Professional ethics?"

"I see," Ded coolly countered. "It's ethical for you to reveal Jerusalem had instructed you to liquidate the trust's assets, but not whom he wanted as his successor trustee?"

Urizen was silent, his question-firing mechanism briefly jammed by apprehension.

Ded hauled the sail farther in, causing the dinghy to heel farther to the leeward and thus Urizen to inch farther up the windward side of the boat. "Was it somebody on the plane that night?"

The man whom Ickey had described in the bequest film as "a thief in a cave" was not only no longer questioning, but now seemed incapable of answering.

Considering his next query, Ded saw the swift current was continuing to take him off course, so although the sailboat was pointing in the same compass direction as before, Alcatraz was now off to the windward.

"Ready to come about!" Ded declared.

Urizen looked at him.

Ded shoved the tiller leeward. "Hard-a-lee!" The dinghy tacked into and then through the wind. As the gusting breeze caught the other side of the sail, the boom swung across the cockpit, grazing Urizen on his shiny head and reversing the heel of the boat.

The lawyer scrambled up the new windward side like a hydrophobic hippo.

"What are you trying to do?" he demanded, rubbing his huge head. "Kill me?"

"Sorry," Ded said perfunctorily as he manhandled the tiller back to the center. "I had to take a different tack, since the one I was on wasn't getting me where I wanted to go."

He hadn't intended his statement to sound the way it did. But from the look of alarm it engendered in the hippopotamusian attorney, he realized he might achieve a better response to his questions by pretending the head bopping had been the result not of mere incompetence but of malice aforethought.

Ded gave his passenger a cold, animal-trainer look. "Doesn't the attorney-client privilege *die* with the client?" He drew out the word "die" with great emphasis.

Urizen's already phobic eyes widened farther until his upper eyelids pulsed against their limit in perfect time with his minimally opening-and-closing mouth.

Ded sheeted in the boom even closer, so the dinghy canted even farther from the vertical. "I repeat, was the successor trustee somebody on the plane that night?"

Urizen grabbed the raised edge of the boat. "Yes," he gasped.

"Who?"

Urizen held his answer in.

Ded heaved in the mainsheet, causing the sailboat, which was now racing along the swells, to heel so much that seawater began slopping over the leeward gunnel.

The terrified lawyer gave up. "Bromion Ulro."

Ded registered his surprise. "Why would Jerusalem want Dr. Ulro to be his trustee?"

"I don't know," Urizen replied in a begging tone.

Dr. Ulro, Ded mused. The man who seemed to despise everything Jerusalem stood for. Who got along with none of Jerusalem's family or friends. It didn't make sense. Ded combed his upper lip with his lower teeth. *Except… by the time Dr. Ulro would become the trustee, the trust would already be empty!*

Ded reached into his inside suit jacket pocket, took out the silver pen with the initials "BU," and held it toward his cowering passenger. "Is this yours?"

Urizen started at the sight. He leaned forward to get a closer look. "Yes, it—"

A huge swell hit the raised underside of the vessel, causing the rotund lawyer to lose his balance and flop heavily onto the interior of the lowered side of the dinghy. Water poured over the edge. As Urizen desperately tried to clamber back up, the boat slowly turned onto its side.

CHAPTER 35

THE REVOLVING PLANETS

The dinghy lay half-submerged on its side, its still-implanted mast floating with the sail on the surface of the Bay. Bacon Urizen was thrashing about in the rolling waves near the front of the horizontal mast, holding his monocle high above him in the hand above the wrist bearing his Rolex watch.

Ded, who had surfaced behind the water-filled sail, was pondering whether, in line with his earlier boom-swinging coming about, he should pretend he'd tipped the dinghy over on purpose. He pressed his dripping glasses against his face with his index finger to get a better view of the lawyer's wildly emoting eyebrows. *No,* he concluded. *This time, it is probably wiser to disclaim all responsibility.*

Treading water, Ded clipped the silver ballpoint back into his jacket pocket and steadied himself by placing his hand on the sideways-floating rudder. "See if you can get up onto the mast," he called out.

The floundering lawyer frantically paddled closer to the base of the floating mast. With his free hand, he reached to the gunwale directly above. Huffing and puffing with the strain, he managed to manhandle himself up so his bottom rested on the mast.

"Well done," Ded reassured him. "Now, all you have to do is sit tight and wait for a boat to come to our aid."

In the light of the fact Urizen's wet weight was a pound or two greater than the buoyancy of the mast, Ded's reassurance was, to say the least, a wee bit premature. The attorney, once again holding his monocle over his head with his watch arm and now moaning faintly, gradually sank with the mast under the sea, carrying the hull of the upturned dinghy over on top of him.

ð

Ded held his spectacles in place with his left hand, dove beneath the capsized boat, and with his extended right hand located the two chubby legs tightly wrapped around the inverted mast. Tracing upwards with his fingers, he discovered two chubby arms wrapped farther up the mast, and above that, out of the water yet inside the hull, the lawyer's gargantuan, nude head.

Ded rose to the surface. It was pitch dark. "Mr. Urizen?"

After a moment of silence, the lawyer spoke slowly in his resonant bass. "Your suggestion that I sit on the mast, Mr. Smith, was not a good idea."

"Yes," Ded said, unable to think of anything else to say.

A sigh hissed in the darkness. "Not much of a future here, I suppose."

"No," Ded agreed. "We'll run out of air fairly soon. We've got to get out from under the hull."

The shattered lawyer sighed again.

Although Ded still had a few questions to ask, he decided now was not the time.

"When I count three, you swim to the outside *that* way." Ded pushed the lawyer's shoulder to show him the direction. "I'll go the other way. When we surface, we should be on opposite sides of the boat. I'll count to three again, and we'll both reach up, grab the centerboard and haul ourselves up onto the hull at the same time. There, we'll wait for help."

ණ

When the harbormaster arrived in his speedboat, he found the two men clinging to the centerboard, their respective torsos draped down opposite sides of the upturned hull, their legs submerged, and their wet-trousered buttocks bobbing in and out of the swells.

"You're not going to right the boat that way," the harbormaster said with a laugh as he maneuvered behind Urizen. "You've both gotta pull on the same side."

Exhausted, Urizen looked over his shoulder at the harbormaster. "I am not trying to right the boat," he stated weakly. "I am trying to stay alive." He reached out toward the speedboat. "I've got a heart condition."

The harbormaster shook his head, his craggy face breaking into a scornful grin. "How come you went sailing with a heart condition?"

"Jesus, man!" Urizen snapped. "This is no time for a Socratic dialogue. Get me into your boat, now!"

The harbormaster shrugged and moved his speedboat around. On the back of the boat, an elevated winch arm dangled a hammock sling. The harbormaster lowered the sling behind Urizen's gigantic buttocks. On instruction, the lawyer pulled his feet up onto the upturned hull, released his grip on the centerboard, and flopped backwards into the sling.

"You're lucky I kept an eye on you guys," the harbormaster gloated as he hauled Urizen on board with all the sophistication of a cargo of overripe Honduran bananas. "We don't get a lot of people here who go sailing in their business suits."

Urizen, slumped in the back of the speedboat, gave Ded a black look.

The harbormaster helped Ded right the sailboat. Then, he unspooled a hose from his speedboat onto the floor of the flooded dinghy and turned on a pump near his outboard engine. When the water level was down to about four inches, he told Ded to climb into the righted vessel and take the tiller. He hooked a line from his speedboat to the prow of the dinghy. After making sure Ded was settled, he began towing the *Icarus* back to the marina.

"Let the sail move freely," the harbormaster ordered when Ded started to adjust the boom.

Ded let the mainsheet go and sat back, holding onto the tiller, shivering in his drenched suit, and blinking through his salt-stained glasses as the canvas luffed noisily and erratically on the freely swinging boom.

Out on the Bay, Ded was not particularly disturbed by the fluttering racket of his uncontrolled sail, but upon entering the marina, he found it increasingly discomforting, not so much due to its disorderly effect on his thought processes as due to the harbormaster's circuitous route back to Jerusalem's berth. It seemed designed to pass every occupied yacht in residence, as though Ded, under a giant flapping flag, was a barbarian captive being paraded through the streets of Rome by a returning Caesar.

"The harbormaster won't let me tie the boom!" Ded tried to explain to each gawking yacht owner, raising his voice to be heard over the din of the sail.

&

Despite its ignoble denouement, Ded considered the sailing expedition a major success. The information he'd gotten from Urizen was helpful, and absolutely invaluable was what he now grasped in the hand he sheltered in his lower right suit jacket pocket. It was a small piece of evidence he'd discovered while clinging to the upturned hull of the dinghy—something that had been right there, all along, tacked to the side of the centerboard.

It was a key.

And from the "#4, Zoas Depot" printed on its flat bow, Ded had a good idea what the key was for.

&

Some time later, Urizen and Ded sat in the harbormaster's office, huddled in blankets, their clothes drying in front of the electric heater. Through the filthy window, they could hear their weather-beaten host outside, abusing some unfortunate sailor who'd mistakenly requested assistance.

Ever since Urizen had heaved into the room, he had been wholly unresponsive to his former sailing companion, refusing to acknowledge Ded's comments about the nice weather they were having or the sparseness of the office's interior decoration. Even when Ded asked whether he might now want to take up sailing as a hobby, the rainy-faced lawyer had merely stared out the window, grinding his teeth.

Ded, growing impatient with the delay in his gathering of the proof he needed, decided to put a little more substance into his interrogations.

"The night Jerusalem died, Mr. Urizen, when you got onto the plane, did anybody see you had a plastic cleaning bag over your overcoat?"

His huge bulk covered with a blanket from head to toe, Urizen swung slowly around, gave the recently disgraced dinghy captain a look of disgust, and swung slowly back.

Doggedly, Ded tried again. "Do I take it, then, you're not interested in helping to determine exactly how Jerusalem died?"

The attorney swiveled again and stared at Ded with haggard eyes. Although Urizen obviously thought the claims adjuster an idiot, the last thing he, as a prominent attorney, would want was to be seen as obstructing an investigation into the death of his client.

"Anybody could've seen me carry it on," he relented in a spent voice. "Mr. Jerusalem noticed it for certain."

"How do you know?"

"On the way to the closet, I accidentally dropped it in the aisle next to his seat. Mr. Jerusalem picked it up for me."

"Did he say anything?"

"Just that it was good I kept my overcoat in a plastic bag if I intended to drop it on floors."

"What did you say?"

"I thanked him for his assistance. The purser came up and said he'd hang the coat in the closet. I returned to my seat."

Urizen opened his blanket to pull it more tightly around him, giving Ded a brief glimpse of two naked, pendulous breasts drooping over an equally drooping stomach.

Ded wiggled his naked toes. The sea had washed his black policeman's clodhoppers, socks wadded inside, from the cranny next to the Styrofoam floats on the *Icarus*. Staring at his bare feet, he imagined what it must have been like to be in Jerusalem's shoes. Then, he looked back up into the waiting monocle. "I've got one more question and then I'm done. Rahab Oothoon says she was the friend who rescued you from throwing yourself off the balcony Saturday night, and she spent last night with you because she was afraid of her husband. Is that correct?"

"Yes." Bacon Urizen sighed. "She drove me to the office this morning. Now, if you don't mind," he breathed wearily, "I have to call my secretary."

He struggled to his feet and hobbled to the phone on the wall of the harbormaster's office, then dialed a number.

"It's me. Any messages?" The lawyer moved his flabby lower lip unconsciously as he listened. "Okay, thank you." He hung up, returned to his seat, and flopped down into it.

"Any messages to do with Jerusalem?" Ded asked.

"One." Urizen waited a moment to catch his breath after his strenuous round trip to the phone. "Before I left the office, I asked my secretary to check with the trust's account officer at the bank to make sure he'd properly identified Mr. Jerusalem when the money was withdrawn."

"And?"

"The bank officer confirmed he had. The withdrawal was so large, the Bank of California didn't have enough paper money to handle it. So, they had to arrange ahead of time for Bank of America to get it from the Federal Reserve Bank of San Francisco. The B of C officer, who was acquainted with Mr. Jerusalem, went over to the B of A to make sure of his identity. He even helped him load the money into the hearse."

Ded mulled this information over, then, surprised to see from a clock on the wall that it was just after 3:30, he got up, padded across the room to the phone, and rang Officer Jarvis to speak to Gwendolyn Heva.

Jarvis reported he had met Miss Heva off her flight and taken her to his office. However, when she discovered he hadn't been sent by the four people she'd expected to meet, but instead by someone investigating Ickey Jerusalem's death, she immediately quit talking—except for a request to use the office phone to call her employer in New York to book her a flight home.

"She wasn't under arrest," Officer Jarvis explained to Ded, "so I couldn't keep her."

Ded thanked Officer Jarvis and hung up. Thinking over what the security officer had just said, he pulled the evidence-bagged photograph of Miss Heva from his jacket pocket and studied the conservative way she was dressed, tie and all, and then read the stamped name and address on the back again. All at once, everything he now knew about Miss Heva came together. He understood who she was and who she was supposed to be meeting.

Ded dialed Inspector O'Nadir.

"Good you called," the inspector said after the initial pleasantries. "The bullet analysis is done on everything—from the stage at Mount Tamalpais, the tree trunk at Macondray Lane, the anthology of poetry, and your ceiling at the Holiday Inn—and all the bullets are from the same gun. Plus, get this, from the markings on the slugs, the gun seems to have a barrel longer than a normal pistol but shorter than a normal rifle."

"That fits. What about the prints you were looking into?"

"No third-party prints on the death note, apart from Jerusalem's, and none in your room. From the various smudges, Ben thinks the culprit in both was using disposable surgical gloves. There's no way to match them."

Noticing Urizen's ear cocked in his direction, Ded turned away and spoke more softly into the phone. "What did your academic say about the leather glove prints?"

"So far, he's only looked at those on the plastic bag and our special briefcase," O'Nadir answered, popping his gum, "and they appear to be a perfect match. Looks like your friend, Tharmas Luvah, will have some real explaining to do."

He's not the only one, Ded thought as he considered how the lab results fit into his theory.

"Dr. Ulro is here to discuss the exploding golf club but refuses to give his fingerprints without us arresting him first, which we don't yet have the evidence to do. Fortunately, his prints have arrived by courier from the California Medical Board. Meanwhile, we've been able to get the Tongan's prints from San Francisco Immigration and Naturalization. I've sent both sets to the lab to see if they match the large fingerprints we found on the plastic bag. In a little while, I plan to go down and get the final results."

"Before then," Ded said so Urizen could hear, "could you do something for me?"

"Sure."

"Could you see if the airline can provide us with a parked 747 we can use for an hour or so tonight? I'd like to get everyone together to re-create Jerusalem's death."

"What time?"

"Around six-thirty?" Ded gave the eavesdropping Urizen a questioning look. The lawyer nodded. "Mr. Urizen can come," Ded spoke into the phone. "And I'm sure Beulah Vala and hence Adam Ghostflea can, too. They're outside at the moment, waiting for us. Could you check Thomas Luvah? He should be up at his place. And you've got Dr. Ulro there with you."

"Will check with both Luvah and the doctor. By the way, you should know that Rahab Oothoon has not yet shown up. The doctor said she was coming in her own car."

"Think she's flown the coop?"

"Looks that way."

"Okay, I'll give you a call in a bit to get the final lab report on the prints and to see whether we're on for tonight at the airport."

Forty-five minutes later, Bacon Urizen and Ded put on their damp clothes and walked out onto Marina Green. Beulah was sitting on a stone bench facing away from the Bay, next to a high pressure, impact lawn sprinkler, spraying back and forth over a bare patch in the grass before her. Scofield slept at her feet, just out of range of the spray. Adam Ghostflea was standing in the sprinkler-free middle of the green, flying a Chinese kite high in the sky.

The lawyer and the claims adjuster stood for a moment, observing the chauffeur, for whom the primary pleasure of the sport appeared to be, rather eccentrically, not in watching the kite in the air, but in watching the winder in his hand. The kite, sperm-shaped and with a large golden sun painted on the front, tugged fiercely at the long thin cord, trying in vain to break free from the firm grip of the indifferent Ghostflea and soar into the heavens.

"I haven't flown a kite since my youth," Urizen said pensively. He shuffled off towards the chauffeur, ostensibly to have a try.

Ded went over to sit next to Beulah, announcing himself as he neared.

"You took a long time," she commented in her friendly, schoolgirl voice.

"We went for a sail." His tone was as flatly matter-of-fact as he could make it.

"Did you find the money there?"

"No. It wasn't there."

Ded felt the breeze on his face and his bare feet. His suit was damp and cold, having not had enough time to thoroughly dry from the heater. "Tonight, at six-thirty, we hope to have a get-together at the airport to re-create on a 747 precisely what happened that night. Can you come?"

Beulah, the breeze fluffing her strawberry-blond hair out over the back of the bench, appeared to debate the matter before answering. "Sure."

Without thinking, Ded started to reach for her hand, stopping before he made contact. It was important he keep in investigator mode.

The sprinkler stopped.

On the green, Urizen took over the kite-flying from Ghostflea. Marshaling his limited strength, the lawyer jerked the winder down. The kite, high in the sky, fell precipitously in response and then soared back up.

Urizen repeated the process again. And then again.

Unlike Ghostflea, the lawyer appeared to take pleasure in watching the kite in the sky.

As an intrigued Ded watched, Urizen gave the winder an especially vicious yank. The string snapped. The paper sun hesitated in midair and then fell, tumbling several hundred feet to the ground. The long, thin cord the kite had been fighting against had, in reality, been the very thing that allowed it to fly.

❧

A dejected Ghostflea, who had left the green as soon as Urizen took over the kite, walked by the bench where Beulah and Ded were sitting, on his way to the hearse.

Ded glanced at the bare patch of ground where Ghostflea was leaving fresh shoeprints. One heelprint had a cross and the other a line producing a backwards cloven hoof.

Ah, yes, Ded thought. *That fits the facts perfectly.*

"Ghostflea, just a moment." Ded got up from his bench. "I have a question for you."

The chauffeur stopped and waited for Ded, who pulled him out of Beulah's earshot.

"You know a lot about firearms, don't you?"

"Yes."

"I need your opinion as to the type of gun that's been taking shots at us the last few days." Ghostflea looked pleased to be consulted, so Ded laid it out for him. "The bullets are 45-caliber, but the shots are much more accurate than one would expect from a pistol. Plus, the firing noise suggests a sound suppressor, which would make a pistol even less accurate. When I saw the sniper in the woods yesterday steadying his aim on the roof of a car, I could see the gun was longer than a pistol but shorter than a rifle, which has been confirmed by analysis of the bullets. At Macondray Lane, it seemed at the end the shooter lost control of his weapon and started shooting rapidly and wildly. Then, this morning, someone fired a rapid line of shots through the window of my hotel room. I saw the shooter on a nearby roof entering a stairwell compartment holding a flat, rectangular, canvas carrying bag. Knowing all that, what type of firearm would you guess?"

"Easy." Ghostflea's soba-noodle tongue shot out of his mouth and then withdrew. "An M3 suppressed submachine gun. On Macondray Lane and yesterday in the woods, the dampened report and instant reload sounded exactly like the M3 my father used to have. The Grease Gun, he called it, because of the way it looked. The favorite weapon of the CIA during World War II before it became the CIA. He kept it in just such a canvas carrying bag."

"Wow, Ghostflea," Ded said. "You know your stuff. That info is exactly what I needed."

Adam Ghostflea headed the hearse out of the marina parking lot with Scofield in the front, and Urizen, Beulah, and Ded in the back, all sitting in silence.

Ded picked up the car phone and dialed Inspector O'Nadir. "I'm heading to my hotel. Any luck on a plane?"

"The airline's chief of security arranged it right away," O'Nadir reported, sounding pleased with himself. "The very plane Jerusalem was on that night. It's being used for a flight that arrives at five this evening. We've got it to ourselves from six-fifteen to seven-thirty. Gate 58. Thomas Luvah and Dr. Ulro have confirmed they'll be there."

"Great job," Ded said. He consulted his watch. "Pick me up in an hour at the hotel."

"Will do," O'Nadir said. "In the meantime, I got two interesting bits of info."

"Wait." Ded pressed the upper part of the headset to his ear with his hand over it and turned, to make it more difficult for Urizen and Beulah to overhear. "Okay."

"First, right after you hung up, I got a call from the St. Francis Memorial Hospital emergency room. An hour ago, Rahab Oothoon showed up saying she'd been poisoned."

Ded flashed back to Louie's, when Dr. Ulro poured everyone's tea.

"She was anxious, salivating, shaking, vomiting, and alternating between rapid and slow heart rates, which then progressed into full seizures. The doctors have no idea what she consumed. They've pumped her stomach for forensics to look at."

"The last time I saw those poisoning symptoms," Ded said, "the victim was a dog. It was saved by a veterinarian flushing its alimentary canal with water."

"That's what the doctors are doing. They say it's still touch and go whether she'll make it."

"Has she said anything about it?"

"She kept pointing at a large square of wrinkled wax paper she had stuck under her headband. The doctors removed the headband and called homicide to look for prints and any other evidence from the paper. Ben has the headband and paper now."

"Could you ask Ben to check the center of the headband's golden sunburst brooch against anything else he's seen recently? Ideally, before you and I leave for the airport."

"I'll put a rush on it. And now, the most interesting thing: I went to the lab, as scheduled, and—"

"Tell me about it later," Ded cut in, noticing Ghostflea slowly sliding open the glass divider, and Urizen and Beulah leaning toward the claims adjuster.

"Well, I just thought you might want to know the glove pr—"

"Let's discuss it on the way to the airport," Ded interrupted, hanging up before O'Nadir could say anything more.

Ded had a good idea what O'Nadir was going to say.

❧

Ded looked at his companions. Ghostflea was now peering at him curiously in the rearview mirror. Urizen, at the far end of the rear seat, had turned away to gaze studiously out his window. Between the lawyer and the insurance man, Beulah was resting her head on her seatback, her cherubic face toward the ceiling, lost in an internal reverie of some sort. Her lips were moving in a murmured chant:

> I found them blind I taught them how to see
> And now they know neither themselves nor me

A tear materialized below the rim of her dark glasses and rolled down her cheek.

CHAPTER 36

REACHING FOR THE STARS

A little after 5:30 p.m., having picked up an envelope from O'Nadir at reception, Ded showered, changed his suit, and put on his spare shoes.

Tying up a few other loose ends, he first looked up Zoas Depot in his room's phonebook. Next, down at hotel reception, he checked for flights to and from L.A. in the big volume of USA flight schedules kept for guests. Once he found what he was looking for, Ded went outside just as Inspector O'Nadir arrived in his car.

On the drive to the airport, O'Nadir informed Ded he'd been able to get the business and economy class passenger lists, and they contained none of the names Ded had mentioned: Theo Jerusalem, Rahab Oothoon, Los Jerusalem, or Cousin Ijim. The two stewardesses were still unaccounted for. And the internal police department mail had delivered to O'Nadir an anonymous note posted more than a week before, accusing Dr. Ulro of being the murderer.

O'Nadir then eagerly filled Ded in on the final report regarding the multifarious prints, what Ben saw in Rahab's brooch, the info about the orangey-red liveried taxi company, the contents of Rahab's stomach, and the good news that Rahab was thought to be on the mend.

Ded steepled his fingers and lightly bounced the nails of his index fingers against his front teeth. "It all fits," he concluded. "Precisely as I thought."

"It does?" The Irish-American cop crinkled his brow. "How?"

Ded turned solemnly in his direction:

> God Appears & God is Light
> To those poor Souls who dwell in Night
> But does a Human Form Display
> To those who Dwell in Realms of day.

O'Nadir risked a glance away from the road as he said with a straight face, "Thank you, Dr. Deadly. I'm so grateful for your explanation." The inspector's eyes took the great circle route back to the road.

"Patience," Ded chided O'Nadir. "This evening, on the plane, all the supposed contradictions will at last be resolved."

Ded looked out the side window at Twin Peaks, San Francisco's almost thousand-foot-high, north-south-oriented natural landmark. The evening sun was resting in the bottom of the "V" between the two top knobs, like a bead in a gun sight. Ded remembered standing in the same place once. The view from that position—eastwards over working-class homes and industrial lots toward the muddy, land-filled edge of the Bay—was one of the highest and ugliest in the city.

O'Nadir started to say something, but at that moment the freeway dipped lower and, as if in censure, the sun appeared to set behind Twin Peaks. The two investigators continued down the highway in shadow and silence, conversing again briefly only after a necessary stop in South San Francisco and a carphone call by O'Nadir to a relevant airline employee.

ꕥ

By the time they reached the airport, Ded had all the evidence he needed. He could have canceled the final gathering, returned to his hotel, written up his report, sent Inspector O'Nadir a copy in the morning, and flown away without ever seeing anyone involved in the case again.

After all, final gatherings in detective cases were seldom necessary. Occasionally, a movie detective's skillful questioning produced the required confession: "Yes, yes, it was me. I cut the whiskers off a sleeping tiger at the zoo where I work, put them in Godfrey's pepper grinder, and then served him an under-spiced fettuccini Alfredo. Due to my intentionally leaving the door to the tiger cage ajar, the massively displeased beast soon turned up at our house, where, smelling his missing whiskers on Godfrey's breath, he promptly performed a full body organdectomy on the ill-starred spice lover. A terrible way to go, I agree, but I just couldn't take any longer Godfrey's continual failure to remove completely the tinfoil cover from the communal yogurt pot."

Even when there was such a confession in the movies, nine times out of ten, before the detective opened his mouth to deliver his final spiel, he already had them by the short ones (ground up or not).

Accordingly, Ded, not one to follow convention over logic, had never once bothered to have a final gathering of the people involved in his investigations. People were merely facts to fit into his theories. As soon as he had done fitting them in, he had no further interest.

The case of Ickey Jerusalem, however, was different. As Ded had realized at the lunch at Louie's, he liked these people a lot, each in their own way. But for Ded, it wasn't merely a matter of liking them. From the first interviews at the airport, he had become immersed in a subculture more intense, more varied, and more emotionally powerful than he'd ever encountered before. In addition, the whole way he perceived the world had been irrevocably changed. The richness of his interactions with those he had been investigating had produced in him a strange sense of communal obligation. He couldn't simply vanish, leaving everyone with nothing but an abstract, disembodied report to read. He had to be there. In person.

A cynic might say this was only because he wanted to hear everyone say, "Thank you, masked man," to his Coke-bottom-spectacled, ultimate-outsider face, whereupon, waving his white hat, he would jump onto his silver plane and zoom off into the sunset.

But even before the Ickey Jerusalem case, Ded was not one for cynical self-aggrandizement. In his own peculiar manner, he'd always been a truth-seeker. And now, knowing that as soon as he finished the case, the Apocalypse, pulsing deep down inside him in its temporary net of categories, would likely free him forever from his alienation, the idea of flying far away from human relationships no longer held any attraction for him.

❧

At 6:25 p.m., Ded left the toilet where he'd gone to drain his bladder before his expected exposition, then strode through the terminal and out onto the concourse to Gate 58. Inspector O'Nadir had gone ahead to escort everyone onto the plane. By the time Ded entered the poorly lit jetway, darkness had fallen. As he walked, he felt an increasing dread, as though he was descending an ever-narrowing cavern toward a tomb big enough only for his coffin.

Ded entered the aircraft and crossed the galley to the far aisle. He turned toward the front and quietly drew the curtain to first class aside. On his immediate left was the entrance to the first-class toilets. On his right, the closet where Urizen's overcoat had been hung.

O'Nadir was supposed to have directed each person to take the seat they'd had the night of Jerusalem's death. In front of the closet, next to the poet's empty aisle seat, sat the lovely Beulah, wearing the same outfit she had at Urizen's office, now *sans* hat, and reading her Braille anthology.

Ded sat down in the poet's seat.

"Who's that?" Beulah asked chirpily.

"Ded," he answered, feeling a stir of emotions deep inside his compressed web of abstractions.

"You're sitting in Ickey's seat," she reprimanded mockingly. "Inspector O'Nadir will not approve."

"I'm trying to get a feel for what Jerusalem saw that night," Ded explained stiffly. He leaned forward, briefly mimicked the intense writing of a poem in an imaginary notebook, and then looked around. His view of the rest of the cabin was blocked, either by the wall of the central section containing the toilets and galley, or by the seat in front.

"May I?" Ded took the poetry book from Beulah's hands. In a quiet, monotone voice, he read the printed page opposite the Braille:

> But in the Wine-presses the Human grapes sing not, nor dance
> They howl & writhe in shoals of torment; in fierce flames consuming,
> In chains of iron & in dungeons circled with ceaseless fires.
> In pits & dens & shades of death: in shapes of torment & woe.

When he looked up, Beulah was smiling sweetly. He continued, a few lines down:

> Forsaken of their Elements they vanish & are no more
> No more but a desire of Being a distracted ravening desire,
> Desiring like the hungry worm & like the gaping grave
> They plunge into the Elements the Elements cast them forth
> Or else consume their shadowy semblance Yet they obstinate
> Tho pained to distraction Cry O let us Exist for
> This dreadful Non Existence is worse than pains of Eternal Birth.

Her smile unchanged, Ded handed the book back to Beulah. "Took the words right out of my mouth." He glanced down at the date window on his watch. It was, after all, October 31st, the official date for Halloween.

Leaving Jerusalem's seat, Ded walked up the aisle to the front where the two rows came together. Instead of being in his seat beside Urizen, Tharmas stood next to Inspector O'Nadir.

"Tell me, Ded," O'Nadir said as the claims adjuster approached. "Where does someone with two seats sit?"

His mind still on the "dreadful Non Existence," Ded mistook O'Nadir's question for a joke. "I don't know," he replied innocently. "Where *does* someone with two seats sit?"

The inspector looked at him hesitantly. "In the seat he was in at the time of the victim's death?"

As a courtesy, Ded managed a little chuckle. *O'Nadir's punchline delivery is hopeless,* he reflected, noticing that other than himself, no one else was even attempting to laugh. They seemed satisfied, instead, to stare queerly at Ded.

Ded considered asking O'Nadir to explain the joke, but having learned how the explanation of poems failed to catch their true meaning, he realized the explanation of a joke could never be funny.

"What I wanted to know," Inspector O'Nadir tried again, displaying great forbearance, "is whether Tharmas Luvah should sit next to Bacon Urizen, where he spent the first half of the flight, or back with the purser, where he spent the second half of the flight."

Ded gave the goateed business manager a furtive glance. "Oh. Of course." He made a vague gesture to the back of the cabin. "Tharmas should sit where he was sitting when Jerusalem died."

"Right," Tharmas accepted in his nasal voice. With his long, seductive tongue clamped lightly between his teeth, he prepared to head off.

"But Robert N. William isn't here," Ded said, purposely not going on to disclose to the unfortunate reason why. "For the sake of authenticity, we should have someone stand in for him."

O'Nadir looked around.

Ded didn't say a thing. He let the inspector come to his own conclusion.

"Shit," O'Nadir said. "That purser was one obnoxious guy. But hey, since he's not here, like you say, I guess I can use my best efforts to do him justice. Luckily, as you know, when it comes to gays, I don't have a prejudiced bone in my body."

O'Nadir began limbering up like a method actor getting ready to go on as King Lear.

Tharmas Luvah winked at O'Nadir and led the way down the aisle to the seats at the back of the cabin. The inspector sighed and followed, performing a type of fingers-out, ballroom-dancer's glide designed solely, as far as one could tell, to create the impression his jockey shorts were lighter than air.

When O'Nadir reached the rear seats, he turned to hold up a thumb towards Ded, a questioning look on his face.

Ded returned the thumbs up, not having the heart to tell the inspector that by the phrase "stand in for" he meant for O'Nadir only to position himself where the purser had been, not to replicate Robert N. William's mannerisms in a way that—while an honest attempt on the inspector's part—might have caused offense to quite a number of people, had they been present.

ഗ

Once everyone was in place, Ded, ready to begin his objective analysis of the death of Ickey Jerusalem, stood at the front of first class and studied each member of his audience in turn.

Sitting at the back on Ded's left, across from the toilets and galley where he had left her moments before, was Beulah Vala. All Ded could see was the top of her bent, reddish-blond head as she read her Braille book of Jerusalem's poems with her fingers.

On Ded's left, in the first row, was Dr. Brom Ulro, wearing a powder-blue track suit, clay-colored running shoes, and a meticulous blond toupée. He was scowling in his usual constrained manner, seemingly unhappy his valuable time was being wasted, or perhaps worried about his earlier police grilling about the exploding golf club.

Seated at the back on Ded's right, blocked off from the toilets by a partition, Tharmas and the purser-imitating O'Nadir were engaged in some kind of amusing—although stilted, on O'Nadir's part—repartee.

Midway up the aisle on Ded's right, the dog-tired, bald-headed Bacon Urizen was sunk into his seat as far as his body could go, waiting to hear what would come next.

Adam Ghostflea sat the next aisle seat up.

His eyes met Ded's.

One at a time.

Ded pulled out his handkerchief and took off his glasses. In a blur of myopia, he watched himself methodically cleaning his lenses. Then, as he replaced his glasses and everything came into focus, he noticed something odd. All at once, he was no longer watching himself from the outside, but from within. As though his whole consciousness was peering out from that lingering, apocalyptic, black hole of his emotions crushed deep within his subjective inside, straining to escape.

Swirling around him were so many intense, mixed-up emotions under such massive pressure that he couldn't be sure what he felt, apart from a general, inchoate apprehension over what was to come.

Ded cleared his throat and solemnly raised his hand for attention.

"No doubt, you're wondering why I called you here tonight," he began, falling into the clichéd movie detective role.

"Why would we wonder that?" Dr. Ulro's unpleasant, falsetto voice intruded. "Didn't you say you wanted to recreate the circumstances of Ickey's death?"

"Yes, you're right," Ded stumbled at this interruption. He took a moment to collect his thoughts before proceeding. "As you know, for the last few days, I've been investigating the puzzle of what happened on Ickey Jerusalem's last flight. Thanks to your cooperation, I've managed, I think, to gather all the pieces. Tonight, I'll put them together."

"Wait, wait," Tharmas called. "Let me get my pencil out." The business manager's head disappeared. "Aaaahhhh," he sighed loudly a moment later, "that feels good."

Inspector O'Nadir dropped his hand in a limp salute. "Oh, you're such a hoot, Tharmie," he giggled, as he imagined Robert N. William would have done.

"When I first became involved in this case," Ded restarted, feeling he was not getting the respect a master puzzle-solver deserved, "Jerusalem's death seemed a simple suicide. He'd locked himself in the toilet, put a plastic bag over his head, snared his wrists behind his back, and suffocated."

Ded waited for a smart comment from the back, but none was forthcoming. "But there was a problem," he continued. "Nobody could give me a good reason why Jerusalem would have wanted to take his life. He had money. He had recognition. And he had the love of a beautiful woman." Ded glanced at the top of Beulah's head. The rest of her remained hidden. "As I got deeper into the case, I learned Jerusalem had developed an intricate metaphysics, capable, it seemed, of explaining almost everything in existence. On the hope it might explain his death, I made a determined effort to learn more about it."

As Bacon Urizen opened his curious eyes and aimed his brow-pinched monocle at the Buffalo-State-College-educated speaker, Ded took on a more professorial tone.

"I'll be the first to admit I had a difficult time understanding Jerusalem's metaphysics. On the face of it, though, I could see nothing to suggest he would have wanted to commit suicide. On the contrary, his whole system seemed to promote life, not as mere existence, but as its full expression—creativity, spontaneity, freedom, and the immediacy of experience. Except, that is, for one part of his metaphysics I kept coming back to: Satan Incarnate, the abstracter from Hell who keeps smothering the creative imagination. I tried to figure out who Satan was, but it was hopelessly confusing. Different clues pointed to each of you. Then, in his bequest film, Jerusalem seemed to be pointing at *all* of you. Following the film, I recalled Jerusalem's painting, *Satan Exulting over Eve,* which I'd seen among other pictures on Tharmas's VW bus just before the funeral Saturday morning. I compared my vague recollections of the floating Satan in that painting with each of you, but none of you fit, causing me to conclude it was purely symbolic. Shortly thereafter, at the Louie's lunch, Mr. Urizen and Beulah gave a detailed description of Satan that actually caused me to suspect myself—driving me into a claustrophobic panic, leading to a personal apocalypse in Louie's cloakroom while I was reading a poem to Scofield."

"You read poetry to a *dog*?" Dr. Ulro's Central-Valley ancestry was more evident than normal in his rapid, disbelieving countertenor. "You really did have a personal apocalypse, didn't you?"

"Interesting," Urizen said, "I've always assumed, perhaps foolishly, that Scofield is a philistine."

Realizing further discussions of his personal apocalypse weren't going to help his image as the master detective, Ded continued as though he had not mentioned it at all. "During the hearse ride to the marina this afternoon, I looked at the *Satan Exulting over Eve* painting in a photo O'Nadir had left for me at Louie's, this time seeing much more there, in part because I now had more background knowledge than I'd had when I saw it on Tharmas's VW bus before the funeral and in part because the photo possessed more detail than my fuzzy memory at the bequest meeting. The result was I could now recognize that the painting was *not* purely symbolic but, in fact, presented the spitting image of a real person whom over the last few days I've gotten to know well. Someone with brushed down, tousled hair; a full face; large eyebrows; broadly positioned eyes framing a classically Greek nose; fleshy lips and a curved chin, both no wider than the nostrils; plus a physically toned body in its prime."

Ded paused to look slowly around his audience. "In short," he concluded, "none other than Ickey Jerusalem himself."

CHAPTER 37

A GALAXY FAR, FAR AWAY

Tharmas stood up at the back. "What? Are yuh saying Ickey is Satan Incarnate? That's ridiculous."

"See for yourself," Ded said, holding up the photo of the painting and then, starting with Dr. Ulro, moved down the aisle on his right to the back, giving everyone a chance to see it up close (except, of course, Beulah, who was blind).

Dr. Ulro, Ghostflea, and Urizen, although indicating in different ways they hadn't paid much attention to the painting before, agreed the floating man appeared to be Jerusalem.

When Ded approached Tharmas, the business manager refused to look, as though despite his protestations on the way to the country club about not understanding any of the VW bus paintings, he already knew the identity of the floating man. "Sure, there might be some resemblance, but that's purely coincidence. After all, why would Ickey, the anti-Satan, paint himself as Satan Incarnate?"

"I don't know," Ded said. "Maybe he was going through emotional turmoil at the time. It was done five months ago, not long after the failed birth of Ololon, his child with Beulah. Or maybe he did it as a joke. Or he was unaware the image he was creating was of himself. What matters is that he did it, and thereafter, prompted by the idea that Jerusalem was Satan Incarnate, I was able to independently fit all the facts into place to prove it."

"Prove it?" the business manager said. "There's just no way that Ickey can be Satan Incarnate."

"Don't be so sure, Tharmas," Dr. Ulro drawled, sitting sideways on his armrest. "While I customarily discount the views of people who recite poetry to dogs, I think Mr. Smith may be onto something. After all, who but Satan Incarnate would hire an immoral degenerate like you to be his business manager?"

Tharmas gave the doctor a withering look.

The doctor smiled back with mock tolerance. "I'm sure you of all people will understand that once I saw that you were a mere reflection of the unfallen God in the mirror of the fallen, I had no choice but to play the Old Testament prophet and make you see what you really are."

"Yuh... yuh," Tharmas faltered, glaring at the sacrilege of the doctor's paraphrase.

"Could you two cut it out?" Urizen broke in. "Some of us would like to hear what Mr. Smith has to say."

Tharmas started to argue but, thinking better of it, shook his head in disgust and sat.

"Now," Urizen said evenly to Ded, "please explain what you're talking about."

All leaned forward to hear what was coming next.

"Let's look at Ickey Jerusalem's history," Ded said, and began precisely reciting Urizen and Beulah's lunchtime description of Satan Incarnate, adding here and there in deadpan-voiced parentheticals the precise application of each description to the poet. "Jerusalem was born in a place known for its traditional social values {Eden}. Raised by a dutiful father and a devout mother {Los and Enith}. Spent most of his early life alone in his room. Reducing the world he saw outside to simple abstractions {called words} sketched on paper {in the form of rhyming couplets}. He then went on to college {Oxford}. There, making few acquaintances and no friends {due to being treated as a hick by his sophisticated classmates}, he was inculcated with a complete, prefabricated world view {known as poetry}, in which he was taught to believe everything everywhere could be reduced to abstractions {words} on paper, albeit somewhat more complex abstractions than those he had produced in his youth. And from those abstractions, he could see what those wrapped up inside their world could not see."

Urizen bobbed his bald pate in agreement that, yes, the Satan Incarnate description did seem to fit Mr. Jerusalem.

Emboldened by the cautious acceptance of his interpretation, Ded strode on. "Imbued with the fervor of a new convert, Jerusalem left college for the real world, only to find himself soon packed into a crowd of humans, all the same and extending indefinitely in every direction {living with Bromion Ulro in the San Francisco fog belt's unending, serried rows of tract homes}. At the same time, pressed up against him, was a young woman {Rahab Oothoon}. Wrapping her arms around his neck and her legs around his hips, she introduced the young man to lovemaking and drew him down into the mundane."

Dr. Ulro slipped from his armrest into his seat and glowered at the bulkhead in front of him.

Ded felt bad, but nothing could stand between him and the description of the truth as he saw it. "For the next several years, with Jerusalem's perspective confined by this woman and the others pressing in around him {Rahab binding him down with the bonds of lust, Brom with the bonds of conventionality, Los with the bonds of duty, and Enith with the bonds of spiritual devotion}, he lost all interest in reducing to paper anything that had not already been so reduced before he got to it {quitting poetry writing and confining himself to his job as an engraver, copying any letters, figures, and other such symbols he was given}."

Ded took pleasure in uttering the next thought. "If things had continued in this manner, Jerusalem would, no doubt, ultimately have been able to pass for a normal person."

Encouraged by Urizen's continual nodding, Ded plowed on. "But then, he who preceded him {Uncle Urthon Spectre, having rocketed out his hospital window} fell from the sky, crashed down, and died, changing Ickey's life forever {as all of Mr. Spectre's millions poured into the trust}. Jerusalem, stepping onto what was left of the dead one {his uncle's fortune}, freed himself from those who were keeping him down {by moving out of the fog belt to the higher elevations of Telegraph Hill and hiring Tharmas Luvah as his business manager}. For the first time in his life, Jerusalem could see unobstructed in all directions. A multitude of images, experiences, and insights {the psychedelic hippies, the anti-war movement, the ghetto riots, the radical lesbians, the topless bars} began flooding into his freshly freed mind, resonating with his being in a druglike rush of Orc-like euphoria. He tried to make sense of it, giving report after exhilarated report {writing poem after exhilarated poem} about what he was seeing to those left behind. But he found it hard to keep up. Ultimately, overdosed on the inflow of inputs, he lost track of where he was, and found his jumble of perspectives so wide and all-encompassing, he could imagine himself everywhere other than where he was." Ded paused to take a breath.

"Or," he added, "as you, Tharmas, put it to me at your party, Jerusalem 'opened up his self so wide that it soon disappeared, swallowed up by the ability of his creative imagination to take in any thing, any time, any way, any where, no matter what.'"

Ded took another deep breath. "Jerusalem continued for several years in his joyous creativity, stimulated by the multifarious inputs. During this period, however, as his collection of inputs piled up, he began to see connections, and from those connections, he constructed random and disjointed theories {of imagination, spontaneity, freedom, and the immediacy of experience} into which the incoming inputs could fit, all related to his ability to see what others, with their limited perspective, couldn't."

Ded went on. "And then, a little over three-and-a-half years ago, Jerusalem's joy was cut short by a highly painful rejection coming out of nowhere {the vicious attacks on him and his poetry by San Francisco critics and fellow poets jealous of his calling himself 'Poet Laureate'}, causing him to try to isolate from the source of the pain {by moving out of the liveliness of North Beach to the Oakland Hills}. Over the next several months, however, his devastating suffering not only continued but also got worse, and worse, until, just when he thought he could no longer stand it, he had a revelation {when first making love to Beulah, pondering how she, due to his poem, went blind while perceiving the Heavenly Host in the sun} that rapidly brought together all his accumulated ideas into one Grand Unifying Theory {the parable of the sleeping God}, explaining everything in the universe and his part in it—a theory that relieved his pain by distancing himself emotionally from others and his own experiences, so he thereafter {although his theory nominally advocated imagination, spontaneity, freedom, and the immediacy of experience} related to them solely by comparing, generalizing, categorizing, and abstracting them, reducing their multidimensional humanity to desiccated, paper-thin imprints, and then bringing those imprints back into his mind to be neatly fitted into his theory. {As Jerusalem did this morning in his filmed bequests, deftly reducing each member of his coterie to an archetype and then placing that archetype into its own special folder, filed under the divider marked 'Pretenses,' exactly as the keeper of a well-kept filing cabinet would do.} "

Tharmas scowled at Ded, presumably at the impertinent suggestion his personality could ever be reduced to a mere two dimensions.

"Unbeknownst to Jerusalem, at the moment of his revelation, his whole being instantly inverted, morphing him from Orc into Urizen—the full-blown, upside-down Satan Incarnate. As with the Satan Incarnate discussed at our Louie's lunch, from that moment on, Jerusalem's head was trapped between the two surfaces of his Consolidation of Error—'below,' the screen of pure abstraction, filtering out all but the lowest-common-denominator generalizations from his fellow human beings—and 'above,' the black void of pure theory, his Grand Unifying Theory's supposedly unobstructed view of reality."

"Black?" Tharmas objected. "Weren't yuh listening this morning when Ickey said in the film that his metaphysics was a mixture of every possible-to-imagine color?"

Ded stared at Tharmas and then, with great deliberation answered his question. "What Jerusalem actually said was that his metaphysics was a *disturbing* mixture of every possible-to-imagine color. And do you know why he used that adjective?"

"Nope."

"Because a mixture of every possible-to-imagine color, as Jerusalem, the painter, well knew, produces solid black, the color of the entrance to the deepest and most light-free pit of Hell."

Ded's right hand closed into a fist. His voice continued, slowly and firmly. "Over the next three years, isolated, alone, overwhelmed by an increasingly suffocating sense of claustrophobia, Jerusalem, working on his epic poetry, withdrew emotionally into the space between the two inner surfaces of his Consolidation of Error, where he thought he could feel safe experiencing life as a mere concept."

Tharmas stood up again at the back of the first-class cabin. "This is hogwash, Smith. I knew Ickey well and I never saw him withdrawing emotionally between two planes!"

Ded took a deep breath. This was one part of the story he understood intimately. "Then why did Jerusalem become paranoid about everyone being out to murder his creative imagination," he asked Tharmas, "and so increasingly cut himself off, for instance, by installing a glass divider in the hearse, moving into the closet-sized Lambeth guest bedroom, and becoming drunk and stoned every time he had to meet you? Wasn't he unconsciously trying to escape the only way his relentlessly-pushing-inwards, dual-plane Consolidation of Error would allow? By pulling the thickening bottom plane up from his chin to increase his distance from the illusions of humanity crowding him from below? While pulling the thickening upper plane down through the top of his head {via his ever more convoluted epic poetry}, trying to get closer to the solace of his theory's unobstructed view of reality? Until, reduced to jabbering miserably to his dead brother, Orc, he became nothing more than the infinitely wide, infinitesimally shallow boundary between the two planes?"

"Holy mackerel!" a facetious Tharmas couldn't resist observing. He threw the back of his hand to his forehead in a waggishly dramatic gesture. "No wonder the poor schmuck committed suicide."

Ded smiled bleakly. "Merely being locked up in Hell was not enough of a reason to kill himself," he explained. "For that, Jerusalem would have had to *know* he was locked up in Hell."

Ded turned to the rest of his audience. "Which brings me to the broccoli."

"Broccoli?" Dr. Ulro couldn't help scoffing in his castrato voice, his slow eyes a burlesque of despair. "Don't tell me you were reading poems to vegetables as well?"

Ded disregarded the interjection. "On Saturday, when I was looking through Jerusalem's stuff at Lambeth, I found a bronzed, flattened piece of broccoli, inscribed with the phrase, 'Whence came the truth that all things must pass.' I didn't think anything about it, until this morning, when I heard Jerusalem proclaim the exact opposite in the bequest film: 'For every thing exists & not one sigh nor smile nor tear, One hair nor particle of dust, not one can pass away.'"

Ded looked around the room. "Since Jerusalem went on to describe his bronzes as freezing forever moments of change in his life, the broccoli must have represented such a moment, a moment which, according to the date inscribed on the bronze's bottom, occurred on Monday, October 10th."

Beulah, who was now standing at her seat, put a trembling hand to her mouth.

Ded shifted his eyes to a seat on the other side of the plane. "Ghostflea, when you were driving Jerusalem back from the meeting with

Mr. Urizen on that date, there was a small piece of flattened broccoli Jerusalem was using as the bookmark for a poem he then read out loud to you. On our drive to the funeral Saturday, you described the poem as being something about night, day, God, human."

"Yes."

"Was this the poem?"

Ded recited from memory what he had read to Scofield at Louie's, at that time vaguely recalling that someone had told him about it before, but not remembering who, until, in the hearse on the way to the marina, he caught sight of Ghostflea's small head through the partition.

God Appears & God is Light
To those poor Souls who dwell in Night
But does a Human Form Display
To those who Dwell in Realms of day.

Ghostflea started in his seat. It *was* the same poem.

Ded swept his gaze over the rest of his audience. "According to Ghostflea, after reading the poem out loud, Jerusalem said nothing more. He just stared at the opened anthology in silence, until the hearse stopped in Lambeth's driveway, when he suddenly sucked in air very loudly, opened his eyes wide, took the piece of broccoli from the book, and ran with the anthology into his house."

Ded surveyed his audience. "What was going on?"

No one volunteered an answer, so Ded began revealing all he had learned parsing the poem through from different points of view that afternoon in the hearse on the way to the marina.

"When Jerusalem wrote the poem months before, my guess is he intended its meaning to be that people dwelling in the fallen world's night see God as a separate abstraction, like light, but those dwelling in the unfallen world's day see no distinction between God and humans. However, on Monday, October 10th, on the ride from Urizen & Fallen,

Jerusalem was in a deep depression, due to doubts sown by his lawyer's questions. Isn't that right, Mr. Urizen?"

Urizen looked guilty.

"As a result, even though Jerusalem had written the poem, he was no longer certain what it meant, and now reread it with a hopelessly questioning, analytical mind. Given I have precisely that type of mind, my guess is his thought processes were along the following lines: While people can glimpse the unfallen world, they can't really dwell there until after the Apocalypse. But after the Apocalypse, the fallen world no longer exists. So, everything in the poem must be taking place before the Apocalypse, in which all the bifurcations such as night and day, light and dark, and God and human are still there. If in the poem's fallen world, those in night see God, and He is light, while those in day see a human form, then although the poem doesn't say so explicitly, since bifurcations are always opposites, the displayed human form in day is necessarily dark. Not that being dark has much import here, since the human on display is actually God in disguise. Why God disguises Himself as a human in day when He's happy to be seen as light at night, Jerusalem is not sure. Maybe He avoids being a light during the day for fear people would have difficulty seeing Him due to the brightness of the sun. That, however, assumes those in the day are going to be looking for God *outside* the sun rather than *in* it. At this point, Jerusalem recalls his earlier poem leading to Beulah's blindness, in which he looks up at the sun and sees not a human (dark or otherwise), but the Heavenly Host, a.k.a. God, plus, a whole lot of light—the exact opposite of what the night/day poem says should happen to those in day. Jerusalem then realizes that in the same way, the night/day poem gets it wrong with respect to those in night. It's a basic axiom that you can't have the sun in the night. Otherwise, it would be the day. So, by definition, the light those in night are seeing must be much dimmer than the sun. In fact, given the constraint requiring the maintenance of night, the light they see is likely no brighter than a flashlight. Not something anyone, even in night, would readily start worshipping. Certainly, if a few hours before, they saw the sun blazing during the day.

"Despite Jerusalem having just destroyed the night/day poem with his impeccable logic, he can't believe the poem is wrong. After all, the poem is a permanent glimpse of the highest level of God's consciousness, as is the Heavenly-Host poem that directly contradicts it. So, Jerusalem decides he must be looking at the night/day poem the wrong way. Accordingly, on the rest of the drive back from Dr. Ulro's office, he struggles manfully to filter and refilter the poem up through his screen of pure abstraction 'below,' trying to produce a conceptual description able to fit precisely into his sleeping-God void of pure theory 'above.' But each time, he fails in the task—even after attempting to make the filtered description so highly generalized, it conveys no information whatsoever, and thus, the contradiction with the Heavenly-Host poem seems to disappear—like the contradiction between the parable morals 'Out of sight, out of mind' and 'Absence makes the heart grow fonder,' disappearing into the informationless, super-moral 'You'll miss what you used to have unless you don't miss what you used to have.' And then, all at once, as the hearse enters the driveway at Lambeth, Jerusalem is struck by the total absurdity of what he is attempting, and at last comprehends how shallow he, the difference between the two planes, has become, and how that shallowness is the exact opposite of the unlimited freedom, as well as the imagination, spontaneity, and immediacy of experience, promised by his own Consolidation of Error. *He* is the poor soul who dwells in night, in the deepest most light-free pit of Hell. The poor soul who, having created his own system rather than be enslaved by another's, has ended up enslaved by his own. Trapped inside a self-constructed Tree of Mystery—mechanistic, predictable, repressive, and in the end, thoroughly mysterious behind its complex logical abstractions."

The upturned faces in the cabin were looking at Ded as though he was speaking in an arcane code most of them knew well. A code from the grave.

Ded continued. “Drawing in a sudden breath of recognition so loud that even his chauffeur can hear it, Jerusalem sucks the two opposing surfaces of his Consolidation of Error through his wafer-thin self, causing them to meet, and like matter and antimatter, to annihilate. Now, without his view being blocked, he can at last behold, by immediate perception, the ultimate Consolidation of Truth in all its stark reality. There is no sleeping God. There is no Golgonooza. There is no unfallen world. There is no way to unify subject and object, time and space, energy and form, emotion and reason, mind and matter, life and death. The sun is nothing more than a burning ball of gas. The creative imagination is nothing more than the ability to associate ideas on a suggestive basis. Poetry is nothing more than a combination of words that please or emotionally stimulate some of the people some of the time. And contrary to what he declared during the filming of his bequest six months before, everything, be it a man or a sigh or a smile or a tear or a hair or a particle of dust, will someday pass away.”

Ded took in a breath. “Seeing, at last, his metaphysics as but a dream, Jerusalem awakes, obliterating all the illusory divisions that seemed so real, until his perception once again encompasses all reality.”

The claims adjuster stopped to let his words sink in.

“All in all,” Dr. Ulro said to no one in particular, “I think I prefer Miss Marple.”

Bacon Urizen was jiggling his jowls in contemplation. “I hesitate to ask, Mr. Smith, but other than the bronzed broccoli, what proof do you have that Mr. Jerusalem had come to your enumerated conclusions?”

“You mean apart from his conversations with this dead brother, Orc, suddenly becoming happy.

“Yes, I did notice that. But hardly proof of the Apocalypse, I’d say.”

Ded shifted his gaze from Urizen. “Ghostflea, the morning after you brought Jerusalem back from Mr. Urizen’s office, he took your shoes and then gave them back in the afternoon.”

"Yes."

"Was there anything different about the shoes?"

"Yes, the heels had markings. I thought he might be saying something bad about me, so I didn't tell anyone."

"I saw your shoeprints this afternoon, one heel with a cross and one with a straight line making the heel look like the backward-facing cloven hoof of the upside-down Satan."

Ghostflea said nothing, seeming uncertain whether this was good or bad, and where in the hell the upside-down Satan guy came into it.

Ded prudently had not mentioned seeing Ghostflea's shoeprints outside Beulah's bedroom window where the chauffeur had stood, most likely after tracking the escaped Scofield. The last thing Ded wanted was for the chauffeur to describe what he'd seen through the window at the night's denouement.

"In the bequest film played today, Ghostflea," Ded said, "Jerusalem described you as focusing solely on the here and now as comprehended by the five senses, with no imagination or abstractions."

Ghostflea looked back at Ded blankly.

"In the hearse, when Jerusalem gave up his metaphysics, he disavowed both God's imagination and Satan's abstractions, putting him on a par with you. So, what better way to demonstrate his change of heart without yet announcing it to the world than to gouge symbols of both into your heels, so that you, whom he'd named after the first human, created from the earth's red clay, would thereafter trample both God and Satan underfoot when he walked?"

Ghostflea blinked uncomprehendingly.

Urizen raised his hand as though he were in a classroom. "There might be other reasons Mr. Jerusalem would have marked the shoes."

"Like what?"

"Perhaps Mr. Jerusalem wanted Ghostflea, when walking, to print God and Satan's symbols on the earth."

"Why would he bother to do that if he still believed in his metaphysics? If he wanted to spread his ideas of God and Satan, wouldn't it have been much better for him to pay for the distribution of his poetry to every household in the world?"

Urizen did not answer.

"Jerusalem's behavior the last two weeks of his life showed he was no longer interested in distributing his poetry. He drained the trust that would have funded everything. Gave notice of termination to everyone who could have helped him. At the New York book launch, instead of talking up his idea, he was, according to Tharmas, just going through the motions, as though he had some big plan up his sleeve unrelated to his poetry. And then, on the flight from New York, he wrote the four epigrams the police later found in his pocket."

Ded took Jerusalem's spiral notebook from his inside jacket pocket, pulled the four torn-out pages projecting from it, and read the first to hand. "'Attempting to be more than Man, We become less.' Jerusalem realized this was precisely what he had attempted with his parable of the sleeping God, and its actual result."

Ded went on to the next. "'The tygers of wrath are wiser than the horses of instruction.' This one proves Jerusalem now saw his Grand Unifying Theory has having reduced the Palace of Wisdom's cherished unrestrained freedom of experience to a mere domesticated pedagogy."

And then next. "'I found them blind I taught them how to see, And now they know neither themselves or me.' He knew what had happened to him had also happened to his followers."

And then the last. "'The Bat that flits at close of Eve, Has left the Brain that won't Believe.'" Ded began putting the loose pages into the notebook as he concluded, "Ickey Jerusalem was admitting he no longer believed."

Urizen raised his hand partway up. "How do you know he meant those epigrams to refer to his metaphysics?"

"Because after he wrote them, he penned one final, complete poem. The ultimate expression of his awakened consciousness. The final confirmation that, as Tharmas told me, Jerusalem's whole attitude had changed. A poetic satire comparing his dismissed metaphysics with a flatulence contest."

Looks of surprise filled the room.

Ded turned Jerusalem's notebook upside down and opened it at the back. He read Jerusalem's last poem aloud, with particular emphasis on the poet's bifurcation into the "English Blake" and the country hick "Klopstock," and the subsequent decline of everything into trumpetfuls of turning farts, belches, churning bowels, and shite.

At the poem's conclusion, it was Bacon Urizen who spoke first. "I guess we now know why, when Mr. Jerusalem came to commit suicide, he did it on the toilet."

"Yes," Dr. Ulro agreed, with simulated gravity. "He clearly wanted to go out in a burst of glory."

"Wait. Wait." The guttural Ghostflea held up his chapped, red hands for everyone to stop. "Mr. Jerusalem killed himself because of my shoe heels?"

"No, Ghostflea," Ded said, "I don't think Jerusalem killed himself at all."

Ded returned the poet's spiral notebook to his inside pocket. "It was possible that without his metaphysics, Jerusalem no longer felt he had any reason to live. But the various changes he was instituting during the last two weeks of his life suggests just the opposite. For instance, why would he kill himself before the changes were made to his trust and will?"

No one had the answer.

"And if he'd intended to kill himself, why, when he drained the trust, did he then hide the paper money where he could get to it later?"

With a swagger, Ded reached into his pocket, pulled out his fist, and opened his fingers, palm up. "This is a key I discovered tacked to the centerboard of Jerusalem's sailboat." He held it up by its end. "'#4, Zoas Depot' is what's stamped on its bow. A self-serve ministorage in South San Francisco. This key unlocks Unit Number Four. On our way here, Inspector O'Nadir and I went to the unit and found in it the missing hundred million dollars, packed in four large suitcases."

Ded held the key up as everyone gazed agape, and then he put the key back in his pocket. "No, Jerusalem's death on the plane wasn't a suicide."

"What was it then?" Tharmas asked, as though afraid of the answer. "An accident?"

Ded laughed scornfully and ran his hand sideways through the air, fingers splayed, as if over a huge headline. "Ickey Jerusalem, Noted Poet, Tries to Tie Shoelaces in Airplane Toilet—Mistakenly Kills Himself Instead."

He lowered his hand, looking coldly at the assembled suspects from eye to eye. "No, it wasn't an accident. It was murder."

CHAPTER 38

THE ENORMOUS BLACK VOID

Immediately after the word "murder" escaped Ded's lips, a loud gasp emanated from the group. Up to that point, nobody—well, nobody but Ded, O'Nadir, and the murderer—had thought of Jerusalem's death as anything other than the intended or unintended consequence of a visionary or perhaps deranged poet acting out of unfathomable motives. Now, all of a sudden, the picture changed.

Urizen leaned forward challengingly. "I assume you have some evidence of this supposed murder?"

"I do." Ded pulled out his own loose-leaf notepad and flipped the cover over. "Let's start with Jerusalem's fingerprints on the plastic bag. First was his left handprint on the shoulder of the sealed end of the bag, consistent with his removing the bag from the hanger and carrying it into the cubicle. Second were the set of prints on the right and left side of the bag's open end. These were thumb prints on the inside and fingerprints on the outside, prints consistent with him pulling the bag over his head with both hands."

"Yes," Urizen agreed. "Strong evidence of suicide, wouldn't you say?"

"Not when you look closer," Ded replied. "Take the print on the sealed end of the bag. If Jerusalem was going to handle the bag with only one hand, it's unlikely he would have used his left. Jerusalem was right-handed." He looked to the back of the cabin. "You did say, Beulah, that while Jerusalem sat on your left, he was writing in his notebook and his elbow kept brushing against you?"

"Yes," Beulah confirmed.

"Even if Jerusalem had been ambidextrous, however, the creases on the bag show it had been folded up into a small square, a task impossible for Jerusalem to have accomplished without leaving fingerprints all over it."

"But then where did his handprint at the top come from?" Bacon Urizen asked.

"It was made at the beginning of the flight, when you accidentally dropped your bag-covered overcoat on the floor next to Jerusalem, who was sitting in the aisle seat. Jerusalem would have picked the bagged garment up at the top with his nearest hand. His left hand."

"And his prints near the opening?" Tharmas rushed in, as though anxious to discount the theory of murder.

"He didn't put them there by pulling the bag over his head, that's for sure." Ded glanced at his loose-leaf notepad to check his details. "To start with, the forensic analysis of those prints showed no traces of soap, which should have been evident if he had pulled the bag over his head after writing the goodbye message on the mirror."

"So, how did the prints get on the bag?" Tharmas asked.

"For the answer, we have to look at the evidence relating to Jerusalem's shoes and shoelaces. According to the suicide theory, after pulling the bag over his head, Jerusalem slipped his wrists behind him in the shoelace noose because he feared he might rip the bag from his head, if he panicked as he began to suffocate—and who wouldn't? The horrible expression on his face when he was found and the violent scuff marks on the door from his running shoes reveal that he *had* panicked as death drew near. The problem, however, is that despite his violent kicking that caused bruises on the underside of his toes and the balls of his feet, his at that point loose, laceless shoes weren't thrown off, and despite his struggling panic, there wasn't a single bruise anywhere else on his body, including around his wrists where the shoelaces were tied. How could that have been?"

Ded waited for dramatic effect. "Because Jerusalem had been suffocated *before* the shoelaces had been removed from his shoes and tied around his wrists. Suffocated by the murderer."

"But how did Ickey's prints get on the opening of the bag?" Tharmas asked again, clinging to his last hope.

"The same way the soap message got onto the mirror." Ded focused on Tharmas's hawklike face. "The murderer guided Jerusalem's dead hands—first onto the bag opening to make his death look like suicide, and then onto the soap to write the two-letter farewell. It was just done in the wrong sequence."

Tharmas sat back and everyone else remained still, absorbing Ded's evidence.

"Yes, Jerusalem was murdered," Ded stated with certainty, "and the person who did it is sitting in this cabin."

Everyone looked at everyone else while Ded waited for their attention to return to him. When it did, the claims adjuster stared straight at Adam Ghostflea. The chauffeur drew back.

After an appropriate pause, Ded moved his eyes to Bacon Urizen.

Then, to Tharmas Luvah.

Then, to Beulah Vala.

And then, to the last one in the group, Dr. Bromion Ulro.

❧

Ded pointed his finger at the doctor. "You hated Jerusalem."

The plastic surgeon's face froze into a featureless mask, hiding contempt and concern in equal measure.

Ded's accusing finger moved closer to its prey. "Not only did Jerusalem represent everything you despised as one of those unconventional fruitcakes you told me needed to be snuffed out before they destroyed our civilization, but he was also the biological father of your twin boys. You had tolerated his continuing to live because when it came to the showdown, Rahab had chosen to marry you. But then, Jerusalem started having sex with your wife again."

Doctor Ulro exhaled as though hit in the midsection by a hard-thrown medicine ball. Not because the consorting between his wife and Jerusalem was something he didn't already know, but because Ded's public disclosure of the fact undermined the "happy family" image he always tried to project. "My wife is a chaste woman," he murmured through clenched teeth, not very convincingly.

Ded was breaking the promise of confidentiality he had made to Rahab Oothoon, but he knew that Dr. Ulro would be going away for a long time and to a place where he could not harm his wife. "Ever since the stillbirth of the five-headed Tirzah years before, after which you renounced having sex with your wife, you allowed her to have sexual relations with other men who paid for her services and who were not acquaintances, as long as the full proceeds were turned over to you."

The plastic surgeon's crumbling face collapsed into horror at the dual disclosure of his decade-long inability to make love to his wife and of his living off the proceeds of her immoral earnings. In one fell swoop, Ded had ripped away the doctor's carefully constructed cover of conventionality. Dr. Ulro peered around the cabin and met the equally horrified eyes peering back, including those of Bacon Urizen, who had naïvely assumed he was the only one having carnal knowledge of Rahab.

"Although Jerusalem was an acquaintance," Ded persisted, "you accepted the relationship because he paid twice the going rate for Rahab's services and you knew he wouldn't tell anyone because using a prostitute was a violation of his metaphysics."

The doctor tried to stand to storm out but didn't have the strength to muster the required indignation.

"Based on the detailed description of the fruitcakes you gave me during our golf game yesterday, however, despite your own acceptance of the relationship, when you were listening outside your wife's door to Jerusalem quoting poetry at the top of his lungs as he brought your home aquarium's pygmy electric eel into the act, you had the idea of snuffing out Jerusalem in order to preserve civilization."

"I never listened outside my wife's door," Dr. Ulro protested weakly.

"But none of that was sufficient to tip you over the edge into murder," Ded noted. "That did not occur until during the heat of an argument in your office, Jerusalem told you of his plans. Plans which I figured out with the help of a Miss Gwendolyn Heva."

"Who?" Dr. Ulro asked.

"An attractive young woman I've never met, although I did hear her on Jerusalem's answering machine and later found a formal photograph of her. She was scheduled to meet Jerusalem at SFO this evening at 3:30 p.m., she had a ticket to the Cayman Islands, and she apparently was not aware Jerusalem was dead. When she arrived at the airport, though, she refused to talk, but did let slip she expected to be met by four people, and her employer was in New York. Perusing her photo again, I realized the stamped name on its back I'd previously assumed was for the photographer's studio was actually for her employer. That evocative name, 'Poppins & Partners,' plus Miss Heva's upper-crust, NewYork accent and the picture showing her very primly dressed, wearing a tie, gave me the answer. Miss Heva was a governess. Probably arranged for by Jerusalem when he was in New York."

"So, she was a governess," Dr. Ulro said. "Who cares?"

Ded ignored the challenge. "Three things flow logically from Miss Heva's vocation. First, the four others she expected to meet at SFO must have included Jerusalem's biological sons, Hand and Hyle. Jerusalem, having given up his poetry, his metaphysics, and his friends, and thus no longer thinking of children as a drag, was now intending to spirit them out of the country, away from you. Second, since a governess is usually required when normal schools are not available, Jerusalem must have been planning for the boys to be traveling for a very long time and without settling anywhere. Finally, given the age of the boys and the length of the trip, the children's biological mother, Rahab, must have been the fourth person coming along, if only to support the ultimate custody battle against you."

"Rahab loves and respects me," Dr. Ulro mumbled hopelessly, despairing as the last shred of his public dignity disappeared. "She would never take the kids and run off with an undependable poet like Ickey."

"Even if the poet had a hundred million dollars, and unlike you, I suspect, had promised her that he would not only sleep with her, but encourage her to take as many free or paying partners as she wanted?"

Dr. Ulro, unable to argue the point, switched tack. "Even if Rahab was planning such a thing, there's no proof I was ever told about it."

"But there is. After lunch at Louie's today, Rahab confirmed to me in a cryptic note that Jerusalem told her the argument you and he had at your office was about you losing Hand, Hyle, and her. My guess is, in the early part of the appointment, Jerusalem hadn't cared at all about your attacks on his metaphysics, because by that point, he secretly agreed with what you were saying. But then, during your lecture on the benefits of conforming to the rules governing our existence, when you smugly included in your list of 'possessions' a fashionable wife and two beautiful children, he couldn't resist letting you know what he was planning."

"Yes, but," the doctor hesitated, the total shame of Ded's various exposures leaving him on the edge of becoming a broken man.

"Who would have blamed you for killing Jerusalem?" Ded asked rhetorically, in what he meant to sound like the *coup de grâce*. "Under the circumstances, it was, by far, the easiest way to keep him from absconding with your wife, and more importantly, your hand-molded sons. It also prevented your public humiliation. Therefore, that night, you concocted your plan: book a flight to New York for a supposed medical convention, book a return seat for yourself on Jerusalem's flight at the last moment, board late, wait until everyone was asleep, open the little black medical bag Ghostflea saw you take from your case, inject Jerusalem with a paralyzing drug, drag him into the toilet, and suffocate him with a cleaning bag."

The doctor was sweating in his seat and shaking his head in extreme agitation.

"And because merely killing Jerusalem would not satisfy you enough," Ded continued, "beforehand, you decided to send him a pasted-letter death-threat designed to strike fear in his heart. Since you didn't want to incriminate yourself, you wore disposable surgical gloves while composing the note and couched the threat in imprecise, religious-nut terms about having sex with someone to whom he was not married—going so far as to apply the threat not only to Jerusalem but anyone else sleeping with that 'someone.' You left out anything about Jerusalem taking Hand and Hyle. And you signed the note with the ambiguous 'N.' All of which, despite the obfuscations, meant that Jerusalem, knowing of the argument at your office, your atheism, and your high school nickname, 'Nobodaddy,' the jealous god, would clearly understand who was making the threat and for what reason."

"But, but—" the doctor stammered in little peeps.

"But," Ded cut him off, "there is one problem." He broke into a satisfied smile. "You didn't do it."

Dr. Ulro, at once, opened his eyes with confoundment and contracted his eyebrows with distrust.

"Despite my story, the evidence just isn't there," Ded explained. "The autopsy showed no evidence of any sort of drug in the body. Even if you'd brought your own plastic cleaning bag, you had no way of knowing about Urizen's bag, the one used for the murder. You boarded the plane late, after Urizen's overcoat had been hung in the closet, and you had no reason thereafter to look in there. You stored your parka in the overhead compartment above your seat, and you used the upstairs toilet, rather than the one next to Jerusalem. More crucially, the police's forensics examination completed today, after they got your prints from the California Medical Board, found no trace of your fingerprints on the bag. The one set of large handprints we thought might have been yours belong to the employee who packed Urizen's overcoat at the New York cleaners." Ded put his hands in his pockets and leaned back on his heels. "And while there *are* glove prints on the bag, which, under old forensic technology, meant they could have been anybody's, the San Francisco police now engage the services of a cutting-edge UC Berkeley academic who has identified the glove prints on the bag as belonging to another party."

As his alarm receded, Dr. Ulro's face slowly defaulted into its Marin-County, condescending friendliness mode, which, given Ded's earlier revelations about the doctor's private life, was not enough to qualify as authentic.

"Of course, this doesn't mean you *didn't* come onto the plane intending to kill Jerusalem," Ded added. "It's just that by the time you got around to it, he was nowhere to be found. Someone else had beaten you to it."

The doctor was about to protest this accusation, but having gotten off the hook on the big charge, remained silent.

CHAPTER 39

WHAT DIDN'T HAPPEN

"It follows," Ded continued, "that the murderer of Ickey Jerusalem is someone other than Dr. Ulro."

Ghostflea's crossed eyes widened as the claims adjuster's gaze landed on him.

"Your position as chauffeur to Ickey Jerusalem, Ghostflea, was a great source of pride for you, wasn't it?"

"Yes," the chauffeur agreed cautiously.

"So much so that when you were chauffeuring me to the funeral, and I asked you what Jerusalem had thought of your driving, you neglected to mention he had given you your notice the day he died because of how you'd driven the limo in New York."

Ghostflea looked distressed. He glanced around at the others in the cabin in the vain hope they hadn't heard, and then sank back into his seat, totally mortified.

Ded stepped down the aisle toward the chauffeur. "Being fired must have caused a tremendous loss of face for you."

Ghostflea buried what was left of the latter in his hands.

"And we all know what such a loss means. You told me so yourself, last night. If you were in danger of losing face, you said, you would have no choice."

The man Ickey Jerusalem had called Adam lifted his head and peered at Ded like a loyal dog that had been kicked by its master.

"Sitting alone on the plane," Ded went on ruthlessly, "it was easy for you to slip to the back, paralyze Jerusalem with a Kung Fu pinch like the one you used on the man at our dinner outside St. Helena, drag him into the toilet, take the cleaning bag from Urizen's overcoat, and complete the supposed suicide."

Chagrined, Ghostflea nodded. A few seconds later, he froze, furrowed his sloping forehead, and began vigorously shaking his head in denial.

Ded stepped back, his aspect lightening. "Yet, how could you have known the trick about locking the toilet door from the outside? The flight to New York had been your first in an airplane. And even on that flight, you had had little chance to learn much, since you spent most of your time knocked out with sleeping pills. On the flight back to San Francisco, according to the purser, none of the first-class toilets were out of order or used to store stuff during takeoff, the two most likely situations in which you might have seen a flight attendant locking a lavatory door from the outside."

Ghostflea nodded. Then, he hesitated, a confused look on his face, and began shaking his head, before hesitating once again, nodding, then hesitating, and then shaking his head.

"A man of conflicting opinions," Bacon Urizen noted impartially.

"On top of that," Ded asked the chauffeur, "how could you have slipped the plastic bag over Jerusalem's head without leaving any fingerprints?"

"Gloves?" Ghostflea suggested obligingly.

"According to the forensics examination this afternoon," Ded informed him kindly, "your glove prints don't appear on the bag."

Ghostflea seemed confused about which way he should move his head. He looked up at Ded. "So, I didn't kill him?"

"No," Ded replied. "Because, you see, the simple fact is the murderer has to be someone whose prints were on the plastic bag." Ded turned and focused his gaze on the person who most fit that description. "Someone like you, Mr. Urizen."

Bacon Urizen acknowledged Ded's designation with a barely discernible raising of his monocle-holding right eyebrow.

"Your prints were everywhere. On the plastic bag. On the toilet seat. On the sink. On the mirror. On the wall. One would have to conclude that if you didn't kill Jerusalem, you must have employed some exceptionally interesting ways of taking a pee."

The fleshy San Francisco Brahmin's eyebrow raised no farther.

"There's more. As confirmed by the fiber analysis, the bag was yours. You knew where it was hung, and, as you told Inspector O'Nadir and me, to avoid climbing the spiral staircase, you went back to the toilet opposite the closet several times during the flight. And since, as you also told us, you've been traveling by plane for years, you would at some point have seen flight attendants locking the bathroom door from the outside."

Urizen let his eyebrow drop with apparent unconcern. "What possible reason would I have for wanting to kill Mr. Jerusalem?"

"On Monday, October 10th, the last time Jerusalem met with you in your office, you gave him a copy of the trust's financial books to take home with him."

The pale lawyer warily concurred.

"Last Saturday, when I searched through his belongings at Lambeth, I discovered a worksheet on his desk. At the top, he'd written 'RWB,' followed by a long number and a question mark. Below that were a stack of lines, each with a three-digit number, a date, and a number out to two decimal points. I copied several of them down."

Urizen's eyebrows were beginning to show some unease.

Ded spelled out the prosecution's evidence. "After lunch in Chinatown today, you paid the bill by check. The name on the checkbook cover was the Redwood Bank, which caused me to suspect a connection with the RWB on Jerusalem's worksheet. Later, at the marina, when I noticed the waterproof plastic container in Jerusalem's sailboat, I got the idea that if I could talk you into sailing, I could get you to give me your checkbook for safe storage, and in the process, I could sneak a look. Which is exactly what happened."

Bacon Urizen's eyebrows rose to high anxiety.

"While you were gazing up at the *Devil* and the deep blue *C*," Ded gloated, "I compared your checkbook with my notes. The number on Jerusalem's worksheet is your account number. The dates and amounts I had copied matched the deposits in your check register."

Urizen's monocle fell onto his protruding stomach and then slid down into his lap.

"What's even more interesting, Mr. Urizen, is that following each deposit from the trust into your personal account, you appear to have written a check for the same amount to the Golden Sun City Development Corporation."

Half-looking at Ded, the senior partner urgently felt around the portion of his lap hidden by his stomach, searching for his monocle.

Ded went in for the kill. "You were taking funds from the trust to make good on a guarantee of Cousin Ijim's loans, weren't you? And Jerusalem found out. That's why you killed him."

"Mr. Jerusalem approved those transfers as loans," Urizen protested, finding his eyepiece hiding in the folds of his trousers above his left testicle. "He felt responsible for my predicament, because he had introduced me to his cousin and had urged me to guarantee the loans since the trust couldn't invest in the project of a relative."

"Did Jerusalem give his approval in writing?"

"No," Urizen conceded, cleaning his monocle with his handkerchief. "That's why he took the books home. I had asked him to check them over, so he could confirm them in a letter. He died before he could do it."

"And before he could remove you as trustee," Ded added.

Urizen pretended to be too involved with his monocle to rise to the bait.

"You know what I think, Mr. Urizen?"

The bloated attorney quivered his huge, shiny head back and forth in a "*No*."

"I think the evidence against you is so total, it's impossible to believe you're guilty."

Urizen re-inserted his monocle and peered at Ded, unsure whether he had heard correctly.

"If you were embezzling money, why would you pay it into an account under your own name where it could be easily traced? Why would you have volunteered to me that Jerusalem wanted you removed as trustee? Why, for that matter, if Jerusalem had found out you were embezzling, would he have bothered removing you as trustee, since he had taken all the money out of the trust anyway? Why, if you wanted to suffocate Jerusalem, would you have used your own cleaning bag with your fingerprints all over it? Why would you have waited until after the bag was hung in the closet before you removed it from your overcoat, increasing the risk of discovery, when you could have easily pocketed it back in your New York hotel room? Why would you, a lone, out-of-shape cardiac patient, have chosen a method of murder requiring you to overpower a much younger man and drag him into a toilet cubicle? Why, if you did murder Jerusalem, would you then put your fingerprints all over the toilet cubicle?"

Throughout Ded's *tour de force*, Urizen kept nodding in increasing agreement.

"Of course," the life insurance investigator allowed, "you could have intended to make it look like you did it, so no one would think you did it, but then you could not have been sure someone might not have thought you did not intend to make it look like you did it, or worse, you intended to make it look like you did it so no one would think you did it, and thus, you did it."

Urizen's visage showed he found this last statement hard to refute, or even, truth be told, understand.

"That's the problem," Ded declared. "It all depends on what you intended, which is something no one but you can know for sure. Which means the only way to prove you didn't kill Jerusalem is to prove someone else did." Ded looked to the back where Tharmas Luvah and Inspector O'Nadir, the faux purser, were sitting. He raised his voice. "Someone else whose prints were also on the plastic bag that suffocated Jerusalem."

O'Nadir, hamming it up, raised his hands to either side of his head, and with his straight fingers rapidly wiggling, dropped his face and clamped his lower palms onto his temples. "Oh, no-o-o-o-o," he moaned.

Ded fixed his eyes on O'Nadir's seatmate. "Tharmas, you had a motive for killing Jerusalem, didn't you?"

"I did?" His voice was guarded.

Ded gave the business manager his all-knowing detective look. "The day everyone was to leave San Francisco for New York, Jerusalem came by your house with a picture for you. During his visit, you began to suspect Jerusalem was up to something. Perhaps it was how he hurried away after dropping off the picture, driving the hearse himself. When he left, you followed. You saw him collect the hundred million in cash from the bank."

Tharmas rolled his dark eyes. "I can see now my opinion of yuh has been flat out wrong. Yuh *do* have a creative imagination." He dropped the insincere smile and stared sternly at Ded. "Because there ain't no evidence whatsoever I saw Ickey take that money."

"Then, when we were walking to lunch at Louie's," Ded stared back, "how did you know Jerusalem took the money from the *Bank of America*? The trust's bank is the Bank of *California*. Urizen himself didn't know until late this afternoon that the Bank of California, short of cash, had arranged for the Bank of America to dispense the funds."

Tharmas opened his mouth to answer, made a few false starts, and then closed it.

"After Jerusalem left the Bank of America, you followed him to the mini-storage warehouse and watched him unload the money. You then tailed him to the marina. You were the man the harbormaster saw, weren't you? Wearing the Jesus beard you later used for Halloween. Unable to see Jerusalem's boat from the gate, you watched through the coin-operated binoculars on the seawall. You saw Jerusalem tack the key to the raised centerboard, before lowering it back down. In the process, you left your glove prints all over the binoculars."

Ded was bluffing about the prints. But it didn't matter. He knew he was right.

"Even if I *did* see Ickey take the hundred million," Tharmas said, "it don't mean I killed him."

"No? Let me give you a scenario. After witnessing Jerusalem's curious performance, you are uncertain what to do. So, you don't do anything. The following day, in New York, Jerusalem informs you that when he gets back to San Francisco, he will no longer require your services."

Tharmas looked down, so all Ded could see of his suspect's head was the dome of his greasy, black curly hair.

"After everything you've done for him—given him ideas, encouraged his poetry, promoted him into celebrity, invested his money for him—your reaction to Jerusalem's cursory dismissal is understandable. Hurt. Anger. Hatred. Thoughts of revenge."

Luvah looked up, his face betraying exactly the combination of emotions Ded had described. The claims adjuster had guessed right.

"All at once, you remember the money and a plot begins to take form. Murder Jerusalem in a way that looks like suicide. After his death, it will be discovered he took all the trust's money out in cash, but nobody will be able to find it. The sailboat will pass to you, and with it, the key to the storage unit."

"How could I have known Jerusalem would bequeath me the

sailboat?" Tharmas objected, looking up and nervously tugging at his goatee.

"Because he promised you he would, according to this morning's screening of the bequest film made six months ago."

Tharmas rubbed his lips together.

"In New York, before the flight," Ded continued confidently, "you become friends with the purser. For a cut of the loot, he agrees to help you in setting up the suicide. He sends the two stewardesses false messages that will make them miss the flight. You plan to use your own plastic bag you got from the cleaners, but upon seeing Urizen enter the plane with his drycleaned overcoat, decide to use his. That way, if anybody suspects foul play, they'll go after Urizen first."

"Not true," Luvah hissed.

"Not true," a purser-imitating O'Nadir chimed in.

"In the middle of the night, you and the purser, who are conveniently sitting together at the back, get up, go around to the other side, overpower the sleeping Jerusalem, take him into the toilet, and suffocate him, setting his body up to look like suicide (in the process, the purser accidentally leaves his fingerprint on the top of the plastic bag). To gild the lily, you take a piece of soap in Jerusalem's dead hand and write the misspelled farewell message, 'BI,' on the mirror."

"Not true!" Tharmas bawled, leaving his seat and charging up the aisle. "Not true! Not true!"

"Not even poetically true?" Ded grinned as Tharmas advanced.

The business manager stopped in his tracks.

Inspector O'Nadir, the consummate actor, hurrying up the aisle behind Tharmas as fast as the invisible hobbles on his knees would allow, collided with his former seatmate, gave off a little shriek of surprise, and rebounded onto the floor, his pinkie fingers flying in all directions.

Tharmas did not look back. "I maya kept my mouth shut at the will reading about where the money was in hopes I'd be able to get the key and keep the loot for myself," he admitted, "but I didn't kill Ickey."

"Are you suggesting," Ded asked, "the false messages received by the stewardesses weren't sent by you, but instead were invented by them as an excuse for their oversleeping after you'd kept them awake all night making love?

The self-confessed libertine hesitated and then indicated yes.

"Isn't it true," Ded continued, "under company procedure, a flight attendant receiving a message is supposed to call the airline back to confirm they got it? Something they failed to do?"

Tharmas, catching Ded's drift, enthusiastically ratified it.

"Are you suggesting, Tharmas, the purser's handprint on the top of the plastic bag was made not while helping you suffocate Jerusalem, but when taking Urizen's overcoat to hang in the closet at the beginning of the flight?"

Tharmas agreed, as did the purser-playing Inspector O'Nadir, who had finally managed to get upright again.

"Are you suggesting the glove prints on Inspector O'Nadir's briefcase you handed me at the reading of the bequests this morning, which forensics identified as being the same as those on the plastic bag, were not yours?"

O'Nadir looked at the business manager's gloved hands.

Tharmas hid them in his pocket and looked expectantly at Ded.

"Are you suggesting the glove prints matching those on the plastic bag came not from the *middle* of the briefcase where you had gripped it but from the *top*? Where the case was touched, momentarily, at the reading of the bequests, by someone sitting next to me? Someone who had accidentally bumped into the case and knocked it over because that someone didn't see it? Didn't see it, because she was blind?"

Tharmas Luvah turned, as did everyone else, to Beulah Vala, who was now standing before her seat, her folded, white-suede-gloved hands resting on the seatback in front of her.

"I think," Ded stated as he looked deep into the black void of Beulah's floral-rimmed glasses, "I must agree."

Miss Vala stood immobile, locked by blindness inside her solitary, subjective self.

"But she wasn't wearing no gloves that night," Tharmas argued, turning from Beulah to look at Ded. "Like I told yuh, I kissed her bare hand in the plane."

"She *didn't* have her gloves on when you kissed her hand. Nor for most of the flight. That's why her fingerprints showed up in the next-door toilet. She didn't put gloves on until she was going to murder Ickey Jerusalem. She wore them only to keep her fingerprints from getting on the plastic bag. What she didn't realize was that her gloves would leave prints as well, which the UC Berkeley criminologist found all over the bag. From the top to the bottom."

"Someone else musta borrowed her gloves," Tharmas insisted.

"Beulah has extraordinarily small hands. Nobody else's hands could fit."

"But how could a blind woman kill Ickey?"

Ded looked at Jerusalem's personal assistant. Her delicate, gloved hands, still resting, folded, on the top of the seat in front of her, were now accompanied, on either side, by her two faultless breasts, straining against the soft pastel cloth of her dress. The claims adjuster felt a twinge of regret. "Do *you* want to tell them, Beulah? Or should *I*?"

CHAPTER 40

BOTTOM'S TRUTH

Miss Vala hung her head in answer, her red-tinged, golden hair falling over her moonlike face. It was up to Ded to lay out what happened and hope the evidence would become sufficiently overpowering to force Beulah to confess.

"Miss Vala can't be the murderer," Ghostflea protested. "She's too nice."

Ignoring the chauffeur, Ded buried his misgivings and began. "When Bacon Urizen dropped his overcoat in the aisle next to Jerusalem, Beulah heard Jerusalem's comment about it being good Urizen kept his coat in a plastic bag if he intended to drop it on floors. So, she must have heard the purser take the coat and hang it in the closet. Later, on the excuse of retrieving her own coat, she went to the closet by herself, put on her white suede gloves, took the plastic bag off of the overcoat, folded it up, and put it in a pocket of her silk paisley dress. That's why there were virtually no fibers on the outside of the bag. High-quality silk doesn't shed."

Tharmas stuck out his goateed jaw. "How do yuh know she went to the closet?"

"When she first entered the plane, the purser took her coat and hung it in the closet. But when he checked her after the bout of turbulence, she was wearing it."

This, Ded thought, *is the coat the purser wanted to tell me about on the phone before his friend (Tharmas?) arrived at his door.*

"Someone else coulda gotten the coat for her," Tharmas pointed out.

Ded looked around the cabin. No one volunteered.

"How about Ickey?" Beulah's champion persisted.

"If she had ended up with only her coat, it's possible," Ded agreed. "But she ended up with something else." He strolled to the back, reached around Beulah where she stood, and picked up her book of Jerusalem's poetry. "This was the very book from which, this afternoon in Louie's cloakroom, I read the night/day poem."

Ded waited for yet another derogatory comment from Dr. Ulro about reading poetry to a dog, but this time, none came. "I'd taken the book from beneath Beulah's blazer in the cloakroom. As I was reading the poem a second time, I noticed on the page before me—" The claims adjuster opened the book and removed a pink slip of paper with a number printed on it and staple holes near the top. He held it up. "Right away, I knew what it was. But to confirm, I took out my notepad and opened it to the page on which I'd earlier recorded the number Inspector O'Nadir had given me."

He pointed out to his audience the printed number. "This is the New York cleaner's pink slip that was stapled to the plastic bag covering Bacon Urizen's overcoat."

Ded ceremoniously returned the slip to the book, placed it on the seat in front of Beulah, and turned back to the group. "The slip must have fallen off when the plastic bag was in her pocket. Later, when she discovered it there, Beulah assumed it was merely scrap paper and used it as a bookmark."

Tharmas, glancing questioningly at Beulah, turned back to Ded. "But that still don't explain how she could drag Ickey into the bathroom and kill him."

"Correct," Ded concurred. "Which brings me to the question of why, when Jerusalem was found, he was sitting on top of the toilet lid with his pants down."

"And the answer is?" Tharmas demanded.

At that moment, Beulah lifted her face so her sightless dark glasses stared imperturbably in the claims adjuster's direction. Ded stared back from the minuscule, Apocalyptic bolthole deep within his subjective inside. "After everyone had gone to sleep, Beulah, you snuggled up to Jerusalem and began whispering the erotic words I know from personal experience you're so skilled at."

There was a collective "Huh?" as the rest of those in the cabin looked at Ded with new eyes.

Ded kept his attention on Beulah. "Continuing to whisper those erotic words, you began stroking him with your gloved hands. On his cheek. His neck. His shoulder. His arm. His inner thigh. Until Jerusalem—who, after all, hadn't slept with you for over six months, and now, having abandoned his metaphysics, had no further reason not to—was persuaded to take you into the lavatory and attempt a mile-high union to end all unions."

Beulah's face communicated nothing. Ded's voice cracked a little as he went on.

"Jerusalem sat on the toilet seat's lid with his trousers down and you sat on his lap, facing him, your legs on either side of his torso. You told him to relax, to close his eyes, while you enveloped him in your warm and tender love. Unsuspecting, he dropped his eyelids, put his arms down by his sides, and let you wrap your legs around him.

"Lulling him with your gentle rhythms, you reached into your dress pocket, took out the plastic bag, and yanked it over his head. Jerusalem opened his eyes with a start. He squirmed. He twisted. He bucked. But he couldn't break the hold of your legs on his arms. Few people ever had. Even sober ones. It was the hold you'd perfected when you were a nude wrestler on Broadway. The hold you were using in the photograph I saw at Lambeth. A hold that allowed you to counter a man's much greater upper body strength with your even more powerful lower body strength."

Miss Vala took this accusation in without the slightest flicker of distress.

"Jerusalem tried to stand, but you gripped the toilet seat securely on either side with your fingers, leaving the smeared glove prints found by police forensics, who mistakenly thought they were caused by someone lifting the seat."

Ded turned to O'Nadir. "Who do you know who lifts the toilet seat with both hands?"

He turned back to Miss Vala. "In his panic, Jerusalem lurched from side to side, banging the outside of your knees against the wall, causing the small bruises that I noticed when I first met you. It was over in a few minutes. There were no bruises on his body because you had held him with your thighs. The only signs of a struggle were the scuff marks from his shoes where he had kicked the bottom of the door and his facial expression, neither of which you could see. You got up, and pressed his hands and fingers to the lower part of the bag to make it look like he had committed suicide. Then, you took the soap bar from the built-in dish and wrote the farewell message on the mirror. Being blind, you began the B in the lower left corner of the mirror, orienting your letters with the vertical and horizontal edge. You then rinsed the soap, pressed the bar into Jerusalem's hand, and dropped it into the sink. Next, you removed Jerusalem's shoelaces, tied slipknots at either end, and bound his wrists behind his back. Then, you removed the ballpoint from Jerusalem's shirt pocket where you knew he had placed it after finishing his writing, left the cubicle, closed the door, and slid the lock with the point of the pen. You had learned the latch trick several years ago as a kid, when, as you recollected at your airport interview a little over a week ago, a stewardess had heard you banging and got you out."

Ded peered at Miss Vala's face. She still hadn't cracked.

The others in the cabin were looking back and forth between Beulah and Ded to see what would happen next.

"You put the ballpoint in your pocket and forgot about it until you got home. Because Bacon Urizen's initials were flush with the surface of the pen, you couldn't feel them. Thus, you didn't know the pen was his. So, you left it by your phone for your sighted guests to use, which is where I picked it up, the first time I visited Lambeth."

Ded reached into his pocket, pulled out the pen, and held it up with an expression of triumph, hoping by this demonstration of the completeness of his case to provoke Beulah at last into a confession. Obviously, being blind, she couldn't see either his expression or the pen. Ded sheepishly returned the ballpoint to his pocket.

"So, you see, Beulah—" He started over. "So, you *understand*, Beulah, we know exactly how you killed Jerusalem. Do you want to tell us why?"

Beulah gave no response.

Deaf now as well, are we? Ded taunted her in his mind. He already knew her motive.

"Strange, isn't it, that of the hundreds of poems in the anthology, the one that caused Jerusalem to reject his own metaphysics was the same poem bookmarked in your anthology today at Louie's. Why? Had Jerusalem told you on the plane about his rereading of the poem and its effects?"

Ded turned to the others. "As I outlined earlier, at the metaphysical level, Jerusalem's realization that he was the poor soul who dwelled in night had caused him to awake, obliterating his beliefs. But at the level of the concrete and particular, I think there was another poor soul who dwelled in night, to whom God had appeared, filling her world with light. No matter that to everyone else who dwelled in day, Ickey Jerusalem did a human form display. To Beulah the blind, he was the Heavenly Host in the sun. When, at last, Jerusalem awoke from his dream and displayed to her his human form, she was by then so locked inside his system that rather than lighting up with the day, her world went completely dark. Desperate to bring back the light, she did the only thing allowed to her by the logic of Jerusalem's system. She put her God back to sleep. This time forever."

Poor Ickey Jerusalem, Ded thought, *having seen the ultimate truth of the void, he returned to the Cave to be killed by the one prisoner who believed most fervently in the shadows on the wall, the one who could least accept the truth of what the poet had seen.*

"Of the five of Jerusalem's circle on the plane that night," Ded said, trying once more with Beulah, "four of them—Bromion Ulro, Adam Ghostflea, Bacon Urizen, and Tharmas Luvah—have admitted that Jerusalem announced his intention to sever his relationship with them. So estranged did they feel that in the plane, all except the infirm Urizen used the less convenient upstairs toilet, just so they would not have to pass Jerusalem on the way. Why were you, Beulah, the only person who did not mention receiving such a notice?"

Slight lines of strain creased across Beulah's otherwise opaque face.

Ded pressed on. "Is it because Jerusalem, who was terminating his relationship with everything connected with what he now saw as his Consolidation of Error, was still interested in preserving his relationship with the one person most devoted to that error? Or, Beulah, is it because you're hiding something from us?"

The audience stared at Beulah, but there was no response.

"This afternoon, in the hearse on the way from the marina, I overheard you reciting under your breath, 'I found them blind I taught them how to see, And now they know neither themselves nor me.' The same words as the couplet I read out earlier. Composed just prior to Jerusalem's death, and thus, I've assumed seen since by nobody but Inspector O'Nadir and me. The only way for you to have known the words was if Jerusalem read them to you on the plane."

The lines on Beulah's face became wrinkles of intensity.

"When he *did* read them to you, you must have understood exactly what he meant. The bat had left the brain that no longer believed."

Beulah's folded hands were pressing hard in upon each other, but still she didn't confess.

Ded tried another approach. "The two letters in soap on the mirror, positioned as they were, starting in the lower left corner of the glass, were not intended as initials. They were the beginning of a word. After you began the second letter, though, the bar slipped from your hand into the basin. When you picked it up, you realized you couldn't relocate your last mark on the mirror in order to write the remainder of the letters. So, you had to stop."

Beulah's lips parted.

Ded waited, but she did not speak. "It must have been an important word." He moved next to Jerusalem's empty former seat. "What was it? The word to be written with soap on the reflection of reality? The reflection you couldn't see? Was the second letter not an 'I' at all, but the beginning of an 'E'? Was the word 'BEULAH'?"

Ded stopped. Before his eyes, the personal assistant seemed to wilt like a sick rose.

"I was..." she faltered in her Orlando-girl voice, "I was just trying to get something clear in my head." She wrung her white-gloved hands. "Ickey had once written that everything in eternity had a vortex, opening outward into its mental reality in our minds. As we descend into the fallen world from eternity into time, we pass through the apex and see each thing only from the point of view of the thing itself, making it look as though it has an existence outside our minds. In effect, we are turned inside-out, so the vortex appears to us as a globe. Thus, we feel surrounded everywhere by remote globes, and are unable to see that the earth is but one infinite plane."

Dr. Ulro started to sneer something, but Ded silenced him with a finger to his own lips.

"What I was asking Ickey on the flight that night," Miss Vala continued earnestly, "was whether in eternity, since the perceiving mind was omnipresent, the globes were to be found *inside* the body." She unfolded her hands and placed the right one on top of the left. "Ickey took my hand solemnly in his. 'Personally, Beulah,' he told me, 'I take the popular view on this matter, that once the blinders have fallen from your eyes, even you should be able to see it is all complete and utter bullshit.' And then he laughed.

"He told me about his rereading the night/day poem, leading him to the realization that everything he'd been preaching had been a joke, an elegant slapstick, with a punchline so obvious he'd been totally unable to see it. He'd taken an insignificant phenomenon, the ability of a poet to put words together in a way that's enjoyable to the reader, and given it a seriousness far beyond its reality, building around it an intricate, crystalline thought-cathedral, the sole purpose of which was to suppress 'the tygers of wrath' with 'the horses of instruction. He described himself as the genuine Satan Incarnate, floating airily above as his metaphysics coiled like a serpent around my supine body."

Beulah sighed. "Then, Ickey read me the hideous toilet poem he'd just composed." She crossed her arms. "When he finished, he told me he was giving up poetry forever. He had taken all the trust money out of the bank, not to fund the distribution of his poems throughout the world, but to deposit it in the Cayman Islands, to fund his jetting off with Rahab, their two sons, and a governess, spending the rest of his life in permanent travel, flying first-class from one exotic destination to another, dropping into each place for a few weeks at a time, soaking up the available novelty by immediate perception, before flying on to the next. Ickey said that having seen the bleak truth of his meaningless metaphysics, and being unable to put his blinders back on, the only thing that made sense for him was a rootless existence above it all, never again becoming trapped inside any community, anywhere, anyhow."

How ironic, Ded thought. *In the end, the poet, Ickey Jerusalem, ended up as a convert to my now defunct Grand Unifying Theory.*

"Ickey did let me know he was giving me Lambeth," Beulah said, "so I wouldn't have to move."

"You must have been terribly upset," a sympathetic Urizen said.

"I was, but not by his going off with Hand and Hyle. I mean, they were his children, and if he could now abide them, so be it. As for Rahab, if I had no problem with Ickey having had sex with her rather than me for the last six months, his permanently taking off around the world with her was not all that much bigger a step. Without beliefs, morals, or cerebral understandings, their relationship was still—as I described it to Ded earlier, and as with the sex in the Orc poems between the fictional Urizen and the fictional Rahab—just pure, physical, unadulterated lust. Ickey didn't have to worry about cutting himself off from her, because he was never attached. She was merely an object for him. A sex object. And crucially, also the means for him to take Hand and Hyle away from Brom."

"But still, you would no longer be living with Ickey," Urizen said.

Beulah lifted her beautiful head with a wry smile. "Living with Ickey had never been easy. He focused his life intensely on his poetry. At best, he saw me as a mindless, sensual source of nebulous inspiration he could dip into, or not, at his pleasure." She dropped her head. "Most of the time, though, he hardly saw me at all."

Beulah's words caused a lump of sympathy to rise from Ded's heart to his throat. Had he treated Beulah in exactly the same way? He wanted more than anything to step up and take her in his arms. But his job was to stay where he was and get the whole story.

"If he wished to run off with Rahab and the kids, it made no difference to me," Beulah said, after a moment. "I had continued to live with Ickey for one reason, and one reason only. I was in love. Not with him. But with his vision. His exquisite, all-encompassing, passionate vision. Ickey Jerusalem, the man, may have been selfish, unfaithful, and uncaring, but his vision was perfect."

She opened her arms imploringly, like a childlike angel before the court of the Lord. "So, how could I allow him to mock his divine vision with his sacrilegious epigrams and evil, fart-filled poem? Allow him to characterize his previous poetry as a mere combination of enjoyable words? Allow him to destroy the foundations of my faith by declaring his teachings to be complete and utter bullshit? To bring his entire metaphysics crashing down, leaving nothing but a hopeless, purposeless void? An unending, sunless blackness from which I could never escape?"

She lowered her arms. "I had only one course of action. The consignment to oblivion of that part of Ickey existing in time and space.

In order that nothing, absolutely nothing, would remain but Ickey's eternal and infinite creations—unharmed, untouched, unmoved."

Ded stepped into the foot space of Jerusalem's former seat.

Beulah put her palms together and raised them to her lips as though to pray. A single tear streamed down her holy cheek.

"The word I was writing on the mirror," she murmured, "was BLIND."

ණ

Inspector O'Nadir entered the row in front of Beulah, took her hands over the seatback between, and slipped a set of handcuffs around her wrists. "Thank heavens," he said to Ded out of the side of his mouth. "For a moment there, I thought the word might've been BROCCOLI."

ණ

Having proved what he'd set out to prove after his epiphany in the cloakroom at Louie's, the claims adjuster's specific job in the fallen world was over. Beulah, as Jerusalem's murderer, could not collect on the Olympian Life Insurance policy. Ded, nonetheless, put out a hand to stop the inspector from leading her away. "There are still a few items we need to clear up."

He then addressed the others. "Let's start with the attempted murder of Bacon Urizen."

Dr. Ulro, Tharmas, and Ghostflea gave voice to their surprise as they turned to the lawyer.

"Pursuant to Urizen's request, we kept the attempt quiet until we had solved the case. Having now solved it, we can tell you that on Saturday night, someone sent Urizen a gift coated—unbeknownst to him—with pure LSD crystals, accompanied with a recording that, once he was sent tripping by touching the crystals, urged him to fly off his balcony."

Dr. Ulro clucked his tongue. "And the someone who sent the gift is?"

Ded moved his eyes back to Beulah and touched her wrist.

She did not respond.

"How could Beulah get pure LSD crystals?" Tharmas asked. "That's not the kinda thing sold on the street."

"In Orlando, Miss Vala grew hydroponic marijuana so successfully for a local hippie drug lord that she earned his eternal gratitude. In the wastebasket of the office at Lambeth, I found a pristine toy figurine of the bad boy, Lampwick, from the movie, Pinocchio. A Disney character so obscure it was likely to have been bought only at Disneyworld or Disneyland. Forensics says Beulah's glove prints were all over it, and inside were traces of pure LSD crystals, suggesting that her former employer had sent her the crystals, at her request. After taking the prepared present to Tharmas's party Saturday night, she talked Robert N. William into delivering it to Urizen's apartment building."

"So, that's why yuh were looking for Robert," Tharmas said.

Ded dipped his head in the affirmative. "The writing on the accompanying notes—one on the outside, saying it was from Orc, and one on the recorder with instructions to play it first—had been done between two rulers, as a blind person would do to keep their letters from wandering. And as with Jerusalem's death-scene evidence, Beulah's glove prints were all over the box and the recorder."

"But Beulah," Urizen said, "why would you want to kill me?" Beulah turned to answer the lawyer, but Ded squeezed her wrist to stop her. "That discussion will be more worthwhile once we've gone through the other items." Ded's eyes fell on Tharmas Luvah. "Like the garroting of the purser Saturday morning in your VW bus."

"What?" Tharmas blanched. "Robert was strangled in my bus?"

Bacon Urizen, Dr. Ulro, and Adam Ghostflea looked suitably aghast.

"Yes, not long after you gave him the keys."

"That's horrible," Tharmas said as though genuinely moved. "Poor guy. Who coulda done it?"

"You were supposed to visit Beulah yesterday morning, but because you'd lent your car to the purser, you decided to come with me to the Three Heavens country club in Marin, remember?"

"Yeah."

"And when you rang Beulah to let her know, there was no answer?"

"She was in her garden."

"No. In fact, she had taken a cab from Lambeth to the Taylor Street end of Macondray Lane. There, she found your VW bus in its normal parking place, probably felt the license plate 'LUV TREE' to make sure, and then, unknowingly leaving a perfect glove print behind, opened the uphill side door and crawled in behind the front seat. When Robert N. William came to the vehicle, he couldn't see her because of the Red Dragon painting that covers the left side windows. As soon as he got into the driver's seat, Beulah sat up, looped a thin rope over his head, and pulled back with all her strength against his neck. The purser didn't have a chance."

"Christ," said Tharmas. "So, she killed him to stop him talking about the package for Urizen?"

"No, I don't think she intended to kill the purser at all. She thought he was you."

"Me? But Beulah, why would yuh want to kill me?"

"As I said," Ded cut in, "we'll get to that later. However, it's clear she would have had no idea the purser would be driving your bus. Instead, since she had arranged for you to meet her at eleven, she had every reason to believe that between ten and ten-thirty, you would get into your vehicle to drive to her house."

Tharmas put his full hand to his throat and stared, horrified, at Beulah.

"And then there's Dr. Ulro's exploding golf club," Ded went on, "sent to him at his clubhouse, supposedly as a gift from Rahab."

"Exploding golf club?" It was now Bacon Urizen's chance to raise his eyebrows.

"The sender had to be someone with bomb experience," Ded explained. "And the only person in Jerusalem's coterie fitting that description is Beulah, whose favorite uncle was an Army Explosive Ordnance Disposal specialist. It's likely that when he used to horse around with her in Orlando, he showed her how to make triacetone triperoxide—TATP—from common hydrogen peroxide, acetone, and acid. At the reading of the bequests this morning, she bore the lingering fruity smell that is the sign of having handled TATP. All she needed to do was drill a hole at the end of the club's handle and pour the crystals into the space, then carefully patch the hole. TATP can be set off by a blow, so all it would take would be for the club to strike the ball."

"But how did she get it to the clubhouse?" Urizen asked.

"By cab." Ded gestured toward Inspector O'Nadir. "From what the country-club staff told us of the taxi's distinct orangey-red livery color, the inspector tracked down the cab company. The dispatcher revealed that the driver had picked up Beulah with a golf-club-sized package from Lambeth at 9:45 a.m., dropped her off at the Taylor Street entrance to Macondray Lane, gone on to deliver the package to the country club in Terra Linda, and returned an hour and fifteen minutes later to take Beulah back to Lambeth. The note, though nominally signed by Rahab, was written in the same script as Urizen's LSD gift note. And once again, Beulah's glove prints were all over everything."

Dr. Ulro didn't go through the motions of asking Beulah why she would have wanted to kill him. He'd find out soon enough.

"Which leads us next," Ded continued, "to the poisoning of Rahab Oothoon."

Now, Dr. Ulro came out of his seat, shaken. "My wife's been poisoned?"

Tharmas Luvah, Bacon Urizen, and Adam Ghostflea looked similarly shocked.

"Don't worry. She's recovering. She ingested poison at Louie's of Grant Avenue."

Dr. Ulro, who had been so solicitous in serving everyone the Chinese tea at lunch, sank ambiguously back into his seat.

"Once O'Nadir told me her symptoms," Ded said, looking from

face to face, "I knew how it had been done. According to the hospital, Rahab had been anxious, salivating, shaking, vomiting, and alternating between rapid and slow heart rates, which then progressed into full seizures. Precisely the symptoms I saw once in a dog that had eaten a toad."

"Rahab was fed a toad at Louie's?" Bacon Urizen asked.

"No. She was fed bufotoxin milked from the external parotoid glands behind the ears of a garden toad. Roughly a hundred garden toads, to be more accurate. Kept by Beulah in a cage in her back yard."

The witchlike image of the personal assistant milking a hundred toads shot through the minds of the people in the cabin.

"At Lambeth yesterday morning, I found in the kitchen cupboard a bag of shelled walnuts, a big bar of cooking chocolate, a packet of mint Life Savers, and jars of wild cherry jam and ground aniseed. These are all ingredients known to mask bitter tastes such as that of bufotoxin, and traces of which were found when Rahab's stomach was pumped. At lunch today, Beulah sent me to the cloakroom to get her anthology of Jerusalem's poems, even though when I returned, she had no need for it. It was then that I noticed Rahab picking at crumbs on her plate, and she had small, chocolate-brown smears at the corners of her mouth. Crumbs and chocolate are not usually associated with *dim sum*. Later, after I heard about the poisoning, I realized that when I was out, Beulah must have taken advantage of Rahab's self-admitted sweet tooth by offering her some home-cooked confectionery. This was confirmed when forensics examined the waxed paper wrapper Rahab had kept and found Beulah's glove prints."

Ded's mind flashed back to Louie's where Beulah's white-gloved hands were mimicking the two planes squeezing his depth to nothingness. When the image faded, he slowly swept his eyes across his super-attentive audience, coming to rest on Jerusalem's lovely personal assistant. "So, Beulah, what do you have to say about all this?"

Beulah did not hesitate. "It's true. I did everything you described. And I'd do it all again. Except for the purser. You're right, I mistook him for Tharmas. I feel really terrible about that."

"But why were you trying to kill Mr. Luvah," Urizen asked, "and Dr. Ulro, and Ms. Oothoon, and me? What had we ever done to you?"

"I think," Ded broke in on her behalf, "it's more a matter of what you'd all done to Jerusalem. Am I correct, Beulah?"

She nodded.

"Jerusalem laid it all out in his bequests film, didn't he, Beulah? Reiterating to the camera what he must have pointed out to you many times." Ded addressed the others. "To Ickey Jerusalem, each member of his coterie—each of you—represented a particular area of the fallen world's pretense of the unfallen world, out to murder his creative imagination in its own peculiar way."

"Yes, that's right," Beulah said earnestly. "They were responsible for Ickey giving up his vision. If it weren't for them, Ickey would have continued creating. They had to pay for what they had done to the consciousness of God."

"And those who had to pay were not just the four people you've gone after so far," Ded said. "Jerusalem also picked out Los, Enion, and Ghostflea."

Beulah acknowledged Ded's point, her jaw firmly set. "I would have gotten to them, eventually."

The chauffeur inhaled sharply, understanding for the first time that the person he most admired had been just waiting to kill him.

"Which finally brings us to the razor wire," Ded said, relentless in his pursuit of the truth. "A line of razor wire was strung across Beulah's front door at neck height in the apparent hope that she, being blind, would walk straight into it."

There was some wincing around the room.

"And who do you believe did that?" Urizen asked.

"I didn't think much of the clues at the time," Ded said, addressing Beulah, "but after I realized in the Louie's cloakroom that you killed Jerusalem, I could see from the clues that you'd set up the wire yourself. You easily navigated the coils of razor wire around your garden, and the wire cutters, a screwdriver, and suede gardening gloves were available in the tool shed. A blind person would almost certainly use a screwdriver to install the wire, since it affords much more control than swinging a hammer at a nail. Shortly after you almost walked into the razor wire, when I described the trap setup to you, you didn't seem surprised. You even characterized it as a practical joke. You insisted I not tell the police, which makes sense if you didn't want an outside investigation cramping your style as you went about trying to kill everyone. And when I asked Ghostflea to get some tools to remove the wire, you told him to get a screwdriver, even though I had not said how the wire was attached. Lastly, in this evening's final forensics report, the only prints other than mine on the screwdriver turned out to be ones from your extra-small gardening gloves."

Beulah smiled. "You're very good, Ded Smith."

Ded ignored the compliment.

"But why would she set up a wire like that?" Tharmas asked.

Bacon Urizen offered an answer. "Maybe she did it simply to draw suspicion away from her for the other attacks coming."

"Could be," Ded said, keeping his eyes on the personal assistant, "but I think there's a better reason. Isn't there, Beulah? In Ickey Jerusalem's bequest film this morning, among those guilty of trying to murder his creative imagination was you—your murder weapon being a pretense of love cloaked in the language of his poems. If I remember correctly, he said the more he made love to you, the deeper his dissipating creative imagination sank into the warm soil of your femininity. He became passive, helpless, and unable to create his epic poetry."

"What Ickey said about me was true," Beulah admitted. "I am as guilty as anyone. And so, I also need to be punished. However, I decided to leave the *when* up to God."

"God?"

"I positioned the razor wire, and then brought you back with me from the funeral. If you didn't spot the wire, God wanted me to die then and there. If you did spot it, then God wanted me to live in order to dispose of those who had murdered Ickey's creative imagination—after which, because I really didn't care about getting caught, I'd end up being tried and executed for my crimes."

Beulah raised her chin in a defiant gesture, tinged with a great sorrow.

Ded couldn't resist. He put his arm around Beulah's stiffened shoulders and kissed her on the forehead. *Was it on the forehead that Judas kissed Jesus? In the garden, outside Jerusalem's wall?*

The Bible didn't say.

Following Inspector O'Nadir's instructions, Officer Jarvis, who had appeared at the back, stepped up and took Miss Vala away.

❧

Ded looked around at the remaining people in the cabin, reacting to what they had just heard.

"I always said that bitch was a loony," Dr. Ulro glowered.

"'Loony' is a little harsh," Urizen said, "though I am shocked she could have done such a thing. I didn't expect it at all. I'm just glad it's all over."

"It's Ickey's fault," Tharmas said. "If he hadn't given her all that crap about everyone murdering his creative imagination and then announced he was leaving her, everything coulda gone on as before."

Ghostflea put a hand up. "What about the gunshots?"

Ded drew himself up, feeling the impatient, tiny, black hole deep inside, straining against his constricted web of abstractions. "Yes, somebody *has* been shooting at me the last few days."

Nobody looked surprised.

"And to make a long story short, I have concluded the 'somebody' is Dr. Bromion Ulro."

Everyone looked at the doctor, who started coming out of his seat, ready to object.

Ded waved him back down and stepped closer to stand over him. "Based on what I've learned during my investigation about your classic, absolutist doctor's mind, my take is as follows."

The doctor scoffed, ready to tear apart anything Ded might say.

"While you were happy to take the proceeds of your wife's activities, you lived in fear someone who knew you would find out and blow your all-important cover of conventionality. Therefore, you made the rule that Rahab could not have sex with acquaintances. A rule that was always followed, except where you were certain the client was so embarrassed by what he was doing he would not tell anyone."

Dr. Ulro rolled his eyes. As this information had already been revealed, there was not much the doctor could say.

"Worried that Rahab might breach the rule, you constantly shadowed her to check on her clients. That's why you were at the Holiday Inn Friday night. Your antiseptic odor gave you away."

"I was at a medical convention in L.A.," the doctor objected. "I gave you the receipts."

"True, your receipts proved you flew to L.A. Thursday night on a *Pacific Southwest Airlines* flight, checked into a hotel, registered for a medical conference, and flew back on the same airline early Sunday morning. But those receipts didn't preclude you flying back to San Francisco on Friday morning and then back to L.A. at midnight on Saturday night. After I checked the possible flights on my hotel reception's flight guide, Inspector O'Nadir rang a friend at *United Airlines* from his car phone and the friend was able to give him your specific flights."

The doctor spluttered, unable to verbalize a response.

"At the Holiday Inn, you covered the lights at the far end of the corridor beyond the room where Rahab was entertaining her clients. Hidden in the darkness there, waiting to check out the three guys when they exited, you saw Rahab approach me as I peered around my door. Given my thick glasses and skinny body, you easily recognized me from the interview after Ickey's fatal flight. The message my home office left on your answering machine had already confirmed I was a life insurance claims adjuster."

"Even if what you say is true, which I totally deny," Dr. Ulro said, "none of it indicates why I would want to kill you. After all, you were neither a client nor an acquaintance."

"Yes," Ded said, "at that point, I knew only that I'd been approached by an unnamed prostitute. However, you could foresee I was highly likely to discover who the prostitute was during my subsequent investigations, and in doing so, might blow your cover of conventionality. Thus, by your absolutist rules, I had to die before I connected the dots."

"Hmph," the doctor disagreed.

"After you'd shot at me at the funeral and on Macondray Lane, I did, as you feared, meet Rahab at the country club. But I then told you during our golf game that I hadn't said anything to anybody yet. As a result, you figured you could still shut me up in time. Hence, the subsequent attempt in the woods and—after you ransacked my hotel room in search of a draft report for my home office or any other such evidence—this morning's shots through my window."

"Pure speculation," Dr. Ulro said dismissively.

"Speculation, yes, as any theory about what goes on in someone's mind must be. But not *pure* speculation. Especially when you take into account the mountain of facts proving you are the shooter."

"What facts?"

"When, still a medical student, you discovered Jerusalem was having an affair with Rahab, you took a shot at him with your father's World War Two gun, which you supposedly threw away as part of a peace deal brokered by Rahab. But I suspected you hadn't really thrown it away. So, earlier today, I gave Ghostflea, an expert on guns, all the facts we knew about the shots over the last few days—caliber, barrel length, accuracy, report sound, reloading sound, firing speed, and canvas carrying case. He said, without a doubt, the gun shooting at me was an M3 suppressed submachine gun, the favorite weapon of the CIA before it became the CIA."

"My father wasn't in the CIA."

"No, but according to Beulah's description of your family in Eden, during World War Two, your father was in the Office of Strategic Services, the predecessor of the CIA."

"That doesn't prove anything. There are lots of M3s around."

"You're right. In order to prove it was the same gun, I asked police forensics to examine the golden sunburst brooch Rahab wears on her headband. My hunch was right. The grey, striated, stubby phallus at its center was the bullet you'd fired at Jerusalem years ago, the one Rahab had dug out of the couch and put on prominent display as a reminder to you of how close you had come to going to jail. The bullet's markings match those of the bullets recovered from the recent crime scenes."

"That doesn't prove it was me shooting the gun," Dr. Ulro countered. "It could've been Rahab."

"No. It could not have been Rahab. During the first shooting from the top of the amphitheater, she was down at the funeral with Tharmas. During the shooting at Macondray Lane and in the woods, Rahab was at or on her way to Urizen's apartment. Plus, Rahab was too short to be the shooter I saw aiming over the black car's roof in the woods. And this morning, the sniper I saw on the flat roof of the building below my hotel room window had to duck down when entering the stairwell compartment, something Rahab would not have had to do."

On top of that, Ded thought, *Rahab didn't want to kill me. She was counting on me to put you away.*

"So," Dr. Ulro protested, "the person must have been somebody else who found the gun when I threw it away years ago."

Ded smiled. "Except I don't think that would explain why the gun is now in your car parked outside."

"You searched my car?"

"Not yet. But after shooting at me this morning, there was not enough time, given morning rush-hour traffic, for you to drive across the Golden Gate Bridge to store the weapon at your home in Marin County and then return to San Francisco for the reading of the bequests. Consequently, the gun is likely still on this side of the bridge. It could be at your office, but there are too many other people around there. After the bequests, you walked to Louie's. After that, you immediately went to your car and drove to the Hall of Justice to be interviewed by O'Nadir about the exploding golf club. Then, you went back to your office for your open clinic between four and five-thirty. Thus, most likely, you took the easy way out and left the gun in your car, say, under the floor of the trunk next to the spare tire."

"Got a warrant?"

"No. But given all the evidence above, Inspector O'Nadir has more than enough probable cause to search your car without a warrant or simply impound the car until a warrant is obtained."

"If there is a gun in my car, then someone's planted it."

"With your fingerprints all over it?" Ded retorted. "The shooter this morning was holding the gun bag with an ungloved hand."

Dr. Bromion Ulro stood, his mouth opened to say something, but he seemed to have run out of counterarguments.

O'Nadir stepped up with a pair of cuffs for the stunned Dr. Ulro.

"And while Inspector O'Nadir is at it," Ded called to the doctor, "he will take prints of the soles of your shoes and of your tire treads to see if they match those at the scene of the forest shooting."

As the second criminal was escorted out of the airplane's cabin, Ded let out a long, quiet breath in recognition of having finished every last task he had set out to do.

Closing his eyes, he at last released the web of abstractions compressed around the tiny, black hole deep inside, and felt the overpowering rush of the Apocalypse exploding upwards and outwards through his being on its multidirectional way toward encompassing everything that could ever be imagined.

EPILOGUE

The near-empty 747 droned on through the night sky. The drinks service, the meal service, and the movie had all finished. Ded Smith looked at his watch. It was one minute to midnight.

Five years after Ickey Jerusalem's death, exactly, he noted, *and here I am. Still a life insurance investigator. In a plane. High above it all. Doing what I'm good at. Coasting around the circumference of the earth.*

He looked out the aircraft window through his reflection into the pitch-black night.

ɷ

Three days after Inspector O'Nadir had taken Beulah into custody, Bacon Urizen posted her bail and she was let out into the cautious custody of Adam Ghostflea. Rather than go home, she asked to be driven to the viewing area at the Marin County end of the Golden Gate Bridge. Ghostflea obliged. Once they arrived, she left Scofield in the car with the chauffeur, and using the railing as her guide, walked to the center of the bridge's span. It was early evening. The sun had just sunk beneath the horizon. Billowing, white fog was creeping under the bridge into the Bay.

Not that she could see it.

As the security cameras recorded her every move, Beulah took out her anthology of Ickey Jerusalem's poetry, opened it to a particular page, and let her fingers sensuously read the single Braille poem. When she finished, she folded her dark glasses, placed them in the book, and carefully laid the anthology on the walkway. Then, casting her sightless eyes to the heavens, she slipped effortlessly over the railing and fell into the formless cotton amoeba below.

When Inspector O'Nadir arrived at the scene, he picked up the undisturbed anthology.

"I'm not sure what it means," the inspector told Ded later as he presented him with the book, "but I thought you might want to know what she was reading before she jumped."

The dark glasses still marked the page. Ded opened the anthology to see the poem he had first encountered when investigating the case:

The Sick Rose
O Rose thou art sick.
The invisible worm,
That flies in the night
In the howling storm:
Has found out thy bed
Of crimson joy:
And his dark secret love
Does thy life destroy.

Ded—recalling the airplane view a week before of the brilliant-white fog shrouding the Bay Area, so like the snow and ice smothering that small North Dakota community, the one with a woman's old-fashioned name—understood precisely what the poem meant.

After Dr. Ulro's fingerprints were found on the gun in his car's spare wheel compartment (along with his blue knit cap), and his shoe prints and tire treads were shown to match those at the forest shooting, he was convicted of trying to kill Ded. During the trial, forensics evidence came out showing that he had, in the past, shot and killed several of Rahab's johns who might have blown his cover of conventionality.

The subsequent trials, plus the wide disclosure of the doctor's unconventional private life, caused him to finally conclude, like the Sicilian virgin, that he had been irreparably ruined, and thus, was better off dead. In the end, one juror did not agree, so Ulro was sentenced to life without the possibility of parole—forced until death to conform to the brutal dictates of an entirely new convention and, when gang leaders would make him remove his false teeth, the soulless mechanics of nature.

Since the $100 million dollars in cash was outside the trust after Ickey Jerusalem's death, it passed under his will to Theo, Jerusalem's eldest surviving brother. Very quickly, Rahab Oothoon divorced her imprisoned husband and returned to beg forgiveness of her first love. Although initially uncertain, Theo relented after Rahab, being the perfect height, demonstrated a form of oral sex much more satisfying than the obverse directional one she had introduced him to all those years ago in his moving convertible.

After Theo remarried his ex-wife, he put Grandma Enion into a luxury care home and joined Rahab, Hand, Hyle, and the governess, Miss Gwendolyn Heva, in the doctor's former house in Marin County. There, thanks to Theo's naïveté, they all lived happily ever after.

Los and Enith, having, with the deaths of Orc and Ickey, lost a full one-sixth of their sons, decided to lay off Theo about a duty to mankind and the emperorship of the universe. They focused instead on their grandsons, Hand and Hyle—the former getting the short straw of a duty to mankind, while the latter got the carousel of life's gold ring, involving—as Enith repeatedly predicted—millions of adoring masses throughout the cosmos hailing Hyle as their one and only Emperor.

⁂

Bacon Urizen, still trustee of the Urthon Spectre Trust, repaid his debt to it when Cousin Ijim's Golden Sun City became a roaring success. He stayed on at Urizen & Fallen for a few years until it was his turn to fall face-first into the Baked Alaska, whereupon the firm's disputatious lawyers parsed the firm into so many factions it disappeared.

⁂

Adam Ghostflea got a job chauffeuring the Grateful Dead around the Haight-Ashbury neighborhood. They liked the hearse, they loved his disturbing appearance, and luckily for Ghostflea, they were continually stoned, so they never seemed to notice he couldn't drive.

⁂

Tharmas Luvah, thanks to his knowledge of the Bible, his experience dressing up as Jesus, and his tolerance for closet libertines, became the manager for a budding TV evangelist. Utilizing his previously noted, infinite pool of unconscious energy, Tharmas tutored the novice, on-screen devil-dodger on how to explode through the lid of conventional behavior with just the right amount of the uncontrolled power of chaos to get those nickels and dimes rolling in.

"Jesus woulda been proud," Tharmas boasted to Ded when they met by chance at an airport. Needless to say, the business manager and the evangelist soon became exceedingly rich.

⁂

As in the case of the Knife, Ded gave Inspector O'Nadir the credit for the solution to Ickey Jerusalem's murder. Consequently, the inspector was promoted to Division Head. The position wasn't a good fit for him, being, as it was, a new division specializing in crimes against gays and lesbians. However, despite his Catholic upbringing, O'Nadir's subsequent success in curbing the rise of gay-bashing crimes made him a local hero.

To his discomfort, he was invited to nearly every event in the gay community, no matter how small, and over his protests, the most prominent of the gay baths put his picture and name on a huge billboard over the downtown entrance to the Market Street tunnel, gratefully proclaiming him an "Honorary Homosexual."

༄

And then, there was Ded Smith.

Releasing his compressed Apocalypse inside changed Ded forever.

He still thought that as a Grand Unifying Theory addressed to a person's reason, Jerusalem's metaphysics of the sleeping God was wrong, being merely another abstract system in which one could become trapped. But as a parable addressed to the whole person, unreduced to a one-line moral, he now felt it possessed a great truth.

From his Apocalyptic epiphany, Ded understood truth is found not merely by widening your perspective as far as your reason can go within the physical universe until you recognize you are but a speck floating aimlessly in an infinite and eternal black void, but truth also includes widening your ways of perceiving beyond mere reason, using the emotional, the creative, the intuitive, the associative, the moral, the spiritual, the empathetic, the beautiful, the imaginative, and so on, allowing you to perceive infinity and eternity in the here and now with a much deeper, more complete, and more intensely satisfying experience of the world as a unified whole.

He knew analytical, reductive reasoning was still king when making predictions about the operation of the physical world, and hence, should be used for everything from solving murders to preventing the other ways of perceiving from straying outside their holistic realms and foolishly trying to make physical world predictions themselves.

But for human beings, reason is not enough. Reason may claim that the other ways of perceiving are merely Sicilian Illusions, resulting from evolution or chemistry or social conditioning or whatever. However, no matter what the cause, they exist in our conscious minds, by immediate perception, as surely as if they had been created by God, and hence, their existence has a major impact not only on our understanding and well-being, but also on the understanding and well-being of those with whom we share them. Unless we embrace those other ways of perceiving the world as a whole, we will be less-than-complete human beings, and our lives will be less worth living.

Thus, these days, whenever Ded found himself dipping into a community, he marveled at the beauty of its landscape and the vibrancy of its citizens, and then reached out and enfolded everyone he met with his love and friendship, drawing them back into his heart, filling himself with happiness, sorrow, moral outrage, empathy, anger, and all the other human reactions to life he had suppressed for so many years.

This approach was not confined to Ded's business travels.

Which was how the other major change in his life had occurred.

He now had a home.

Within two days after Beulah and Dr. Ulro were taken away, Ded had tracked down the white stick-style farmhouse with the attached red barn, surrounded by vineyards. He walked up the driveway and knocked on the farmhouse door.

A week later, following a full-press, passionately holistic courtship, he married the young woman who owned the house: a barefoot widow in a simple cotton frock.

He now spent every weekend at home, sitting on the porch in an old rocking chair, gazing contentedly over the vineyards, while a gaggle of his own bespectacled children played happily at his feet.

Without warning, Ded's plane hit an air pocket. Then another. Then another. The seat belt sign came on. And just like that, the plane flew into a howling storm.

Ded glanced across the cabin, beyond the empty center section to the window seat on the far side, where a young man was sitting bolt upright, gripping the armrest. The man looked as though one more huge air pocket would send him leaping up, screaming, "This is it! This is it! We're going down!"

But when the next huge air pocket hit, he didn't. Or, more truthfully, he didn't in a noticeable way. His leap was limited by his seat belt to no more than three-quarters of an inch, and embarrassment confined his scream to an inaudible facial contortion only Ded noticed.

The claims adjuster understood how the young man felt. Here, high above the earth where he normally dwelled, he felt exposed and unprotected. He longed for the swaddling clothes of his life down below.

Before the Apocalypse, Ded might have tried to reassure him by calling out, "You shouldn't be so concerned. If the plane crashes, your death will be too sudden to feel any pain."

Now, post Apocalypse, Ded's heart went out to him. He wanted to comfort this terrified young man, to let him know turbulence was merely one part of the unified whole that is the joyously exuberant experience of life, and that someday, he would indubitably be lucky enough to develop such a truly broadened perspective that he, as well, could unite his mind with a Sicilian Illusion as it flew too close to the sun.

Which is what Ded did.

He let him know precisely all that, calling it out to him across the dark, near-empty cabin.

The young man stared back in Ded's direction for a moment, and then, turning to face the seatback in front of him, abruptly started screaming at the top of his lungs.

ACKNOWLEDGEMENTS

I would like to give grateful acknowledgment to:

Those who have read my drafts at various stages of development and provided me with their helpful comments: Amanda Hay, Michael Hay, Ozro Childs, Lee Hassig, Lesley McDowell, Kaytie Lee, David Llewelyn, Michael Manahan, Lorraine Reguly, PJ Brown, and James Gingell.

The William Blake Archive, my primary source of Blake's written words. If you want to explore more of Blake's work for free, I suggest you check out their site (http://blakearchive.org).

The J. Paul Getty Museum for allowing under its Open Content Program the use of Blake's 1795 painting, *Satan Exulting Over Eve,* which forms the basis for the cover art.

And, finally, all the characters in *Who Killed Jerusalem?*, who, as I got deeper into writing the book, took on a life of their own, often leaving me, the author, struggling to catch up. They will reside in my heart for the rest of my life.